P9-DDF-965

TANGLED THREADS

"Interesting storylines, alluring world, and fascinating characters. That is what I've come to expect from Estep's series. . . . Easily the best of the series to date."

—*Yummy Men and Kick Ass Chicks*

"The story had me whooping with joy and screaming in outrage, just as all really good books always do."

—*Literary Escapism*

VENOM

"Estep has really hit her stride with this gritty and compelling series. . . . Brisk pacing and knife-edged danger make this an exciting page-turner."

—*RT Book Reviews* (Top Pick!)

"Gin is a compelling and complicated character whose story is only made better by the lovable band of merry misfits she calls her family."

—*Fresh Fiction*

"Since the first book in the series, I have been entranced by Gin. . . . Every book has been jam-packed with action and mystery, and once I think it can't get any better, *Venom* comes along and proves me completely wrong."

—*Literary Escapism*

WEB OF LIES

"The second chapter of the series is just as hard-edged and compelling as the first. Gin Blanco is a fascinatingly pragmatic character, whose intricate layers are just beginning to unravel."

—*RT Book Reviews*

"Packed with pulse-pounding action and suspense, this urban fantasy truly delivers."

—*SciFiChick.com*

JENNIFER ESTEP

WID✲W'S WEB

AN ELEMENTAL ASSASSIN BOOK

POCKET BOOKS

New York   London   Toronto   Sydney   New Delhi

Pocket Books
A Division of Simon & Schuster, Inc.
1230 Avenue of the Americas
New York, NY 10020

This book is a work of fiction. Names, characters, places, and incidents either are products of the author's imagination or are used fictitiously. Any resemblance to actual events or locales or persons, living or dead, is entirely coincidental.

First Pocket Books paperback edition September 2012

POCKET and colophon are registered trademarks of Simon & Schuster, Inc.

For information about special discounts for bulk purchases, please contact Simon & Schuster Special Sales at 1-866-506-1949 or business@simonandschuster.com.

The Simon & Schuster Speakers Bureau can bring authors to your live event. For more information or to book an event contact the Simon & Schuster Speakers Bureau at 1-866-248-3049 or visit our website at www.simonspeakers.com.

Manufactured in the United States of America

10 9 8 7 6 5 4 3 2 1

ISBN 978-1-4516-5177-5
ISBN 978-1-4516-5179-9 (ebook)

To my mom, my grandma, and Andre—for everything

To my papaw—you will be missed

ACKNOWLEDGMENTS

Once again, my heartfelt thanks go to all the folks who help turn my words into a book.

Thanks go to my agent, Annelise Robey, and editors, Adam Wilson and Lauren McKenna, for all their helpful advice, support, and encouragement. Thanks also to Julia Fincher.

Thanks to Tony Mauro for designing another terrific cover, and thanks to Louise Burke, Lisa Litwack, and everyone else at Pocket and Simon & Schuster for their work on the step-back cover, the book, and the series.

And finally, a big thanks to all the readers. Knowing that folks read and enjoy my books is truly humbling, and I'm glad that you are all enjoying Gin and her adventures.

I appreciate you all more than you will ever know.

Happy reading!

WID✣OW'S WEB

❋ 1 ❋

Breaking into the building was easy.

Too easy for an assassin like me.

Hell, I didn't even really have to break in—I could have walked right through the front door, waved at the guard stationed behind the reception desk in the lobby, and taken the elevator up to the appropriate floor. Stroll into an office building holding a vase of flowers, an oversize teddy bear, or a couple of pizza boxes smelling of grease, pepperoni, and melted mozzarella, and no one looks too closely at you. Except to wish they were the ones who'd thought to order pizza.

The delivery ruse was one I'd used countless times before, and I would have done it again today—except my target knew that I was coming for him. He was on his guard, and everyone entering the building was being checked and double-checked for weapons and to see if they even had the right to be there in the first place.

Besides, I preferred to be subtle about these things—to creep around in the shadows, leap out, take down my target when he least expected it, and then vanish back into the darkness once more. As the assassin the Spider, I had a reputation to uphold—that I could get to anyone, anywhere, anytime.

Something I planned on proving once again this evening—no matter how tight the security was.

It had taken me the better part of a week to scout out locations where the hit might go down. Home, office, the route in between, restaurants he liked to frequent, even Northern Aggression, Ashland's most decadent nightclub, where he spent some time after hours. I'd eventually decided to do the job in his office, which was housed in one of the city's downtown skyscrapers. He probably thought he was safe there, but he was going to learn exactly how wrong he was.

It had taken another week, and been a bit more difficult than I'd expected, getting my hands on the building's blueprints and figuring out a way to get close to him, but I'd managed. I always managed. I wouldn't have been the Spider otherwise. Besides, I always enjoyed a challenge.

Now I was into the third week of the operation, and it was finally time to put my plan into action, since the job had to be done before the end of the month. Normally, that wouldn't be a problem, but the target knew about the looming deadline and that I was gunning for him. Every day that passed meant that security got that much tighter and my job that much more difficult.

I strolled into a downtown parking garage, wearing a black pantsuit and matching heels. I'd pulled my dark, chocolate-brown hair up into a high, sleek ponytail, while black glasses with clear lenses covered my cold gray eyes. I looked like just another corporate office drone, right down to the enormous black handbag I carried.

This particular garage lay on the opposite side of the block from the front entrance to the skyscraper I wanted, but thanks to the blueprints I'd looked at, I'd discovered the two were connected by a series of maintenance corridors, which meant I didn't have to go anywhere near the skyscraper lobby to actually get inside the building.

Always take the most unexpected route. That was something my late mentor, Fletcher Lane, had told me more than once, and I expected it to work just as well this evening as it had so many other times.

Still, I'd thought that my target might have a few guards stationed in the garage, hence my business attire, but I didn't see anyone as I walked down the ramp from the street to the basement level. A few security cameras swiveled around in slow loops on the walls, their red lights blinking like malevolent eyes, but it was easy enough for me to walk through their blind spots. Sloppy, sloppy of him not to make sure the entire garage was covered, even if it was on the other side of the block. This was Ashland, after all, the city that showcased greed, violence, corruption, and depravity in all their deep-fried, Southern glory.

My heels cracked against the concrete as I headed toward the elevator, the harsh sound bouncing around like a Ping-Pong ball someone had tossed into the garage. Despite the fact I was in the business district, muggings weren't unheard of here, and my eyes scanned the shadows, just in case there was anyone lurking around who shouldn't be. Assassin or not, I had no desire to get blood on my clothes before I'd gotten close to my target. I was the only one getting away with any violence tonight.

As a final precaution, I reached out with my magic and listened to the stone around me.

People leave behind emotional vibrations in their surroundings, in the places where they spend their time, in the houses, apartments, and offices where they live, love, laugh, work, and die. All those feelings, all those emotions, especially, sink into stone, whether it's a concrete foundation of a house, the gravel that constantly crunches under the tires of a convertible, or even an expensive marble sculpture prettily perched in a living room.

As a Stone elemental, I can pick up on those vibrations as clearly as if the person who had put them there was standing beside me, telling me all about how he'd used that marble sculpture to bash in his wife's brains for the life insurance payout.

I reached out with my magic, and the usual sharp, worried murmurs echoed back to me. Nobody much cares for parking garages, and the low mutters told me just how many folks had fearfully clutched their bags and briefcases to their chests as they hurried to unlock their cars—and how many hadn't made it before they'd been beaten, robbed, and left for dead. Par for the course in this garage and so many others like it.

Still, there were no recent disturbances in the stone, and no indication that someone had set his sights on me. Satisfied, I shut the murmurs out of my mind, rounded the corner, and reached the elevator that led from the garage up into the office building on this side of the block.

A man wearing a suit and carrying a briefcase waited in front of the elevator, watching the numbers light up as it descended to our level. I gave him a polite nod, then pulled my cell phone out of my bag and started tapping the buttons on it, sending a message to no one.

The elevator arrived, and the man stepped inside, holding the door open for me.

"Going up?" he asked.

I waved him off. "I need to finish this text first. My reception always gets cut off in there."

He nodded and let the doors slide shut. I hit a few more buttons on my phone, just in case there was anyone else behind me heading toward the elevator, but no one appeared. When I was certain I was alone, I put the phone away and headed to the far end of the corridor and a door marked *Maintenance Only*.

I looped my bag across my shoulder so my hands would be free, held my palm up, and again reached for my magic. Most elementals are only gifted in one area—Air, Fire, Ice, or Stone—but I had the rare ability to tap into two areas. So now, instead of using my Stone magic, I grabbed hold of my Ice power and used it to form a specific, familiar shape—one that would help me get through this locked door.

A cold, silver light flickered in my palm, centered on the scar there, one that was shaped like a small circle surrounded by eight thin rays. A matching scar was embedded in my other palm. Spider runes—symbols for patience. My assassin name, and so many other things to me.

A second later, the light faded, and I clutched two slender Ice picks in my fingers. Still keeping an eye and ear out for anyone else in the garage, I went to work on the door. I wasn't as good at jimmying locks as my sometimes partner, Finn, was, but I got the job done in under a minute. I threw the Ice picks down on the concrete, where they would soon melt away. Then I slid through the opening and let the door close behind me.

In the long, narrow hallway, flickering bulbs gave everything an ugly, sallow tint. I paused, listening for the footsteps of the maintenance workers who used these corridors. But I didn't hear any scuffles or whispers of movement, so I started walking. Even if I ran into someone, I'd just claim to be a lost worker bee, desperately trying to find my way back to the hive.

For once, my luck held, and I didn't see anyone as I hurried through the hallways. Eventually, I wound up in the basement of the skyscraper housing my target's office. After that, it was just a matter of picking another door lock and taking the service elevator up to the second floor, above the guards in the lobby. Then I leisurely walked the rest of the way up the emergency stairs until I reached the top floor.

Cracking open the stairway door, I looked out over a sea of cubicles divided by clear, plastic walls. I'd gotten here right at quitting time, and everyone was trying to wrap up their work for the day so they could be out the door by five sharp, get their kids, get dinner, and get home. Everyone was hunched over their phones and computers, sending out a few last messages, so no one noticed me slip out of the stairway, softly pull the door shut behind me, and stroll into their midst.

I kept to the edge of the cubicle area and walked down

a hallway until I came to a corner office that, thanks to a scouting trip I'd made here earlier this week, I knew was being used to store supplies. The door was open, and I stepped inside like I had every right to be there. I looked over my shoulder through the inner window, but no one so much as glanced in my direction, so I went into the attached private bathroom and closed the door behind me.

I stood behind the door, counted off the seconds in my head, and waited, just waited, to see if anyone had spotted me and alerted security. *Ten . . . twenty . . . thirty . . . forty-five . . .* After the three-minute mark, I felt safe enough to move on to the next part of my plan. Now that I was on the appropriate floor, all that was left to do was get to my target's office.

I removed a small, electric screwdriver from my bag, climbed up onto the bathroom counter, and used the tool to open one of the grates on an air duct high up on the wall. Of course, I could have gotten into the air ducts down in the maintenance corridor. The only problem was that those grates were all wired into the security system. The second I popped one open, an alarm would have sounded, and lobby guards would have come running with their guns drawn and plugged me full of bullets.

But my target hadn't bothered with alarms on the grates up here in the rarefied corporate air. Few people thought to properly secure the doors, windows, and air ducts on the upper levels of their homes or offices, figuring that preventing someone from getting inside on the ground floor was good enough.

Not when it came to the Spider.

Once the grate was open, I climbed back down,

stripped off my suit and glasses, reached into my bag, and put on my real clothes for the evening—cargo pants, a long-sleeved T-shirt, a vest, and boots. All in black, of course. Yeah, wearing head-to-toe black might be a little cliché for an assassin, but you went with what worked— and best hid the bloodstains.

I put the suit, glasses, and heels into the bag, looped it around my chest, climbed onto the counter, and hoisted myself up and into the air duct, making sure to reach back and close up the grate behind me. Like many buildings in Ashland, the ducts here were made slightly oversize, just in case a giant maintenance worker ever had to squeeze inside, so I didn't have any problems moving through them. I slowly, carefully, quietly, crawled through the air ducts until I reached the office I wanted. Then I eased up to the grate there and peered down through the slats.

My target certainly had an impressive office. A large desk made out of polished ebony stood in the back of the room. Pens, papers, a monitor, two phones. The usual office detritus covered the surface, while two black leather chairs crouched in front of the desk. Matching furniture in varying shades of black and gray filled the rest of the room, along with metal sculptures, while a fully stocked wet bar took up the better part of one wall. Behind the desk, floor-to-ceiling windows offered a sweeping view of downtown Ashland and the green-gray smudges of the Appalachian Mountains that ringed the city.

The office was empty, just like I'd anticipated, so I didn't have to be quite so quiet as I used my screwdriver to undo the grate on this duct and put the loose screws into a pocket on my vest. I practiced removing the grate from its frame until I was sure I could do it without making any noise, then I slid it back into place. I also reached into my bag and drew out my weapon for the evening—a small gun made out of plastic.

Normally, I carried five silverstone knives on me—one up either sleeve, one against the small of my back, and two tucked into the sides of my boots. I liked my knives, and they were the weapons I used on the majority of my jobs. But my target had an elemental talent for metal, which meant he could sense whenever the element was near, just like I could the stone around me. In fact, metal was an offshoot of Stone.

Since I didn't want to give my target advance notice that I was here, I'd decided to leave my knives at home tonight. I wasn't as good with a gun as I was with a blade, but the one I'd brought along would get the job done in the office's confined space.

As a final touch, I reached into my bag and pulled on a pair of black gloves, making sure the thin leather covered the spider rune scars embedded in my palms. The scars were really silverstone that had been melted into my skin years ago by a particularly vicious Fire elemental. I didn't think my target would be able to sense the metal in my palms—not through the ductwork—but the gloves offered another small bit of protection, and I wasn't going to take any chances.

With the grate and my gun in position, all that was left to do was settle down and wait.

I'd been inside the air duct for almost an hour when the office door opened and two men carrying briefcases stepped inside. Both wore expensive tailored suits and shiny wing tips, marking them as the movers and shakers they were. My target was having an after-hours meeting with his moneyman to go over company financials and other sundry things.

Too bad it was a meeting neither one of them would live through.

Through the grate, I watched a third man step into the office—a giant who was almost seven feet tall. He wore a uniform marking him as one of the building's security guards. The two businessmen hung back while the giant did a sweep of the office, peering behind the desk and the wet bar, then going into the private bathroom and repeating the process with a glance into the shower. The nightly sweep was another reason I'd chosen to make my approach through the air duct, rather than just hiding in a dark corner somewhere.

A moment later, the giant stepped back out into the office. "All clear, sir," he said. "The rest of the floor has been checked and is empty as well."

My target nodded his thanks, and the giant left the room, closing the door behind him.

The second man immediately moved over to the bar, grabbed a bottle of Scotch, and poured himself a healthy amount in a tumbler. He swallowed the amber-colored liquor and nodded his head in approval. Then he turned his attention to his friend.

"Any sign of her today?" the drinker asked.

The target shook his head. "Nothing so far."

The drinker grinned. "Well, since the Spider hasn't come to call yet and it looks like you get to live another day, let's get down to business. I happen to have some-one waiting up for me tonight. I'm sure you know what I mean."

My target smiled at that, and the two men opened their briefcases. They spread the papers inside over a table in front of the bar, then sat in the chairs on either side and got to work.

"Now," the drinker began, "as you can see from these latest tax and earnings figures . . ."

I waited until the two men were thoroughly engrossed in their conversation before I slowly, carefully, quietly, removed the grate from the air duct opening. I paused, waiting to see if they'd noticed the slight, furtive move-ment above their heads, but of course they didn't. Few people bothered to look up—even those knowingly being hunted by a notorious assassin like me.

I put the grate to one side of the duct and made sure the gun was within easy reach in its slot on the front of my vest. Then I slowly wiggled forward until I was at the edge of the opening. I drew in a breath, let it out, and slid forward.

I let my weight and gravity pull me down before grab-bing the edge of the duct, flipping over, letting go, and landing on my feet facing the two men. They'd barely had time to blink, much less get to their feet, before the gun was in my hand and trained on my target.

Puff-puff.

I double-tapped my target in the chest, and he dropped to the carpet without a sound. I trained my gun on the second man, who leaped to his feet, put up his hands in a placating gesture, and started backing away.

"Hello, Finn," I said in a mocking voice to the drinker. "Weren't expecting to see me here, were you?"

Finnegan Lane, my foster brother, looked at me, a clear plea in his eyes. "You don't have to do this. You've proven your point by icing Owen there already. This whole thing was your lover's brilliant idea, not mine. Don't blame me for his mistakes."

I gestured with the gun at Owen's prone form. "That's not how I remember things. In fact, I distinctly recall *you* being the mouthpiece behind this whole situation. You were the one who kept pushing and pushing me. Well, tonight, I finally push back."

When he realized I couldn't be reasoned with, Finn decided to try another tactic—bribery. "I'll pay you whatever you want to put the gun down and walk away, you know that."

"I do know that." A cold, cruel smile curved my lips. "But walking away is not nearly as much fun as this is. You know that as well as I do."

"No, please, don't—"

I pulled the trigger twice, cutting off his protests, and Finn joined my lover on the floor.

✲ 2 ✲

Silence.

Then Finn let out a loud, unhappy sigh and climbed to his feet.

"Really, Gin, did you have to ruin my suit?" he said. "This was a Fiona Fine original."

He stared down at the bright red paint splattered across the black fabric of his suit jacket and gray shirt. Then Finn raised his head and glared at me, his green eyes bright in his ruddy face. I didn't bother pointing out that the paint had also splashed onto his face and up into his walnut-colored locks. He was just as obsessive about his hair as he was about his suits, and it just *wouldn't do* for Finnegan Lane to ever look anything less than perfect.

"I agree with Finn," Owen rumbled and sat up. "I didn't think our little experiment would get quite so messy."

Owen Grayson got to his feet, his chest covered in just

as much red paint as Finn's was. Still, despite his ruined suit, my eyes traced over him, from his blue-black hair to his intense violet eyes to his strong, muscled body. No amount of paint could dampen Owen's rugged appeal or the way he had of making me feel like I was one of the most important people in the world to him.

I walked over, leaned against the desk, and pointed my paintball gun at Owen. "You should have known better than to let Finn talk you into drinking so much at Northern Aggression. Drunken challenges issued to assassins rarely end well for the challenger. Or challengers, in this case."

Finn stopped trying to scrub the paint off his shirt long enough to glare at me again.

"As I recall, I wasn't drinking alone, and you and I had quite a bit of fun later on that night," Owen said in a husky voice.

"Maybe." I agreed with a grin. "But Finn was the one who bet me dinner at Underwood's that I couldn't kill you both by the end of the month. So you only have yourselves to blame."

Finn sniffed his displeasure. "You still didn't have to ruin my suit."

"No," I agreed. "I didn't *have* to ruin it. That was just an added bonus."

He narrowed his eyes, but I just gave him my most innocent, gracious, beatific Southern smile.

"Well, it's getting late, and I'm supposed to head over to Bria's," Finn said. "And I obviously can't go looking like *this*."

I rolled my eyes at his put-upon tone, but Owen just laughed.

"Go," Owen said. "Get cleaned up. We can finish our business tomorrow."

"Say hi to Bria for me," I added in a sugary-sweet voice.

Finn grumbled something under his breath about what I could do with certain parts of my anatomy before packing up his papers and briefcase and leaving.

"Well," Owen said after Finn had shut the office door a little harder than necessary. "You got us both, just like you said you would."

I grinned again. "That's what people pay me for. Or used to pay me for."

He raised an eyebrow. "Good to know retirement hasn't lessened your skills any."

I shrugged. We both knew I couldn't afford to let myself get rusty. Not now, when so many folks in Ashland and beyond would love nothing more than to see me dead. Back in the winter, I'd finally killed Mab Monroe, the Fire elemental who'd run the Ashland underworld for years. Pro-fucking-bono, as it were. Mab had murdered my mother and sister when I was thirteen, and her death had been about revenge to me more than anything else. But the Fire elemental's demise had left a power vacuum in the city, and now every lowlife and not-so-lowlife was clawing for that power, position, and prestige. Some of them thought the best way to get all that was by killing me, Gin Blanco, the semiretired assassin known as the Spider.

So far, I'd put all the challengers in the ground along with Mab, but they just kept on coming. A few weeks ago, I'd brought up the idea of testing and updating the security at all the places I frequented, including Owen's home and office. There was no point in making things *easy* for my would-be murderers. Then Finn had piped up and suggested we make it into a contest—with him and Owen trying to outwit me. Of course, that hadn't turned out exactly like Finn had planned, but I was happy with the outcome. I always liked to win, no matter the game.

"So give me the rundown," Owen said. "Exactly how did you get into that air duct?"

I recapped my wanderings through the parking garage, maintenance halls, stairwell, office, and air ducts.

"Overall, your security's sound," I said. "All we have to do is fix a few holes here and there, and no one will be able to get to you, me, or anyone else in here without bringing down the whole building."

His eyes were fixed on mine, but there was a blank look on his face, as though he were only listening to my words with half an ear. I know it wasn't the most romantic talk, detailing how I'd just paintballed my lover, but this wasn't the first time he'd spaced out on me in the last few days. Something was on Owen's mind, and I didn't know what it was. That concerned me more than I would have liked, especially since I'd given him plenty of openings to tell me what was bothering him—openings he hadn't taken.

"Owen?"

Something flashed in his eyes then, something that almost looked like worry, but it was gone too quickly for me to pinpoint exactly what it was. He shook his head and focused on me once more.

"Sorry," he said. "What were you saying?"

Owen shrugged out of his suit jacket, the muscles in his arms and chest bulging with the motion. Suddenly, I was interested in playing something besides a war game. Something that would be far more entertaining and pleasurable—for both of us. Not to mention keep him firmly in the here and now with me. I didn't like playing second fiddle any more than the next woman did, especially when I didn't know exactly what was going on with my lover.

Owen started to loosen his tie, but I put the paintball gun down on the desk and strolled over to him. He stopped what he was doing to watch me, and I put an extra shimmy into my hips. Heat sparked in Owen's gaze—heat that matched the warmth that was flaring up inside me as well.

"Allow me," I said.

Owen watched with dark, hooded eyes as I unknotted his tie and let it fall to the floor. Then I ran my hands across his chest, marveling at the warm muscles there, before reaching up and undoing the top two buttons of his shirt. I pushed the fabric aside, leaned forward, and pressed a soft kiss to the hollow of his throat. Owen's arms snaked around me, pulling me close, and his fingers began pressing into my back, urging me on. I definitely had his full attention now.

"Why don't I help you get out of that ruined suit?" I murmured. "In addition to killing people, this assassin also happens to be exceptionally good at cleanup."

A sexy grin spread across Owen's rugged face, softening the scar that slashed underneath his chin. "Really? That's something I'd be very interested in seeing."

I led him into the bathroom. The door didn't even shut behind us before my lips were on his and I forgot about everything but the pleasure we could give each other. There would be time enough to figure out what had Owen so worried—later.

Much, much later.

☀ 3 ☀

Our war games finished, it was time for me to collect my prize—dinner at Underwood's.

The next night, Owen and I took his car over to the restaurant, which was located in a classy, older building in the city's financial district. Owen pulled up to the sidewalk where a crimson awning bore the restaurant's name, and we got out of the car. While he handed the keys off to a valet, I stood on the sidewalk and reached out with my Stone magic, curious about what I might hear. The brick of the building whispered of money, power, and plots, mixed with lighter notes of dishes and silverware tinkling together. Not unpleasant sounds, but ones that told me just how many dark, deadly schemes had been hatched here over dinner, dessert, and a nice bottle of wine.

Owen took my arm, and we went inside and rode the elevator up to the third and top floor, where the maître d' escorted us to a corner table. Crimson linens covered the table, which had been set with fine white china, delicate wineglasses, and silverware that had a more highly polished luster than some diamond rings. Three crimson tapers shaped like forks burned in a crystal candelabra in the center of the table. The fork was the restaurant's rune, representing all the good meals that could be had there, and the symbol was etched into the plates and silverware, as well as being stitched into the linens in gold thread.

Underwood's prided itself on its excellent food, service, and luxurious trappings, but what I appreciated most was the view. The brick had been stripped from the walls and replaced with floor-to-ceiling windows, letting diners look out over the Aneirin River, which wound through this part of downtown. The shops and lights along the river made the surface of the water glimmer like a silver ribbon unspooling into the black velvet embrace of the night. In the distance, I could just make out the white gleam of the *Delta Queen* riverboat casino. From this angle, the riverboat looked lovely, pristine even, but, as with so many things in Ashland, what lurked beneath the pretty, polished surface was a different story.

A waiter took our drink orders—whiskey for Owen, gin and tonic for me—and handed us each a leatherbound menu. No prices were listed on the creamy white pages. Underwood's was Ashland's fanciest and most expensive restaurant, the kind of highfalutin place that charged you an exorbitant amount just for drinking tap water—and even more if you wanted a refill. But Finn was paying tonight, so I had no qualms about ordering whatever I wanted and enjoying every single sip of it.

"Too bad Finn and Bria couldn't make it," Owen said.

I snorted. "Please. Finn could have put off his meeting if he'd really wanted to. He just didn't want to sit through dinner and listen to me gloat about how I'd won our contest *and* ruined his suit. Can't say I blame him."

"Well, then, I suppose you'll just have to make do with my company tonight," Owen teased.

I reached over and threaded my fingers through his, enjoying the warmth of his skin against mine. "Oh, I think I can manage."

We talked and laughed all through dinner. The food was excellent—black-pepper-crusted steaks, along with soft, sweet sourdough rolls, perfectly grilled vegetables, and mashed sweet potatoes generously slathered with honey butter and sprinkled with cinnamon. Our waiter was attentive without intruding, and none of the other patrons paid us much attention. Even though crime bosses like Ron Donaldson and Lorelei Parker were also eating here, they merely glanced in our direction and went back to their meals and dinner companions, content to leave well enough alone—at least for tonight.

Owen and I were having a lovely evening. Until Jonah McAllister walked into the restaurant.

Among those in the underworld, McAllister was probably the person who hated me the most—with good reason. Last year, I'd killed his son, Jake, for trying to rob the Pork Pit and then wanting to rape and murder me. Plus Jonah used to be Mab's lawyer, so I'd cut off his meal ticket and a good deal of his power and influence as well when I'd taken her out.

Rumor had it that McAllister was at loose ends these days, looking for a new crime lord or lady to serve, but he was also gunning for me. A few weeks ago, he'd sicced a sadistic vampire named Randall Dekes on me, but I'd managed to put the vamp in the ground instead.

Needless to say, Jonah was at the top of my to-kill list now. All that was left was for me to decide when and where to take him out—and just how much I wanted to make it *hurt*. My only regret was that it wasn't going to be tonight. But I wasn't ruining my evening with Owen, especially not for the likes of Jonah McAllister.

The maître d' led him to a table about fifteen feet away from ours. Despite my hatred of him, I had to admit that the lawyer cut a trim, confident, impressive figure in his impeccable black suit. Plus, his thick, perfectly styled coif of silver hair gleamed luxuriously underneath the restaurant's muted lights. Nobody in Ashland—male or female—had better hair.

McAllister sat down and glanced around, checking out who else was there. He tipped his head at Donaldson and Parker, who both politely nodded back at him, even though their smiles were nothing more than mocking sneers. Not too long ago, McAllister had tried to have me and the two of them killed at Mab's funeral. At least, I was convinced he was the one behind that sneak attack, even if nothing had ever been proven. I was mildly surprised that neither boss had retaliated against McAllister yet. Perhaps they didn't realize that he was probably behind it. Or perhaps they simply thought he was beneath their notice these days. Either way, the lawyer was still breathing when he shouldn't have been.

Finally, he spotted Owen and me. He stiffened in his chair, and his mouth puckered downward the faintest bit in displeasure, but the rest of his features didn't move with his lips. Despite the fact that he was in his sixties, McAllister's face was smoother than mine was at thirty, given his regimen of Air elemental facials. Vanity, thy name was Jonah McAllister.

"Well, well, well," I murmured. "Look who's here. I'm glad we had dinner already, or I would have lost my appetite."

"Ignore him," Owen said. "Just pretend he's not sitting there. I don't want him to ruin our night. I don't want to give him that satisfaction, and I know you don't either."

"Of course not. We both know he's not worth it."

So we focused on our menus and ordered dessert—a classic New York cheesecake with strawberry topping for Owen and a decadent black cherry and chocolate parfait for me. I ate my parfait slowly, letting the light, airy layers of cherries and chocolate melt on my tongue and savoring every sweet bite. All the while, though, I wondered if I could possibly lure McAllister into one of the restaurant bathrooms and stab him to death with the knife in my evening bag. A pleasant daydream on my part, since he would never go anywhere willingly with me, but the lawyer's days were numbered—even if he didn't realize it yet.

All through dessert, I kept an eye on McAllister, but he seemed determined to ignore me. Judging by the way he kept checking his expensive watch, the slick lawyer was waiting for someone—and whoever it was looked like they were late. Aw, I just hated that for him.

I'd just put my spoon down and pushed away my empty parfait glass when a series of hushed whispers rippled through the restaurant, as though everyone was trying very hard not to talk about someone and failing miserably. I looked out across the room, wondering who or what the fuss was about.

And that's when I saw her.

There were plenty of beautiful women in the restaurant, the belles of the underworld, the society pages, and all the social circles in between, all of them decked out in the finest evening gowns and jewels they or their husbands' money could buy. But this woman was in a class by herself. She was simply that stunning—the kind of woman who looks almost too beautiful to be real.

She was tall and willowy, with sun-kissed skin and golden hair that rippled halfway down in her back in soft, silky waves. A slinky, sequined, sky-blue gown clung to her curves in all the right places, the slits in the top and the bottom showing off the generous swell of her breasts and the long, lean lines of her legs. A silverstone cuff bracelet flashed on her right wrist, some sort of design etched into the metal.

Every head in the room turned to watch her, and a small, satisfied smile played across her rosy lips. Whoever she was, she knew exactly how stunning she was and enjoyed the attention.

The woman stopped at McAllister's table, which surprised me, since she definitely looked out of his league. The lawyer jumped to his feet, and she coolly offered him her hand, which he shook with all the enthusiasm of a shyster sidling up to his next victim. The two of them exchanged what seemed to be a polite greeting, although I couldn't hear the exact words over the clatter of the dishes and the continued whispers of the other diners.

Even though she was talking to McAllister, the woman was well aware of the stir she'd created. In fact, she encouraged it, slyly glancing at one diner, then the next to judge how eagerly they were ogling her. She even went so far as to subtly pose this way and turn that way to show off all her ample assets. A hip curve here, a flash of leg there, a faint pout of her lips. It was quite a show, better than a movie star preening for the cameras.

Finally, her eyes met mine. When she saw that I was merely curious and not completely enraptured by her, the woman's gaze went past me. But that same small, satisfied smile curved her lips again. Instead of taking the chair McAllister had pulled out for her, she headed in my direction.

I grabbed my purse from where I'd put it on the table. It only took a second for me to flip open the top and palm the silverstone blade nestled inside the black satin fabric, just in case. She was here with McAllister, after all. That didn't necessarily make her my enemy, but it certainly didn't make her my friend either.

Owen was engrossed in eating the last bite of his cheesecake, so he didn't see her approach us and stop on the opposite side of the table from where we were sitting. I'd thought the woman would say something to me, perhaps even make some snide, clichéd comment about my being the Spider, but I was surprised once again when she ignored me and fixed her gaze on my lover instead.

Owen pushed his plate away and sighed with contentment. "I know we're here on Finn's dime, but that cheesecake was worth every penny—"

For the first time, he realized someone was staring at

him. Owen looked up at the stranger, and his face went white with shock—as pale and stunned and bloodless as I'd ever seen it. His eyes widened, his mouth fell open, and the napkin he'd been about to put on the table slipped from his suddenly slack fingers and fluttered to the floor.

All the while, the mystery woman just stared at him, that small, satisfied smile still on her lips, stretching a bit wider and looking far more smug now.

"Hello, Owen, darling," she said.

Owen just sort of—sagged. His hands thudded down on the table, and his whole body pitched forward, as if the mere sight of her had turned his bones to jelly. He continued to sit there, a stunned expression on his face, as though he couldn't quite believe there was a woman standing in front of him—that *this* particular woman was standing in front of him. Whoever she was, he obviously knew her and was floored by her appearance—as floored as I'd been when I'd seen Donovan Caine, an old lover of mine, a few weeks ago. Hmm.

"Don't you have anything to say?" she asked. "Or perhaps a hug for an old friend?"

Her voice was soft, sweet, and utterly feminine, with the kind of faint dulcet chiming that made me think of water rushing down a mountainside. A hypnotizing voice—one that could persuade a man to do all sorts of things. Up close, I could see that her eyes were somewhere between blue and green—aquamarine, some folks might say. Their color seemed to constantly shift from one to the other and back again, churning like the sea.

"Owen?" she asked again.

"Of course," he said in a faint voice. He pushed his chair back and got to his feet.

Owen hesitated, then held out his hand, but the woman ignored his gesture and stepped into his arms, molding herself to his body and pressing her breasts against his chest. He hesitated again, then awkwardly patted her on the back before stepping out of her embrace as fast as he could. Amused by his attempts to disentangle himself from her, she did everything she could to slow his getaway.

Her antics did not amuse me—not one little bit. Especially since the woman was staring at my lover like she'd very much like to have him for dessert. Like it was almost a forgone conclusion that she *would,* despite my presence at the table.

Finally, she tore her gaze away from Owen long enough to glance at me. "Aren't you going to introduce me to your friend?"

"Of course," he echoed again. "Salina Dubois, this is Gin Blanco. Gin, Salina."

I discreetly tucked my knife back into my purse, closed the top, and put it down on the table. Then I got to my feet. Salina held out her hand to me, the same remote expression on her face that she'd shown McAllister—the one that told me just how very far beneath her and unimportant she thought I was.

Still, I took her hand. Even assassins could be polite on occasion. Her grip was firm, and her fingers felt cool against my own. I felt the tiniest trace of magic emanating from her, so faint I wondered if it was just my imagination.

Some elementals constantly gave off invisible waves of magic even when they weren't actively using their power, like embers throwing off heat. I concentrated, and once again I felt a faint flicker of magic. So Salina was an elemental, then. For a moment I thought that perhaps she had Ice magic, but her power didn't seem quite cold enough for that. No, her magic felt . . . softer and more fluid, like a raindrop sluicing across my skin. Perhaps she was just a weak Ice elemental, or maybe she was gifted in an offshoot power, like water.

We shook, but I didn't immediately let go of her hand afterward. Instead, I held on and turned it to the side, staring at the silverstone bracelet on her right wrist. The cuff was more than two inches wide and had a vaguely Egyptian design to it, like something an ancient queen might have worn. Delicate loops and whorls had been etched into the center of the cuff, along with a rune—a mermaid with long, flowing hair, a curled-up tail, and a serene smile.

Elementals, dwarves, giants, vampires—practically all of the magically inclined in Ashland and beyond used runes to identify themselves, their power, their families, and their businesses. So it didn't surprise me that Salina had her own personal rune. In fact, it seemed especially suited for her, since a mermaid was the symbol for deadly beauty. I could easily imagine Salina perched on a rock somewhere, wearing nothing but a seashell bra and a smile, luring sailors to their watery deaths with a mere crook of her finger.

What bothered me was that it seemed like she'd done the same thing to Owen once upon a time, judging from the way he couldn't stop staring at her.

But more than that, something about Salina's mermaid rune seemed familiar to me, like I'd seen the shape somewhere before—and her too. I could almost feel a memory wiggling around, trying to break through to the surface of my mind. Strange, because I should have remembered meeting someone like Salina. She was the sort of person who was hard to forget, if the reaction of all the men, and some of the women, in the room was any indication.

"What a beautiful bracelet," I murmured.

I traced my left index finger over the mermaid rune and realized that I was getting the same sensation from the bracelet I was off Salina's hand—one of cool, constant motion. So she used the cuff to store her magic then, like so many elementals did their silverstone rings, watches, and necklaces.

Salina pulled her hand out of mine and made a pointed show of rubbing my fingerprints off the cuff's glossy surface. "A family heirloom."

"Charming."

We smiled at each other, being painstakingly polite the way Southern women so often were, even though our eyes were flat and emotionless. Instant dislike on both sides.

Salina stared at me, taking in my simple black evening gown with its long, swooping, poet sleeves and full tulle skirt, which hid the two knives I had strapped to my thighs. Her gaze lingered on my own silverstone jewelry, the ring on my right index finger, which had my spider rune stamped into the middle of it and contained my Ice magic. But apparently, my ring wasn't as impressive as her bracelet, because she didn't comment on it. Instead, she focused her attention on Owen again.

"I'm so glad I ran into you tonight," Salina purred. "Especially since you never returned the message I left at your office last week about my finally coming back to Ashland."

I looked at Owen, who winced. He'd never told me about any message he'd gotten from her.

"Anyway, now I can give you my good news in person," Salina continued in her soft, sweet voice. "Before, I said I was only coming for a visit, but I've decided to move back to Ashland permanently. Isn't that wonderful?"

"Wonderful," Owen echoed, his voice even fainter than before.

Salina smiled and moved even closer to my lover. She reached out and smoothed first one side, then the other of his jacket, before bringing her fingers up and toying with his lapels. "The two of us will have lots of time to catch up now. I'd like that, wouldn't you?"

Over at his table, McAllister pointedly cleared his throat, saving Owen from answering that loaded question. Salina turned to send the lawyer a cold, withering look and held up a finger, indicating that she'd be there in a minute. Then, she focused her attention on Owen again, all smiles and sunshine once more.

"Call me, darling. You have my number. Any time, day . . . or night."

Wow. Subtle she was not. I don't think her meaning could have been any clearer than if she'd hiked up her dress and asked Owen to do her right there on the table.

Salina winked at him, then sashayed back over to McAllister's table, where the lawyer was still standing, his hands now clenched around the back of the chair he'd pulled out for her. He didn't like being ignored any more than I did. The two of them sat down, and McAllister started talking, although Salina was only half listening to the lawyer, her gaze repeatedly drifting over to Owen.

My lover sighed and looked at me. "About Salina—"

I reached over and straightened his tie, giving him the same killer smile Salina just had. "Not while we have an audience, *darling*. There'll be plenty of time to chat in private on the drive home."

I told the waiter to put the bill on Finn's tab, and Owen and I left Underwood's and got into his car. We didn't speak on the drive over to Fletcher's house—my house now. Owen steered his Mercedes Benz to the top of the driveway and put the car in park, but he didn't turn off the engine. Instead, he stared out the windshield into the darkness—brooding.

I wondered what he was seeing—what he was remembering about Salina. The time they'd been together, the things they'd shared, how she'd made him feel when they were alone in the dark, their skin touching, their hands exploring, their bodies arching into each other.

My heart pulsed with jealousy at the thought of them together, but I stayed quiet. Owen hadn't been a virgin any more than I had been when we'd gotten together. We both had pasts—Owen had just seen more of my dark, violent one than I had of his.

He finally sighed. "Ask away. I know you want to."

"You and Salina?"

He nodded. "Me and Salina."

"How long ago?"

"A lifetime," he murmured. "Maybe two."

I waited for him to go on, to talk about how they'd met, the time they'd spent together, or even why they'd broken up. He didn't say anything, but his face, his whole body, was tight and tense with emotion—with pain. Whatever had happened between them, it hadn't ended well. Still, I kept quiet, waiting for Owen to tell me about them in his own way, in his own time. That's what he'd done for me when I'd run into Donovan while on vacation in Blue Marsh. I figured I owed Owen the same courtesy.

He sighed again. "Anyway, it's over, and it has been for a long time now. I hadn't seen or heard from Salina in years . . ."

"Until she left that message at your office last week."

He nodded. "Right."

And that would have been about the time Owen had started acting distant and distracted. Ah. *Lightbulb finally on,* and a bloody little slice on my heart and ego to go along with it. To realize that Owen had been preoccupied because of Salina—and that my lover hadn't told me the first thing about her until forced to tonight. Reunions with old lovers rarely went well, and it seemed like there was more history between the two of them than most. Still, I didn't care too much about Owen's past with Salina, as long as he knew that I was his present—and, most importantly, his future. Something I planned on showing him tonight.

I reached out and trailed my fingers down his face. "Come in?" I asked.

He hesitated. "I really shouldn't. I've got an early meeting tomorrow."

"I understand," I murmured, keeping my face smooth and hiding the hurt that pricked my heart.

Owen gently reached for my hand and kissed my palm, right in the middle of my spider rune scar. "Rain check?"

"Of course." This time, I was the one with the faint voice.

Owen hesitated again, then leaned over and pressed his lips to mine—but he pulled back far too soon, like he'd been guessing how long he should maintain the kiss and the allotted time was up. I managed to smile at him, pretending I didn't notice the sudden distance between us, distance that Salina had somehow created just by walking into the restaurant.

I got out of the car and shut the door behind me. Owen put the vehicle in gear and turned it around. He paused to wave good night to me, and I lifted my hand in return. A moment later, the car disappeared down the driveway.

I stood there alone in the dark and wondered who the hell Salina Dubois really was, why she seemed to have such an effect on my lover, and what I was going to do about her. Because this was a matter of the heart—and one problem that all my knives and all my prowess as the Spider wouldn't help me solve.

�֎ 4 ✲

Despite my unease and questions about Salina, the next day was business as usual at the Pork Pit, the barbecue restaurant I owned—right down to me checking for booby traps.

It was just before eleven, and I'd spent the last twenty minutes looking at everything in the restaurant storefront, from the well-worn but clean blue and pink vinyl booths to the long counter that ran down the back wall to the framed, blood-spattered copy of *Where the Red Fern Grows* that hung on the wall beside the cash register. I peered underneath each one of the tables and chairs, examined the front door for any signs of tampering, and checked every single one of the windows for the slightest hint of a crack, chip, or break. I even got down on my hands and knees and followed the paths of the faded, peeling, blue and pink pig tracks on the floor all the way back to the men's and women's restrooms. Then I examined both of those areas top to bottom as well, just to make sure nothing was hidden in a trash can or taped to the back of a toilet.

"Anything?" a harsh voice rasped.

I walked back out into the storefront and looked at the source of the voice: Sophia Deveraux, the dwarf who was the head cook at the Pit and chief Spider-related body dumper. Sophia had sat in one of the booths, calm and cool as could be, while I checked for traps, but she was causing quite a stir on the street outside, as people saw her through the windows and stopped to stare at her.

That's because Sophia was Goth. Today, the dwarf wore her usual black boots and jeans, topped off by a white T-shirt that had a bright red cherry bomb in the center of it—one with a lit fuse. The bomb's scarlet color matched the spiked silverstone collar ringing her neck and the cuffs on her wrists. Her lipstick was as black as her hair, and smoky shadow arched over her dark eyes as well, making her face seem as pale as the moon in comparison.

I eyed the cherry bomb T-shirt, wondering if Sophia had worn it as some sort of joke, given the volatile nature of the Ashland underworld these days. It was hard to tell with her sometimes. The dwarf didn't talk much due to her voice, which had been ruined years ago when she'd been forced to breathe in elemental Fire.

"Anything?" Sophia asked again, sounding like there was a cheese grater scraping against her vocal cords.

"Nope," I replied. "Nobody left us any nasty surprises. So you can go into the alley out back and tell the waitstaff to come on in."

Sophia nodded, got up, and walked the length of the

restaurant before pushing through the swinging double doors that led into the back.

I looked over the storefront a final time, double-checking to make sure I hadn't missed anything. Checking out the Pit was something I did every morning now, given all the folks who would love to see me dead. In addition to using them as their personal or business symbols, elementals could also imbue runes with their magic and get those symbols to flare to life and perform specific functions—like firebombing my restaurant and hopefully killing me in the process. It would be far too easy for a Fire elemental to casually stroll by the restaurant late one night, pause a moment, and trace an incendiary rune into the wooden doorframe that would erupt in flames as soon as I opened the front door the next morning.

So far, no one had tried that particular trick, but it was only a matter of time before someone thought of it—and I planned to be ready when they did. That was why I checked the restaurant, and it was why I kept an eye on all the diners who scarfed down the thick, hearty, barbecue sandwiches and other greasy Southern treats Sophia and I served up at the Pit.

Satisfied that no one had laid any traps for me, I flipped the sign on the door over to *Open* and moved back behind the counter to start cooking for the day.

Given the warm, bright, inviting May sunshine, it didn't take long for folks to leave their offices, head outside, and flock to the restaurant in search of an early lunch. Catalina Vasquez and the rest of the waitstaff seated everyone and took their orders, before bustling back over with their drinks a few minutes later. Meanwhile, Sophia and I manned the ovens, the stoves, and the french fryers. I also mixed up a batch of Fletcher's secret barbecue sauce and set that pot on one of the back burners to simmer away. I breathed in, enjoying how the sauce's spicy cumin kick mixed with all the other rich, dense flavors in the air.

In between cooking and dishing up food, my gaze went from one diner to the next, but they were all focused on their meals and companions. Oh, they still watched me, of course, giving me quick glances out of the corners of their eyes when they thought I wasn't looking. After all, I was rumored to be the Spider, the assassin who'd killed the supposedly unkillable Mab Monroe. The whispers were more widespread among the underworld denizens, but they were slowly starting to circulate among regular folks as well. Hell, I was something of a tourist attraction in Ashland these days, and people came from near and far just to get a glimpse of me, sit in my restaurant, and eat my food. I'd even heard rumors that some particularly enterprising soul was selling T-shirts with the slogan *I ate at the Pork Pit . . . and lived!* emblazoned on them, but so far no one had been bold enough to wear one inside the restaurant.

I gazed around the storefront once more, but none of the current crop of customers looked like the type who'd come here to cause trouble or try to murder me, so I went back to my cooking. Maybe today would be a calm day. I hoped so. I needed some time to think about Owen, Salina, and what her reappearance might really mean to my lover—and how I could keep her from messing up what I had with Owen.

But it wasn't to be—because Phillip Kincaid strolled into the restaurant around two o'clock.

Kincaid had sandy blond hair that was slicked back

into a low ponytail and strong, pronounced cheekbones a model would have been envious of. He wore a dark blue suit that showed off the strength of his tall, thick body, and he looked almost as good in the expensive threads as Finn did in one of his designer duds. Kincaid wasn't movie star handsome—not like Finn—but there was something about him that caught your eye and made you take a second look. Something in the easy, confident way he carried himself, and the coldness in his vivid blue eyes.

Despite his striking looks, Kincaid was on my radar for another, less pleasant reason: he happened to be one of Ashland's top underworld sharks, with a network of giant enforcers and other rough types who worked for him. Kincaid had been one of the few heavy hitters who'd dared to go toe-to-toe with Mab when she'd been alive. Now that the Fire elemental was dead, Kincaid had even more power, as he'd spent the last few months picking up some of the pieces of her old empire and consolidating them into his own operations.

The last time I'd seen Kincaid had been on his luxe riverboat casino, the *Delta Queen,* back in the fall. I'd gone to one of his parties to kill Elliot Slater, a giant who was stalking and terrorizing a friend of mine. I'd never spoken to or had any real interaction with Kincaid, other than watching him smile at me at Mab's funeral, but we both knew who the other was.

I expected to see a giant bodyguard or two step into the restaurant behind Kincaid, but the door swung shut behind him. Phillip Kincaid, walking into my gin joint all by his lonesome. Interesting. Somehow, though, I didn't think he was here for the food, no matter how good it was.

Sophia heard the bell over the front door chime when Kincaid opened it, and she looked up from the warm sourdough buns she was slicing. She recognized him too, her black lips flattening out into a thin, hard line.

"Trouble?" the dwarf asked, her fingers tightening around the bread knife in her hand.

"We'll see," I murmured. "Stand by for now."

Sophia grunted and went back to her slicing.

Kincaid scanned the inside of the restaurant, looking over everyone and everything, much as I'd done earlier. Then, to my surprise, he walked over, unbuttoned his suit jacket, and took a seat at the counter right in front of where I was slicing ripe tomatoes, sweet red onions, and crispy lettuce for the day's sandwiches.

Catalina grabbed a menu and started to go over to Kincaid, but Sophia headed her off and pointed her to a customer who needed a drink refill, leaving him to me.

Kincaid sat at the counter and watched me slice the vegetables. The surprising thing was that I didn't sense any judgment or rancor in him. Not like when Jonah McAllister came in. The lawyer always sneered at me, but Kincaid just looked at me with curiosity—and wariness.

I chopped my way through a head of lettuce, amusing myself by imagining it was McAllister I was cutting into, before he finally spoke.

"Gin Blanco." His voice had a slow, seductive Southern drawl to it, the sort that would make a woman melt on a hot, steamy night, although I could hear a faint twang in his words, as though he'd been raised more poor country than his slick city suit let on.

"Phillip Kincaid." My tone was as frosty as his was warm.

His eyebrows arched up. "You know me."

"And you know me. So let's cut the fake surprise and niceties and get down to business. What do you want?"

"Well, right now, I want a sweet iced blackberry tea, a bacon cheeseburger, potato salad, baked beans, and a slice of that cherry pie in the cake stand. It looks absolutely delicious. And would you be so kind as to bring it all out together, please? I always hate waiting for dessert."

I gave him a hard, flat stare, but Kincaid just smiled, revealing perfect white teeth. He didn't show a hint of doubt or fear in the face of my wintry gray gaze. If anything, his own eyes brightened in what looked like delight, as if I'd passed some sort of secret test by not responding to his obvious charms. Well, if that was the game he wanted to play, I'd be more than happy to oblige him—right up until I stuck one of my knives in his chest the second he showed his true colors.

"Why, coming right up, sugar," I said in a drawl that was as slow and syrupy as his.

Kincaid's eyes narrowed at my mocking tone, but he kept his smile on his face. He had balls, I'd give him that, coming into my restaurant and acting like just another customer. Then again, so did all the other lowlifes who did the exact same thing. I wondered if Kincaid had more brains than the others did. One would assume so, given how long he'd managed to survive swimming in the underworld muck. You didn't achieve Kincaid's level of staying power and success by being a pushover or stupid.

Sophia helped me fix Kincaid's food, and a few minutes later I set his plates in front of him. He wasted no time in tucking a white napkin in at his chin and digging into his bacon cheeseburger, side dishes, and pie. He ate them all at once, taking a bite of burger, then one of potato salad, then beans, and finally one of pie, instead of waiting to eat his dessert after he finished everything else. Every once in a while, he'd break up the pattern with a swig of tea. Curious. So was the fact that he ate so quickly, as if he was afraid I was going to reach across the counter and snatch away his plates before he'd had his fill.

The way he wolfed down his meal reminded me of myself when I'd been living on the streets as a kid. Back then, I'd crammed food into my mouth as rapidly as Kincaid was doing now. Most curious indeed.

We didn't speak as he ate, and I moved back and forth behind the counter, fixing drinks, dishing up food, and helping Sophia and the waitresses with whatever the other customers needed. But through it all, I kept an eye on Kincaid.

All the while, I kept waiting for some of his giant bodyguards to show up, for someone to try and take a shot at me through the bulletproof storefront windows . . . hell, for something, anything, dangerous to happen—but nothing did. For all intents and purposes, Phillip Kincaid had just come here for lunch.

The problem was, I didn't believe that any more than I believed the moon was made of green fucking cheese.

Several minutes later, as I was whacking my way through another head of lettuce and still indulging in my murderous daydreams, Kincaid finished his meal and let out what sounded like a satisfied sigh, as though he'd truly enjoyed the food. He removed the napkin from the collar of his shirt, dropped it on the counter, and pushed his plates to the side.

I finished with the lettuce and moved on to the next vegetable on my list, potatoes that needed to be peeled and cubed so I could make another batch of potato salad.

"That was a mighty fine meal," Kincaid said, sounding quite sincere. "Best one I've had in a long time. In fact, that's why I came here today."

"Oh?" I said, putting as much withering disbelief as I could into that one word.

"I'm holding a little get-together on the *Delta Queen* in a few days' time. And I want you to cater the event."

This time, my eyebrows were the ones that shot up. "You want me to cater a party? On your riverboat?"

"I do. Everyone says you make the best barbecue in Ashland, so I decided to see for myself. You've sold me on your little place. Consider me a loyal customer from now on."

He gave me another winning smile, as if that seemingly innocent expression could somehow lure me into swallowing the absolute bullshit he was spouting. He rather reminded me of Finn in that moment. The difference was, I trusted my foster brother.

"Don't you have your own chefs?" I asked. "From what I hear, the food on your little boat is some of the best in the city, close to rivaling Underwood's. Surely your own staff could cater."

He shrugged. "Perhaps. But I think the patrons of this particular event will enjoy something a little more . . . down-home and relaxed than champagne and caviar. I'm prepared to pay you quite generously for your time and culinary expertise, of course."

"Of course."

I looked over at Sophia, who was stirring the barbecue sauce I'd put on the stove earlier. The Goth dwarf was standing close enough to hear Kincaid's catering offer. She glanced at me and shrugged, telling me she didn't know what he was up to any more than I did, but that she'd go along with whatever I wanted to do. She was a good friend that way.

I concentrated on my potatoes, giving myself a few seconds to think. Try as I might, I couldn't imagine what Kincaid was plotting. He'd never made any problems for either Gin Blanco or the Spider before. Just about every other crime boss in Ashland had sent some goons after me, trying to eliminate me, but Kincaid was one of the few who hadn't. I'd thought it had just been common sense on his part, but now I was wondering if it was something else—if he had some other kind of trap in mind for me. Either way, it made me curious enough to want to find out—and to upset whatever apple cart Kincaid had so thoughtfully arranged. I rather enjoyed being petty that way.

"When is this little shindig of yours?" I finally asked.

His eyes gleamed with sly triumph. "Thursday, three days from now."

"And how much food do you think you'll need?"

He quoted me some figures about expected guests, what he wanted to see on the menu, and when he wanted the food to be served. We also hammered out the payment, which was far more generous than it should have been for a job like this one. Then again, nothing about this was what it seemed to be—except rotten.

"Excellent," Kincaid said when we'd finished our discussion. "Let's take care of the money right now."

He reached into his jacket, and my hand tightened around the knife I was using to cube the potatoes. Just in case he was going for something other than his checkbook.

But that was exactly what Kincaid drew out of his jacket, along with a silverstone pen, and he wrote me a check for the catering gig and his lunch. He even added an obscenely generous tip on top of everything. Oh yes, he was definitely up to something, but that didn't keep me from taking the slip of paper from him, folding it, and sliding it into the back pocket of my jeans. Finn would never let me hear the end of it if I passed up all that money.

"It's been a pleasure doing business with you, Gin," Kincaid said, putting away his checkbook and pen, getting to his feet, and buttoning his suit jacket once more.

I gave him a thin smile. "I doubt I'll say the same before this is all said and done."

For a moment, worry filled his eyes before he was able to mask it, although the pleasant expression never dropped from his lips—not even for a second. Oh, yes. Phillip Kincaid could definitely give Finn a run for his money in the suave department.

Kincaid nodded at me, did the same to Sophia as well, then turned and headed out of the Pork Pit. He stopped and held the door open for someone coming in, and I realized it was Finn. The two men stood in the doorway and stared at each other, before Kincaid moved past Finn and stepped outside, letting the door swing shut behind him.

Finn frowned, walked over to the counter, and slid onto the stool the other man had just vacated. "What the hell was *he* doing here?"

"I don't rightly know," I said, watching Kincaid stroll down the sidewalk and out of sight of the storefront windows. "But I'm going to find out."

❖ 5 ❖

That Thursday I found myself staring up at the *Delta Queen* riverboat casino.

The riverboat was a massive structure, with six decks of gleaming, whitewashed wood, red- and blue-painted trim, and polished brass rails. At the rear of the boat, a giant paddle wheel rose up from the water and loomed over the topmost deck like a white whale about to crash down and sink the whole ship. Globe-shaped lights wrapped around all the rails and dropped from one level to the next, swinging back and forth in the warm spring breeze.

The *Delta Queen* was docked in the downtown district in front of a wooden boardwalk lined with old-fashioned iron street lamps and benches. Several uppity art galleries, overpriced antique stores, and cutesy cafés could also be found along the walkway, their windows and outdoor seats offering views of the boat and the Aneirin River that it slowly bobbed up and down upon.

The boardwalk and shops were an attempt by the city planners to gentrify the area, despite how close it was to Southtown, the dangerous part of Ashland that was home to the city's down-on-their-luck bums, deadly gang-bangers, vampire hookers, and their violent pimps. So far, the upscale stores and pristine landscaping had stuck, thanks in part to the security force Kincaid paid to watch over the *Delta Queen* and surrounding parking lots. After all, it just wouldn't do for someone to get mugged before he could board the riverboat and lose his money in the casino.

"Pretty lights," Sophia rasped beside me.

"Yes," I murmured. "The lights on the riverboat are certainly pretty."

I just wondered what darkness waited for me on board.

I'd asked Finn to find out everything he could about Kincaid and what was going down on his riverboat to-night. My foster brother had an impressive network of spies, snitches, and folks who owed him favors in Ashland and beyond, and Finn loved digging up dirt on people more than a gardener enjoyed planting his prize roses.

Still, despite all his sources, Finn hadn't been able to find out much. Kincaid had appeared on the underworld scene as a teenager, doing whatever dirty job he was asked to and ruthlessly working his way up through the ranks of various criminal organizations until he'd struck out on his own. Today, he controlled the market for all the gambling operations—legal and otherwise—in Ashland.

Kincaid was rumored to be as dangerous as they came, despite the fact that he wasn't an elemental. Then again, you didn't need elemental magic to kill—just an intense desire to make someone quit breathing and the will to make it a reality. Kincaid wouldn't have gotten where he was and stayed there all these years without having both of those in spades.

Good thing I did, too. I'd be more than ready for whatever trap the casino boss had in store for me tonight.

"Well," I said to Sophia, "let's go make some barbecue."

Sophia and I spent the next fifteen minutes unloading our supplies from her classic convertible and the Cadillac Escalade I'd borrowed from Finn's fleet of cars. Together, the Goth dwarf and I carried everything we needed up the gangplank and on board the riverboat . . .

And right into the middle of a frat party.

Guys and girls in their late teens and early twenties filled the riverboat's third deck, which formed an open U shape that jutted out past all the other decks and curved into the bow of the boat. Everyone had on flip-flops and sandals, along with the tightest T-shirts and the shortest shorts they could get away with. A banner hanging down from the fourth deck read *Charity Rocks! Give 'Til It Hurts!*

That was the other strange thing about tonight. I'd expected Kincaid to be throwing some fancy gala, but instead here was a fund-raiser for an animal shelter being put on by some sororities and fraternities at Ashland Community College. Well, perhaps *fund-raiser* was too generous a term. *Kegger with a cause* would have been more appropriate, given the students who had brought along their own beer and were already stumbling around like the boat was actually moving instead of being secured to the dock.

Games had been set up on deck, everything from poker to roulette to craps. A twenty-dollar cover charge got you on board the riverboat, all the food you could eat, and a stack of chips. They didn't have any monetary value tonight, but if you won enough chips playing the games, you could redeem them for prizes. Raffles of donated items were also being held, and screams of delight rippled through the crowd every time someone won something, rising above the loud, constant, ringing *ching-ching-ching* of the slot machines.

The kids who weren't drinking or gambling were amusing themselves by hooking up, as though standing by the railing meant that no one could see them sticking their tongues down each other's throats or would notice all the wandering hands disappearing beneath skimpy outfits.

It all looked so real, so legit, so damn *convincing*, that I would have almost believed this was a bona fide catering job—except for the fact Kincaid had personally come into the Pork Pit to hire me. Men like him didn't do things like that—that's what underlings were for. The casino boss was definitely up to something; I just didn't know what it was yet.

"Gin! There you are!"

Speak of the devil. Kincaid pushed through a door that led into the riverboat's interior and headed in my direction. From my past explorations here, I knew the inside of the boat was hollow and ringed with a series of balconies, so folks on the upper decks could see the stage here on the third floor and watch the elaborate shows put on there. Kincaid offered a full, Vegas-style experience, right down to the leggy showgirls Finn always lusted after whenever he watched a performance here.

Kincaid walked toward me, followed by a giant with pecan-brown hair, matching eyes, and olive skin. Both men wore light, summer-weight suits, and each had a large pin in the middle of his silk tie. Kincaid's pin was made of silverstone, while the giant's was gold, but both were shaped like a dollar sign superimposed over an out-line of the riverboat—Kincaid's rune for his casino and the buckets of money it netted him. A little garish and too in-your-face for my tastes, but it didn't surprise me that the casino boss liked to flaunt his wealth. He'd earned it, clawing his way up through the underworld.

More giants circulated through the crowd, all wearing suits and the same gold tiepin. They closely monitored the students and games. Despite the fact that he'd opened up his riverboat to the college crowd, Kincaid wasn't let-ting any of the kids cheat or swipe chips from their fellow gamblers. How noble of him.

Kincaid stopped in front of Sophia and me, his blue eyes flicking over our boots, jeans, and long-sleeved T-shirts. Once again, I got the sense he was highly amused about something whenever he looked at me, although I had no idea what that could possibly be. There wasn't anything amusing about me—or the knives I'd brought along.

"This is Antonio Mendez, my second-in-command," Kincaid said, gesturing to the giant beside him. "If you need anything tonight, just let him know."

Antonio nodded his head at Sophia, then turned to

stare at me, sizing me up. Despite the neutral expression, I could sense the coiled strength in his seven-foot body. Finn had actually been able to find out more about Kincaid's men than about Kincaid himself, so I knew Antonio could be ruthless when need be. The giant wasn't someone you wanted to fuck with.

Then again, neither was I.

I returned Antonio's searching stare with a cold, hard one of my own. After a moment, the giant nodded his head again, indicating I'd passed his little mental pissing contest. As if I cared. I didn't have anything to prove to the giant or anyone else, but I'd have been happy to show him exactly who he was messing with if he got an inch out of line or threatened either Sophia or myself in the slightest way.

Antonio turned his attention to the Goth dwarf, and his eyes widened at her black lipstick and the purple streaks she'd put in her hair. "Here. Let me help you with those," he said, reaching for the stack of boxes in her arms.

Sophia let out a low, threatening growl. With her ruined, raspy voice, she sounded like a mythological Fenrir wolf about to sink its teeth into a hunk of fresh meat. Antonio froze. Sophia let out another growl, and the giant dropped his hands to his sides and stepped away from her. Smart man.

Kincaid stayed silent throughout their exchange, then made a sweeping motion with his hand. "This way."

He led us over to the far side of the deck, the one facing out toward the Aneirin River. A large cooking station had been set up there, complete with pots, pans, utensils, a couple of burners, coolers filled with ice, and everything else we would need. Kincaid had been thorough, if nothing else. His accommodating nature only made me that much more suspicious about what he really wanted—and how many people I might have to kill to make it through the night.

"I thought we would set you up out here so you can see all of the action," he said. "Keep you right in the thick of things."

His voice was as bland as could be, but something in his words bothered me. It almost sounded like he was expecting trouble tonight, but I couldn't imagine what problems the drunken frat boys and girls could possibly create that his giants couldn't handle.

"Like I said, let Antonio know if you need anything."

Kincaid gave me a thin smile, then moved off into the crowd. Antonio nodded at us and walked away too, although he didn't go far, planting himself against the rail about twenty feet from the cooking station. Keeping an eye on us.

"This gets stranger by the minute," I said to Sophia.

The dwarf grunted her agreement, put down her boxes, and started unpacking them. I did the same. Whatever Kincaid was up to, there was nothing to do now but see it through to the end.

The next hour involved reheating the dishes Sophia and I had made earlier in the day, creating some last-minute ones on-site, and then serving everything up to the hungry kids.

I recognized more than a few folks and said hello to those I knew, since I was also a student at Ashland Community College. I was always taking a course or two at the college, like the literature class I'd signed up for this summer. Sophia and I had just finished feeding the first wave of students when I spotted two very familiar faces in the crowd—Eva Grayson and Violet Fox.

Eva was Owen's nineteen-year-old sister, and Violet was her best friend. The two girls were pretty much inseparable, despite how different they were. Eva looked a lot like Owen, with her blue-black hair, while Violet was all frizzy blond hair and glasses. Like everyone else, they were dressed in shorts, T-shirts, and flip-flops. In fact, Eva's T-shirt bore the name of the sorority that was hosting the fund-raiser, making me wonder if she'd been involved in the planning.

I wasn't particularly surprised to see them at a college function, but the troubling thing was that the two girls were talking to none other than Kincaid himself. The casino boss said something, causing both Eva and Violet to laugh. Eva, especially, seemed interested in what he had to say, tossing her hair over her shoulder and smiling at him—something her big brother would definitely not approve of.

Owen had a protective streak a mile wide when it came to Eva, just like I did when it came to my younger sister Bria. Owen would definitely not want Eva cozying up to a casino mobster, but that was exactly what she was doing—and Kincaid seemed to be enjoying every second of her attention.

I dished up the last of the macaroni salad in my tin pan and turned to Sophia. "Can you handle things for a while? I see something I need to take care of."

The dwarf followed my gaze, frowned, and nodded. She didn't like the two girls being close to Kincaid any more than I did, especially since we still didn't know what he was plotting.

"Go," she rasped.

I undid my blue work apron, lifted the strings over my head, and tied them to the brass railing behind me. Then I skirted around the cooking station and headed for Kincaid. Antonio, who'd been leaning against the railing and idly ogling the pretty young girls who walked by, snapped to attention as I stalked past him.

"Down, boy," I drawled. "I just want to talk to your boss a second. I'm not going to kill him."

Yet.

The word wasn't spoken, but the threat must have shown in my cold face, because Antonio followed me over to where Kincaid was holding court with Eva and Violet.

Violet saw me first and winced, like the jig was up. She tapped Eva on the arm, trying to get her attention, but Eva was too interested in what Kincaid had to say to pay her friend any mind. That changed, though, the second I shouldered my way in between Eva and Kincaid, not so subtly bumping the casino boss away from her and making him take several steps back.

"Why, hello, Eva," I drawled again. "I had no idea you were going to be here tonight."

"Gin!" Eva sputtered, her blue eyes widening. "What— what are you doing here?"

"Catering. And you?"

It took her a second to recover, but when she did, she gestured at the other kids. "Overseeing the fund-raiser."

"Really? This is *your* fund-raiser? I don't remember you telling me anything about it when you and Violet had lunch at the Pork Pit yesterday. I'm surprised you wouldn't mention it to me, if the cause was so very important to you. But I'm guessing you told Owen all about it, right? And where you were going tonight?"

A guilty flush stained Eva's pale cheeks. *Busted.* Eva realized as well as I did that Owen wouldn't want her near anyone as dangerous as Kincaid, but here she was all the same. I couldn't help but wonder why. Was the fund-raiser being held on the riverboat just a coincidence? Or was there something else going on? Something between Eva and Kincaid, as unlikely as that seemed? I didn't know, but I was going to find out.

I had to hand it to her, Eva wasn't easily intimidated, not even by the likes of me, and she raised her chin. "I needed somewhere to host the fund-raiser, somewhere cooler and more interesting than the student center, so I called Philly and asked him if we could use the riverboat. He said yes."

"*Philly?*" I asked, arching an eyebrow.

Kincaid squared his shoulders and looked me in the eye. "Philly. It's an old nickname Eva gave me when we were kids."

This time, both my eyebrows shot up. According to Finn's sketchy file on him, Kincaid was my age, thirty, which made him about eleven years older than Eva. Even if you disregarded the age difference, they didn't exactly move in the same social circles. So what was going on here? How did they know each other? And more importantly, why was Eva being so nice to Kincaid? Cozying up to him like he was a long-lost friend?

I was opening my mouth to ask those very questions, when a scream ripped through the crowd.

❖ 6 ❖

One second, everything was normal. Kids were laughing, talking, drinking, eating, and playing games. The next, everyone had stopped what they were doing, puzzled expressions on their faces as they tried to figure out why someone was interrupting their buzz. Then, when the screams didn't stop, panic rippled through the crowd, until all the kids were pushing, shoving, and lurching around the deck, trying to put some distance between themselves and whatever horrible thing was happening.

I immediately palmed one of my silverstone knives and turned toward the source of the disturbance, although I made sure to keep Kincaid in my line of sight as well, just in case this was some kind of trick to distract me. He might be the boss here, but I wouldn't have put it past him to pull a gun or knife on me and get his hands dirty himself.

"Back, back, back!" I yelled at Eva and Violet, pushing

the two girls until they were up against the closed doors that led inside the riverboat.

Knife in hand, I put myself in front of them, protecting them from whatever the danger might be—and that's when I realized the screams were coming from Antonio.

Given their tall, strong, thick bodies, giants were tough to injure and even tougher to kill. Sure, you could take one down with a gun or knife, but you usually had to work to do it. But Antonio was bent over double in the middle of the deck, his hands clutched to his head as though he had the worst migraine imaginable. He just kept screaming and screaming, and I couldn't figure out why. He didn't appear to have been stabbed, and I hadn't heard any gunshots ring out. He didn't seem to have so much as a paper cut. So what the hell was wrong with him?

Antonio finally lifted his head and straightened up. Once again, I looked him over, searching for any injuries and what might have caused them. I didn't see any blood or wounds—not so much as a nick or a bruise—but wait . . . There was something wrong with his skin. It looked . . . wet.

And that's when I felt the first gust of magic swirl through the air.

The elemental power slid against my skin as cool, slick, and gentle as water dripping off waxed paper. It wasn't an unpleasant sensation—not at all—but I didn't welcome it either. Because magic most always meant trouble.

I focused, concentrating on the feel of the other elemental's magic, but I couldn't tell exactly where it was coming from or who in the panicked crowd was wielding it—just that it was concentrated on Antonio.

After a few more seconds, the giant's screams faded to garbled gasps. He was having trouble getting words out, and then his voice dried up altogether. He stood in the middle of the deck, his dark eyes empty, his body swaying from side to side like a tree about to topple over.

And he literally melted.

I watched as his skin, which had seemed damp before, took on a glossy sheen, as though he'd just run ten miles uphill and was sweating profusely. But it wasn't sweat slicking down Antonio's face, neck, and hands. It was water—all the water in his body, leaving.

"A water elemental," I muttered, although my voice was lost in the commotion of the crowd.

I knew there were elementals gifted with water magic, and I'd heard of the ways such people used their abilities for everything from sailing, skiing, and fishing to more serious matters like flood control. But I'd never seen anything like this.

The human body was mostly made of water, and giants' bodies were no different. More and more water beaded upon Antonio's skin until it dripped off the ends of his fingers, his chin, hell, even the tip of his nose. His soaked suit was plastered to his body, and water leaked out of his wing tips and slowly spread across the deck. Well, that explained his agonized cries. Having the water forced out of every single cell in your body would make anyone scream, even a giant.

Without all that precious fluid, there wasn't much of Antonio left. The giant's face took on a gaunt, hollow look, and his whole body seemed to slowly deflate, like a tire that had sprung a leak.

It was sickening to watch.

Antonio wasn't screaming anymore—but everyone else was. Even I had to bite back a snarl of disgust, especially when the elemental used their magic to pop the giant's eyeballs right out of his head. The orbs splattered onto the deck and oozed over the glossy wood like white, runny eggs. That was a little excessive, if you asked me, a bit of showing off, especially since the giant was already so close to dead.

In less than a minute, it was all over. Antonio had been reduced from a rough, tough, seven-foot-tall giant to a pile of loose skin topped by an eyeless skull. The giant's mouth opened once more, as if he wanted to scream a final time, but he never got the chance.

Antonio collapsed onto the deck, his skin and bones resting in the puddles of water that had just been forced out of him.

✲ 7 ✲

I stood there, still shielding Eva and Violet, and stared at the wet, floppy thing that had been a man just seconds before. Poor bastard. He'd never had a chance.

Kincaid fought through the screaming crowd of students and went down on one knee by Antonio, not caring that he was getting his pants wet with, well, Antonio. He started to touch the giant, then thought better of it. There was nothing that could be done for the man. Not now. Disgust and pity filled Kincaid's face, along with rage—so much rage.

My eyes narrowed. That look told me that the casino boss knew exactly who had done this and why—things I planned on asking him just as soon as I got Eva and Violet to safety.

By this point, Sophia had managed to shoulder her way through the students over to my side.

"You get the girls off the boat!" I yelled at her. "I'll handle Kincaid!"

Sophia nodded. The dwarf reached out and clamped a hand on Violet's trembling arm. Sophia started to do the same to Eva, but the girl twisted away from her.

"No!" Eva shouted. "I'm not leaving him behind. Not again!"

Again? What did she mean by that?

Before I could grab her and ask, Eva shoved away from the doors and ran toward Kincaid as fast as she could, given the people still trampling over each other. Now, instead of just running around in a blind panic, everyone was racing toward the gangplank, determined to get off the boat before what happened to Antonio happened to them too.

"Stay with Violet. I'll get Eva!" I yelled to Sophia.

Knife still in my hand, I headed after Eva, dodging and darting between the stampeding students. The giants that made up the casino's security force weren't any calmer. Their heads swiveled left and right as they shouted at each other, all trying to stay as far away from Antonio as they could, lest they end up just like him. Some of the giants even shoved kids out of their way in their mad dash to safety.

Up ahead, I saw Eva reach Kincaid's side. She stared at the dead giant and the pools of water under his body, then turned away and threw up all over the deck.

Kincaid cursed, got to his feet, and reached for her. "Eva, it's okay—"

And that's when I felt another gust of that cool, deadly magic sweep across the deck. Only this time, it was focused on our host.

I didn't know exactly how it happened. One second,

Kincaid was reaching for Eva. The next, his feet had gone out from under him, and he was on his back on the deck, clawing at something around his throat. Eva must have seen him fall out of the corner of her eye, because she wiped her mouth and turned her head in his direction. Her eyes widened, and her already pale face whitened that much more.

"Philly!" Eva screamed. "Philly!"

She dropped to her knees beside him, tearing at his neck with her nails, just as Kincaid himself was doing. I surged past a frat boy and sprinted over to the two of them. My eyes flicked left, then right, looking for the source of the danger, looking for the elemental who was behind this, but all I saw and heard were screeching kids and panicked giants.

Since I couldn't immediately eliminate the danger with my knife, I squatted down next to Kincaid. Something translucent shimmered around his throat, and it took me a second to realize that it was . . . *water*.

Somehow, a long, thick stream of water—of Antonio, really—had attached itself to Kincaid's neck and solidified there like a noose, slowly digging deeper and deeper into his throat and cutting off his air. The casino boss clawed and clawed at the water, but it was stuck to his skin like a coat of wet plaster. The water even looked like a noose, the length of it taking on a braided, twisted design and forming a tight knot in the center of Kincaid's neck. The elemental definitely had a sick sense of humor.

"Gin!" Eva screamed at me, tearing at the water and trying to peel it off just as hard as Kincaid was. "Do something! Help him!"

Eva was a strong girl, a tough girl, who'd been through a lot in her life, including the murder of her parents, but she looked absolutely terrified right now. Like Kincaid was the most important person in the world to her and she'd be absolutely devastated if she lost him. What was going on between them? And why didn't I know anything about it? Eva and I might not have been best friends, like she and Violet were, but we talked, and I dated her brother. I should have known *something* about her relationship with the casino boss.

Kincaid's eyes met mine. I could see the pain in his gaze—and the hope that I could somehow save him.

Part of me knew the smart play was to let the elemental finish the job—to let Kincaid die. With him dead, there'd be one less bad guy in Ashland, one less person to come after me. If it had been Jonah McAllister, I wouldn't have hesitated. I would have gotten myself a drink, leaned against the railing, pulled out my cell phone, and recorded the whole thing for repeat viewing. But to my knowledge, Kincaid had never made any moves against me or mine, except for luring me here tonight, and I was starting to get a glimmer of an idea why he'd really done that.

Maybe it was Eva's screams, or maybe it was the hope in the bastard's eyes—the one emotion I could never quite disregard or turn away from. Either way, I knew I had to help him.

I bent down closer to Kincaid, looking at the noose around his neck. Both his and Eva's fingers dipped into the water time and time again, but they weren't having any luck grabbing onto the stream and yanking it away. All they were really doing was getting their hands wet, and the water was slipping through their fingers and snapping right back into place like a rubber band. It almost seemed like the elemental was playing with them, solidifying the water just enough for them to think they had a chance to rip it away, then letting it dissolve and run through their hands only to re-form the deadly noose again. No doubt the elemental was enjoying every second of this sick game.

I couldn't rip the thing off with my hands, any more than Kincaid and Eva could, and my knives wouldn't be any help either. That left only one option.

"Eva, stop! Stop! Kincaid, quit fighting, and hold still," I said.

Eva reached for him again, but I shouldered her back and out of the way. Despite the fact that he was the one being strangled, Kincaid was calmer than she was. He managed to nod, although his face was tinged with blue by this point.

I put my hand down on the noose, feeling the water writhe like a snake against my fingers. Then I reached for my Ice magic, letting the power rise up out of the deepest part of me. A silver light flared in my palm. The other elemental would sense me using my magic and probably realize what I intended to do with it, but there was nothing to be done about that right now. I just hoped our assailant didn't have enough magic left to try to suck the moisture out of anyone else on deck. Probably not, since it took a lot of power to do that sort of thing, and the elemental hadn't tried the same trick on Kincaid already.

It only took me half a second to completely freeze the noose around Kincaid's neck and turn all that shifting, sloshing water into a solid ring of elemental Ice. I sent out another burst of magic, shattering the Ice around his throat, and Kincaid quickly sucked down breath after breath.

He looked at me, his blue eyes cold and furious. "Find her," he rasped. "Kill her . . . now . . . before she . . . gets away. . . ."

Her? So the other elemental was a woman. Good to know. I didn't need to be asked twice. My head snapped up, and I scanned the deck once more. Off to my right, out of the corner of my eye, I saw a slender figure sneaking onto the walkway that lined the rear of the boat.

Sneaky people were always up to no good. I knew from years of being that way myself.

"Stay here!" I yelled at Eva.

Then I palmed another knife, got to my feet, and raced after the fleeing figure.

Rounding the corner, I sprinted onto the back walkway. It was darker on this side of the boat, with only the moon above and a few globes wrapped around the brass rails to light the way, but a woman pounded down the narrow strip about a hundred feet ahead of me. Just like Kincaid had said. She opened a door that led into a glassed-in sitting area, ran through that, and then shoved through the door on the other side.

I chased after her. I didn't bother shouting at her to stop. Waste of breath, and we both knew it.

But she was fast. She sprinted down the walkway like she knew her life depended on it, which it did.

She reached the far end of the walkway and rounded the corner, stepping out onto the back deck and disappearing from sight. I put on another burst of speed and ran after her. There was nowhere for her to go, unless she decided to take a header into the Aneirin River. And even if she did that, I could always jump in after her. One way or another, I was getting some answers about Eva, Kincaid, and why he'd really asked me here tonight, and I was willing to bet the elemental knew a lot more about all that than I did.

I drew in a breath, left the walkway behind, and rushed onto the back deck, my knives up and ready to injure, at the very least, or kill, if absolutely necessary.

But she was gone.

My eyes cut left and right as I scanned every shadow, peered into every dark nook and cranny, but the deck was deserted. I craned my neck up and looked at the three levels above my head, but she wasn't climbing up the side of the boat. I even darted over to the paddle wheel and peered at the wide slats, thinking that she might have somehow lowered herself down.

But she wasn't there—she wasn't anywhere on board.

Whoever the mystery woman was, she wasn't on deck anymore. So where had she gone? I hadn't heard a splash that would indicate she'd leaped into the water—

Water. Of course.

Out of the corner of my eye, I saw something move out in the river. I rushed over to the railing, thinking that the elemental had done a very quiet swan dive after all and was now swimming across the dark river.

I was right, and I was wrong.

She'd gone over the side, but she wasn't swimming in the water—she was walking on top of it.

* 8 *

The elemental was at an angle to me, and I leaned over the railing and stared at her, wondering if she was really doing what I thought she was. But the woman casually strolled across the rippling surface of the Aneirin River like it was as sturdy as the wooden boardwalk Sophia and I had trudged across earlier. Every time she put her foot down, the water in front of her solidified into a square just big enough to keep her from sinking, allowing her to cross the river as easily as I could the street outside the Pork Pit.

Hell, she wasn't even getting her flip-flops wet.

You had to be gifted in one of the four main areas— Air, Fire, Ice, and Stone—to be considered a true elemental, but lots of folks could tap subsets of those areas. I'd once fought an assassin named Elektra LaFleur who'd had a talent for electricity, which was an offshoot of Air.

And now, I'd crossed paths with someone with water

power, which was a subset of my own Ice magic. That was why the elemental's power had felt cool and wet when I'd sensed it on the main deck earlier. That was why it hadn't made me grind my teeth together like I would have if she'd had some sort of Air or Fire magic—because her power was similar to my own.

And she'd wielded it with deadly efficiency. Disgusting, given what she'd done to Antonio, but definitely effective.

The water elemental reached the far bank of the river. The translucent, watery walkway underneath her feet vanished the second she stepped back onto dry land. She hurried forward, heading for the woods, not stopping for a second, not even to glance over her shoulder to see if I was watching her. Her plan had gone to hell, and she was running away, distancing herself from the scene of the crime as fast as she could. Five seconds later, she was in the trees and out of my line of sight, vanished like she'd never even been there at all.

I hadn't gotten a good look at the water elemental, had only seen that she seemed to be wearing white shorts and a dark T-shirt, the better to help her blend into the college crowd. Normally, that would have frustrated me, but not tonight.

Because I had a suspicion that I already knew exactly who she was.

In a way, magic was just like a fingerprint, in that everyone's power had a slightly different feel. Sure, the magic emanating from Fire elementals would usually feel hot and be able to burn you, but there would still be subtle differences in strength, skill, and how the elementals chose to wield their power. Besides, water magic wasn't as common as Fire power was, and I was willing to bet that I'd been in close proximity to this elemental before. If I was right about her identity, well, things had just gotten a whole lot more complicated for me.

Since I had no hope of catching her, I tucked my knives up my sleeves and hurried back to the main deck. It looked like a tornado had swept through the area. The gaming tables, the chairs, even the cooking station Sophia and I had manned. Everything was turned over on its side and had been trampled into a splintered, broken mess. All those precious chips the students had been vying for earlier now littered the deck like forgotten bits of confetti. Oh yes. The party was definitely over.

By this point, most of the college students had left the riverboat, although I could see them milling around on the boardwalk below, still stunned by what they'd seen. Many of the giants who made up the riverboat's security force were down there with them, although most of the giants looked just as shell-shocked as the kids did. Shootings, stabbings, and beatings were as common as the sunrise in Ashland, but this—this display of magic and malice had just been downright *vicious*. Probably more vicious than anything Kinkaid's men had ever seen, much less done themselves. No, Antonio's death had been particularly cruel, and would have impressed even Mab.

I walked over to where Sophia and Violet hovered next to the doors that led inside. Someone had thrown a white tablecloth patterned with small gold imprints of the casino rune over Antonio's corpse, something the few students and giants still on board were trying very hard not to look at.

And then there was Phillip Kincaid.

The casino owner stood a few feet away from the sheet covering what was left of Antonio. He has his arms wrapped around Eva, who was sobbing into his shoulder. But the most surprising thing was that Kincaid was actually . . . comforting her.

"It's okay, Eva, it's okay," he said, patting and rubbing her back the way one might soothe an upset child. "She's gone now. She can't hurt you anymore."

And on and on it went, with Eva crying and Kincaid murmuring platitudes into her ear. Not at all what I'd expected to find. Then again, nothing about tonight was turning out like I'd thought it would.

"What is *that* about?" I asked Sophia in a low voice, jerking my head at Kincaid and Eva.

The dwarf shrugged. So I turned to someone who might be able to give me some answers.

"Violet," I said in a dark tone, making sure she heard all my questions loud and clear in that one word.

She sighed and ran a hand through her blond hair, making it frizz out a little more. "I'm not supposed to say anything."

"I know this is going to make me sound like somebody's mom, but right now, I don't fucking care. You either tell me what you know, Violet, or I'm going to call your grandfather and tell him that you've been keeping company with one of Ashland's most notorious crime lords. Somehow, I don't think Warren will like that."

I might have been the Spider, might have been one

of the scariest folks in Ashland, but even I couldn't hold a candle to the force of nature that was Warren T. Fox. The old coot was just as tough as I was, and he wouldn't hesitate to give Violet a severe tongue-lashing for hanging out with Kincaid. Maybe it was judgmental of me, thinking the casino boss was such a bad guy when I was an assassin myself, but I would never hurt Violet. I'd do everything in my power to protect her, just like I had in the past when she'd been threatened. And I'd do the same for Eva. I wondered what Owen was going to make of his sister's friendship with Kincaid—and the fact she'd witnessed such a brutal murder because of that association.

Violet sighed again, knowing she was beaten. "It was a fluke, really. Eva and I were out shopping a couple of weeks ago over in Northtown, and we ran into Phillip."

Northtown was the uppity part of Ashland, where the yuppies and all the other folks with money, power, influence, and magic to spare lived. The area was full of themed shopping developments and exclusive, trendy restaurants designed to cater to folks with expensive tastes and help them spend as much of their money as quickly as possible.

Violet drew in a breath. "Anyway, we'd finished shopping, and we'd decided to get coffee and dessert in this café. Eva saw Phillip sitting by himself having an espresso and insisted that we go over to him. I thought she was out of her mind, wanting to talk to someone like him, but he actually smiled at her, like she was a friend he hadn't seen in a long, long time. The two of them started talking, and one thing just sort of led to another—"

"Until we all wound up on the riverboat tonight," I finished.

Violet nodded.

I looked at Kincaid, who was still murmuring to Eva. Whatever he was saying was working, because her sobs had died down to faint sniffles.

"How does Kincaid even know Eva to start with?"

"Eva's been sort of . . . vague on the details. She just said that she knew him from when she and Owen were living on the streets."

Well, well, well, the surprises just kept coming and coming tonight, and my eyebrows shot up once again. If they kept doing that, there were going to get permanently stuck there.

Violet's words made me once again think about Mab's funeral back in early March. The whole underworld had turned out for the service, and everyone had been looking at and speculating about me and my role in the Fire elemental's death. Kincaid had gone so far as to smile at me that day, which had been strange enough, but I'd also seen him talking to Owen after the service was over. I'd been distracted by other things—namely, the dwarves who'd tried to kill me at Mab's coffin—and I hadn't thought much of it at the time. Owen had brushed off my questions, saying that the two of them had just been exchanging idle chitchat, but it was clear there was more between them than I'd ever suspected.

"And let me guess," I said, looking at Violet again. "Eva told you not to mention Kincaid to me. And, I'm guessing, especially not to Owen."

A guilty look filled her dark brown eyes, which was all the confirmation I needed.

Kincaid drew back from Eva and whispered something

into her ear. She wiped the tears off her cheeks and nodded. I scanned the rest of the deck, taking in the kids, the giants, the ruined remains of the fund-raiser, and the body sprawled in the middle of it all.

What a fucking mess. But there was nothing to do now but deal with it—starting with Eva.

I pulled my cell phone out of my jeans pocket and called Owen. He answered on the third ring.

"Hey," his low, sexy voice rumbled in my ear. "Done with your catering job already?"

I stared at Antonio's still-wet wing tip peeking out from underneath the tablecloth. "You might say that."

"Where did you say it was again?"

I hesitated. Eva wasn't the only one who'd keeping secrets. I hadn't told my lover that I was catering an event for Kincaid. I hadn't been sure what game Kincaid had been playing, and I hadn't wanted him to worry. Besides, Owen and I hadn't seen much of each other these past few days, except for when he'd come to the Pork Pit for a quick lunch.

We'd both been busy with work, but that wasn't really the problem. Ever since our dinner at Underwood's, there had been this distance between us. I kept waiting for him to open up about what was bothering him, to tell me about Salina and all the ghosts she'd brought back to Ashland with her, but Owen hadn't said a word about her. Now, that awkward talk had morphed into a necessity—for all sorts of reasons.

"Gin? Are you still there?"

"Yes, I'm still here." I drew in a breath. "I'm on the *Delta Queen,* and Eva's here with me. She's fine, but there was an . . . incident. Someone tried to kill Phillip Kincaid."

Silence. Then—

"I'll be there just as quick as I can," Owen said, his voice as cold, dark, and furious as I'd ever heard it. "Whatever you do, you keep Eva away from Phillip. The man is dangerous—more dangerous than you know. Promise me that you'll keep her safe from him—and keep yourself safe, too."

"Of course, I'll protect Eva. You don't have to worry about that, but what—"

I didn't get a chance to ask my question. My lover had already hung up on me.

While I waited for Owen to arrive, I made a few other calls. I dialed Finn and let him know what had happened, and I also phoned Jo-Jo Deveraux as well. I wasn't injured, so I wouldn't need the dwarf's Air magic to heal me, but I still wanted her in the loop. Because whatever was going on with Kincaid and the water elemental, I was smack-dab in the middle of it now—and I had a suspicion that Owen was too.

I'd just hung up with Jo-Jo when Kincaid led Eva over to where I was standing with Violet and Sophia. Violet hugged her friend, and the two girls started whispering. Kincaid turned his gaze to me.

"We need to talk," he said. "In private."

"Why, I thought you'd never ask, sugar," I drawled. "Sophia, would you please stay here and make sure Eva and Violet are okay?"

The dwarf grunted, letting me know she was there for me.

Kincaid jerked his head. "My office is this way."

I followed him through the doors and into the ballroom. The crimson curtains were drawn across the stage, and the lights on the balconies above our heads were dim, since there weren't any shows scheduled for tonight. Kincaid strode down the center aisle of the ballroom, then went over to a side door and punched in a code on a keypad. The door opened, and we walked down a flight of narrow stairs. The lower two decks of the riverboat were enclosed and housed the cages where the money and chips were counted on an hourly basis.

I let Kincaid go first and put my feet down exactly where he did, just in case there were any trip-wires or magical runes hidden on or underneath the stairs. I certainly would have rigged up a few, given how much cash came through this place every day.

We made it down to the second deck without any problems, and Kincaid led me to a thick wooden door at the end of a long hallway. I eyed the wide silverstone strips that crisscrossed the wood and surrounding walls. Not nearly as sturdy as the granite and silverstone door on Fletcher's house, but it would still be tough to try and pound your way through, even for a giant or a dwarf.

Kincaid punched in another code on the keypad on the wall, opened the door, and stepped inside. I followed him and shut the door behind me. No sense in leaving it open and my back exposed. Besides, Kincaid had said he wanted to talk in private, and so did I—because depending on what he said, the casino boss might not be leaving the room alive.

The office was exactly what I expected it to be—the

inner sanctum of an underworld figure with a lot of money, power, and influence. The antique desk in the back of the room was expensive, but functional, while the laptops, monitors, and phones atop it were the best money could buy. Dark blue cushioned chairs crouched in front of a high-end flat-screen TV mounted on one wall, while a wet bar off to one side held every kind of pricey booze you could ever want to drink.

Yes, Kincaid's office was exactly what I expected— except for the toys.

Apparently, Kincaid was something of a movie buff. Lots of posters of classic and popular films decorated the walls, everything from *Casablanca* to *Casino Royale*. A couple of glass curio cabinets held action figures, both plastic ones and more costly stone molds of superheroes and other fantasy characters. Stacks of DVDs filled a bookcase, while popcorn and cotton-candy machines stood guard on either side of it.

Underworld figure. Casino boss. Geek.

Kincaid walked over to the bar and poured himself a shot of whiskey, which he threw back. I moved so that I was standing at the other end of the bar, close to him but still able to see the door at the same time.

"Care for a drink?" he asked, pouring himself another shot. "Because I plan on having several."

"Need a little liquid courage after Antonio?"

Kincaid shrugged. "Don't you?"

This time, I shrugged. He downed another shot, then grabbed a bottle of gin, along with some ice and a lime. His movements were quick and efficient, and a minute later, he plunked a gin and tonic down on the bar.

"Gin for Gin, right?" Kincaid said. "My sources tell me it's your drink of choice and that you even introduce yourself to people by comparing yourself to it. What is it you say? *Gin, like the liquor.* A bit cliché, don't you think?"

"Mmm." I made a noncommittal sound. "And what else do your sources say about me?"

He started working on his own gin and tonic. "Lots of things. Everyone in Ashland knows you as Gin Blanco, owner of the Pork Pit barbecue restaurant, but your real name is Genevieve Snow. Quite a tragic backstory you have. Mab Monroe murdered your mother, Eira, and your older sister, Annabella, when you were thirteen. Apparently, Mab and your mother had been enemies for years, which is one of the reasons why she decided to kill your whole family. Or tried to, anyway, since you somehow miraculously survived. Reports are sketchy as to exactly how you managed that, much less got your younger sister, Bria, away from Mab before she burned your family's mansion to the ground."

He didn't have all the details exactly right, but the broad strokes were correct. Looked like Kincaid had the same sort of sources Finn did. Worrisome, to say the least. I had enough people coming after me without Kincaid throwing his hat into the ring.

He finished mixing his drink, but instead of slugging it down like he had the others, he cradled it in his hands and stared at me. "Of course, we both know you're more than just a simple restaurant owner. Everyone in the underworld knows—or at least strongly suspects—that you're really the assassin the Spider, the woman who killed the mighty Mab. Why, you're a legend now. Everyone's still whispering about how you killed Mab with . . . what was it, exactly? Ice magic? Or did you use your Stone power as well?"

I palmed one of my silverstone knives and started flipping it end over end in my hand. "Actually, I shoved my knife into the bitch's black heart. It was one of the most satisfying moments of my life."

He watched me turn the knife over and over again. "I bet it was."

After a moment, he drew in a breath and continued with his dossier. "Everyone knows about your supposed . . . skills, but what's really interesting, at least to me, is that you've been seen out and about on the town with Owen Grayson these last few months. I wouldn't think an assassin like you would indulge in such a relationship—any relationship, really. But the two of you seem quite taken with each other."

Kincaid's voice was smooth, but his tone darkened when he said Owen's name, as though it left a bitter taste in his mouth. A small tell, but a tell nonetheless in this verbal game we were playing.

"That's it?" I asked when he didn't say anything else. "That's all you know? You're not going to stand there and tell me what my favorite color is or how I always wanted a puppy when I was a kid?"

Kincaid gave me a thin smile, but he didn't respond to my taunts.

"Well, I have to hand it to you, *Philly*. It looks like you know everything there is to know about me. But you're not the only one who's been doing his homework."

He made a sweeping gesture with his hand. "Please. Enlighten me."

"Phillip Kincaid, owner of the *Delta Queen* riverboat casino and one of the richest and most powerful men in Ashland. To most folks, you're a self-made man, a guy with nothing who came from out of nowhere and built a massive fortune. In addition to the *Delta Queen,* you also have riverboats in several other cities, including Memphis and New Orleans, and there are rumors you're starting a new project down in Blue Marsh."

Kincaid grinned. "I suppose I have you to thank for that last one, don't I, Gin? Now that Randall Dekes is no longer an issue down there. It seems the Spider never takes a vacation. At least not without killing someone."

I ignored his words. "But there's a lot more to you than just your portfolio and the official rags-to-riches story on your corporate website, isn't there, Philly?"

"Like what?"

"Like the fact that you're an orphan. Supposedly, your father was a dwarf and your mother was a giant, which means you're probably quite strong, at least stronger than a regular human would be. You certainly have the solid physique and thick muscles for it. But who your parents were doesn't much matter since you never knew either one of them, does it? You got anonymously dropped off at a church when you were about two years old. From then on, you bounced around from foster home to foster home, going from one bad situation to the next. Tell me, did those cigarette burns on your arms ever heal up?"

Kincaid blinked in surprise. Apparently, he hadn't thought I'd be able to find all the skeletons in his closet as easily as he had the ones in mine, but I had, thanks to Finn. Sometimes I thought my foster brother must be part bloodhound, the way he could track down leads and run them to ground with only a whiff of information to go on.

"You got those burns when you were thirteen, right?" I said. "And a whole lot of other injuries. Cuts, bruises, a few broken bones. At that foster home where the man of the house drank like a fish and liked to smack around his wife and the kids in his care when he'd had a few too many. Funny thing about that guy. Shortly after child services noted the burns on your arms, a robber broke into the house and almost beat that man to death with a metal pipe. That's what the wife claimed in the police report, anyway. But you know what I think, Philly? That thirteen wasn't an important year for just me."

His blue eyes glittered with a cold light, but he didn't respond.

"Don't get me wrong," I said. "I think the bastard got exactly what he deserved. Actually, I'd say he got off easy. I would have stabbed him to death."

Kincaid snorted, but he didn't say anything, so I continued.

"Maybe you were scared the cops would put you in juvie for what you did to that guy, maybe you were scared of him beating on you again when he got out of the hospital, or maybe you just decided you'd rather fend for yourself. Either way, there's no record of you in any foster home after that. In fact, you dropped off the map entirely for a few years there, which leads me to believe you were living on the Southtown streets and scrounging for whatever food, clothes, and money you could find, cheat, beg, borrow, or steal. Eventually, you joined some of the lower-level crews in Ashland, working your way up through the ranks until you decided to branch out on your own. Somewhere along the way, you dreamed up the idea for the *Delta Queen* and made it a reality. Even more impressive is the fact that you've managed to hang on to it all these years despite Mab and other folks trying to wrestle it away from you. So bravo to you."

I stopped twirling my knife long enough to walk over and pick up the gin and tonic from the bar. I toasted him with the drink, then used the glass to gesture at all the action figures and movie posters. "Now, seeing your office, I assume you growing up as poor and shitty as you did is the reason for all of this. The posters, the movies, the popcorn machine. That you're indulging yourself now with all the things you didn't have as a kid. I also assume that's the reason you gulped down your food at the Pork Pit the other day like you were afraid I was going to take it away from you. Because you have had your food taken away in the past. Because you've gone to sleep hungry more times than you'd care to remember."

Kincaid looked around the office as if he was seeing all the things inside it for the very first time—and, more important, what they revealed about him. His mouth twisted with disgust, but I couldn't tell if it was with himself for being so easy to read or with me for dredging up so many bad memories. Then his gaze dropped to the drink still in his hand, and he tossed it back as easily as he had the whiskey before. He put the empty glass down on the bar.

"Well, it seems like you've got me all figured out, Gin. Want to tell me what my favorite color is? Although, for the record, I wanted a kitten, not a puppy, when I was a kid."

"Not quite," I said. "As interesting as our life stories are, they don't explain what happened to Antonio tonight. So why don't we save the reminiscing and one-upmanship for some other time, and get down to business, with me asking the questions and you giving me the answers just as quick as you can."

"And if I don't want to answer your questions?"

I put my gin down on the bar and bared my teeth at him in a predatory smile. "Then I hope you enjoyed that drink, because it's the last fucking one you'll ever have."

Kincaid eyed the knife I'd started flipping over and over in my hand again. "You'd kill me just for not answering your questions?"

I shook my head. "No. Like you said, everyone in the underworld knows who I am, or at least who they think I am. I expected you to come after me sooner or later, just like everyone else has. Targeting me is one thing, but you put my friends, my family, in danger tonight—Eva, Violet, and Sophia. And that is what is unacceptable to me. *That's* what I'd kill you for and not think twice about it."

For a moment, I almost thought I saw a glint of respect in his eyes, but he kept his face as cold, remote, and impassive as mine was.

"First question?" he finally asked.

"Who's the water elemental who killed Antonio?"

Kincaid eyed the empty glass on the bar like he wished it was still full. "What makes you think I know who it is?"

"Because your second-in-command was murdered right in front of you, and you didn't bat an eye. Water elementals aren't uncommon, but the way this one used her magic was especially creative and vicious. But you just looked at Antonio, or what was left of him, and you weren't surprised in the least. So that makes me think you know exactly who this elemental is and what she's capable of. Not to mention the fact that you asked me to go after *her*. Not the elemental, not whoever had done this, but *her*."

Kincaid kept his gaze on the glass, so I decided to push him even more.

"And then there's Eva, who said that she wasn't leaving you behind *again*. Which, naturally, implies that she did leave you behind at some point before. Add that to everything else, and it seems that you know a hell of a lot more about what's going on than I do. I don't like to be kept in the dark, Philly—or worse: used. Believe me when I tell you that a person only ever does that once to me."

A muscle twitched in his cheek, but that was his only reaction. I thought Kincaid wouldn't answer me or that perhaps he was thinking of some lie or some way he could spin what had happened to Antonio. But after a few seconds, he shrugged again and gave me the answer I'd been expecting all along, although he did add a caveat that took me by surprise.

"Her name is Salina Dubois," he said, lifting his head and looking at me. "And I want you to kill the bitch for me."

❋ 9 ❋

So my suspicions were correct, and Salina Dubois was a water elemental—one who could use her magic to kill as easily as I could with my own Ice and Stone power.

I'd thought as much, given the distinctive feel of the water elemental's magic—magic that had felt exactly like the power that Salina had subtly given off when I'd shaken her hand at Underwood's. At the restaurant, I'd thought that perhaps Salina was a weak Ice elemental or gifted in some subset, like water. Now, I knew exactly what kind of magic she had—and that she wasn't weak at all.

But Kincaid's confirmation raised even more questions. Did Owen know about Salina's magic? Did he know what she could do with it? Could my lover be in danger from her? And how did Eva and Kincaid fit into all of this? What tied them all together?

Kincaid watched me closely, waiting to see what effect

his bombshell and subsequent request would have on me, but I didn't give him the satisfaction of reacting.

"Didn't you hear me?" he asked. "I want you to kill her for me. I want you, the Spider, to kill Salina Dubois."

I laughed. "And what? You think I'm going to do it just because you ask me to? Oh, Philly. You should know better than that."

"Of course not," he said in a smooth voice. "I know what a . . . professional you are. You deserve to be richly compensated for your skills and expertise. Believe me when I tell you that money is no object. Name your price, and I'll double it. Triple it, if necessary."

I shook my head. "There's not enough money in the world to get me to work for you."

"Ah, but money's not the only thing I can offer you. I think we'd both agree there are things that are far more precious than money, especially to people like us."

"And what would these *precious things* be?"

Kincaid grinned. "A little peace and quiet."

"What do you mean?"

His grin widened. "Consider this a tit-for-tat deal. You kill Salina, and I take care of all the folks who want to take out the Spider. That's a win-win for everyone, I'd say."

I looked at the casino boss. "Let me get this straight. In return for my killing Salina, you'll agree to what—call off every other lowlife in Ashland? I don't think you have that much pull, Philly."

"I have quite a bit more than you think, Gin," he said. "At the very least, I can give you some breathing room. It's been two months since Mab's funeral. How many people have you had to kill since then? A dozen? Two?"

I hadn't been keeping count. It wasn't like I was getting paid to kill people anymore—I had to do it simply to survive. But the constant barrage of blood and bodies had been enough to make me tired—so tired. That was the reason I'd gone down to Blue Marsh a few weeks ago, just so I could get away from everyone in Ashland who wanted me dead. But of course my vacation had ended up being just as dangerous. Still, I had to give Kincaid credit. His offer was tempting—far more tempting than he knew. It looked like the casino boss was shrewder, smarter, and more devious than I'd realized.

"Go on."

"Go on?" he asked. "And say what?"

"Oh, I don't know," I said. "Like maybe *why* Salina wants to kill you. I'm the one asking the questions, remember? Now, I'm assuming that you were her ultimate target, since it's your fancy riverboat we're on. I'm also guessing that offing Antonio the way she did was just fun for her, and that's why she didn't kill you to start with. Or maybe she killed him first to sucker you into going over to his body so she could use what was left of him to wrap that water noose around your neck. Personally, I like to be more straightforward about these things, but Salina seems a little ostentatious when it comes to her magic. Either way, she had no qualms about dropping two bodies here tonight."

He snorted. "You have no idea what Salina's idea of fun is."

"So enlighten me."

"All right," Kincaid said. "Since you've made it so clear what will happen if I don't answer your questions."

I just smiled and kept twirling my knife in my hand.

He drew in a breath. "Salina and I have been enemies for years. No real reason, just a mutual distaste for each other. It's not as dramatic as your victory over Mab, but I count the day Salina left town as one of the happiest of my life. But over the past few months, I've been hearing some rather disturbing rumors that she'd finally decided to come back to Ashland, rumors I was able to confirm a few days ago."

"And do you know why she's come back? Why now, after all these years? Why did she even leave town in the first place if this was her home?"

"Apparently, Salina's determined to start up her father's business again," he said.

"Who's her father?"

"Benedict Dubois."

I frowned. "Why does that name sound so familiar?"

Kincaid hesitated. "Benedict Dubois ran most of the gambling operations and bookies in Ashland for years. At least, until Mab decided those operations should belong to her. Benedict thought he could take her on and win, but I'm sure you can imagine how that turned out for him."

"Not well."

He nodded. "Salina . . . left town after his . . . death."

I looked at him. "But with Mab gone, you now run all the gambling operations in town. So you're telling me that Salina wants you dead because you're standing in the way of her re-creating her daddy's empire?"

He shrugged. "Something like that."

Kincaid wasn't telling me everything. Hell, he wasn't telling me a *fraction* of what I wanted to know. His answers were much too vague for that. Oh, I could believe Salina desired him dead because they were old enemies and she wanted to take over his business interests. That was par for course in the Ashland underworld. I couldn't even fault her for it, not really, not considering all the people I'd killed for money.

But that still didn't explain why Kincaid had asked me to cater the fund-raiser tonight. And the most telling thing, the big red elephant in the room, was Eva. Kincaid hadn't mentioned her at all, much less explained why Eva seemed to be as familiar with Salina's water magic as he was, or why he'd taken the time to comfort a girl he shouldn't have even known in the first place.

Before I could voice my suspicions and demand he tell me everything, one of the phones on his desk rang. Kincaid raised his eyebrows in a silent question, and I gestured for him to go ahead.

He walked over and picked it up. "What?" he growled into the phone.

A voice murmured something indistinct on the other end.

"Tell them I'll be right there." Kincaid hung up and looked at me. "Apparently, the police are here and want to talk to me."

He looked as thrilled by the prospect as I felt. As a semiretired assassin, I didn't exactly count the members of the po-po among my best friends. But I supposed I didn't have anything to hide tonight, since I hadn't actually murdered anyone on the riverboat. Why, I hadn't so much as gotten my clothes good and bloody. Definitely a slow night for the Spider.

We left Kincaid's office, walked back up the stairs to the ballroom, and stepped out onto the main deck. While I'd

been gone, Sophia, Violet, and Eva had packed up the catering supplies—what was left of them. All the pots, pans,
and utensils had been knocked to the deck and trampled
during the stampede, along with the tins of food. More
than a few had been kicked overboard and had disappeared into the murky depths of the river. But that was
the least of my problems right now.

I looked over the railing at the new arrivals on the scene.
A couple of cop cars sat in a parking lot next to the boardwalk, their blue and white lights flashing over the students
and giants still milling around down there. As I watched, a
dark sedan pulled in behind the other vehicles. The doors
opened, and two familiar figures got out. One of the cops
was a giant roughly seven feet tall with a shaved head, a
thick, muscular body, and ebony hair, skin, and eyes. The
other cop was a woman about my size, with a shaggy mane
of blond hair, rosy skin, and cornflower-blue eyes.

I smiled. Well, at least one thing was going to go right
tonight.

The two cops stopped to talk to one of the uniformed
officers who was taking witness statements. He pointed
at the riverboat, so the two of them walked up the gangplank. One of Kincaid's giants stopped them at the top,
but the female cop showed him her badge and he let them
board. She stood by the railing, scanning the deck, the
people on it, and the body lying in the middle of everything.

Her gaze landed on Sophia, and she did a double take
before her eyes met mine. Her lips quirked up into sort of
a rueful smile, but her expression was warm as she walked
over to me.

"Gin," she said. "I didn't expect to find you here to-night."

"You know me, baby sister," I drawled. "Always in the thick of things."

Detective Bria Coolidge scoffed a little at that; then she turned and called out to her partner. "Xavier, look who we have here."

The giant was talking to one of Kincaid's men, and he waved at Bria, letting her know that he'd seen me and Sophia. He also gave me a wink, which I returned. Xavier was more than just Bria's partner on the force—he was a friend and part of my extended family.

"Was the dead guy gunning for you?" Bria asked in a soft voice, nodding at the body.

I shook my head. "Nope, this is someone else's handi-work tonight. You know I don't like to stick around after the fact—or leave behind any bodies for the cops to find."

A grimace crossed her face before she was able to hide it. Despite the fact that Bria knew I was an assassin, she was still a cop at heart—one of the few good, honest ones in Ashland. She spent most of her days chasing after all the bad folks who called the city home. Having one of them for a sister was hard on her sometimes, especially these days, when most everyone walking in the shady side of Ashland life suspected who I was.

"Tell me what happened."

I laid it out for her. The only thing I didn't mention was that Salina appeared to be the murderous elemental in question and that Kincaid wanted to hire me to kill her. I wanted to talk to Owen about Salina—and a lot of other things—before I dropped the dime on that.

While Bria took notes on a small pad, Xavier crouched down next to the body, pulled up the tablecloth, and peered underneath.

The giant let out a low whistle. "That is one nasty mess. Did you say a water elemental did this?"

Something in his voice made me frown. "Yeah. Why?"

Xavier waved his hand at Bria. "Come take a look at this."

My sister moved over, and Xavier raised up the tablecloth again so she could see Antonio's body. Bria's face tightened, and she nodded at the giant.

"It looks exactly the same as our other victim," she said.

My eyes narrowed. "What other victim?"

"Katarina Arkadi," Bria replied. "I'm sure you know the name."

Oh, I knew the name all right. Katarina Arkadi was another one of the underworld movers and shakers, someone who was trying to consolidate her power base of late. If the rumors were to be believed, Arkadi had actually proposed some sort of cease-fire in the city until everything could be divided up between all the folks who had a seat at the table.

I glanced at Kincaid. Another rumor that Finn had told me about linked Arkadi with the casino boss in some hush-hush deal. I'd heard Arkadi had been found dead, but I'd been so preoccupied with Owen and Salina, and now Kincaid, that I hadn't really paid too much attention to the news stories surrounding her untimely demise.

"Arkadi's been dead how long now?" I asked, working through the timeline in my mind. "A week?"

"Four days," Bria corrected me. "Her maid came into her room to clean Sunday morning and found her in bed. Coroner said it looked like she'd died of sudden, extreme dehydration, like all the water had somehow been pulled out of her body. She was a mess, just like this giant is."

I looked at her. "You don't believe in coincidences any more than I do."

She gave me a grim smile. "Not in the least. Not in Ashland."

Bria nodded at Eva, who was still standing with Violet and Sophia. "You want to tell me what Owen's sister is doing here? And Violet along with her?"

I shook my head. "I know why Eva says she's here, but not the *real* reason why. But believe me when I tell you I'm going to find out."

"Well, fill me in when you get your answers," Bria said. "I'll have enough problems dealing with Kincaid. You wouldn't want to do me a favor and . . . motivate him to cooperate, would you?"

I grinned at her. "You're getting rather violent in your old age, baby sister. Last year, you never would have even suggested something like that."

She grinned back at me. "What is it that Finn says? Violence seems to run in our family? Might as well use what we seem to be so good at to get some results, especially when I've got two dead bodies to explain to my boss."

"Well, then, beauty before age, sweetheart." I held out my hand.

Bria shook her head, but she was still grinning as we walked over to where Kincaid was standing. Eva hovered nearby, Violet and Sophia a few feet behind her. By this point, Eva had wiped the last of the tears from her eyes and regained her composure, although she kept trying very hard not to stare at Antonio's body. Her blue gaze kept going to it and then sliding away, as though it brought up too many bad memories for her to bear to look at it.

Bad memories were something else I was intimately familiar with. I just wondered how many more I'd make before this was all over.

Bria pulled her badge off her belt and flashed it at Kincaid. "Mr. Kincaid, I'm Detective Bria Coolidge with the Ashland Police Department. I'd like to ask you a few questions about what happened."

Kincaid stared at her, then his gaze flicked to me. "I know exactly who you are, Detective. Why, I was discussing your tragic family history with your sister just minutes ago. Interesting, the wildly different paths the two of you have chosen in life. I bet it would make for a fascinating psychological case study."

Bria and I both stiffened at his words, and I stepped forward, meeting Kincaid's cool, smug gaze with an even colder, more murderous one of my own. "Apparently, you didn't hear what I said about putting my friends and family in danger, *Philly*. Or perhaps you just didn't realize the same rules apply to mocking them as well. So I suggest you cut the wiseass routine, or you'll be too preoccupied with trying to stuff your innards back where they belong to answer Detective Coolidge's questions."

Kincaid smirked, but before he could open his mouth to respond to my threat, another voice jumped into the mix.

"Eva! Gin!" Owen's voice floated up from the boardwalk.

I stepped away from Kincaid. "Up here!"

Footsteps pounded on the gangplank, and Owen surged into view. The giant guarding the entrance looked over his shoulder at Kincaid, but the casino boss waved his hand, telling his man to stand down.

Owen stood there, looking at Eva, then me, and back again. Once he realized we were both okay, his face hardened, and his jaw tightened with fury. Eva lifted her chin and glared right back at him, which only made Owen's violet eyes blaze that much brighter. Then his gaze went to Kincaid, and he noticed how close the other man was standing to his sister.

"You!" Owen shouted, stabbing his finger at Kincaid. "Get away from her, you son of a bitch!"

Shocked, I watched as my lover stalked over, drew back his fist, and punched Phillip Kincaid in the face.

"You bastard!" Owen snarled, punching Kincaid again. "I told you to stay away from Eva!"

Owen started to hit him a third time, but Kincaid blocked the blow.

"I've been paying for your blind stupidity for years now," Kincaid snarled. "And I'm sick of it!"

He snapped his elbow into Owen's face, and the fight was on.

The two men went at each other, no holds barred, punching and kicking for all they were worth. I was so surprised by Owen's violent reaction to Kincaid that it took me a few seconds to move to break up the fight.

"That's enough," I said, wading in between them. "That's enough!"

I pushed Owen away from Kincaid, while Sophia kept

the casino boss from coming after my lover again. They'd only been fighting for a minute, but they'd made it count. One of Owen's eyes was already starting to blacken, while blood dripped from Kincaid's nose. Anger shimmered in their hot gazes as they glared at each other, and I had no doubt they'd happily pound on each other until they were both nothing but bloody smears on the deck.

"What the hell is going on between you two?" I asked Owen.

He shook his head. "Not here. I'll tell you about it later, when we're safe. All I care about right now is getting Eva away from him. Eva, come here, please."

Eva gave Kincaid a guilty look, but she walked over to her brother's side. Owen put his arm around his sister and hugged her close for a moment.

"Are you okay?" he asked.

She sighed. "I'm fine, Owen. Philly didn't hurt me. He would *never* hurt me."

Owen's face tightened even more. "Don't you even say his name. Do you understand me?"

Eva opened her mouth, but the fury in his eyes made her bite her lip and keep quiet. Desperate, she looked at the casino boss for help.

Kincaid stepped forward. "Owen, I—"

Owen stabbed his finger at the other man again. "I don't want to hear one word from you. Not one fucking *word*. I didn't believe your excuses then, and I won't believe them now. Don't come near Eva, Gin, or me ever again—or I will kill you. Do you understand me, Phillip? This time, I *will* kill you."

✳ 10 ✳

Everyone on deck froze. All the giants, all crime scene techs, all my friends and family. Even I was a little stunned by the venom in Owen's voice. I'd never seen him so angry. Not to mention the fact that he'd just threatened to kill someone in front of a bunch of cops. Not exactly a smart thing to do, even if corruption ran rampant in the police department and most members of the po-po were more interested in where their next bribe was coming from rather than in actually stopping crime.

Bria stepped in front of Owen. "In case you didn't notice, I've got a dead body here. Right now, that trumps whatever history and vendetta you have against Kincaid. So you can either keep quiet, or I can have you escorted off the riverboat by force. Do you understand me?"

Owen glared at her, but after a moment he nodded. Satisfied, Bria turned back to Kincaid.

"Now, Mr. Kincaid," she said in a deceptively friendly tone, "why don't you tell me who tried to kill you?"

"Why would you think that anyone wants to kill me, Detective?" he answered.

She smiled at him, but there was a hard edge to her expression. "Oh, I don't know. The fact that your number-two man is lying ten feet away from us, literally a former husk of himself. Or maybe it's the fact that you would be dead right now if my sister hadn't used her Ice magic to freeze that water noose someone tied around your neck."

Owen frowned. "Water noose?"

Kincaid looked at him. "Yeah, a water noose. Sound familiar?"

Owen didn't respond, but for the first time, I noticed something in his eyes besides rage—doubt. Just a tiny spark of it, so faint I wouldn't have even seen it if I hadn't been looking at him, but it was there.

The casino boss turned back to Bria. "It's true. I was very lucky Gin was on board tonight, wasn't I?"

"Luck had nothing to do with it, you bastard," Owen growled. "You probably planned the whole thing, including the so-called attack."

Kincaid opened his mouth to snipe back, but Bria held up her hand, cutting him off.

"Enough," she snapped. "That's enough. From both of you. I've got two dead bodies, and I want some answers as to who made them that way. Unlike some of my brethren, I actually like to earn my paycheck. So start talking, Kincaid. Now."

"Or what?" he smirked. "You'll get your sister to pull out one of her famous silverstone knives and make me?"

"Oh, Philly," I drawled. "If you knew anything about me, you'd realize that I wouldn't even have to use my knives."

"And if you knew anything about me, Kincaid," Bria added, her voice even frostier than mine, "you'd realize that I don't need Gin to fight my battles. I do just fine on my own."

Kincaid eyed Bria, then me, and I let the cold violence that was always lurking just below the surface leak into my features. Still, it wasn't enough to motivate the casino boss, since he didn't start singing like the proverbial canary.

"Her name is Salina Dubois," Eva said in a soft voice.

Eva's confession didn't shock me like it did the others. While they all looked at her in surprise, I stared at Owen, trying to get a sense of what he was thinking, of what he was feeling. But all I saw in his face was weariness, as if this was a battle he'd fought many times before.

Bria raised her eyebrows. "Okay, so now we have a name. Progress, at last."

Owen sighed. "Eva, you don't know that it's Salina just because Kincaid claims a water elemental is involved—"

"Yes, I do, Owen!" she hissed. "Yes, I do!"

Eva shuddered and wrapped her arms around herself. Owen reached over and started to put a hand on his sister's shoulder, but she jerked away from him before he could touch her. Frustration filled Owen's face. His fingers clenched into a fist, which he lowered to his side. Kincaid watched them, and his mouth turned down with a hint of sadness.

"And Dubois is a water elemental? How do you know her?" Bria asked.

Eva looked at Owen, then at Kincaid. She bit her lip, her eyes drifting over to Antonio's body once more. She shuddered again.

Kincaid sighed. "We all know her, Detective. Some of us far better than we'd like to."

"And why is that?" my sister asked.

Kincaid sighed again. "Because we grew up with her."

Violet had said something before about Eva and Owen knowing Kincaid from when the two of them had lived on the streets, but I still stared at my lover in surprise. Owen and Kincaid? Growing up together? With Salina in the mix as well?

Owen didn't talk much about his past, but I knew his childhood had been just as hard as mine; his parents had also been murdered by Mab. The Fire elemental had burned the Graysons' house to the ground, with them inside, because of a gambling debt Owen's father owed her. Though his parents had been killed in the fire, Owen had managed to get himself and Eva out of the house. He'd been about seventeen then, Eva only two. After that, the pair had lived on the streets. Eventually, thanks to Fletcher and his machinations, Owen had gotten a job with a dwarven blacksmith who lived up in the mountains above Ashland. Owen had worked hard for the blacksmith, before striking out by himself and building his own business empire. Something eerily similar to what Kincaid had done, now that I thought about it. I wondered what else the two men had in common.

I knew Owen had his secrets, just like I did, and I'd respected his privacy, just like he had mine. We both had things we didn't like to talk about, things we'd rather forget. But now, it seemed like his past was forcing its way into the light whether he wanted it to or not.

Whether I wanted it to or not.

"And what can you tell me about Dubois?" Bria asked Kincaid.

"Salina is a cold, calculating bitch who likes to use her water magic to kill people," he snarled. "That's all you really need to know about her, Detective."

Bria's eyes narrowed at his tone. "Oh, I think I know that about her already, Mr. Kincaid. Since I was the one who got called out to come and see what was left of Katarina Arkadi, and now your friend here."

Owen sucked in a breath. "Katarina's dead?"

Kincaid stared at him. "You hadn't heard?"

Owen's mouth flattened out. "I don't exactly run in the same circles as you do anymore, Phillip. Or should I say the same gutters?"

Kincaid jerked his head at me and smirked again. "Oh, your legitimate business interests—the mining, the timber, the metal manufacturing—they may be on the up-and-up, but you could have fooled me when it comes to your personal life, given the company you're keeping these days. Then again, you always did like them a little dangerous, didn't you?"

Owen stiffened, but he didn't respond to the other man's taunt.

Bria glanced at the two men, then at me. I shrugged my shoulders, indicating to her I didn't know what they were talking about either.

"Why do you think Dubois killed Katarina Arkadi?"

Bria asked Kincaid. "Why do you think she wants to kill you?"

His mouth twisted. "You'll have to ask her that. I never did understand what Salina was thinking. Or some other people, for that matter."

Owen glared at Kincaid, but he still didn't respond to the mocking tone in the casino boss's voice.

Bria looked back and forth between the two of them once more. Then she sighed and shook her head, as if she knew that this night was just getting started.

❈ 11 ❈

Bria had us run through the story again and asked Kincaid several more questions, but he claimed not to know anything useful, like why Salina had killed Arkadi, who she might go after next, or what else she might be up to. He didn't mention that he thought Salina wanted to murder him so she could take over his business interests. I supposed Kincaid wasn't any more comfortable sharing information with the po-po than I was.

Despite his lack of answers, Bria did the good-cop thing and offered the casino boss police protection, which he declined. Couldn't blame him for that. Most of the cops would have sold him out in a second to his enemies, if the payday were big enough.

Finally, Bria declared that she was done with Kincaid and headed over to see if the coroner was finished examining Antonio's body yet.

Owen pulled his keys out of his pocket and handed

them to his sister. "Eva, go on down to the car. You too, Violet."

"Packed up," Sophia murmured, pointing to the supplies she'd managed to salvage.

I nodded at the dwarf. "Thank you."

Eva shot Kincaid a sympathetic look, but for once she didn't argue with her brother. The girls grabbed a few of the lighter supply boxes, while Sophia carried the heavier ones, and the three of them walked down the gangplank and out of sight. Owen turned to me, but I beat him to the punch.

"Go on ahead and look after the girls," I said. "I want to talk to Kincaid for a minute."

Owen stared at the other man, then at me. "Gin, I can explain all of this. It's not what it seems like. Whatever he's told you, it's a lie. He hates Salina. He's had it in for her for years. Even if she really did try to kill Phillip tonight, well, it was no less than he deserved after what he did to her."

"And Antonio?" I asked in a soft voice. "Did he deserve what Salina did to him too?"

Maybe me questioning a murder was strange, given all the people I'd killed myself. But when I went after someone, I put him down as quickly as possible. No drawing things out for my own amusement. No toying with my targets. No torture. But Salina had done all those things tonight. I wondered how long she would have played her choking game with Kincaid if I hadn't frozen her water noose. I was willing to bet she would have made his death throes last as long as she could.

Owen looked over at the dead giant. The coroner had removed the tablecloth and was trying to figure out some way to lift Antonio's slack, floppy remains into a black body bag without spilling him everywhere. Owen's jaw clenched, and he didn't say anything. He didn't have an answer for that one.

"Just be careful, okay?" he said. "Kincaid fooled me for years, and it looks like he still has Eva fooled."

I nodded. "Don't worry. I can handle myself."

Owen didn't like it, but he headed across the deck and trudged down the gangplank. That left me and Kincaid standing by ourselves while the cops milled around Antonio's body.

"Well, that was just as unpleasant as I thought it would be," Kincaid murmured. "And here I am without my drink to console me."

I didn't respond. Instead, I leaned back against the railing, more than willing to wait him out. Ten seconds passed as we looked at each other, then twenty . . . thirty . . . forty-five . . .

Kincaid had more patience than I'd imagined, because he made it to the ninety-second mark before he opened his mouth again. "So what was it you wanted to speak to me about?"

I cocked my head to the side. "You are one clever bastard, aren't you, Philly?"

A humorless smile lifted his lips. "I can't even begin to imagine what you're talking about."

I held my hands out. "I'm talking about this, tonight, and this little spectacle you engineered."

"Please," Kincaid sneered. "Enlighten me once again. Because I am not in the business of engineering *spectacles* of any sort."

I crossed my arms over my chest and stared him down. "Here are the facts. Four days ago, Katarina Arkadi was murdered, most likely by your mysterious water elemental friend, Salina Dubois, for whatever reason. She didn't like Katarina, she knew the two of you had business dealings together, whatever. The next day—*the very next fucking day*—you stroll into the Pork Pit and offer me an obscene amount of money to cater an event on the *Delta Queen.* Strange enough, but then I find out that instead of hosting some swanky society gala, you've actually let college students take over your casino. Not only that, but I find you looking oh so cozy with Eva."

"So what?" Kincaid scoffed.

"So, this whole time, I thought you were running some scheme, plotting some way to kill me and dump my body in the river. Hell, I thought you might even be in cahoots with Jonah McAllister. Whatever your motives, taking out the Spider would go a long way toward cementing your position as the new king of the Ashland underworld."

Kincaid shrugged, modestly agreeing with me.

"But that's not it at all. You don't care one damn thing about killing me. After I saved your ass, I thought maybe you wanted me here in case Salina made a move against you, as sort of a backup bodyguard just on the chance she managed to slip past your giants. Although, if that was true, you were taking a big risk, counting on me to save your miserable hide when we've never said so much as *how do you do* to each other. But in a way, that was true. You wanted me here tonight to protect someone, but it wasn't you—it was Eva."

I'd give Kincaid this—he had a hell of a poker face. The only thing that gave him away was a faint narrowing of his eyes. If I hadn't been watching for it, I would have missed it altogether. But I knew I'd struck a nerve, and I decided to press my advantage.

"Now, Eva's a beautiful girl, and I'm sure you enjoy smooth-talking the ladies as much as the next guy. But for some reason I don't fathom, you actually seem to care about Eva—quite deeply, from the way you were comforting her. You should have kept your distance, Philly. You gave yourself away, holding her like you did."

He opened his mouth to deny it or perhaps make some snide quip, but I cut him off.

"Don't play games with me, Kincaid. Eva and Owen are my family, and they're in neck-deep with whatever feud you have going on with Salina. And if there's one thing you should know about me, it's this—that I take care of the people I love, no matter what."

Kincaid looked at me, then let out a harsh, bitter laugh. "Well, apparently I'm not as clever as I thought I was."

"No," I said in a quiet voice. "No one ever is."

By this point, the coroner had managed to scoop Antonio's remains into the body bag. We watched while he zipped it up and got his assistant to help him load it onto a gurney, which the assistant pushed across the deck. Kincaid winced as the wheels rattled over the wood. I wondered if he was thinking that it could have just as easily been him inside that body bag tonight.

"Look," he finally said. "Owen's right about one thing. Salina and I never liked each other, but I'm not the villain he thinks I am. It was Salina—it was *always* Salina.

She could twist Owen around her finger like nobody else ever could, not even Eva. So if I were you, Gin, I'd worry less about me and more about her. Because now that she's back in Ashland, it's only a matter of time before she sets her sights on your boy again. And believe me when I tell you that Salina Dubois will do whatever she has to in order to get what she wants."

His ominous warning delivered, the casino boss stalked over to one of his giants and started speaking to the other man in a low voice. A few feet away, Bria was talking with the coroner, while Xavier was taking statements from some of the giants who'd been on deck when Antonio was wrung out like a wet dishrag. I glanced over the railing. Down below in the parking lot, Violet was helping Sophia put the last of the supplies from the Pork Pit into the dwarf's convertible, while Owen and Eva stood off to one side, arguing.

I looked at them all in turn, thinking. Then I pulled out my cell phone and called Finn again. He must have been waiting by the phone, because he picked up after the first ring.

"Gin? What's happening? What's going on?" Finn asked. "Have you killed Kincaid yet?"

"Sadly, no."

"Why not?"

I let out a breath. "Because as shocking as this sounds, he's actually the victim tonight—and has some strange connection to Owen and Eva. Right now, I'm not sure if I know the bad guy from the worse guy."

"Who could be worse than Kincaid?" Finn asked.

"Salina Dubois," I said. "I want you to get your hands

on everything you can about her. Right now. Then meet me at Fletcher's house. And you might want to put a pot of coffee on when you get there. It's going to be a long night."

There was nothing else for me to do there, so I said my good-byes to Bria and Xavier. My sister promised to call or drop by my house if she had any news, but I knew she'd be busy well into the night tracking down Salina and seeing what she had to say for herself. Even then, at this point, it was Salina's word against Kincaid's, which meant there was nothing Bria could do anyway—to either one of them. Sure, I'd seen what had happened to Antonio and Kincaid, but assassins didn't exactly make the best witnesses in a court of law.

I walked down the gangplank, across the boardwalk, and into the parking lot. The police cars were still on the scene, their bright lights swiveling around and around in endless loops, but all the students had left. I headed over to where the others stood by Sophia's convertible.

Owen looked at me. "I'm so sorry you got dragged into the middle of this, Gin. Eva should have known better than to go anywhere near Kincaid, something we will discuss in further detail when we get home."

"No," Eva said. "I want to stay at Gin's house tonight."

"Eva—" he started.

"Gin's house is the safest place I know," she said, her voice trembling just a bit. "I need to feel safe right now, Owen, and I won't at home. Not when I know Salina's back in Ashland and that she could show up at the house at any time—that you'd *let* her into the house at any time."

Owen opened his mouth to argue.

"It's okay," I cut in. "You both know you're welcome to stay with me anytime. I'd love to have the company."

I didn't add that them coming home with me tonight was for the best anyway, since we had a lot to talk about.

"Fine," Owen muttered. "We'll stay with Gin tonight. But don't think this gets you out of the punishment you have coming for going behind my back and talking to Phillip."

Eva's eyes narrowed, and the siblings glared at each other. Normally, the two of them got along like gangbusters, but whatever had happened in the past had driven a Kincaid-specific wedge between them, one that was still there, even now, all these years later.

Sophia offered to take Violet home. Violet and Eva hugged and exchanged a few whispers before Violet got into Sophia's car, and the two of them left. I wasn't surprised when Eva immediately pivoted in her flip-flops, marched over to Finn's Escalade, threw open the door, and got into the passenger's seat without another word— or a single glance at her brother. I looked at Owen, who just shrugged, letting me know it was fine.

"I'll follow you over there," he said, then pulled me into his arms. "I'm just glad you're safe, Gin."

My arms tightened around him, and I breathed in deep, letting his rich scent, the one that always made me think of metal, fill my nose. For a moment, I let myself forget about everything that had happened tonight and just concentrated on Owen—on the feel of his hands on my back, his warm body next to mine, his lips resting against my temple.

Then I exhaled and put all those soft emotions away, because the night wasn't over yet, and I still hadn't gotten the answers to any of my questions—answers that I needed now more than ever.

I drew back and looked at him. "I'll see you at Fletcher's. Don't worry. We'll straighten everything out."

Owen nodded and headed across the parking lot to his car. I rounded the Escalade and opened the driver's door. But before I got inside, I looked up.

Phillip Kincaid was leaning over the railing of the *Delta Queen*. The bright globes on the decks above him made his slicked back hair gleam like gold, even as the lights cast his features in darkness and caused his long, ominous shadow to stretch out onto the boardwalk below. No doubt he'd seen the whole thing—Owen and Eva arguing, Eva getting into my car, Owen leaving. I wondered what the casino boss thought of all that, if he'd been pleased Eva had taken his side over her brother's, if he even knew why she'd done such a thing in the first place.

Kincaid raised his hand to his forehead and gave me a mock salute before stepping away from the railing and disappearing from sight. Once again, I wondered what game he was playing—and why I had a feeling he wasn't quite the monster Owen said he was.

❊ 12 ❊

Eva didn't say a word in the twenty minutes it took for me to drive across town. Instead, she stared out the window and brooded. I didn't try to question her. There would be plenty of time for that at home.

I turned off the road and steered the Escalade up the rough gravel driveway, leaning into the familiar lumps and bumps as the SUV rocked from side to side. In my rearview mirror, the headlights on Owen's car bounced up and down as he did the same thing. Eventually, both vehicles chugged to the top of the ridge, and Fletcher's place came into view.

The old man had left me his ramshackle house, and the sight of it never failed to lift my spirits, even after a night like this one. A light burned on the front porch, illuminating the white clapboard, brown brick, and gray stone that joined together at crazy angles to form the sprawling structure. The house had passed through a lot of hands over the years, and each of the folks who'd lived here before had added on a room or two onto the structure; hence the mishmash of materials and styles.

The house looked quite a bit worse for wear these days, thanks to all the bullet holes that peppered the front and sides like tiny black eyes. Back in the winter, bounty hunters hot on the trail of the Spider had laid siege to the house. I was still digging bullets out, but I didn't mind. Fletcher had spent years fortifying his home to withstand just such a standoff, and it had more than held up against the hail of gunfire.

Still, that didn't mean someone couldn't be lurking around, waiting to make a run at me. Most of the fools who came after the Spider limited their murderous attempts to the Pork Pit, but a few of the braver ones had sought me out here at home. I supposed I could have moved to some anonymous apartment where folks would have a harder time finding me, but the house was one of the last pieces of Fletcher that I had left, and I'd be damned if anyone was going to make me leave it behind.

"Stay in the car for a minute," I told Eva as I opened the door and got out.

I motioned for Owen to sit tight in his vehicle as well, then walked around the SUV, placing myself between it and the house. My eyes swept over the landscape, from the black maw of the woods on my left to the flat yard that stretched out to my right before abruptly falling away in a series of jagged cliffs.

I didn't see any dark figures or shadows that weren't supposed to be there, although I did spot Finn's silver Aston Martin parked on the far side of the house, which meant he was inside already. Good. Hopefully by now Finn had information on Salina that would shed some light on who she was—and why Owen and Eva were mixed up with her and Kincaid.

As a final precaution, I reached out with my Stone magic, listening to the gravel underfoot in the driveway, the rocks scattered at the edge of the woods, and the brick, granite, and concrete that made up the house. But the stones only whispered back of the cars rolling over them, the animals scurrying to and fro in the underbrush, and the spring heat that was building bit by bit and would soon bake them once more.

Satisfied we were safe, I gestured to the others that it was okay for them to get out of the cars. I led Eva and Owen over to the front door, which was made out of solid black granite. The door was strong enough by itself, but thick veins of silverstone also swirled through the stone, adding another layer of protection. No matter how much water magic Salina had, she'd have a tough time using it to blast through the door or pry apart the silverstone bars that covered the windows.

I'd just started to reach for the knob, when the door abruptly opened. Finn stepped outside, a manila file folder tucked under one arm and a steaming cup of coffee in his right hand, despite the warmth of the night. The chicory fumes drifted over to me, making think of his father, since Fletcher had drunk the same rich, dark concoction before he'd died. I wished the old man was here tonight to help me sort out what was going on—and how I could make everything right again, especially between me and Owen.

Despite the fact that I was the one standing right in front of him, Finn leaned to one side and favored Eva with a dazzling smile.

"Why, hello, Eva," he said in a smooth tone. "You're looking exceptionally fine this evening. Love the flip-flops."

Finnegan Lane was many things—an investment banker, an information trader, a greedy connoisseur of all the fine things his ill-gotten gains could buy him, but sometimes, I thought his chief pursuit in life was that of a shameless womanizer. He might have been involved with Bria, but Finn still liked to charm all the women who crossed his path. And he didn't limit his attention to just the pretty ones. No, Finn was an equal-opportunity flirt—old, young, fat, thin, vampire, human, dwarf, giant. Finn didn't care who they were or what they looked like as long as they were female.

"Hi, Finn," Eva replied.

She gave him a wan smile, and the small encouragement caused Finn's grin to widen that much more. At least, until Owen stepped forward and frowned at him.

"Ah, evening, Owen," Finn added in a hasty tone. "I didn't see you standing there."

"You never do," Owen murmured.

Finn stuck his head outside a little more, scanning the front porch. "Where's Kincaid? I thought Gin would hog-tie him and bring him here so we could question him at our leisure."

Eva and Owen both shifted on their feet. No one said anything. The faint hum of the crickets and cicadas hidden in the grass rose up, but their high-pitched songs did little to ease the tension between us all.

"Well," Finn drawled, "don't everyone speak up at once."

"You have no idea," I muttered. "No idea at all."

I walked inside, down a hallway, and into the den in the back of the house. Owen trailed right along behind me, but Eva dawdled behind us, peering into all the rooms that branched off the hallway and staring at all the furniture that was stuffed inside. Even though she'd been here before, there was always something to look at that she hadn't noticed before. Fletcher had been a bit of a pack rat, and lots of odd dishes, interesting carvings, unusual sculptures, and other quirky knickknacks crowded into the rooms. The old man had been dead for months now, and I still hadn't had the heart to go through much of the house. Throwing away his things seemed like I would be ripping part of Fletcher out of my heart as well—and that was something I just couldn't bear to do yet.

We reached the den, with its worn furniture, but instead of sitting down, Eva went over to the mantel, where a series of framed drawings were propped up, the runes of my family members—dead and otherwise. A snowflake, an ivy vine, a primrose. Eva walked past the first three runes before stopping to look closer at the fourth one, a neon pig.

"I like the Pork Pit sign the best," she said. "It makes me think of how I first met you in the restaurant."

I smiled at her. "Me too, sweetheart."

The sign also reminded me of Fletcher and everything he'd given me, everything he'd taught me over the years. I stared at the drawing and let myself remember the old man for a moment before putting those memories away and focusing on the here and now.

"Y'all make yourselves comfortable," I said. "I'm going to fix us a snack."

Once again, nobody said anything. Eva kept looking at the runes, while Owen sat down on the end of the plaid couch and turned on the television, staring at it without really seeing it. I jerked my head at Finn, who followed me into the kitchen.

Finn put the folder he'd been carrying down on the table, right next to his open laptop, then poured himself what was probably his fifteenth cup of coffee of the day. I started pulling things out of the cabinets, in the mood for something sweet, crispy, and crunchy, all at the same time. Besides, cooking almost always soothed me. The simple motions of mixing, measuring, and stirring comforted me and gave me time to work out whatever was bothering me—and there were plenty of things on my mind tonight.

Home-canned apples, flour, buttermilk, salt, sugar, and more soon crowded onto the counter, and I filled a pan with oil and let it start warming on the stove. I combined the flour and buttermilk to form a soft, sticky dough, used my biscuit cutter to divide it up, and rolled out the sections into several, large, flat rounds. A heaping scoop of apples went into the center of each piece of dough, which I then folded over, crimping the edges together with a fork, making a half-moon-shaped pie.

I repeated the process until I'd made a dozen pies. Then, one by one, I dropped them into the sizzling oil and let them cook until they were light, fluffy, and golden brown. When they were done, I slid the fried apple goodness onto a plate.

"So lay it out for me," I finally said to Finn as I topped the pies off with powdered sugar, cinnamon, and a few drizzles of sourwood honey.

He snatched one of the pies off the plate before I could stop him. "Don't you want to wait until we go back in the den with the others?"

I shook my head. "No, I want to hear what you have to say first without any interruptions. Eva and Owen aren't exactly objective here. You should have seen Eva after Salina worked her magic on Antonio and then tried to do the same to Kincaid. She was terrified. Yeah, watching Antonio get wrung dry wasn't exactly pleasant, but it seemed like there was more to Eva's reaction than just simple shock, fear, and disgust. So tell me what you found out about Salina."

"Nothing good," Finn said in a quiet voice, making sure his words wouldn't carry into the den, where Eva and Owen were. "From what I can tell, Salina Dubois has never worked a day in her life—she hasn't had to, thanks to all her husbands."

"'Husbands'? As in, more than one?"

Finn nodded and took a bite of his pie. "Since leaving Ashland, Salina has had not one, not two, not three, but four husbands. Each one richer than the last, and each one dead under suspicious circumstances. Hubby number one, Rodgers, slipped and fell in the bathtub, cracking his skull open. Numbers two and three, Smythe and Steele, died in boating accidents. Number four, Henley, drowned while swimming in his own pool. *He* managed to make it all the way to his third anniversary with Salina. None of the others lasted more than two years with her."

"So she's a black widow, then," I murmured. "One who likes to use her water magic to kill her husbands for their money, because she's bored with them, or for whatever other reason she might have."

Finn polished off his pie and shot his thumb and forefinger at me. "Bingo. All of the deaths were suspicious, though the police could never pin anything on Salina. Along the way, she's collected an impressive fortune in insurance money, as well as what her hubbies left her in their wills. If I had to guess, I'd say that money is helping fund her return to Ashland. That might even be why she married all these men in the first place."

"So she could return to town one day in lavish style?"

He nodded. "And there's one more interesting thing about Salina and her hubbies. Here, see for yourself."

Finn grabbed the folder off the table and handed it to me. Curious, I opened it and started flipping through the pages inside. Most of the sheets were copies of newspaper and magazine articles about Salina's husbands that Finn had printed off the Internet. Business deals. Civic awards. Wedding announcements.

"Keep going until you see the obituaries," he said.

I did as he said. *One, two, three, four.* I skimmed through the obits, but there was nothing out of the ordinary about them, just a headshot of each man and some facts about his life and those he'd left behind. So I went through the pages again, slower and more carefully this time, studying each one of the headshots, and I finally realized what Finn was talking about.

Black hair. Blue eyes. Nice smiles. Rugged good looks. Every single one of Salina's husbands had the same coloring and the same features. They were so similar they could have been brothers—and they all looked more or less like Owen.

I sucked in a breath, but it wasn't enough to banish the cold, sick feeling that filled my stomach.

Finn gave me a sympathetic look. "They say you never really get over your first love. Seems like Salina's taken that to heart more than most. I'm sorry, Gin."

I stood there, absorbing the news, then grabbed some forks, napkins, and a large tray out of the kitchen drawers and cabinets, along with an ice pack from the freezer for Owen's black eye. I added a pitcher of milk from the fridge to my tray, along with some glasses. I reached for my Ice magic and used it to frost each one of the glasses, so the milk would stay nice and cold inside them, but I wasn't really thinking about what I was doing. All I could focus on was the four men Salina had married, and how they'd all appeared to be substitutes for Owen.

Still on autopilot, I carried everything into the den, with Finn following along behind me. Owen and Eva were exactly where I'd left them—him on the sofa staring at the television and her standing in front of the mantel.

"Eat up," I said, putting the tray on the scarred coffee table between them. "Because we need to talk."

Finn didn't have to be told twice. He sat in a chair, leaned forward, grabbed two of the apple pies and wolfed them down, along with a glass of milk. I ate a pie as well, although the buttery, fried dough and sweet apples failed to satisfy me like they usually did. Owen only picked at his before grabbing the ice pack and holding it against his bruised face. Eva didn't eat anything at all, although she did finally sit down on the opposite end of the sofa from her brother.

After a few minutes, we all gave up the pretense of eating, except for Finn, who never let awkwardness get in the way of something as important as his appetite. He was finishing another pie when I wiped my hands on a napkin, turned off the television, and stared at Eva.

"Why don't you tell me how you know Kincaid, and why he said that Salina tried to kill him?"

Instead of answering me, Eva glared at her brother, her blue eyes cold and accusing. "Ask Owen. He's the one who brought Salina into our lives, and he's the one who always took her side over everyone else's—no matter how wrong it was."

I knew that Owen and Salina had been involved, but Eva made it sound like there was more to the story than just an old relationship—a whole hell of a lot more. I turned to Owen, letting him see the questions in my face.

My lover sighed, and his shoulders slumped, as if a heavy weight had just been yoked across them. He slowly lowered the ice pack from his bruised features and put it on the tray. After a moment, he drew in a breath and raised his eyes to mine.

"Salina was my fiancée," Owen said.

✱ 13 ✱

Fiancée?

Salina had been Owen's *fiancée*?

That sick feeling in my stomach spread through the rest of my body, like acid eating away at my insides. I'd known that Owen had had other lovers before me, just like I had before him. But a fiancée was something else entirely, something far more serious—and something I would have expected him to mention before now. Still, I kept my features calm and remote, as if we were talking about a disappointing football game, instead of the fact that Owen had never told me about this part of his past, a part that looked like it was going to be serious trouble— especially for the two of us.

"Fiancée?" Finn said in an incredulous voice. "You were actually engaged to her? Well, knock me over with a feather."

"My thoughts exactly," Eva muttered.

Owen opened his mouth to let loose some retort, but I held my hand up, cutting him off.

"Enough," I said. "Enough. You and Eva sniping at each other isn't getting us anywhere. Start at the beginning, Owen. I want to hear all of it. About you, Salina, and Kincaid."

Owen got to his feet and started pacing back and forth across the den. He did that for the better part of a minute before he raked his hand through his hair and started his story.

"It was right after Mab had murdered our parents," Owen said in a low voice. "Eva and I were living on the Southtown streets, and I had no idea what I was doing. How I was going to take care of us, how I was going to find us enough to eat and a safe place to sleep every night. You know what I'm talking about, Gin."

I nodded. I'd faced the same challenges myself, back before Fletcher had taken me in. But I knew it had been even harder on Owen, since he'd had Eva to take care of and she'd been so young at the time. Still, that didn't excuse the fact that he hadn't told me about Salina before now, and it didn't ease the hurt that I felt—or the sudden wariness.

"Anyway, the days went by, and I got more and more desperate. Eventually, I started stealing food from convenience stores, grocery stores, restaurants, anyplace I thought I could and not get caught. Only one day, I did get caught. I grabbed two apples from a bin at a convenience store. Two measly apples, and the owner was going to beat me to death over them. He would have too—if this thin blond kid hadn't gotten in his way. The kid bumped into the owner, and I managed to break away and run like hell. I went back to the alley where I'd hidden Eva, and to my surprise, that same kid was there— and he had a whole bag of apples with him. Turned out he'd grabbed them while the owner was using my face for a punching bag."

"So that's how you met Kincaid," I murmured.

Owen nodded. "That's how I met Phillip. He'd seen me and Eva around at some of the shelters where I took her to beg for food. He said we could do a lot better if we started working together. So we did."

"So the two of you hooked up and then what?" Finn asked. "It was mayhem on the mean streets of Ashland?"

Owen smiled, his violet eyes soft with old memories. "Something like that. We started small, stealing food and clothes, mostly. Some blankets and toys for Eva, things like that. Just enough to keep us from starving and freezing to death."

I could see them in my mind. Owen already tall and turning into the man he would soon become. Kincaid still a scrawny kid, but one who knew the score better than Owen did. The two of them with seemingly nothing in common but joining forces to survive. Desperation made for strange bedfellows, no matter how old or young you were.

"Eventually, we got bolder, and we moved on to bigger and better things. We started stealing from pawnshops. My elemental talent for metal let me get through most doors, locks, and windows, no matter how many bars they had on them. Phillip would be the lookout and watch Eva while I went inside and took whatever caught my eye. Guns, jewelry, knives, clothes, shoes, whatever. We'd take the stuff we stole to a different shop and pawn it for cash, using that as an excuse to case the place, then go back and hit that shop a week later."

Finn let out a whistle. "Nice scheme for a couple of teenagers."

Owen gave him a faint grin. "We thought so too, but it wasn't just us. There were other kids on the streets or in foster care, boys and girls Phillip knew, and sometimes they helped."

A thought occurred to me. "Folks like Katarina Arkadi?"

Owen nodded. "And Antonio too, although they were both more Phillip's friends than mine."

I wondered if that was why Salina had murdered them—if she'd wanted to hurt the casino boss by taking away the people he cared about before she killed him. That would explain why she'd gone after Antonio first tonight, instead of Kincaid. Cold. Very, very cold.

"Anyway, despite the stealing, it was still tough," Owen said. "Half the time, the three of us were on the verge of starving. Eventually, though, I got a job with a dwarven blacksmith, thanks to Fletcher."

Owen looked at Finn, who nodded. I'd told Finn that his father had taken pity on and helped Owen back in the day. Fletcher always had a soft spot in his heart for folks who were down on their luck. You couldn't get much lower or more desperate than living on the streets with a toddler to take care of.

"Things got better after that," Owen said. "The blacksmith's name was Cooper Stills. He was tough on me, but he was a decent, fair man. An Air elemental too. He took all three of us in—me, Phillip, and Eva—even though I was the only one who could work in the forge as long and hard as he did. He gave us food to eat and clothes to wear and put a roof over our heads, but it wasn't enough for me and Phillip. Not after what we'd been through, so we kept right on stealing and stockpiling our loot and money, just in case Cooper changed his mind and decided he didn't want us around anymore."

"I'm sensing a *but* in there," Finn said.

Owen drew in a breath. "But Cooper was and still is a renowned blacksmith. The dwarf can forge anything he puts his mind to, and all his pieces are works of art, whether they're weapons or fountains or sculptures. Back then, Cooper did a lot of work for a lot of rich people in Northtown, and he would take Phillip and me with him when he went out to meet with clients, take space measurements, or deliver commissioned pieces."

"Naturally, you saw that as an opportunity," Finn drawled. "I certainly would have."

Owen shrugged. "You might say that. So Phillip and I moved up to a higher clientele, as far as the stealing went. Jewelry, artwork, silverware. We took anything we could get our hands on—small things mostly, things we didn't think anyone would miss, at least for a few days. Then, when it was safe, we'd sell the items to someone who wouldn't ask too many questions about where they'd come from. For two years, everything was great."

"And then what happened?" I asked.

"And then he met Salina," Eva muttered in a dark tone.

Owen stared at his sister, but he didn't contradict her

words. "And then I met Salina. By that point, Cooper was letting me make my own pieces, my own weapons and sculptures. Benedict, Salina's father, saw one of my designs for a knife and commissioned a similar piece. When it was finished, I delivered it to the Dubois house. That's how I met Salina."

He didn't say anything else, and I didn't ask what had happened next. Even now, it was obvious Owen had cared deeply about her.

That he had loved her.

Jealousy seeped through my body, venom poisoning me from the inside out, and a bitter taste filled my mouth, but I sat perfectly still, not betraying any of the turmoil I felt.

The Owen Grayson I knew wasn't the type of man who would propose to a woman if he didn't believe he was going to spend the rest of his life with her. His dedication to the people he cared about was one of the things I admired most about him, even as much pain as it was causing me right now to think about him being with someone else—*loving* someone else.

Owen cleared his throat. "Salina was . . . captivating. Beautiful, mysterious, charming, playful, whimsical, everything I thought I'd ever wanted in a woman. She had a wild streak, and it suited her just fine to take up with a poor blacksmith, even though her father didn't approve of me."

"Wait a minute," Finn interrupted. "Her father—you're talking about Benedict Dubois, right? The old mob boss? The one that Mab made such an example out of?"

Owen nodded. "Salina was his only daughter. She was there the night it happened, and so was I."

His words were like a key opening a lock in my head. Benedict Dubois. I'd thought the name had sounded familiar when Kincaid had mentioned it, just like I'd thought I'd seen Salina's mermaid rune before I'd met her at Underwood's. Now I remembered exactly where I knew the name and the symbol from—a scouting job Fletcher had taken me on years ago.

"Salina . . . changed after that," Owen said. "Witnessing her father's murder—it did something to her."

"Yeah," Eva piped up. "It made her even more of a heartless bitch than she already was."

Owen ignored her and looked at me. "After Mab killed her father, I felt even more of a connection to Salina. She had ended up just like the three of us—with nothing. Mab took everything that Benedict had—all his money, all his businesses, everything—and then she left his mansion to just sit there and rot. I'd been saving up enough money to get my own place, so I did, and Salina moved in with me, Eva, and Phillip. For a while, everything was perfect."

"I'm guessing we're about to get to the part where it all went wrong," Finn said.

Owen grimaced. "Something like that. Cooper finally found out we were using him to steal. He was a good man, and he really did care about us. He tried to convince me to stop, but I didn't want to listen to him. For the first time in a long time, I was having fun, and I didn't want it to stop. So I quit working for him, and I started making weapons and sculptures on my own. Then, when I went to deliver the goods, I would case my clients' houses and go back later with Phillip. We would take what we wanted just like we'd been doing all along."

Owen fell silent and paced across the den once more before going on with his story.

"For a while, everything was great, so great that I proposed to Salina, and she said yes. We were planning to get married just as soon as I could get my hands on enough money to pay for the kind of wedding she wanted."

I knew Owen had been involved with women before me—lots of women, given how rich, handsome, and successful he was. But it still jarred me to hear him talk about someone else, especially about how close he'd been to committing to Salina forever. Owen was really the first serious relationship I'd ever had. I'd opened up my heart to him in a way that I hadn't to anyone ever before, and I'd wanted to be the same thing for him. But I wasn't, and it hurt.

It hurt so much, this sharp, aching, bitter jealousy that burned and sputtered like a candle flame right where my heart was.

And that wasn't the worst part. Because even now, I could see something in his eyes, hear something in his voice, when he talked about Salina. Maybe it was just the fondness of first love or the good times they'd shared, or maybe it was something more serious, but it was there all the same—and it worried the hell out of me.

"So what happened?" Finn asked. "What went wrong with your life of love, loot, and larceny?"

Owen stared into space, not answering him. Eva let out a disgusted snort, which roused my lover out of his memories.

"Owen?" I asked. "What happened?"

He sighed and looked at Eva before finally turning his gaze to me. "Phillip tried to rape and murder Salina."

* 14 *

Nobody spoke. Nobody moved. We were all frozen in place by the ugly, ugly thing Owen had given voice to.

Finn let out another low whistle. "And I thought Gin and I had skeletons in our closets."

I shot him a warning look, but Finn just grinned at me.

The reaction that surprised me the most was Eva's. Her blue eyes flashed in her face, angry splotches stained her pale cheeks, and her features pinched together in disgust. She opened her mouth like she wanted to argue with Owen but clamped her lips shut at the last second. I could see her struggling with something, although I had no idea what it could be. Eva noticed me staring at her, and she grew very still, as if a new thought had just occurred to her.

"Not again," she finally muttered and surged to her feet.

Not the reaction I expected from her—not at all. It made me wonder exactly what Eva knew about Salina—and what she was hiding.

Owen sighed. "Eva, don't do this. I know you never liked Salina, but you know what Phillip tried to do."

Once more, Eva pressed her lips into a thin line, as if she was biting her tongue to keep from saying what was really on her mind. Owen started to go over to her, but she backed away from him and shook her head.

"All these years later, and you still have on blinders when it comes to Salina," Eva snapped. "Well, I'm old enough now that at least I don't have to listen to it anymore. I'm going to take a shower and go to bed. Is that okay, Gin?"

I nodded. "You do whatever you need to, sweetheart. You know where everything is. Go help yourself to whatever you want, and curl up in whichever guest bed you like."

Eva nodded, left the den, and stomped up a flight of stairs to the second floor. A minute later, a door slammed, and I heard the water coming on in one of the showers.

Owen sighed and scrubbed his hands over his face, as though the motion could slough all the old, painful memories out of his mind. "I'm sorry about that. Eva might be right about me when it comes to Salina, but she's the same way about Phillip. She was always tagging after him back then, asking him to play with her. She was only about four when it happened, too young to understand what was really going on."

"What do you think happened?" I asked, careful to keep my voice calm and neutral.

His whole body tensed, and his hands clenched into fists as though he wanted to lash out and punch some-one—Kincaid. "I *know* what happened. The bastard tried to rape Salina, and when she fought back, he decided to beat her to death."

Finn let out another whistle, but I remained quiet. I'd been an assassin for a long time, and I'd dealt with a lot of bad people. With most, it was easy to tell what their pre-dilections were—gambling, drinking, beating their wives and husbands, abusing kids, hurting people just because they could. I didn't really know Kincaid, and the tense conversations we'd had these past few days was all the in-teraction I'd ever had with him, but the casino boss didn't strike me as a rapist.

Then again, a restaurant owner didn't strike most peo-ple as being the kind of woman who'd moonlight as an assassin either.

But I'd been fooled by people in the past. Maybe Kin-caid was just better at hiding his true nature than most folks were.

"Tell me about it," I said, determined to keep an open mind.

"It was a typical night," he began. "Phillip and I had scouted a mansion in Northtown. The owners were sup-posed to be gone, so we figured it would be easy pickings. We left Salina behind to watch Eva, but Phillip said he was feeling sick and went back. I went on to the mansion, but when I got there, the whole place was lit up, and the owners were there. So I turned around and headed home."

Rage darkened his rugged features. "I heard the screams

and shouts as soon as I went inside. I thought that maybe someone we'd robbed had decided to get some payback, but instead I found the three of them in the bathroom. Salina had been giving Eva her bath for the night, and Eva was still in the tub, dripping wet. But Phillip was on the floor, on top of Salina. Her face was cut and bloody from where he'd been hitting her. He was . . . he was still hitting her when I pulled him off."

Owen drew in another breath. "Salina started screaming about what Phillip had tried to do to her, about how he'd tried to rape her. Phillip said it wasn't what it looked like, but I didn't believe him. We fought. I was older and bigger and stronger, but Phillip was tough, even back then. He shoved me into the bathroom mirror so hard it broke my nose. The glass shattered on impact, cutting up my face."

Owen reached up and subconsciously touched his nose. I'd always wondered how it had gotten to be just a bit crooked. He'd probably gotten the scar on his chin that same night.

"And then?" Finn asked.

"Then I got hold of Phillip, and I beat the hell out of him," Owen said in a cold, flat voice. "I should have beaten him to death. I would have, if Eva hadn't kept tugging on my arms, crying and screaming at me to stop. I didn't want her to see me kill Phillip, so I dragged him to the front door and threw him out of the house. That was the end of our friendship. Although he goes out of his way to speak to me whenever our paths cross, like it's some great joke to needle me as often as he can."

"Like at Mab's funeral," I said.

Owen nodded. He was looking at the framed drawings on the mantel, but I knew he wasn't really seeing them. No, right now, my lover was remembering the fury he'd felt that long-ago night and how he'd almost killed a man because of it.

It was a horrible story all the way around. Still, I couldn't help but wonder whether or not it was entirely true—especially since it seemed like Eva remembered things far differently than her brother did. But if she did, why hadn't she spoken up tonight? Why hadn't she told me and Finn her side of the story? And why hadn't she tried to get Owen to listen to her back then? There was something going on with Eva, something that was making her keep her mouth shut about Salina. I had no idea what it could be—but I was determined to get to the truth one way or another.

I looked at Finn. He nodded, telling me he had the same questions I did. I had no doubt Owen believed what he was saying, but I had a funny feeling it didn't quite mesh with what had actually gone down.

Owen sighed. "That was the beginning of the end. Two nights later, I came home, and Salina was gone. Just—gone. So were all of her things. All her clothes, all her makeup, all the jewelry I'd bought her, all the money I kept stashed at the house for emergencies, everything. Just—gone. She left me a note saying she needed some time to herself, some time to get over what Phillip had done. Of course, I looked for her for months afterward, but I didn't find her. Eventually, I just figured that she didn't want to be found. I never heard from her again, and she never came back to Ashland."

"Until now," I said.

Owen nodded, but he didn't say anything else.

I got up, walked over, and put a hand on his arm. "It's not your fault. None of this is your fault. Not what happened then, and not what happened on the riverboat tonight either."

He gave me a grim smile. "That's where you're wrong. It *is* my fault that Salina was beaten and almost raped, that she left Ashland, all because I couldn't see the kind of person Phillip really was. I failed to protect Salina from the person I thought was my best friend—my brother, even. I'll never forgive myself for that, Gin. Never."

Nobody said anything. Owen was thinking about old memories, old hurts, old anger. Finn and I were digesting everything that had been said.

Mostly, though, I thought of how Salina had so easily killed Antonio, and how she'd almost done the same thing to Kincaid. If Kincaid had tried to rape her, I could understand Salina wanting to murder him. Hell, I'd happily let her borrow one of my knives if that was the case.

But why kill the giant? Sure, Antonio had been Kincaid's friend, but what had murdering him really gotten her, other than a few minutes of shock value? If she'd wanted to, Salina could have simply used her magic to force all the water out of Kincaid's body in the first place before anyone had been the wiser. So why waste her time and magic on Antonio?

The more people you tried to take out at a site, the riskier it was, and the less chance you had of making sure all your targets got dead. There was always a possibility that things could go wrong, that one of your intended victims could get away from you, or that someone entirely unexpected—like me—could fuck up your plans.

Even more curious was the fact that Kincaid had said he'd heard rumors that Salina was coming back to town, rumors that would have been confirmed as soon as he'd learned how Katarina Arkadi had died. If she wanted to kill Kincaid for trying to rape her, why would Salina murder the other woman first? Why tip her hand like that? Why give Kincaid any clue that she was back in Ashland at all? It just didn't make sense—unless she'd wanted to make Kincaid suffer by watching his friends die before she killed the casino boss himself. Even then, it was still a lot of trouble to go to when she could have just murdered Kincaid first and been done with things.

Settling an old score was all well and good, but Salina Dubois didn't strike me as the kind of person to come back to Ashland just for that. If such simple revenge was all she wanted, she could have blown into town at any time, killed Kincaid, and been on her merry way. Instead, she'd married man after man, making their fortunes her own, and then returned. She had to have some sort of plan in mind to have gone to such lengths. So why was she really here? Why now, after all these years?

Then there was her meeting with Jonah McAllister at Underwood's. I supposed he could have been her lawyer for all these years, handling her finances, perhaps even helping her marry and murder for money. That was just the sort of thing McAllister reveled in. The obituary photos of all her dead husbands flashed through my mind, each of them seemingly a substitute for Owen, and it took some effort to push the disturbing images away.

Maybe McAllister had helped her with her husbands, or maybe not, but one thing was for sure—he needed a new boss. And I was willing to bet Salina would fit that bill nicely. If Salina had cooked up some other scheme with McAllister, it could only mean trouble. No, something else was going on here besides an old feud, something bigger, something I needed to figure out before Salina hurt anyone else, especially Owen.

But there was nothing I could do about any of that right now, especially since midnight had already come and gone.

"Well," I finally said, "I think that's enough secret spilling for one evening."

"Oh, I don't know," Finn said. "Personally, I'd *love* to hear more about Owen's little larceny scheme. Got any of that loot left? I'm sure it's only appreciated in value over the years."

Owen winced.

"Finn?"

He gave me a friendly smile. "Yes, Gin?"

"Do yourself a favor and leave before I throw you out."

He stuck out his lips in an exaggerated pout. "Fine. But I still want to know all about the Grayson Gang. Or was it the Kincaid Crew? Tell me you guys at least had a catchy nickname."

I glared at him, but Finn just pouted a little more when Owen didn't answer him.

I shut and locked the front door behind Finn, then went back into the den, where Owen was. I turned off the lights, and we walked up the stairs to the second floor.

I headed for my bedroom door, but Owen didn't follow me. I looked over my shoulder at him.

"Maybe I should sleep in a different room tonight," he said. "Since Eva's right down the hall."

It wasn't an unreasonable request, but his words pricked my heart like tiny thorns. Eva was nineteen. She knew exactly what Owen and I did when we were alone together. Still, maybe it was for the best. We'd all been put through the wringer in some way tonight. Eva had witnessed a murder; Owen had dredged up memories of how he'd loved and lost his fiancée; and I'd realized that my lover had more of a past and more secrets than I'd ever dreamed of.

"Sure," I said.

I could hear Eva moving around in the bedroom next to mine, so I led Owen to the one at the end of the hall. I flipped the light on and showed him where the extra blankets and pillows were stacked up in the closet. When that was done, we stood beside the bed, neither one of us knowing quite what to say to the other about everything that had come out into the open tonight.

"I'm sorry, Gin," Owen finally said in a soft voice, "for blindsiding you with all this. I never thought Salina would come back to Ashland, or that Phillip would drag you into the middle."

I shrugged. "It's my fault too for not telling you about Kincaid's so-called catering job in the first place. I would have, if I'd known you had any kind of connection to him. So let's just forgive and forget, okay?"

He nodded. "And what about Salina?"

"What about Salina?" I asked, careful to keep my voice neutral once more.

He hesitated again. "I'd like to talk to her—about a lot of things. I *need* to talk to her. At the very least, I need to apologize for not finishing off Kincaid when I had the chance. I owed her that much, but I failed her."

I suspected Owen hadn't failed Salina so much as she'd outright lied to him, but that was neither here nor there. As much as I wanted to, I couldn't say no. Not too long ago, Owen had given me the time and space I'd needed to come to terms with my lingering feelings for Donovan. The least I could do was let him speak to Salina—even if I thought she was far more devious and dangerous than she appeared to be.

"Of course," I murmured. "We'll talk more about that and everything else tomorrow. Right now, we both need to get some rest. It's been a long day."

"Thank you, Gin," Owen said in a soft voice. "For believing me. For trusting me."

I looked at him, at his black hair, his violet eyes, his rough, rugged features that were so appealing to me. All these emotions roared up in my chest. All my love for him, all my caring, all my worry—and all my fear of losing him.

It was that horrible thought, that terrible fear, that spurred me forward. I pressed my body flush again Owen's, drew his lips down to mine, and kissed him for all I was worth, trying to put everything I was thinking, everything I was feeling, into that one single kiss. Trying to make it perfect, trying to make it everything he'd had with Salina—and more.

The fierceness of my kiss seemed to startle him, but Owen's arms snaked around me, pulling me even closer. I kept right on kissing him, trying to tell him I understood the things he'd done and the decisions he'd made, even if I didn't like everything I'd learned tonight about how much he'd once loved Salina.

Sometime later, we broke apart, both of us breathless and aching—for each other and for answers we weren't quite sure of.

"I love you, Gin," Owen whispered in my ear, still holding me in his arms.

For the first time since he'd said those words to me, I doubted them—and him—but I kept my troubling thoughts to myself.

"I know," I whispered back. "And I love you too. We'll figure this out, just like we always do—together."

He nodded, dropped his arms from around me, and stepped back. I walked over and paused in the doorway.

"If you need anything tonight, I'm just right down the hall."

"I know. Sleep well."

Try as I might, I couldn't quite make myself smile. "You too."

I shut the door behind me, but I didn't go to my room. Instead, I stood there, my hand still on the knob, brooding. I knew Owen loved me, that he loved me just as much as I did him.

But I couldn't help but wonder if he still loved Salina as well—and if she'd always had more of a hold on his heart than I could ever hope to have.

❖ 15 ❖

I finally moved away from the door, but instead of taking a shower like I should have, I went back downstairs to Fletcher's office.

I turned on the light and looked out over the familiar mess. Papers, books, folders, and pens covered the battered desk in the back of the room, and more of the same could be found on the shelves of the bookcases against the walls and on top of the filing cabinets that squatted on either side of the door.

The sight of the old man's clutter brought a ghost of a smile to my face. I just hadn't felt like cleaning it, or the rest of the house, up yet. I didn't know when I would. Sometimes Fletcher's murder and the knowledge that he was gone still hurt as much as if it had all happened just yesterday. Having his things around comforted me—or at least tricked me into believing that part of him was still here with me.

But it was late, and I was tired, so I put my sentiment aside and got busy. It took me about twenty minutes of digging through the cabinets before I found what I was looking for: the file on Benedict Dubois's murder.

Even though he hadn't killed Dubois, Fletcher, being Fletcher, had compiled all the information he could get his hands on about the murder and had organized it in meticulous detail. Besides doing recon on the people he assassinated, the old man was always digging into someone, always keeping track of who was moving up in the underworld and who was getting offed. There was probably more information on more murders in this room than in storage at police headquarters. Fletcher had claimed that his obsessive chronicling was a way to stay ahead of our enemies, but I just thought he liked knowing where all the bodies were buried in Ashland—a trait Finn had inherited from him.

Tonight, though, I just hoped the file told me more about Salina and what she might be up to. I took the folder over to the desk, flipped on a light there, sat down in Fletcher's creaky chair, and started reading.

According to Fletcher's notes, Benedict Dubois's murder had been the talk of Ashland for months—if it could be considered a simple murder. Fletcher had chronicled the series of events that had led to his death, all the skirmishes and problems Benedict had had with Mab, all the things that had prompted him to plot against her, but I skipped ahead to the night it had all gone down. Even then, there were pages of information to go through, covering everything from the blueprints of the mansion to exactly where Dubois had died. Given Fletcher's attention to detail, there was even a guest list of everyone who'd been there that night.

I put the list aside to give to Finn to see what connections he might be able to make between the guests back then and what Salina might be up to now. For all I knew, she was working with someone on the list besides McAllister.

Finally, I got to Fletcher's recap of that fateful night. Benedict, an Ice elemental, had thrown an elegant dinner party at his mansion. Just before the soup course, he'd tried to take out Mab by stabbing her in the back with a silverstone knife—only he'd failed. Naturally, the Fire elemental had made an example out of him for his foolishness.

The more I read, the more I remembered that night, until it seemed like every line, every word, caused another image to pop into my mind.

Then I got to the photos.

Fletcher had somehow gotten his hands on police images of Dubois's body. You couldn't even tell that the ashy, smoking thing in the photos had once been a man. It just looked like a collection of blackened bones strung together, topped by a skull baring charred teeth.

I'd seen similar pictures before. Hell, I'd witnessed such things myself when Mab murdered my mother and older sister. My stomach twisted, and the phantom stench of seared skin filled my nose, making me gag, as if Benedict Dubois's corpse were freshly burned and still smoldering at my feet.

I forced myself to flip past the photos and keep reading, but there wasn't anything else to discover. After she tortured and murdered Dubois, Mab hadn't had any more problems for a good long while.

I slid the pictures back in the file, closed it, and put a crystal paperweight shaped like my spider rune on top of the folder. The information might be a window into the past, but it didn't tell me what had really happened with Kincaid and Salina or, more important, what she was doing back in Ashland. So I turned off the light and went back upstairs.

I went through the motions of getting ready for bed—taking a shower, towel-drying my hair, putting on some shorts and an old T-shirt.

Even though I hadn't killed anyone tonight, I was still exhausted from everything I'd learned about Owen, Salina, Kincaid, and their convoluted history. I was so tired I thought I might fall asleep immediately, but as soon as I closed my eyes, the dreams started, the way they always did. Except they weren't dreams so much as glimpses of my past, memories of all the bad things I'd seen and done. I'd been having the dreams ever since Fletcher's murder last year, and I had no idea when they might stop, if ever. I supposed these particular images were triggered by reading through the Dubois file. . . .

No one was supposed to die tonight.

It was supposed to be a simple assignment, one that Fletcher, the assassin known as the Tin Man, could do in his sleep. Slip onto the estate of Benedict Dubois during a dinner party and gather intel on Peter Delov, an Ashland drug lord. See who Delov spoke to, who he snubbed, how close his guards stayed to him. All in preparation for a hit that was to take place later on.

I moved through the halls of the Dubois mansion, calmly, quickly heading toward my destination. As usual, I wore dark clothes, although I'd been forced to don a white tuxedo vest and a matching bow tie over my black shirt, pants, and shoes. The pale fabric felt like a bull's-eye on my chest, and the fact that I was carrying an empty tray instead of one of the knives Fletcher was teaching me to use made me feel even more vulnerable. Still, the vest and the tray were an effective part of my disguise, that of a simple waiter.

Tonight, instead of skulking around in the shadows, I boldly strode down the corridor, passing one giant guard after another and nodding to them all in turn. A few eyed me with obvious curiosity, probably wondering exactly how I'd gotten this job, since at fifteen I was a bit younger than the other workers. But no one stopped or questioned me. Finally, I reached the entrance to the kitchen and showed the guard there my tray. He politely opened the door for me, and I stepped inside.

The kitchen was a madhouse. Several chefs were busy chopping, cutting, peeling, boiling, steaming, and sautéing everything from potatoes to pasta to peaches, and my nose itched from the red pepper, cinnamon, and other spices in the air. The chefs called out orders to each other and the dozens of waiters who were busy moving through the cramped aisles, grabbing trays of champagne and hors d'oeuvres before scurrying back out to the party to serve up the delicacies.

"Soup's up!" one of the chefs called out.

I handed my empty tray off to one of the dishwashers, got a clean one filled with white china bowls, and headed toward the back of the kitchen to the chef who'd spoken. The overhead lights brought out the silver threads in his walnut-

colored hair, while the heat from the ovens and burners had made his cheeks even ruddier than usual.

I put the tray down on the counter next to his elbow and watched while the chef ladled a scrumptious-smelling, gourmet broccolini soup into the bowls.

"Anything interesting?" Fletcher murmured as he used some freshly grated Parmesan cheese and sourdough croutons to garnish each bowl of soup.

"Not really," I replied. "Just Delov moving through the crowd, eating, drinking, and greeting his business associates. The usual. Although Delov looks to be in the market for a new mistress. He's barely glanced at the woman he brought along tonight. Instead, he's been fawning all over one of the women who came with Beauregard Benson."

"Benson won't like that, but I doubt it will stop Delov," Fletcher said. "See if you can find out who she is. Might prove useful later on."

I nodded, pleased he was trusting me with such an assignment. Fletcher often hired himself out for events like these as a way to surreptitiously study potential targets. Usually, he worked as a waiter, but tonight he'd been needed in the kitchen to cook, so the old man had brought me along to be his eyes and ears at the party, which was being held on the lawn outside. It was something he was doing more and more of these days, now that I was two years into my training with him.

Fletcher said that soon I'd be ready to start doing solo scouting jobs. Serving food and drinks to the puffed-up power players of Ashland wasn't exactly the most thrilling way to spend my nights, but Fletcher said that blending in with a crowd and getting close to my targets was a necessary skill to learn. That it would prepare me for more violent, bloodier things later on. I wasn't quite sure I believed that, but the old man had been right about so many things so far that I wasn't going to argue with him. Besides, the waiter money was decent enough, and I almost always got to take home a bag or two of leftovers.

"Be careful," Fletcher warned as he finished garnishing the last bowl of soup. "Be quiet and be invisible just like always. Don't get yourself noticed by anyone, especially not tonight."

The worried tone in his voice made me look at him. "Is something wrong?"

He shrugged, but his green eyes were dark and troubled. "I heard some rumors that something big might go down at the dinner—"

A scream erupted, cutting through the noise and clatter in the kitchen.

Everyone froze, wondering if we'd all just imagined the sound—but we hadn't. More sharp screams sounded, along with a couple of loud, booming crack-crack-cracks of gunfire. But the most troubling thing was that even here in the kitchen, a hundred feet from the doors that led out to the party, I could feel the crackle of magic in the air. A blast of frigid Ice power, followed by an intense wave of Fire, both of them rubbing against my skin like invisible sandpaper.

Fletcher noticed the grimace on my face. "What is it, Gin?"

"Some elementals are using their power," I said in a low voice. "Ice and Fire. They must be strong, really strong, for me to sense their magic all the way in here."

He nodded. "We need to get out of here—"

But it was already too late. The kitchen doors flew open, and giants stormed into the room. Every single one of them had a gun in his hand. There was nothing Fletcher and I could do, no way we could escape without drawing attention to ourselves and making things worse, so we bowed our heads and put our hands up like everyone else did.

The giants marched the entire kitchen and waitstaff outside onto the lawn. When I'd been out here five minutes ago, the area had been pristine, and everything had gleamed, from the fine crystal and china to the elegant, blue-green tablecloths. Now, tables and chairs were overturned, platters of food had been upended, and splintered shards from the broken champagne glasses glinted like razor blades underfoot.

The dinner party guests had been herded into a tight group out on the lawn, and the giants ushered us in that direction as well. No one spoke, although several folks unsuccessfully tried to hold back frightened sobs and whimpers.

"Good," someone purred in a low, feminine voice. "More witnesses."

I couldn't see exactly who was speaking through the crowd of people in front of me, but I saw the shimmer of copper-colored hair and the flash of a gold necklace around a woman's throat. I looked at Fletcher.

"Mab Monroe," he murmured in my ear. "I'd heard Dubois was planning to make a move against her tonight. Looked like he didn't plan well enough. Poor bastard. He'll pay for it now—more than he ever imagined."

I didn't have to ask Fletcher what he meant. The old man had told me all about Mab and her ruthless reputation.

Two giants dragged a man across the lawn, causing mur-

murs to ripple through the crowd. He was a handsome man with blond hair, but his once-impeccable tuxedo jacket hung in smoking tatters on his shoulders, while his white shirt was charred. The holes in his shirt showed the blistering burns on his skin. The giants stopped with him in front of a beautiful stone fountain shaped like a mermaid. Twinkling white lights had been wrapped around the mermaid's elegant form, although they seemed to make the shadows darker, rather than lighter.

It took me a moment to gather my courage enough to drag my gaze away from the mermaid and look at the injured figure again. I knew what was going to happen now. Everyone did.

"Tie him down." Mab's command floated through the air.

Two of the giants moved off to the left and pulled some metal hoops out of the ground and picked up some wooden mallets. A croquet set. I'd seen it on the lawn when I'd been serving champagne earlier. That was what the giants had grabbed, although I had no idea what they planned to do with it.

I got my answer a few seconds later. Four giants held the man down spread-eagled, while two more positioned the metal hoops over his arms and legs and then pounded them into the ground.

Tap-tap-tap. Tap-tap-tap.

The light, ringing sounds were so at odds with what was happening, and every blow the giants struck took on a somber, sinister note in my mind, until all I heard were death knells. We all knew that was what they really were, and so did Benedict Dubois, who started swearing and screaming at the giants to let him go. When that didn't work, he reached for his Ice magic, trying to blast his captors with it. But the giants were ready for that. They punched and kicked him over and over again, breaking his concentration, his ribs, and his nose, and hurting him until he was too bloody and battered to summon any more of his power.

Finally, Dubois raised his head off the ground and looked out at his dinner guests, his friends and business partners. He started yelling at them to help him. But no one stepped forward—no one dared to, not with Mab staring at them.

No one wanted to share Dubois's fate.

Finally, the giants finished their work and stepped back. A hush fell over the crowd, and even Dubois grew silent as Mab walked across the grass toward him.

"Daddy?" a voice called out. "Daddy!"

A girl a few years older than me sprinted across the lawn, her long, blond hair streaming out behind her like ribbons of silk. She must have been in some other part of the mansion, because I hadn't seen her before at the party. A boy with black hair chased after her, catching her just before she reached her father. He wrapped his arms around the girl and held her tight, even though she struggled against him. Smart guy. He knew it was already too late for Dubois, even if the girl didn't.

"Let me go!" she yelled. "We have to help him! Someone please help him!"

But no one did. Instead, they all looked at the girl with pitying eyes.

A couple of the giants moved toward the young couple, probably to try to get the girl to shut up, but Mab held up her hand.

"No," she purred. "Let her watch. Let it be a lesson to her—and everyone else here tonight."

Mab held out her hand, and elemental Fire sparked to life on her fingertips, hissing and crackling with evil intent. I could see the glow of the flames through the crowd, and once again, I felt the invisible waves of her power pressing against my skin. I couldn't tell for sure, but I got the impression that Mab smiled before she bent down.

And then she started torturing Dubois.

I couldn't see everything that was going on, but I didn't need to. I didn't want to. Dubois's screams let everyone know exactly what was happening to him—and just how much it hurt.

The stench of burning flesh filled the warm spring air, reminding me of the night that a Fire elemental had done the same thing to my mother and older sister, how she'd burned them to death. My stomach roiled, and bile coated my throat. For a moment, I thought I might vomit, but I managed to swallow down the bitter liquid that choked me. Other people in the crowd didn't manage to do the same, turning to the side and retching up the food and drinks they'd just downed.

Fletcher put his arm around me and held me close, trying to tell me that it was okay, that he was here with me, that we would get through this, but there was nothing he could do—for me or Dubois.

But the worst part wasn't the stench or the memories or Dubois's pleas for mercy or the heat of the elemental Fire scorching my face. No, the worst part was that through it all, I could hear his daughter screaming—screaming for her family just like I had.

"Daddy! No! Daddy! Daddy—"

The dream abruptly faded, and my eyes snapped open, although I could still hear the faint echo of the girl's screams in my head—Salina's screams.

For a moment, I wondered what had pulled me out of the vivid memory, but then a creak sounded in the corner, and I realized what had woken me up.

Someone was in my bedroom.

✳ 16 ✳

My hand slid underneath my pillow and curled around the knife there. I also reached for my Stone magic, ready to use it to make my skin as hard as marble for when I leaped out of bed and—

"Gin?" a soft voice whispered in the darkness. "Are you awake?"

Eva. It was just Eva. Although she should have known better than to slip into my bedroom unannounced in the middle of the night.

I let go of the knife and sat up in bed, shaking off the last bit of the dream. Eva perched on a rocking chair in the corner, her knees drawn up to her chest and her feet resting in the chair seat. She had her arms wrapped around her knees, hugging them in, as if that small motion would protect her from all the big, bad, scary things out there—things I imagined looked a lot like Salina to her tonight.

"Eva?" I asked. "What are you doing in here? You should be in bed, trying to rest."

"I heard you talking in your sleep," she replied. "I wanted to make sure you were okay."

I shrugged. "I had a bad dream. I have them quite often. You know that. So why did you really come in here?"

Eva didn't say anything. The moonlight peeking in through the curtains illuminated the whole room, painting everything a soft silver. Even though she was curled up in the rocking chair, Eva still looked like a princess straight out of a fairy tale, her black hair gleaming, her blue eyes luminous, her porcelain skin pale and ethereal.

"Do you want to talk about it?" I asked. "About Salina? And what you think happened back then? Because downstairs, you looked like you remembered things a lot differently than Owen did."

"I don't *think* anything," she said. "I know exactly what happened. It's not a figment of my imagination or a nightmare or some story Phillip told me. It's the truth."

"So tell me about it. Let me decide for myself what's real and what isn't."

Eva shivered and hugged her knees in even closer to her chest. "I don't remember a lot from that time. I was only four. Most of my memories are just hazy flashes of Owen and Phillip, the house we lived in, some toys I had, things like that. But when it comes to Salina, everything is crystal clear, and I can still remember what happened like it was yesterday."

She gave me a bitter smile. "Even though I was a kid, I could always tell she never liked me, and I felt the same way about her. But I had Owen and Phillip, and I was happy enough, even if I missed Cooper when we moved out of his house."

"Until . . ."

"Until one day when Salina had on a new dress or maybe a necklace, I don't remember exactly what it was, but she wanted to show it off to Owen. But he'd promised to play dolls with me so he told Salina he'd look at whatever it was later. Salina never liked being ignored, but I remember glancing up at her at that moment and realizing that she was staring at me with this . . . look on her face. It was just . . . evil."

Eva's voice dropped to a whisper, and it took a few seconds for her to regain her composure and continue.

"That night, Owen and Phillip went out. As soon as they were gone, Salina grabbed my arm and hauled me into the bathroom. She said she wanted to give me a bath, but I knew better. She never paid me any attention she didn't have to. I kicked and screamed and tried to get away from her, but of course I couldn't. She stripped off my clothes, forced me into the tub, and turned the water on, filling it all the way up to the top. . . ."

"Then what happened?" I asked.

"She stood over me, and she had this—this *smile* on her face. And then I felt these invisible hands wrap around my arms and legs, like tentacles sucking at my skin. They pulled me down under the water and held me there, and I couldn't break free of them, no matter how hard I struggled. But the worst part was that I could—I could *see* her through the water. Standing beside the tub watching me drown—smiling while I was drowning."

Eva turned her face, trying to hide the fact she was brushing away the tears rolling down her cheeks. She drew in a ragged breath.

"Eventually, Salina got tired of her game and let me out of the tub. I was too scared to even cry by that point. All I could think about was telling Owen when he got home, but Salina must have known that was what I was planning. She got right down in front of me, looked me in the eyes, and told me that this was our new secret game. She said that if I told anyone, anyone at all, that she'd have to play the same game with Phillip—and Owen too. I knew what she meant. That she'd hurt them the same way she had me."

"So you kept quiet."

Eva nodded. "The next night when Owen and Phillip went out again, she took me into the bathroom, made me get into the tub, and did the same thing—torturing me with her water magic over and over again. And the next night, and the next night."

"Oh, Eva, how long did this go on?"

"A couple of weeks," she whispered. "It could have gone on forever . . ."

"If Kincaid hadn't gotten suspicious." I finished her thought.

She nodded again. "I don't know how he figured it out, but he did. Maybe because I was quiet and withdrawn, and I didn't want to play with anyone anymore, especially not Owen. I was terrified that if he paid more attention to me than he did to Salina, she would hurt me that much more. Or that she'd hurt Philly and Owen like she'd said she would."

"So what changed that last night? What happened?"

Eva drew in a couple of breaths and let them out. When she spoke again, her voice was even softer than before. "I was in the tub underwater, watching Salina smile at me, and then suddenly Philly was there. He shoved her out of the way, reached down, and pulled me up and over the side of the tub so I could breathe again. She came at him, trying to shove him into the tub too, and he started hitting her. You know the rest. What she told Owen, what he did to Philly because of her lies."

I believed her. I believed Salina had tortured Eva with her water magic and that Kincaid had managed to save her. I couldn't deny that I *wanted* to believe it, that part of me just wanted Salina to be an evil bitch so she wouldn't be a threat to me and Owen. But as selfish as my motives were, Eva's voice, her words, had a ring of truth to them I couldn't deny. Even more than that, her story added up when what Salina had told Owen simply didn't.

"I thought my brother was going to kill Philly, but he stopped himself," Eva said. "I tried to tell Owen the truth, but Salina was there. While Owen threw Philly out of the house, she grabbed me and told me that I'd better keep my mouth shut. She said that if I ever—*ever*—told Owen what she'd done that she'd hurt him just like she'd hurt me. I believed her, so I've kept quiet like a coward and a fool all these years."

Her fingers clenched and unclenched, like she wanted to rip the arms off the rocking chair she was sitting in. Like she wanted to scream and shout and tear something to pieces—tear Salina to pieces.

"You were a kid, Eva," I said in a soft voice. "There was

nothing you could have done. Salina knew that—that's why she preyed on you. It's not your fault."

Eva's fingers curled around the chair arms again, so tight that I could see the whiteness in her knuckles from my position on the bed. Then, as suddenly as it had come, the anger drained out of her body, and her face twisted into a disgusted expression.

"Maybe," she finally replied, bitterness making her voice harsh. "But that doesn't make it right. So many times, I've thought about telling Owen what happened, about trying to get him to forgive Philly, but I couldn't help but wonder what would happen if Salina ever found out—if she ever came back to Ashland. And now she has, and it's my worst nightmare come to life all over again."

I could have told Eva that I was sorry for what she'd been through, but I knew better than anyone else that *sorry* was just an empty word. It didn't take away the pain—and it didn't banish the memories, especially when they crept up on you when you were all alone in the dark of the night. That was why I spent so many nights tossing and turning before waking up with a scream stuck in my throat. Because part of me would never forget the things I'd seen, done, and suffered through—just like Eva would never forget what Salina had done to her.

"I know she probably killed Antonio and tried to kill Phillip just because she could, but I wonder . . ." It took Eva a moment to find her words. "I wonder if she also wanted to teach me a lesson because I was there tonight. I wonder if she wanted me to remember her promise to me. Poor Antonio . . . what she did to him . . ."

Eva shivered again. She didn't speak for a moment,

but then she raised her eyes to mine. Anger and determination burned in her gaze, and her face looked as hard as marble in the moonlight. I'd seen this look on other people before. I knew what she was going to say next.

"I want you to kill her, Gin," Eva said in a fierce voice. "I want you to kill Salina for me."

Tick-tock, tick-tock.

The slow, steady movement of the clock on the wall was the only sound in the bedroom, although the longer the silence stretched, the more the rhythm seemed to change, until it was almost like someone whispering Eva's words to me over and over again.

Kill her, kill her . . .

Eva kept her blue eyes steady on mine. As I stared into her face, I wondered if she really realized what she was asking me to do—and how her simply asking such a thing would affect her more than she realized.

Finally, I sighed. "Eva—"

"Name your price," she interrupted me. "Whatever it is, I'll pay it. I'll be twenty in a few weeks, and I can access my trust fund then."

"It's not the money, Eva, and you know it. The situation is . . . complicated."

She shook her head. "No, it's not. Whatever Salina's come back to Ashland for, why she's here now after all these years, I don't know, but it can't possibly be good. You saw what she did to Antonio and then what she tried to do to Philly. Who's to say she won't do the same thing to you or me? Or even Owen?"

I didn't have an answer to that. If Salina had come back

to Ashland for revenge against everyone she'd thought had wronged her, then Eva could very well be on her hit list. Owen too, if the water elemental somehow blamed him for her banishment—or for not trying to stop Mab from murdering her father.

"You know that I will do everything I can to protect you, to protect us all," I said in a careful voice.

Eva shook her head. "That's not good enough."

"And you know that Owen won't let anything happen to you," I said, trying a different tack.

She laughed, although the harsh sound seared the air like fire. "Normally I would agree with you, but not when it comes to Salina. Even now, I doubt he would believe that she hurt me back then. Even if he did, if she comes after me again, if she comes after him, he won't be able to fight back, Gin. If it comes down to Owen and Salina in the end, he won't be able to kill her—and then she'll murder him. Without a second thought, she'll drown him or find some other way to use her water magic to kill him just like she promised me she would."

The obituary photos of Salina's dead husbands, the ones who looked so much like Owen, flashed through my mind.

"You don't know that Owen would let Salina kill him," I said, even as my heart screamed at the thought.

"Oh, yes, I do," Eva snapped. "He never could think straight when it came to her. Kind of like you and Donovan Caine. Owen told me you ran into him while you guys were on vacation in Blue Marsh—he said that Donovan wanted to get back together with you, and he could practically *see* the sparks between you—and this is just like that."

I winced. Seeing Donovan had brought up a lot of memories about our often-strained relationship—just like what seeing Salina had done for Owen. But I'd dealt with my unresolved feelings for Donovan, and Owen and I had grown closer because of that. I just hoped he could do the same when it came to Salina.

"I'm over Donovan, and I have been for quite some time now, thanks to your brother," I said. "What makes you think Owen isn't over Salina?"

Eva let out a breath. "I don't know that he isn't, but Salina always gets what she wants—*always*. She did back then, and she will now too. She'll blindside Owen, and he'll believe all her lies again, just like before. And I don't want to take that chance. Do *you*, Gin?"

No, I didn't, but Owen wouldn't like me agreeing to kill someone for his baby sister much either—especially when that someone was his former fiancée. Despite the fact that she was practically grown, Owen still tried to shield Eva from all the bad things in the world—including my activities as the Spider. Although thanks to Salina, Eva had seen and endured more troubles than I would have ever imagined.

Eva sensed my hesitation, so she decided to play her trump card.

"Salina Dubois is my Mab Monroe," she said in a cold, flat voice. "I was four years old, *four years old,* and she tortured me for weeks, Gin, and not for any more reason than that she was jealous of the attention Owen paid me—that and because it *amused her* to hurt me. I want her dead. Simple as that. She deserves it for what she did to me, and even more so for lying and saying that Philly tried to rape her. Owen almost beat him to death for that, and she just stood there and watched it happen, knowing it was a damn lie the whole time."

Eva looked at me, but I still didn't answer her.

"Fine," she snapped. "If you won't help me, then I'll do it myself—I'll kill Salina myself."

"And how will you do that?"

A stubborn look filled her face, and her hands clenched into fists. "I don't know, but I'll find a way. Just like you always do. I'll buy a gun or something. Shouldn't be too hard to find one over in Southtown. I'll just walk over there after classes one day."

It was bad enough Eva wanted to hire me to off Salina. Her planning a trek into Southtown and trying to take out the water elemental herself would be disastrous all the way around. Eva would be dead on those mean streets long before she ever had a chance to get close to Salina. Owen would never forgive me if I let her do something so dangerous—and I wouldn't be able to forgive myself either.

Between a rock and a hard place. A spot I always seemed to find myself in.

I sighed. "All right, all right. You win. Leave Salina to me."

"So you'll kill her then?"

"I don't know," I said. "It depends on what she's really doing in Ashland besides murdering people with her water magic. But I promise you this: if she lifts so much as a finger in your or Owen's direction, I will take her out."

"No matter what Owen thinks?"

I paused. Once again, I wondered if she realized what

she was asking of me, the position she was putting me in—and if I'd be able to go through with it in the end.

"Gin?"

But try as I might, I couldn't say no to the soft plea in her voice. I couldn't say no to the tremulous hope shining in her eyes. I couldn't say no to the chance to quiet her nightmares.

"No matter what Owen thinks," I agreed in a grim tone.

"And Philly?" Eva pressed her advantage. "Will you protect him from Salina too?"

"Phillip Kincaid is more than capable of protecting himself," I said. "Or at least putting enough of his giants in between him and Salina to make things interesting."

"Please, Gin," she said, a pleading note creeping into her voice. "I care about Philly too. He's my friend."

I thought he was a little more than a friend, given the adoring way Eva had been looking at him earlier on the *Delta Queen,* but I didn't mention that. I couldn't do anything about Eva's crush on Kincaid. No matter what I thought of the casino boss, he had tried to protect her tonight, by hiring me to cater the fund-raiser. In his own way, Kincaid cared about Eva just as much as she did about him. It was a big point in his favor.

"We don't have a deal if Philly isn't a part of it," she said.

Despite the situation, I smiled. When she put her mind to it, Eva Grayson was just as tough a negotiator as her big brother was.

"I'll do what I can for Kincaid, providing he decides to play nice with me, but you and Owen come first, agreed?"

"Agreed," Eva said, somewhat mollified. "Thank you, Gin."

"Now go back to bed," I said, sidestepping her thanks. "Try to get some sleep."

Eva nodded, slipped out of my bedroom, and closed the door behind her. Through the walls, I heard the floor creak and the bed frame squeak as she walked down the hall and crawled back under the covers in the bed in the guest room.

I let out a breath and lay down. As much as I would have liked to, I couldn't fall asleep. Too much had happened, and I'd learned too many things for my thoughts to quiet down. So instead, I stared at the ceiling, wondering just how much the devil's bargain I'd made with Eva was going to cost me in the end.

* 17 *

Breakfast the next morning was a tense, quiet affair.

I made chocolate chip pancakes, smoked maple bacon, cheesy scrambled eggs, whole wheat toast with home-made apple butter, and a sparkling grapefruit punch for Eva and Owen. We gathered around the wooden table in the nook that branched off the kitchen.

The three of us ate in silence, except for the rattle of our dishes and polite mutters to ask someone to please pass the bacon. For the most part, Eva ignored Owen's attempts to talk to her. I kept my thoughts to myself, not wanting to sink any deeper into the sibling quicksand. I was already up to my neck in it.

We finished breakfast and split up. Owen had to get to his office, Eva had to get to class, and I had to get to the Pork Pit.

"I'll come by for a late lunch today, and we can talk

some more. Okay?" Owen asked as we stood on the front porch. The morning sunlight highlighted the faint bruise around his eye from his fight with Kincaid.

I nodded, not sure what to say to him, not sure what I *could* say without making things worse. We kissed goodbye; then he got into his car, with Eva already sulking in the passenger seat. She gave me a pointed look through the window, and I knew she was thinking about the promise I'd made to her last night. That look did not make me feel better about anything.

I waved at Owen as he put the car in gear and steered it down the driveway, but my hand dropped to my side the second the vehicle was out of sight, and I started brooding once more. I was just about to go back inside and finish getting ready for work when I heard a car churning through the gravel at the bottom of the ridge.

I paused, wondering if Owen had forgotten something and returned, but instead, a familiar sedan appeared at the top of the driveway. The car stopped, and Bria slid out of the driver's seat. She was wearing sensible black boots and a pair of dark jeans topped by a white, button-up shirt with the sleeves rolled up to her elbows. Her gun was clipped to her belt, along with her gold detective's badge. Her hair was pulled back into a ponytail, and the silverstone primrose rune around her throat glinted in the sun as she walked across the yard.

"Hey, there, baby sister," I said, leaning against the porch railing. "What brings you up here so early?"

Bria smiled at my warm, easy greeting, but her blue eyes were serious. "I thought you'd want to know about the chat I had with Salina Dubois this morning."

I nodded. "Well, come on in then. No use delving into the unpleasant on an empty stomach."

I led Bria back into the kitchen and warmed a plate of food for her. In between bites, she told me how she and Xavier had spent the night tracking down Salina. It hadn't been hard, since Salina hadn't made any attempt to hide. Instead, the water elemental had been ensconced in bed at her family's mansion when Bria had come knocking on her door in the wee hours of the morning.

"You should have seen her, Gin," Bria said. "She floated down the stairs like she was Scarlet O'Hara on her way to a debutante dance—despite the fact she was wearing a blue silk negligee instead of a ball gown."

I thought of the way Salina had strolled into Underwood's and caught the attention of everyone there. "That sounds like her. What did she say?"

"Well, first of all, she just *had* to offer us some hot tea and coffee," Bria said. "She even woke up her personal chef and had the poor man fix us strawberry scones and cucumber sandwiches."

I raised an eyebrow.

"I'm not kidding you. Strawberry scones and cucumber sandwiches at three in the morning, as if we were having a nice little garden luncheon instead of talking about a murder." Bria snorted. "And when we did finally get around to discussing Antonio, she was nothing but sympathy and alibis."

"What alibis?"

Bria shrugged. "That she'd been home all evening, that her giant bodyguards would vouch for her, all the usual. She also went on and on about what a horrible thing it must have been, a man being murdered in such a brutal fashion. She shuddered and everything. It was all very ladylike."

"Sounds like you weren't impressed."

Bria shook her head. "On the contrary, I was extremely impressed by her. She was just as calm and cool as could be, no matter what I asked her. And believe me, I asked her everything, trying to rattle her. The only time she showed any emotion besides polite grace was when I mentioned that Kincaid wasn't dead. Even then, she wasn't scared of me and Xavier realizing she was behind the attack on him. More like pissed off—seriously pissed off. As if Kincaid surviving her attack was some sort of personal affront to her. But even that tiny bit of rage was there for just a split second before she smiled at us again and asked if we wanted another scone."

While Bria finished her breakfast, I showed her the file of information on Salina that Finn had given to me and the one I'd found on her father's murder in Fletcher's office. I washed the dishes while she read through the information, including the guest list of everyone who'd been there that night.

"Creepy how much all her dead husbands look like Owen," my sister said.

"You're telling me. And that's not even the worst of it."

I sat down at the table across from Bria, finally getting to the thing that was troubling me the most. I told my sister what both Owen and Eva had told me about their history with Kincaid and Salina, and how Eva had slipped into my bedroom and begged me to kill the water elemental for her.

Bria was quiet for a few minutes, thinking, before she raised her eyes to mine. "So what are you going to do?"

I shrugged. "I have no idea. By all accounts, Salina is a dangerous elemental who has no qualms about using her magic to hurt and kill people. Then again, so am I. But she's back in Ashland for a reason, at least according to Kincaid, and I'm going to find out what it is."

"And then . . ."

I shrugged again. "And then I still don't know."

Bria hesitated. "I know we don't always see eye to eye, especially when it comes to things like this and what to do about the bad guys, but if you need me for anything, you let me know. Even if it's just to talk. And if you feel like you have to take Salina out to protect Eva and Owen, then go ahead and do it, and I'll help you clean up the mess."

I reached over and squeezed her hand, grateful that she was willing to work with me on this. Not too long ago, I'd thought I was losing Bria for good because of my activities as the Spider, and it was nice that we seemed to be on the same wavelength—for once.

"I appreciate that. Really, I do, but I have to ask why you're being so accommodating on this. Usually you're the one who tells me to hold back and let the law take its course."

Bria stared at me, her face serious once more. "I've met a lot of bad guys over the years, seen a lot of bad things. Usually I can peg people pretty quickly. How dangerous they are, the things they're capable of, what they'll do if you back them into a corner. But Salina . . . she's different."

"Different how?"

"It's hard to explain," Bria said. "On the surface, she seems to be the very epitome of a sweet Southern belle with her tea and scones, even at three in the morning."

"And under the surface?"

Bria's eyes locked with mine. "Unless I'm mistaken, Salina Dubois is one of the most dangerous people I've met in a long, long time."

Bria promised to check in with me if she found out anything else. I did the same, and my sister got in her sedan and headed back to the police station, taking with her the guest list and Fletcher's folder of information to pass along to Finn, since the two of them were supposed to meet for lunch.

Thirty minutes later, I was in the storefront of the Pork Pit, doing my usual check of the restaurant. Tables, chairs, doors, windows. Thankfully, no one had broken in overnight, and nothing was out of place. I didn't need any more problems to deal with today than the ones I already had—especially since I couldn't stop thinking about Owen and Salina.

I loved Owen, but hearing him talk about Salina last night, hearing him tell me that he'd once been in love enough with her to actually want to marry and spend the rest of his life with her, well, it had jarred me a little more than I'd let on—and a whole hell of a lot more than I'd wanted it to.

I didn't begrudge Owen his past relationships, his past lovers, his past emotions, but I got the impression there was something different about Salina—something he couldn't admit to himself even now. I didn't think he had really let go. Salina had left town so abruptly, so mysteriously, that Owen hadn't gotten any more closure than I had when Donovan had hightailed it out of Ashland. Sometimes Owen and I were far too alike for the other's good.

But the hours ticked by, and customers came and went with no signs of trouble, and I was slowly able to lose myself in the rhythms of the restaurant, in the mixing, stirring, and baking that helped soothe me when I needed it the most. And I definitely needed some soothing today.

I might be a woman worried about her lover's ex, but most of all, I was still the Spider. So I did my due diligence and checked in with Finn. He'd gotten Fletcher's folder of information from Bria and was now hot on the trail of some rumor about the water elemental poaching giants from the other crime bosses to build up the ranks of her own fledgling criminal enterprise. He hadn't been able to verify anything yet, but if Salina was doing that, it confirmed my theory that she was back in town for more than just revenge on Kincaid. It would also indicate that she'd been planning her return to Ashland for a while now, that maybe she'd been back in town even before she'd killed Katarina Arkadi a few days ago. Whatever Salina was up to, Finn would figure out what it was, and then I could decide how to act on the information—and whether or not she needed to get dead.

Part of me wanted to just go ahead and kill her for the horrible way she'd tortured Eva all those years ago. She certainly deserved it; if it had been anyone else I would have already been happily plotting her demise. But two things were stopping me. One was how Owen's face had softened when he'd talked about her last night. The other was my own memory of her frantic screams as she'd watched her father being burned to death.

Seeing her father brutally murdered by Mab right in front of her, being forced to fend for herself after that, trying to create a new life, a new family, threatening and killing anyone who did her wrong or got in her way. The irony was as sharp and pointed as one of my own knives twisting into my gut. Because in many ways, Salina and I were quite alike—right down to how ruthless we were with our enemies.

Those were the thoughts that occupied me through the lunch rush, but the day wasn't all doom and gloom, especially since Roslyn Phillips came in around two o'clock.

Roslyn was simply one of the most gorgeous women—inside and out—that I'd ever had the pleasure of knowing. When the vampire stepped into the restaurant, every eye, male and female, turned in her direction. The men were lustful, the women envious. I had a little envy myself when it came to Roslyn. Her toffee-colored skin was as flawless as could be, and smoky black shadow rimmed her eyes, making them seem just a shade darker than her skin. Today, the vampire madam wore a black sundress with white polka dots, along with strappy black sandals with small kitten heels. The simple cut of the gown highlighted the perfection of her body and her generous curves. A glossy white headband held back her black hair, and her red lips formed a perfect heart in her face. Roslyn looked like she'd just stepped out of some old Hollywood movie—she was just that glamorous.

Roslyn smiled and headed in my direction. Putting her white clutch on the counter, she took the seat closest to the cash register that I was perched behind. She eyed the book in my hand.

"What are you reading now, Gin?"

I held up the cover where she could see it. "*Little Women* by Louisa May Alcott. For my next literature class."

"I approve. That's one of my favorites."

I arched an eyebrow. "I didn't know you liked to read, Roslyn. Why, we'll have to start ourselves a little book club."

The vampire chuckled, showing off her small, perfect fangs. "Oh, I doubt I could keep up with you when it comes to that."

I used one of the day's credit card receipts to mark my place in the book. "So what will it be?"

Roslyn ordered her usual grilled cheese and water. Despite her protests, I also gave her some of the chocolate chip cookies I'd baked fresh that morning. We talked back and forth over the counter while I helped Sophia fix her food. Roslyn sank her teeth into the grilled cheese with relish, and she even ate two of the cookies.

Finally, the vamp finished her food and pushed her empty plates away, then met my eyes. "Xavier told me what happened last night on the *Delta Queen*."

I nodded. I'd expected nothing less; she and Xavier had been a couple for some time now.

She stared off into space, a thoughtful look on her face. "You know, it doesn't surprise me that Salina finally came back to town."

I frowned. "You know Salina Dubois?"

Roslyn hesitated. "No, not Salina. But I knew her father, Benedict. Once Xavier told me what happened and that you were involved, I thought I'd come by and tell you what I knew about him. Salina's mother died when she was young, and Benedict was often . . . eager for female company. I was one of his favorites for years, right up until I started Northern Aggression."

Before she'd opened her nightclub, Roslyn had spent years working as a hooker in Southtown, like so many other vampires in Ashland did. All vamps needed blood to live, but lots of them also got a high off having sex or even other people's emotions. For those folks, doing the deed gave them the same sort of enhanced senses, increased strength, and quickened reflexes that other vamps got from downing a pint of O-positive. Thus, the number of vampires involved in Ashland's skin trade. Why not get laid, paid, and powered up all at the same time? And since vamps could walk around in the sunlight just like the rest of us, you didn't even have to wait until dark to get your freak on. All you had to do was walk down the Southtown streets any time—day or night—and you'd find at least one vampire hooker looking for a client, and her pimp waiting in the wings to beat you to death if you didn't pay up promptly for services rendered.

"So what can you tell me about Benedict?"

Roslyn shrugged. "Other than his sexual preferences, not much. He was just another wiseguy who thought he was stronger than he really was. An Ice elemental."

"At least until Mab put him in his place for that mistake."

Roslyn nodded. "That she did."

I asked the vamp a few more questions about Benedict, but she didn't know anything else about the old mob boss. Still, I appreciated her coming by, and I gave her my thanks.

She nodded. "So what are you going to do now? About Salina?"

"It's . . . complicated."

She grinned. "Most things are when it comes to you, Gin. But I'm a good listener, if you need someone to talk to."

This was the second time today someone had offered me her ear, which was something of a new experience for me. Assassins aren't naturally in the habit of spilling their guts to just anyone, and Fletcher had always taught me to keep my emotions bottled up tight. Hell, I'd never even had a real girlfriend before, someone I could talk to about such things. Oh, I knew I could tell Jo-Jo anything, but she was more like a mother to me than anything else. Sophia would listen to what I had to say, but she wouldn't say much in return. Sure, Bria was my sister, but we were still getting to know each other, still working on our relationship. The truth was that Roslyn was the closest thing I had to a female confidant, so I told her about all the bombshells that had been dropped on me last night, including the fact that Salina had been Owen's fiancée.

When I finished, Roslyn let out a soft whistle.

I grimaced. "Now you sound like Finn. All he did was whistle last night. You'd have thought there was a train in the room—one that just kept running over me. Splat, splat, splat."

Roslyn let out a soft laugh before her face turned serious once more. "I don't know what to tell you to do about Owen, but you need to be careful with Salina. I know you've been up against a lot of dangerous folks, but she's something else, Gin."

First Kincaid, then Eva and Bria, and now Roslyn. It seemed like everyone was on the *Salina-is-dangerous* bandwagon but Owen.

"How so? Besides the fact that she uses her water magic to come up with new and creative ways to very painfully kill people?"

Roslyn raised her eyebrows. "Well, there's her history with Owen. Anybody would feel a little threatened by that. But don't let Salina get in your head. If she does that, she's halfway to getting what she wants."

I shrugged. I couldn't deny that I was worried about Owen's past with Salina, but Roslyn was right. I needed to be calm and in control of my emotions now more than ever.

The vamp hesitated. "As to why else I think you should be careful around her, well, it's hard to explain exactly. Just more of a feeling I had about her. From what I remember, Salina had her daddy wrapped around her little finger. Benedict would have done anything for her, as would every other man around her."

I grinned. "I could say the same thing about you. You bat your eyes, and men get all weak-kneed and tongue-tied. Women too. Crook your finger at them, and half of them keel over from shock and awe."

Roslyn smiled at my compliment, but she shook her head. "Maybe, but I don't use it like Salina did. She knew how beautiful she was, and she used it to get exactly what she wanted exactly when she wanted it. But on the rare occasions that didn't happen, she became . . . cruel. I remember seeing her out in the gardens at the Dubois estate one time. The gardener had been pruning the roses, and he accidentally cut one branch too many. Salina saw him, of course, and she went over to talk to him. She never raised her voice, and she never said anything that was unkind—on the surface, anyway—but by the time she was done, the poor man was in tears. He apologized to her over and over again, like it was all his fault that she was so disappointed in him. And all because he hadn't trimmed the roses back exactly the way she'd wanted. Like I said, just . . . cruel."

Cruel. It was such a simple word, but I thought it described Salina perfectly, given what I'd seen her do to Antonio. Elemental magic was never a fun way to die, but having all the water pulled out of your body and your eyes popped out of your skull for an extra thrill, well, that was a little extreme—even by Ashland standards, where elemental duels were common.

"Cruel," I said. "Got it."

Roslyn opened her mouth to say something else, but the bell over the front door chimed, indicating that I had a new customer.

And just like that, Salina Dubois herself strolled into the Pork Pit.

❋ 18 ❋

Salina stood in the doorway, surveying my gin joint. And once again, I was struck by how lovely she was, but her beauty didn't inspire quite the same awe in me as it had before, especially since Roslyn was here.

Where Roslyn's beauty was soft, warm, and inviting, Salina's was hard, cold, and distant. The planes of her face were perfectly proportioned, but the angles were sharp, as though her porcelain skin had been chiseled from marble. Her lips were full and covered with a slick pink gloss, while her eyes were that shifting color somewhere between blue and green. But even they were cold, so cold they reminded me of the glass eyes I'd seen in some dolls not too long ago. Flat, empty, and completely emotion-less.

Salina wore a power suit in a bright aquamarine that brought out the beauty of her sun-kissed skin. Matching stilettos covered her dainty feet, and I could see the gleam of her pink pedicure all the way across the restaurant. Her silverstone cuff bracelet—the one with her mermaid rune etched into it—adorned her right wrist. But the expensive clothes and flash of jewelry almost made her seem a little too polished, a little too perfect, like she was made of wax and would melt if you so much as touched her.

The only thing soft about Salina was her hair, which cascaded down her back in rippling blond waves, reminding me of the water she could so easily control. I'd never been one for long hair myself. Too much trouble to take care of and, in my line of work, too much chance of it getting pulled out during a fight to the death.

"Stay right where you are. Act casual, but whatever you do, don't turn around," I told Roslyn in a soft voice.

The vampire stiffened. "Salina just walked into the restaurant, didn't she?"

I nodded. "And since it seems like she's going around Ashland killing former associates, or at least trying to, I don't want her to see you and remember you used to visit her father. Okay?"

Roslyn nodded and kept facing the back wall, although she pulled a compact out of her purse, as though she needed to powder her nose. She angled the mirror so she could see behind her.

"Yep," she murmured. "That's Salina all right."

The vamp snapped her compact shut and stuck it back into her purse. "So now what are you going to do?"

I picked up a menu and a glass of water, and gave her a wink. "Why, I'm going to go see what she wants, of course. You know how much I pride myself on my stellar customer service."

Salina didn't wait for me or one of the waitstaff to seat her. Instead, she looked around the restaurant a second longer before walking over and sliding into an empty booth by the storefront windows. Then she turned her head in my direction and smiled, a clear invitation for me to come on over.

I looked over my shoulder at Sophia. Roslyn had leaned forward and was talking to the Goth dwarf, quietly filling her in on the situation. Sophia turned in my direction, a clear question in her black eyes, but I shook my head, telling her to stay put. Even if I'd wanted to, I couldn't kill Salina in the middle of the Pork Pit. My customers and staff might have thought I was the Spider, but it wasn't like I wanted to palm my knives and give them a demonstration of my deadly skills.

Sophia nodded at me and said something to Roslyn. The vampire slid off her stool and followed her to the back of the restaurant, probably so she could leave through the alley. Once Roslyn and Sophia were out of sight, I plastered my best, easiest, most unconcerned smile on my face and sidled up to Salina's booth. I put the glass of water down on the table, along with the menu.

"What can I getcha, sugar?"

"Sit down, Gin," Salina said, a clear command in her voice. "You don't have to keep up the charade for me. I find charades to be rather tiresome, don't you?"

I arched an eyebrow at her boldness, but if that was the way she wanted to play things, then that was fine by me. I'd never much liked making nice with or feeding my enemies, even when they were paying for the privilege.

So I slid into the opposite side of the booth from Salina. Up close, she was even more stunning, with a dazzling beauty you just couldn't look away from. I could see why Owen had been so drawn to her. Hell, I could see why any man would be. The fact that she'd been Owen's fiancée cut a little deep.

Salina's eyes flicked over my long-sleeved T-shirt and the blue work apron I always wore whenever I cooked at the Pit. Her pink lips curled up into a faint sneer.

"So you're Gin Blanco, the assassin known as the Spider," Salina finally said. "How . . . disappointing."

I leaned back in my booth, my easy smile still on my face. "And you're Salina Dubois, the woman who likes to use her water magic to pop people's eyes out of their skulls. I'd say the disappointment is mutual."

Bria was right—she was smooth. Salina didn't bat an eyelash at my words. Didn't blink, didn't suck in an indignant breath, didn't pucker her lips in displeasure or denial. It was like I hadn't even spoken for all the reaction she showed. Instead, she reached for the glass I'd put in front of her, took a delicate sip of the liquid, and then wrinkled her nose, as if it left a foul taste in her mouth.

"Tap water," she murmured, carefully setting the glass off to the side. "I should have guessed."

Yes, Salina was good, but I recognized the misdirection for what it was. She was trying to buy herself a few seconds to decide whether or not to lie to me about what had happened on the *Delta Queen*. Apparently I wasn't worth the trouble, because she just shrugged, instead of denying my accusation or placing the blame on Kincaid, like she had with Owen.

Salina seemed a little put out that I wasn't more upset— or perhaps awed—by her appearance, but she got down to business. "Tell me, how is Phillip feeling? I was going to stop by the riverboat this afternoon, but I was in such a hurry to get over here that I just didn't have the time."

I didn't know what she meant by that, or why she had come here in the first place, but I kept my face just as smooth as hers was. Salina wasn't the only one who could play this sort of game.

"Kincaid is doing just fine," I replied in an even tone. "Despite your attempt to kill him."

Salina shrugged again, as if the fact that I'd just accused her of attempted murder was no more worrisome than a piece of lint sticking to her clothes. Given the obvious time, trouble, and energy she'd put into her appearance, I imagined the lint would bother her more.

"I knew I'd sent Phillip a clear message with Katarina's death, but I didn't expect him to be so desperate as to hire an assassin to protect him," Salina said. "I didn't think Phillip was that smart. Katarina certainly wasn't."

"And what was your problem with Katarina?"

Salina smiled. "Nothing in particular, other than I knew she was friends with Phillip. People should be more careful about the company they keep. It can get them into trouble. Just ask Antonio."

So I'd been right, and she'd killed the others mostly to hurt Kincaid. Cold and cruel.

"I let Katarina know in advance I was coming for her," Salina continued, as if that excused murdering the other woman in so gruesome a fashion. "Not that it did her any good. It never does, in the end, when I'm around."

That sounded exactly like something I would say when talking about my prowess as the Spider. She was cocky, I'd give her that. But then again, given what I'd seen her do to Antonio, she had every right to be.

To my surprise, Salina didn't radiate magic as strongly as many elementals did. Whenever I'd been around Mab, I'd always felt like there were hundreds of tiny, invisible, red-hot needles stabbing into my skin. But it wasn't like that with Salina at all. In fact, the only feeling I got from being close to her was a vague sense of cool wetness, like if I reached out and touched her skin, it would feel damp and slick. You didn't have to radiate magic to be a strong elemental, and Salina had more than enough power to be dangerous—even to me.

Besides, like Jo-Jo always told me, it didn't matter how much elemental power you had—just what you did with it. Even the weakest elemental could kill the strongest, if the circumstances were right.

"Is that why you've come back to Ashland?" I asked. "To settle old scores? Like the one you have with Kincaid?"

Salina let out a small, pealing laugh. "Hardly. I'll admit it's been . . . amusing seeing my old . . . friends, but the thrill of that has quickly worn off. I'm here on more serious business. Although make no mistake, I'll get back to Phillip soon enough."

"And what business would that be? I assume it's something that weasel Jonah McAllister is helping you with, since you were with him at Underwood's."

Salina smiled, but the expression didn't quite reach her eyes. "Why, Jonah has just been an absolute *dream* to work with so far. In fact, we had quite an interesting conversation about you, Gin, after you and Owen left the restaurant. Jonah filled me in on all your many . . . exploits."

Once again, I cursed McAllister and the day his path had ever crossed mine. It was bad enough the lawyer wanted me dead, but he was determined to make as much trouble for me as he could in the meantime. If he hadn't known about Salina and Owen before, I was sure he did now—and was delighted by their connection and how it might screw up my relationship. That was just the kind of sneaky, underhanded thing McAllister enjoyed, and he'd have been more than happy to see me suffer on my way to getting dead.

Salina straightened up in her side of the booth. "As to what I'm up to, I see no reason to hide it, not from someone like you, Gin. What I want is simple: to take my rightful place in the Ashland underworld. The place my father held before his unfortunate . . . accident."

"You mean before Mab Monroe staked him out and barbecued him like a pork chop for all his friends to see," I replied. "And you too. Pity, dear old dad getting roasted like that right in front of you."

My words were cruel, heartless even, but I'd meant them to be. So far, nothing I'd said or done had bothered Salina in the slightest, and I wanted to rattle her. I wanted to see the real her and not just the polite mask she'd shown me so far. I *needed* to see the real her—for all sorts of reasons.

Salina's left hand went to her silverstone cuff bracelet, and her fingers traced over the mermaid rune almost as if she was thinking about reaching for the water magic stored in the metal and using it against me. Something flashed in her eyes then, some hint of emotion I hadn't seen her show before. I knew it for what it was, though— rage. Absolute, complete, murderous *rage*. I wondered who it was directed at. Me, for goading her? Mab, for killing her father? Or maybe even daddy himself for not being strong enough to oust the Fire elemental from her position?

Either way, Salina regained her composure in an instant. The rage slid out of her eyes, she dropped her hand from her bracelet, and that cold, remote smile decorated her face once more.

"Yes, well, that's all in the past now. What matters is the present and, most important, the future. And both of those are all thanks to you, Gin. In fact, that's why I came here today. To thank you."

"For what?"

Her smile widened. "Why, for killing Mab, of course. Naturally, I wanted to do it myself and was even planning my long-awaited return to Ashland when I heard the news that you'd done it for me. And I'm not the only one who's grateful to you for eliminating her. To hear the whispers, it seems that Ashland is wide open to new . . . business interests now that that horrible Fire elemental isn't around. I've heard several folks talk about expanding their investments here. Why, you practically performed a public service, killing her the way you did."

I'd jokingly said that sort of thing myself more than

once, and I wondered if she was mocking me. But she actually seemed sincere, as though I really had done her a favor. Her and everyone else. It was bad enough every low-life and his higher-ups in Ashland were already gunning for me. I didn't need out-of-towners adding to the mess too—but that was exactly what Salina was describing. I bit back another curse, wondering just how many more people I was going to have to kill before everyone got the message to leave me alone. Before I could enjoy the retirement and the quiet life Fletcher had wanted for me.

"In fact, I'm going to be hosting a little soiree for my father's old . . . associates tomorrow night at my estate," Salina said. "A business dinner, if you will. Consider yourself invited as well. After all, as an assassin, you have as much right to be there as anyone else in Ashland these days."

I might have inadvertently put myself in the underworld limelight by killing Mab, but I'd rather have eaten raw rattlesnake than attend any sort of event Salina had in mind. Still, I matched her fake politeness smile for smile.

"So I take it you're back in Ashland for good then?" I asked. "Since you plan on picking up your father's . . . business interests?"

"It's my home. And I plan to reclaim what's mine—*everything* that's mine."

I knew exactly what she was referring to, and she confirmed it a second later without saying a word. Instead, Salina lifted her hand. I tensed, wondering if she was reaching for her water magic to use against me, but all she did was wave at someone through the storefront windows.

"In fact, there he is right now," she practically purred.

The bell over the door chimed. A sinking feeling filled my stomach, one that only got worse a second later, when Owen stepped into the restaurant.

Owen spotted us immediately, and my lover paused in the doorway, his gaze going from me to Salina and back again. His face was calm and expressionless, but I could see the tension in his shoulders. This wasn't a meeting he was looking forward to. Couldn't imagine why.

He wore his usual business suit, this one a dark navy blue, and more than one female customer looked at him in appreciation as he walked over to our table. Salina slid out of the booth, got to her feet, and turned her cheek, expecting a kiss, but Owen only squeezed her hand.

"Salina," he said. "I'm glad you could make it."

He'd invited her here? He'd actually asked his former lover, his ex-fiancée, to my restaurant? That bitter, painful jealousy flared up in my chest again, despite my attempts to smother it. But I kept my emotions in check, waiting to see what his reason for this meeting was.

Owen dropped her hand. I moved over, and he sat down next to me. Another flash of emotion flickered across Salina's face—annoyance this time. I wondered if it was because Owen hadn't slobbered all over her like she'd expected or because he'd chosen to sit on my side of the booth instead of hers.

But she recovered quickly, plastering a sunny smile on her face. "Of course, darling. You'd know I'd meet you anytime, anywhere. Even . . . here."

I rolled my eyes. Salina wasn't the first person to sneer

at the hole-in-the-wall atmosphere of my restaurant, but her comment needled me more than most. Or perhaps that was just because of her history with my lover.

Owen raised an eyebrow. "What's wrong with here? The Pork Pit has some of the best food in the city."

"Oh, I don't know. I just thought you might want to catch up in private." Salina's expression turned coy, and she fluttered her lashes.

My lover stared at her for a moment before deliberately reaching over and putting his hand on top of mine.

"We don't have anything to say to each other that Gin can't hear," Owen said in a level tone. "After all, we're just old friends now."

I looked at Owen, who gave me a wink and a slow, sexy smile. I threaded my fingers through his and gently squeezed his hand, silently telling him that I appreciated his words and gestures.

Salina's gaze dropped to our linked fingers. Her smile slipped, and once again, that rage flashed in her eyes momentarily. "Of course," she murmured, rubbing her fingers against her cuff bracelet again.

She noticed me watching her. Salina's hand stilled, then dropped from the silverstone once more.

"So," Owen said, "what have you been up to all these years?"

She gave him another bright, dazzling smile. "Why, darling, I'd thought you'd never ask."

Salina spent the next ten minutes talking about her travels since she'd left Ashland. Apparently, the water elemental had been living the high life, going from one luxurious spot to the next and enjoying all the fine food and scenery the world had to offer. The one thing she didn't mention was the trail of dead husbands she'd left behind, their suspicious, water-related deaths, and how they'd all borne an eerie resemblance to Owen.

"And what about Phillip?" Owen asked after she'd finally wound down with her stories of glitz and glamour. "I know what happened on the riverboat."

Salina didn't miss a beat justifying her actions. "You know what he did to me, Owen. I was just trying to make sure the bastard got what he deserved—what he should have gotten all those years ago."

"But Eva was there," he said. "You scared her, Salina. You scared a lot of people with your water magic. And you killed a man with it—an innocent man."

He was finally confronting Salina about what she'd done to Antonio, but his tone wasn't as harsh and accusatory as I would have thought it would be. As I would have *liked* it to be, truth be told. Instead, Owen was being . . . careful with her. Considerate, even, as if she were some delicate creature who needed shielding from all the ugliness in the world. Almost like he was waiting for her to explain away the whole thing—and hoping that she would. Once again, doubt filled my mind, doubt about Owen's feelings for Salina—and just how much she really meant to him. That worrisome feeling twisted deeper and deeper into my chest, like I was using one of my own knives to saw through my heart.

Salina leaned forward, her eyes widening with seeming sincerity. "Well, then it was a doubly good thing I was there. You wouldn't want Phillip to do the same thing to little Eva that he tried to do to me? Would you, Owen?"

"No, of course not, but—"

"And I don't know why you were so concerned about that giant. The man worked for Phillip, which probably made him just the same sort of heartless bastard. You know what Phillip's attack did to me, how it drove me to leave Ashland, to leave *you*. All I wanted was to make things right; all I wanted was to give myself some closure, some peace. You don't know how hard it's been on me, coming back home and knowing Phillip is still alive."

Her voice trembled, her eyes glistened with tears, and her lips quivered, somehow making her look heartbreakingly vulnerable, and that much more beautiful for it. Salina picked up the glass of water I'd brought her earlier and took another sip of it, her hand shaking just a bit, just enough to be noticeable.

A sick, guilty look filled Owen's eyes, and Salina clearly decided to take advantage of it.

"All I can think about is, what if Phillip comes after me again? Why, I can't even *sleep* for worrying about it. I've even hired bodyguards to protect me, just in case he tries something."

Well, that was a clever way to explain her poaching giants from the other underworld figures. Total bullshit, but clever. Salina needed protecting about as much as I did.

"Phillip won't come after you," Owen said. "I'll make sure of that."

Salina reached over and grabbed his hand, smoothly pulling it away from mine. "Promise me, Owen. Promise me you'll handle Phillip. The way you should have back then."

Wow. And I thought I was good with knives. Salina had just pulled a verbal dagger from out of nowhere and buried it in Owen's chest, then twisted it in for good measure. I could see what Roslyn had meant when she'd called Salina cruel, because that was just what she'd been to my lover, and he didn't even seem to realize it. Instead, more guilt filled his face, and I knew he was thinking he should have killed Kincaid back then.

I thought about what Bria had said this morning. My sister was right. Salina Dubois was dangerous in a way I'd never expected her to be. She was a skilled actress who instinctively seemed to know what buttons to push to manipulate the people around her. But the truly remarkable thing was that she projected such absolute, utter *sincerity* as she spun her web of lies, like everyone she'd hurt had done her some grievous wrong and she was just making things right, no matter how horrible and deadly her own actions were. If I hadn't known better, I might have believed her myself—that was how convincing she was.

Owen opened his mouth, but his cell phone rang, saving him from answering her. He pulled his phone out of his suit jacket and glanced at the screen.

"Excuse me," he said. "I have to take this."

He scooted out of the booth, got to his feet, and walked back toward the bathrooms and away from the noise of the storefront. Salina watched him the whole time, a hungry look in her eyes.

"Bravo," I said, clapping my hands together politely. "That was quite the performance."

Salina kept staring at Owen. "I have no idea what you're talking about."

"Please," I scoffed. "Phillip Kincaid never tried to rape you, and we both know it."

The water elemental's eyes narrowed, and she finally deigned to look at me again. "Why would you say that?"

Better to let Salina think I'd seen through her lies and focus her attention on me, rather than realize that Eva was finally ready to tell Owen how the water elemental had snowballed him. I didn't want Eva in any more danger than she already was.

"Because your story? The one you just got all teary-eyed over? It's complete and utter fiction. I've met a lot of liars in my time, but I have to say that you are one of the best. Very impressive. Really."

Once again, that calculating look flickered across Salina's face, as she debated whether she wanted to try to work her charm on me. I could have told her not to bother, that I knew anything coming out of her mouth was more than likely either an outright lie or a truth she'd conveniently twisted.

Salina Dubois was every inch the sly, dangerous elemental Eva and Kincaid claimed she was. I wondered if she'd always been this way, as Roslyn seemed to think, or if she'd changed because of her father's murder, like Owen claimed.

Daddy! No! Daddy! Daddy—

For a moment, Salina's screams rang in my ears, and I had to breathe in several times to get the phantom, acrid stench of singed skin out of my nose.

It didn't really matter why or when Salina had become the person she was. The real question was, why hadn't Owen seen it? Had he been that in love with her? So devoted to her that it had blinded him to what she was really like and how she was manipulating him? The thought made my heart twist once more.

Still, despite my reasons for disliking the water elemental, I couldn't quite banish the faint echo of her screams. So I decided to give Salina a chance—more of one than she'd given Antonio and Kincaid.

"I don't know what game you're playing—with Owen, with Kincaid, with McAllister—but forget it," I said. "Pack up and leave Ashland while you still can."

Salina smiled yet again. "Why, Gin, if I didn't know better, I would say it sounds like you're threatened by little ole me."

I snorted. "Hardly. I eat haughty, arrogant, manipulative, self-important bitches like you for breakfast, sugar. And then I go back for seconds."

The serene smile flickered for a moment then dropped completely off Salina's face, and the coldness seeped into her eyes, making them glitter like ice.

"And I would suggest you watch your tone with me," she snapped. "I'm a *Dubois*. That name means in something in Ashland."

"Correction," I snapped back. "That name *used* to mean something in Ashland. Not anymore. Not for a long time now. And my mother was Eira Snow, one of the strongest Ice elementals this city has ever seen. So I've got just as much right to claim this grand old family legacy as you do."

This time, Salina snorted. "Keep telling yourself that. Just like you've apparently convinced yourself that Owen cares about you. Maybe he does, but that won't last long.

He always comes back to me in the end because he loves *me*—nobody else. I'm Owen's, and he's mine. That's the way it's always been since the moment we first saw each other, and that's the way it's always going to be. You're deluding yourself to think otherwise."

I wasn't the one here with delusions, but once again, I was struck by the utter sincerity in her voice. Despite the fact that Owen couldn't hear us and she didn't have to keep up any pretense with me, Salina still radiated wounded honesty. It was almost like she actually *believed* all the lies she was spouting, that she had rearranged events in her head to create whatever story she liked best, and everything else, including what had really happened, was just plain unimportant.

Or maybe these were truths about her and Owen that I just didn't want to hear.

At that moment, I couldn't decide if she was crazy—or if maybe I was.

But I didn't let her see my doubts. "You really think Owen won't figure out that you lied about Kincaid? He might not have listened to Kincaid back then, but I'll make sure that he listens to me now."

Salina shrugged. "If Owen can bed down with an assassin like you, then I'm sure he can forgive me for anything I've done—or will do."

"I might be an assassin, but I've never framed anyone for murder. I've never blamed anyone for a crime I committed just to get my way or make things easier on myself. Never tried to, never needed to, never wanted to, but apparently that sort of thing doesn't bother you."

Salina shrugged again. "Your opinion doesn't matter to

me in the slightest. The only one I care about is Owen's, and we all know how . . . forgiving men can be when they see something they want."

To that, I didn't have an answer—and we both knew it.

Salina smiled again, gracefully slid out of the booth, and got to her feet. "As lovely as our conversation has been, I'm afraid I've got to run. I have a meeting with Jonah and some final preparations to make for my dinner party. I'm so looking forward to reintroducing myself to everyone who matters in Ashland."

It took a lot to get to me, but there was something ominous about the way she said *dinner party* that made my skin crawl. I made a mental note to get Finn to check into this shindig Salina was throwing, and to see if he could find out anything about her mental health. It seemed like there was a disconnect going on with Salina, who talked as if framing Kincaid for rape had been of no big consequence and that Owen would just forgive her for doing something so horrible to his best friend, and for killing others.

Once again, I couldn't decide if she was a master manipulator who was supremely confident in her skills or if she just rearranged things in her own mind to suit the situation. Either way, she knew exactly what she was doing when it came to pushing every single one of Owen's buttons. But how could she think that he would come back to her after everything she'd done, especially to Eva? If Salina really did have that twisted a view of reality, if she really believed that what she did didn't matter, then she was even more dangerous than *anyone* had realized—even me.

"It's been a pleasure talking to you, Gin. I'm sure I'll be seeing you again soon," Salina said. "Do be a dear and give my regards to Owen, will you? Tell him I've been thinking about him for *ages* now, and I'm looking forward to finally getting reacquainted again after all these long, lonely years apart."

Her voice was calm, pleasant, as if she'd asked me to say good-bye to Owen instead of let him know that she had set her sights on him again. I wanted to palm one of my knives and drive it straight into her heart, but I restrained myself, especially since the other customers had picked up on the tension between us and were staring at me like they expected me to take her out in the middle of the restaurant.

I entertained the thought but quickly discarded it. I didn't want to upset my diners.

Not to mention how Owen would react to me murdering his ex-fiancée right in front of him with seemingly no provocation.

Salina was unconcerned by my lack of response. Instead, she waggled her fingers good-bye at Owen, blew him a suggestive kiss, and then sashayed over to the front door and out of the restaurant.

And all I could do was just sit there, watch her go, and wonder how I was going to unravel all the lies this black widow had told Owen—as well as the ones it looked like she was telling herself too.

❖ 19 ❖

I stayed in the booth, thinking back over everything Salina had said. All the threats she'd made, all the awful promises she'd so casually dropped. As much as I hated to admit it, she had a right to be confident. With Mab gone, Salina could potentially revive her father's business empire. And if she was willing to use her water magic like she had last night, then she could easily be among the most dangerous people in the city.

And then there was the threat she represented to my relationship with Owen.

The past could be a powerful thing, especially when it came to love lost. I wondered if Salina's past with Owen would trump whatever future my lover and I had together. Thanks to my promise to Eva, I had a funny feeling I was going to find out—one way or another.

Owen finished his phone call, came back over, and sat down in the booth. "Where did Salina go?"

"She had a meeting with Jonah McAllister," I said. "Something about a dinner she's hosting tomorrow night."

"We need to tell her about McAllister, what a snake he is."

I frowned, wondering again at his seeming blind spot when it came to Salina. Did he really think she needed protecting from McAllister? Maybe Salina wasn't the only one disconnected from reality, especially if Owen thought the lawyer was doing anything other than what Salina wanted him to.

I shook my head. "Don't worry. I get the feeling Salina always knows exactly what she's doing."

"What do you mean by that?"

I looked at my lover. I'd had some small, foolish hope the situation might resolve itself. That Owen and I could just go on like we had before Salina came to town. But there were too many people involved in this mess now. Someone had to tell Owen the truth about his ex-fiancée, and it looked like the job had fallen to me. Now came the hard part—convincing Owen that Salina wasn't the victim he'd thought her to be all these years. He hadn't believed Kincaid back then, and I didn't know if he'd listen to me now, but I had to try—for all our sakes.

"I talked to Eva last night after you went to bed," I said in a soft voice. "She told me a very different story from the one you did about the night Kincaid supposedly attacked Salina."

He stared at me. "Eva spoke to you about that?"

"Is that so surprising?"

Owen shook his head. "She never really talked to me

about what happened. . . . All she ever said was that Phillip didn't hurt Salina, but obviously that wasn't true. I assumed she'd blocked most of it out, that it was just too traumatic for her to realize or remember what Phillip had done to Salina. So I eventually gave up trying to get her to talk about it. I didn't want to bring it up over and over and have her constantly be haunted by that night."

I didn't tell him that Eva had been too scared of the water elemental and her threats to confide in her big brother. That was Eva's part of the story to tell—not mine.

I leaned forward. "I believe Eva. She's telling the truth about what happened—and so is Kincaid, like it or not."

Owen didn't say anything, but he shook his head again, and I could see the same weariness in his eyes I had last night.

"Think about it, Owen," I said before he could speak, before he could stick up for Salina again. "Forget your feelings for Salina and really *think* about things. You walked in and found Kincaid beating Salina. No one's disputing that. But he was, what, fifteen then? Still a scrawny kid. And Salina was the same age as you, right? About nineteen, four years older than Kincaid?"

He nodded, confirming the information in Fletcher's file.

"So Salina was older. Not only that, she had elemental magic. Even if Kincaid had tried to rape her, why would he attack her in the bathroom, of all places? With Eva only a few feet away in the tub, a tub with all that water in it? Why didn't Salina use her water magic to fight him off? Why did she insist you beat him to death instead?"

Owen didn't say anything, but I could see him thinking back and struggling to review everything with an objective eye. He sat there, working through it all. I leaned back in my side of the booth and kept quiet, wanting him to draw his own conclusions—the right ones this time.

"It could have happened the way you think it did," he finally said. "Maybe Phillip didn't try to rape Salina. But why were they fighting? Why was he beating her? What did she do to him that was so terrible? Because he would have killed her if I hadn't come back when I did."

Now it was time to rip the scabs off all the old wounds—no matter how much it was going to hurt Owen.

I drew in a breath. "They were fighting because Salina was torturing Eva with her water magic. Salina was using her power to hold Eva down under the water in the bathtub. She was drowning Eva again and again."

All around us, everything went on as usual. The other diners talked and laughed; the waitstaff hurried from one table to another; Sophia dished up plate after plate of food; the chatter of the customers and the *clink-clink-clink* of dishes and silverware sounded; and the air smelled of hot grease mixed with smoky spices.

Yes, the world went on just like it had before. But for Owen, everything had changed.

For a moment, he was absolutely still, as if frozen to where he sat. Then, everything happened at once. All the color drained out of my lover's face, his eyes bulged, and he let out a strangled gasp.

"No—no way. That's just not possible—"

"That wasn't the first night it happened," I said, cutting him off, being brutal, like I had to be right now. "The torture had been going on for weeks. Kincaid finally figured out what Salina was doing to Eva. That's why he told you he was sick, so he could go back home and catch her in the act. He was trying to protect Eva."

Owen flinched, like I'd just zapped him with a stun gun. I reached over and took his hand, trying to bring him the same comfort he had me earlier.

"It's not your fault," I said. "None of this is your fault. Salina fooled everyone."

"But if what you're saying is true . . ."

His voice trailed off, and he couldn't get the words out. That sick, stricken look filled his face again, and I knew he was thinking of what Eva had suffered.

I squeezed his hand. "I know . . . I know this is a lot to take in."

Owen stared at me, but his eyes were dark and distant, and I could tell that he was lost in his memories. Thinking about various facts, clues from that time that might support—or undermine—what I'd just revealed. "I was so sure Salina was telling the truth. It seemed so obvious at the time. But if she wasn't . . . if what you're saying is true . . . Eva . . . Phillip . . . all these years I've blamed him. . . ."

His voice trailed off, and guilt tightened his features at the thought of what he'd done to Kincaid, of how he'd almost beaten his best friend to death because of Salina's lies.

I let him sit there for a minute, thinking about everything. I would have liked to put my arms around him and tell him that everything was going to be okay, but that would have been a lie. The past was done, and we all had to live with the consequences of it. The only thing we could change was the future.

"What if I can prove it to you?" I asked. "One way or the other, who's lying and who's telling the truth. I think I can give you that."

What I hadn't told him was that there was one more person involved in this drama. There had to be. From what I'd seen, Salina had been just as crazy about Owen back then as she was now. She wouldn't have just abandoned him for no reason. No, someone had forced Salina to leave Ashland, and I didn't think it was Kincaid—but I was betting that the casino boss knew exactly who it was.

"How are you going to do that?" Owen finally asked, still staring off into space. "How are you going to give me answers? You weren't even there when it happened."

I squeezed his hand again. "You'll see. But you'll have to trust me. Do you think you can do that?"

After a moment, he focused on me and slowly nodded.

"Good. Then let's get out of here."

"This is a bad idea," Owen muttered. "A really bad idea."

Thirty minutes had passed. Before we'd left the Pork Pit, I'd grabbed a few things I thought I might need from the back of the restaurant and stuffed them into my jeans pockets. Now we stood on the boardwalk in front of the *Delta Queen*. A sign by the gangplank said the casino wouldn't be opening until tonight, I assumed so every last bit of Antonio could be scrubbed off the main deck.

"Certainly," I agreed. "But we both have questions that only Kincaid can answer. So let's pay him a visit."

Owen hadn't said much on the drive over here, but I could see him thinking back, straining to recall everything that had happened that night. Everything everyone had said and done, all the shouts, accusations, truths, and lies. I didn't know what conclusions he'd drawn, but his face had grown darker and darker as the miles passed, until now, his violet eyes almost glowed with rage and guilt—the first over what Salina had done, the second for not realizing what was going on. But those were emotions that Owen would have to deal with himself. All I could do was be here for him—and squeeze Kincaid until he screamed the truth for the whole world to hear.

"You don't have to go in with me," I said.

Owen shook his head, and a stubborn look filled his face. "No. I don't want you going on board alone. And I need to hear what Phillip has to say for himself. I just . . . I need to."

I nodded, undid the red velvet rope that cordoned off the entrance, and walked up the gangplank with Owen. The main deck had been cleared of all the games, tables, chips, and chairs that had been out here last night. The wood underfoot gleamed like freshly minted gold, and the sharp scent of varnish filled the air. Kincaid certainly hadn't wasted any time shellacking over what had happened last night.

Someone must have spotted us coming up the gangplank through the windows, because we'd only taken a few steps forward when a giant stepped out of the double doors and came over to us, his hands out to his sides.

"Sorry, folks. We're closed until tonight."

I smiled at him. "Not for us. Tell Kincaid that Gin Blanco and Owen Grayson are here to see him."

The giant frowned, as if the names were familiar but couldn't quite be placed. So I decided to jog his memory.

I palmed one of my silverstone knives, making sure the giant saw the gleam of the metal in my hand. Then I started casually flipping it end over end, just like I'd done in Kincaid's office last night.

"Is there a problem?" I asked.

The giant stared at my knife. After a moment, he backed up and shook his head. "No problem. No problem at all. I'll tell Mr. Kincaid you're here."

"You do that," I said.

The giant scurried through the double doors and disappeared from sight. He came back less than a minute later and gestured for us to follow him inside. Sometimes it helped to have a reputation as bad as mine.

The giant led us into the main ballroom, where Kincaid sat at a round table in front of the stage, eating a late lunch. The table was covered with fine linens and china, but instead of the lobster and other delicacies I'd expected, Kincaid was chowing down on baby back ribs, grilled sausages, coleslaw, cornbread, and a peach cobbler topped with melting vanilla ice cream. A pitcher of iced tea sat on the table, along with the glass he was drinking out of.

The giant went over and whispered in Kincaid's ear. The casino boss's gaze went to me, then Owen, and he put down his fork. He whispered something back to the giant, who nodded and took up a position several feet behind the table. Sloppy, sloppy, sloppy. The giant should have put himself in between me and his boss, especially with me still twirling a knife in my hand. Good thing I wasn't here to kill Kincaid. He would have been dead before he got to finish his peach cobbler.

"Ah, visitors," Kincaid drawled, pushing his plates

away and pulling the napkin out of the collar of his shirt. "Tell me, to what do I owe this honor?"

"I think you know why we're here," Owen said. "We need to talk."

"Whatever for?" Kincaid asked. "You've spent years going out of your way *not* to talk to me. So why would you want to have a conversation now? Did Gin tell you what a good time we had getting to know each other last night? Is that why you're here? Apparently, I just keep ending up with your women, Owen. Why, they practically throw themselves at me . . . whether I want them to or not."

Kincaid smirked at me. I gave him a lazy look, then kicked his chair over, with him still in it. He'd barely thumped to the floor before I was straddling him, my knife at his throat. Kincaid started to get up, but I pressed the blade against his skin and he froze. They almost always did.

When I was sure he wasn't going to move, I looked up at the giant who'd taken half a step toward his boss. Too little, too late. If I'd wanted it, Kincaid would have been bleeding out already.

"If you even think about reaching for that gun under your jacket, I'm going to be very upset," I told the giant. "Trust me when I tell you that you do not want to upset me. It won't end well for you or your boss."

"It's okay, Rusty," Kincaid said. "Stand down. Gin and I are just having a friendly little chat. What can I say? She's a feisty minx."

"Phillip," I said in a pleasant voice, "your snide comments are getting on my last nerve. So unless you want me to finish the job Salina started, I suggest that you shut the hell up. I don't like getting blood on my clothes this early in the day, but believe me when I tell you that I'm no stranger to it."

Kincaid swallowed at my threat, his Adam's apple bobbing up and down and scraping against the knife in my hand. A mottled, bluish bruise ringed his throat, a reminder of the water noose that had been wrapped around his neck.

"Maybe you should just go ahead and save us all the trouble then," he said. "I'm sure Owen wouldn't object. He'd probably thank you for it."

My lover sighed. "I just want to know the truth, Phillip. I'm giving you a chance to do the right thing."

"I *always* did the right thing," Kincaid snarled back. "You were the one who was too blind to see—"

"Forget that night," I cut in. "What I really want to know is how you managed to run Salina out of town after the fact."

Kincaid blinked in surprise before he could stop himself. "What are you talking about? Salina left Ashland all on her own. I had nothing to do with that."

I shook my head. "No, she didn't, Philly. Why would she leave? She got Owen to believe you tried to rape her and almost got him to kill you in the process. Things went exactly the way she wanted them to go. But two days later, she just up and vanishes, and no one hears a peep from her for years. Since I know Owen didn't send her packing, that leaves you—and whoever helped you."

Owen frowned. "Phillip? Is this true?"

Kincaid didn't say anything, so I decided to encourage

him by pressing the knife a little deeper into his throat. He clenched his jaw, but he still didn't talk.

"I'm going to get the truth for Owen one way or another," I said in a deceptively light voice. "You can be helpful, or you can be dead. Doesn't much matter to me."

He glared at me, his blue eyes practically glowing with cold anger. "What makes you think I had help?" Kincaid finally said.

"Because Salina has water magic, and you don't. You were just a kid back then, one who'd just been beaten to within an inch of his life. She wouldn't disappear just because you threatened her. No, Salina wouldn't leave town unless someone with real power told her to go—someone she thought could really back up a threat."

Kincaid didn't say anything, but I could see the agreement in his eyes.

"Phillip?" Owen asked again.

After a few more seconds, the casino boss sighed. "It was Cooper, okay?'

Cooper Stills—Owen's dwarven mentor, the blacksmith he'd worked for, the one who had taken in Kincaid too. It made sense, and I should have realized it before now. Of course Kincaid would have turned to Cooper to help get rid of Salina. The dwarf had probably been the only person Kincaid had left after Owen had thrown him out.

I pulled my knife away, got to my feet, and held out my hand. Kincaid hesitated, then took it, and I pulled him up to his feet. His bodyguard started to come over to him, but the casino boss waved him off. He took a moment to straighten his suit jacket and tie before he looked at me once more.

"So now what?" Kincaid said. "Have I told you everything you needed to know? Can I go back to my lunch?"

I grinned at him. "Oh, Philly. You'd better put all that food in a doggie bag. Because we're all going for a little ride."

❉ 20 ❉

Kincaid managed to convince his giant guard that we weren't *really* kidnapping him, and ten minutes later, the three of us were in Finn's Escalade, which I was still driving. I thought about calling Finn and telling him what was going on, but I didn't want to distract him from chasing down his leads on Salina.

Owen sat in the passenger seat, staring out the window, while Kincaid sprawled across the backseat. None of us spoke.

I left the *Delta Queen* and the downtown district behind and headed toward Northtown. Driving past all the immaculate estates of that area and then into the Appalachian Mountains north of the city, we soon left the McMansions completely behind and started winding our way up one of the picturesque two-lane roads that dotted this part of Ashland. Trees crowded up to the edge of the pavement, showing off their clusters of spring leaves and painting the world in a fresh green color.

"So tell me about Cooper," I finally said. "What's he like?"

Owen let out a harsh laugh, but a little of the tension eased out of his shoulders. "A lot like Fletcher, I'd imagine. A rough, gruff, tough son of a bitch who worked and pushed me hard but who cared a lot about me too."

"He pushed all of us hard," Kincaid said from the backseat. "Except for Eva. He was like a dwarven Santa Claus to her. He was always giving her candy and treats."

Owen glanced over his shoulder at his former friend. "That's because Eva was a cute little girl and had him wrapped around her finger. She had everyone wrapped around her finger, including you."

A faint grin spread across Kincaid's face. After a moment, Owen's lips twitched up as well, and they actually smiled at each other, the two of them lost in their memories.

"He's an Air elemental, right?" I asked. "I remember you telling me that before. How strong is he?"

Owen shrugged. "When I was a kid, he seemed incredibly strong, but he's pushing three hundred now."

"Middle-aged, then, for a dwarf," I said.

Kincaid nodded. "And he works too hard. He always has. The man isn't happy unless he's at his forge pounding on something. Whenever I come up here to visit him, I always tell him to slow down, but he never listens to me."

"You visit him?" Owen asked, the surprise clear in his voice.

"Of course I visit him. Don't you?"

Owen shifted in his seat. "Yeah. I just didn't think you would."

Kincaid laughed, but the sound was low, harsh, and ugly. "Still determined to believe the worst about me."

Owen didn't respond.

Kincaid leaned forward and looked at me. "But if you're asking if he could stand up to Salina, the answer is yes. I just don't know for how long. Cooper is strong, but even back then, it took everything he had to get Salina to leave town. He should have killed her when he had the chance. We both should have."

Owen didn't say anything, but his mouth tightened, and that troubled look filled his eyes again. He didn't agree with Kincaid about killing Salina, not even now, when he knew what she'd done to Eva.

I wondered what he would think of me when I did the deed for him.

My mind was made up. Maybe it had been from the moment Eva told me what Salina had done to her, but seeing the water elemental this morning, talking to her, had made me realize exactly how dangerous she was. I didn't know exactly what she was up to with McAllister and her mysterious dinner party, but like the others had said, it couldn't be anything good. She'd only been back in Ashland a few days, and she'd already killed two people and tried to off Kincaid as well. It was just a matter of time before she hurt someone else, someone Owen cared about. And I'd be damned if I'd let that happen.

I glanced at Owen, but he was staring out the window and brooding again. Yes, I wondered what my lover would think when I killed his ex-fiancée. If he would be glad she wasn't around to be a threat anymore—or if he would hate me for it.

We rode the rest of the way in silence. I drove past Warren Fox's store, Country Daze, and slowed down so I could take a good long look out the window as we passed. More than a dozen cars filled the parking lot, along with a tour bus, as folks stopped on their way to wherever to get a quick drink or snack or to browse through the mountain crafts and homemade jams, jellies, and honey that Warren sold. I smiled. Nice to see that Warren's business had picked up since I'd gotten Tobias Dawson off his back. One of the many pro bono good deeds I'd done in the last several months. The only ones that seemed to matter to me anymore.

I kept driving up into the mountains. I'd just passed a moving truck and a smaller van parked on the side of the road, their giant drivers standing in between them and conferring about something, when Owen pointed to a turnoff up ahead.

"That's it," he said.

I turned and steered the Escalade onto a bumpy dirt track that seemed to lead into the middle of nowhere. We drove about a mile back into the woods and up a ridge. Tiny flashes of light sparked in the trees to my left, almost like fireflies winking on and off, even though it was the middle of the afternoon. It took me several seconds to realize the flashes were from bright metal shapes reflecting the sun. I squinted, but I couldn't quite make out what the figures were before we rounded a curve and a large house came into view.

It was a massive structure made out of gray river rock, the kind that could be found in the waterways in and around Ashland and the surrounding mountains. The smooth stones fit together beautifully, while the house's A-line roof looked like a blanket of coal that had been thrown over the rocks.

I parked the SUV, and we got out. Owen and Kincaid stood side by side staring at the house, memories filling their faces of all the good and bad times they'd shared here.

Finally Owen shook his head, as if banishing his thoughts. "Come on," he said. "Cooper will be around back in the forge. He always is."

Owen led me to the right, and we walked around the house, with Kincaid bringing up the rear. We stepped into the backyard, which was clear of the trees that crowded around the front of the house. More of the river rock had been shaped into flat stones and placed on top of the grass, forming a patio and a winding path that led over to a forge that was almost as large as the house itself. The forge was made out of the same gray river rock as everything else. Two sides of it were open to the air, and I could see a variety of blacksmithing tools hanging down from the ceiling and stacked on the tables inside. A fire burned low in the hearth, sending out wisps of smoke and adding to the growing heat of the day.

Owen frowned. "It's not like Cooper to go off and leave the forge hot when he's not around. Too much risk of sparking a fire. Maybe he stepped into the house for a minute, after all. I'll go inside and look. He always leaves the back door unlocked."

"I'll go with you," Kincaid said.

I reached out with my magic, listening to the stone around me, but the rocks only whispered of the rivers and streams they'd been plucked out of. They also emitted a faint ringing sound—like a blacksmith's hammer hitting metal over and over again. I concentrated on the deep, throaty, vibrant sound, but there were no uneasy murmurs, no notes of worry, anger, or fear rippling through any of the stones. No one was here who shouldn't be, including Salina. It wasn't out of the realm of possibility to think that she would come after Cooper, especially since he was the one who'd forced her to leave Ashland—and Owen. But she wasn't here now, so I didn't voice my concern to the others.

"You guys go on inside. I'll search out here. Maybe he went into the woods for some reason."

Owen nodded, and he and Kincaid moved off toward the house. I headed over to the forge.

"Cooper?" I called out in a loud voice, not wanting to startle the dwarf in case he was engrossed in his work. "Are you here? My name is Gin, Gin Blanco. I'm a friend of Owen Grayson's. . . ."

No answer.

I walked through the forge, looking at all the tools and the items Cooper was crafting—everything from swords to sculptures to a very large and elaborate metal birdhouse. Once again, sly gleams of metal in the trees beyond caught my eye, and I slipped out of the back of the forge and headed in that direction, searching for the source of the flashes, if only to satisfy my own curiosity. I was rather like Fletcher that way.

A hundred feet into the woods, I found a sculpture garden.

Dotting a wide clearing and the landscape beyond, sculptures perched here and there among the trees. They were shaped like every figure you could possibly imagine. Birds, bears, rabbits, foxes, sunflowers, rainbows, and everything in between. The sculptures were made of various types of metal, from iron to steel to silverstone that glimmered like a star as the sunlight warmed its smooth surface. Iron benches had been placed along the paths that wound through the area, so folks could sit and look at their favorite pieces.

I traced my fingertips over a beautiful statue of an eagle with its wings spread wide, as if it was getting ready to fly away. Despite the fact they were made of silverstone, the wings bore such intricate detail that I almost imagined they were ruffling as the spring breeze danced through the air.

I wandered farther out into the garden, following the path of flagstones wending through the woods, amazed by all the pieces hidden among the dappled shadows. I could see why Owen continued to craft sculptures and weapons in his own forge. He'd been given the skills to do so by Cooper, just like Fletcher had instilled his love of cooking and the Pork Pit in me. More important, Owen shared the dwarf's obvious love for working with raw ore and shaping it into something smooth, supple, and wondrous.

Footsteps slapped on the flagstones behind me. I put a welcoming smile on my face, but then I realized the footsteps were approaching far too quickly for this to be a friendly encounter. Instinct took over, and I ducked to the right.

Good thing, since a red-hot poker hit the sculpture of a bear I'd been admiring just a second before.

Sparks hissed through the air, a few landing on my T-shirt and jeans and creating smoking holes in the fabric. I ignored the sparks, whipped out a knife, and turned to meet the danger.

A dwarf stood behind me. He was tall for his kind, topping out at just over five feet, and incredibly muscled. His chest, biceps, and forearms looked as hard and un-yielding as the sculptures, as though he'd been made from the same metal he could shape so well. His hair was a soft silver, with a few black patches sprinkled here and there, and was spiked to a high, wavy point above his forehead, like he'd run his fingers through the thick locks more than once today. A pair of goggles covered his face, making his rust-colored eyes seem that much bigger and brighter in his tan, speckled face. He wore a blue work shirt and a pair of matching pants, along with brown boots.

Instead of being concerned about the knife in my hand, the dwarf immediately drew back his poker for an-other swing at my head.

"So you're the one who's been sneaking around steal-ing my fountains. I'll teach you a lesson you won't soon forget! That knife won't save you, missy—nothing will!"

He swung the poker again. I ducked behind the statue, and the clang of metal on metal made my ears ring.

"Cooper!" I said, yelling louder than I should have, since I couldn't quite hear myself think at that moment. "Put down the weapon! I'm not here to hurt you!"

The dwarf snorted. "Right. And pretty girls carrying knives just show up on my doorstep and creep around my woods every day of the week, and twice on Sunday."

He stepped around the statue and took another swing at me, forcing me to back up. Normally I would have rushed forward, knocked his weapon away, and put my blade up against his throat. But Owen wouldn't have liked me attacking his mentor, even if Cooper had started things. So I slid my knife back up my sleeve and held my hands out to the side, showing him I was unarmed.

"See there? No more knife," I said in a soft, easy voice, trying to calm him. "Now why don't you put that down so we can talk like reasonable people?"

The dwarf studied me through his thick goggles. "We can talk, all right," he muttered. "After I've bashed your head in."

Despite the situation, I couldn't help but grin. I was starting to like the dwarf. Maybe because he seemed to have the same violent streak Finn always claimed I did.

Cooper came at me with the poker again, but once more, I ducked out of the way. This time, he slammed the rod into the sculpture of another eagle, this one perched on a tree stump. Unfortunately, the sculpture didn't hold up against the dwarf's assault and he knocked the beak right off the bird.

"Damn," he said. "That was one of my favorite pieces. You'll pay for that, missy!"

I sighed and kept up my dance with the dwarf. Around and around the sculpture garden we went, with Cooper trying to split my skull open and me sidestepping out of the way time and time again. Despite the fact that Cooper was nearly three hundred, the dwarf moved with the ease of a much younger man, and all the long hours and years working at his forge had given him incredible strength and stamina. I was already sweating from all the bobbing and weaving, but Cooper looked like he could swing that heavy poker at me all day. He probably could, and sooner or later odds said he was sure to connect.

Still, I held back. We'd already gotten off on the wrong foot. I didn't want to add insult to injury by hurting the dwarf.

Finally, just when I was getting good and tired of playing pin-the-poker-on-Gin's-head, Owen and Kincaid came running into the sculpture garden. Cooper whirled at the sound of their footsteps and raised the rod over his shoulder, ready to take on these new intruders, whoever they might be. The two men skidded to a stop, and Owen held his hands out, just like I had a few minutes before.

"Cooper," he said. "It's me, Owen. Put down the poker, okay?"

Cooper blinked and slowly lowered his weapon. "Owen?"

He nodded and smiled at his mentor.

The dwarf frowned, then looked over his shoulder at me. "Then who is that?"

I just wheezed and leaned against the broken sculpture.

✼ 21 ✼

Owen introduced me to Cooper. It took some convincing, but eventually the dwarf put his poker on the ground and clapped me on the back, almost knocking me over with his great strength.

"Sorry about the confusion, missy," Cooper said in his loud, rumbling voice. "But you can't be too careful these days, even up here in the mountains. These are troubled times, you know. Troubled times."

I thought about all the hoodlums who'd tried to kill me in the last few months and all the others who would keep coming after me. I grimaced. I could tell Cooper a thing or two about troubled times.

"Especially since someone keeps stealing my fountains!"

"Fountains?" I asked. "You make fountains?"

The dwarf nodded. "Not as often as I do sculptures, but I got a commission a few months ago for them. Some guy named Henley wanted seven of them for his gardens, but the guy never showed up with the money."

I frowned. Something about the name *Henley* seemed familiar to me, like I'd seen or heard it somewhere recently. I concentrated, but the memory just wouldn't come to me.

"So I just planted them out in the woods, figuring I'd get rid of them sooner or later," Cooper said. "But one by one, someone's been stealing them. There's only one left now, which was why I was out hiding in the trees, trying to catch the thief. I saw you come out here and thought you might be the person whose backside I need to kick."

"Sorry," I murmured. "Not much use for fountains in my line of work."

Once he decided I wasn't a threat to him or his remaining fountain, Cooper moved over to Owen and Kincaid. He clapped Owen heartily on the back and did the same to Kincaid. Then he put his arms around the two of them in a bear hug and lifted them both up off the ground, letting out a loud roar that made Owen smile and Kincaid laugh.

"It's good to see my boys together again," Cooper said when he finally put them back down.

They didn't say anything, but Owen and Kincaid looked at each other over the top of his head.

Cooper led us back to the house and directed us to some chairs on the patio while he went inside and rustled up something for us to drink. A few minutes later, he came back with a tall pitcher of lemonade and several mismatched cups, some of which were actually repurposed jelly jars.

"It's a bit warm," he apologized, setting everything down on the metal table in the middle of the chairs. "I'm afraid I forgot to fill up the ice cube trays the last time I emptied them. I always forget that."

Kincaid chuckled. "And everything else that involves housework. All you care about is your forge and your latest masterpiece."

The dwarf shrugged, but there was a good-natured smile on his face.

"Let me help with that," I said.

I leaned forward, wrapped my hand around the pitcher, and reached for my magic. A silver light flickered on my palm, and elemental Ice crystals spread out from my hand, ran up the pitcher, and then down into the lemonade below. A second later, the entire pitcher was cold and frosty, so much so that the layer of Ice I'd put on the glass started to steam, the faint wisps of it curling up into the afternoon heat.

Cooper looked at me, his eyes sharp and wary in his lined face. I sat back in my chair and gave him an easy smile.

We sat there for half an hour, sipping lemonade, while the three of them caught up. If the dwarf thought it strange Owen and Kincaid were here together, he didn't comment on it. Instead, he reminisced about Christmas, when Owen and Eva had visited him last. I hadn't come with them then, not wanting to intrude on what was a family celebration, but I was glad I'd been able to meet Cooper today. I only wished the circumstances could have been better.

Finally, we finished our lemonade. The dwarf pushed his glass away and speared Owen with a hard look.

"Now, do you want to tell me the real reason you came all the way up here?" Cooper asked. "Because I know it wasn't just for the pleasure of my company. Not when you came with Phillip, to whom as far as I know, you haven't said a civil word in years. And you still haven't told me about *her*."

The dwarf jerked his head at me. Owen had introduced me before simply as Gin, but now it was time to let the dwarf know who and what I was.

"My name is Gin Blanco."

The dwarf frowned, like he recognized the name but couldn't quite place it, so I decided to help him out.

"I believe you know, or rather knew, my foster father. Fletcher Lane."

The dwarf's eyes sharpened that much more. "Yes, I knew Fletcher. I was very sorry to hear about his passing."

Well, *passing* was a polite way of saying *brutal murder,* but I tilted my head, accepting his condolences.

Owen leaned forward, staring at the dwarf. "We came up here today because Salina is back in Ashland."

For a moment, Cooper went completely, utterly still. He'd been reaching for the pitcher to pour himself some more lemonade, and his hand wavered in mid-air before he dropped it down to the table. Then, he sat back in his chair and shrugged, like it didn't matter to him where Salina was or what she was doing.

"Well, I suppose it had to happen sooner or later," he grumbled. "Although I was hoping for never."

"What do you mean?" Owen asked.

Cooper shifted in his chair. His gaze cut to Kincaid, but he didn't respond to Owen's question. He didn't have to.

"So it's true then," Owen said. "What Kincaid said. That Salina—that she hurt Eva all those years ago."

Emotions flashed across his face like lightning. Shock, disbelief, disgust, and finally anger—so much anger. Owen got to his feet and paced around the patio, stalking from one side to the other, his wing tips clacking on the stones.

Finally, he turned and stabbed his finger at Cooper. "Why didn't you tell me?"

"Because you wouldn't have listened to us—any of us," the dwarf said in a resigned voice. "You loved the girl, and you only wanted to see the good in her. There was no point in making things worse than they already were."

Owen turned his gaze to Kincaid. "And you, Phillip? Why didn't you tell me what she was doing? Hell, why didn't Eva tell me?"

"I tried, but you were too busy beating the shit out of me," Kincaid snapped. "As far as Eva goes, she told me that Salina threatened to hurt me and you too if she said anything. She begged me to keep quiet, so I did. Eva was so upset, so afraid that Salina could come back at any time. She'd already been hurt enough, and I didn't want her to worry any more than she already was. That's the reason I kept my mouth shut back then and all these years. I was protecting Eva."

Something you failed to do. Kincaid didn't say the words. He didn't have to.

That stricken look dimmed Owen's eyes again, and I knew what he was feeling—guilt. Guilt that he hadn't realized what was going on, guilt that he'd taken Salina's side over everyone else's, guilt over what Eva had suffered, guilt that he'd almost killed Kincaid because of Salina's lies. So much guilt. Enough to last a lifetime.

As much as I wanted to go over to Owen, hold him close, and tell him it was okay, I couldn't do that. Nothing I could say would make his guilt go away, and right now I needed to talk to the dwarf about more practical matters.

I looked at Cooper. "So what happened? How did you convince Salina to leave Ashland?"

He shifted in his chair again. "Phillip called me the night Owen beat him. We'd kept in touch, even though Owen and I weren't speaking at the time. I came and picked him up, and he told me what Salina had done. I got the boy patched up, and we waited for Owen to leave the house. When he finally did, we went in and confronted Salina. I told her to leave Ashland and never come back—or I'd kill her. Of course, she didn't listen to me. She tried to use her water magic on me, but I managed to overcome her with my Air power. I held her down on the ground with it while Phillip packed up her things. Then we made her write a note for Owen and threw her out of the house. That was the last time I saw her."

We were all quiet, although I could hear the sudden, loud chirping of the birds deeper in the woods, like something had startled them. A few crows zoomed up out of the tops of the trees and started circling around and around in the sky above.

"Salina might come after you," I told the dwarf. "Especially given how isolated you are here. Maybe it would be better if you stayed with Owen for a few days. Just in case."

"Bah!" Cooper waved his hand. "I don't need protection from her. Besides, I doubt she'd come all the way up here. Salina never did much care for this place—or me."

"All the more reason for her to come after you now," I said. "Salina seems to be going around settling old scores, among other things. You were the one responsible for running her out of Ashland. That's not the kind of thing a person forgets. Especially not someone like her. Trust me. I know a thing or two about grudges. She'll come after you sooner or later."

Cooper shrugged. "And I'll deal with her the same way I did before."

The dwarf looked back and forth between me and Owen. "But the two of you are together now?"

Owen nodded. "We are."

"Then I'd say missy here is in far more trouble than I am," Cooper said. "Salina never did like sharing you, Owen—not with anyone."

Owen didn't respond, but sadness mixed with the guilt on his face. I wondered if he realized what the dwarf was really saying—that Salina would probably come after me too. I wondered what Owen would do in that situation— which one of us he'd choose. I hoped it would be me, but I couldn't quite ignore the cold, creeping dread that it would be Salina instead.

We sat there for another half hour. Owen and Kincaid tried to convince Cooper to come back to Ashland and stay at the Graysons' mansion, if only for the next few days, but the dwarf wouldn't budge, saying he had too many projects to finish.

"I've been up here in this old holler going on two hundred years. I'm not about to let Salina or anyone else drive me out of it."

Cooper winked at me, and I found myself grinning in return. I liked the dwarf, with his loud voice and thick goggles. He reminded me of what Fletcher would have been like if the old man had still been alive—absolutely irrepressible.

Eventually, since he wouldn't come with us, we got to our feet and said our good-byes. Cooper walked us around to the front of the house. I started to get into the car with the others, but he grabbed hold of my arm.

"You be careful with Salina," Cooper warned. "I've heard about you, Gin, and what you can do with your magic. How you killed Mab Monroe. But Salina's tricky. She always has been, and so is her water magic. Fighting her isn't like fighting another elemental. Water power is hard to get a hold on, and it's even harder still to figure out some way to beat it."

I nodded, taking his words to heart. I'd seen what Salina could do with her magic—how she enjoyed using it to hurt people.

"I'll be careful," I said. "I'll take care of Kincaid and protect him from Salina. Eva too. She won't hurt them again. Not as long as I'm still breathing."

Cooper shook his head. "Eva and Kincaid aren't the only ones who need protecting from Salina. I think you know that."

I looked over at Owen, who was already in the car and staring at us through the passenger window. "Yeah, I know exactly what you mean."

I got into the Escalade. Through the open windows,

Owen and Kincaid tried one final time to get their mentor to come along.

But Cooper shook his head again. "I'll be just fine up here. I have been for a long time now, and I don't see that changing anytime soon. But you take care." His gaze flicked to me. "All of you."

I nodded at him, and he nodded back. Cooper knew how these things ended. He knew that one of us would kill the other, and I was determined to be the last one standing—no matter how tricky Salina's water magic might be.

I cranked the engine and backed up the SUV. We all waved at Cooper a final time. I'd just started going down the ridge when the dwarf turned and went around the house, probably going back to his forge.

Kincaid and I were quiet in deference to Owen. We both knew he needed some time to process everything. To sort through and come to terms with all the lies. Still, once again, I wondered how he would react if I told him what Eva had asked me to do, how she'd asked me to kill Salina. If he would let me do it—or if he'd try to stop me.

A murder of crows exploded out of the trees to our right, forcing me to slow down or risk hitting them. Finn would not be happy if I came back with feathers in his grille. He still hadn't forgiven me for trashing his Aston Martin.

The crows flapped across the rutted driveway before taking flight and soaring up into the spring sky, their sharp *caw-caw-caws* ringing through the air. I took my foot off the brake and put it back on the gas.

"What is with the birds today?" Kincaid muttered. "That's the second time something's startled them."

His words made me remember how earlier the crows had taken flight from trees deeper in the woods, even though the four of us had been sitting on the patio. That led to another thought, then another one, until they all seemed like a series of grenades exploding in my mind.

The giants, the moving truck, and the van I'd seen near the bottom of Cooper's driveway. Some guy commissioning several fountains he'd never picked up. Someone else knowing enough about Cooper to steal those same fountains from his sculpture garden. The crows flying away, even though there was seemingly nothing around to frighten them.

And then I felt it, the final piece of the puzzle—a cool caress of magic, like water sliding against my skin. Faint as a whisper, but I knew what it and everything else meant—and what I had to do.

I slammed on the brakes, making the SUV fishtail and skid on the gravel. Rocks sprayed everywhere as the vehicle finally lurched to a top.

"Gin?" Owen asked, his hand braced against the dashboard. "What's wrong?"

I didn't answer him. I was too busy getting out of the SUV and running back toward the house.

☀22☀

"Gin!" I heard Owen shout behind me. "Gin!"

Instead of answering him, I quickened my pace, sprinting up the driveway as fast as I could. Behind me, Kincaid shouted at Owen to get in the driver's seat and back the SUV up the ridge.

I didn't bother yelling and trying to warn Cooper. I was still too far away for that. If the dwarf was working in his forge, he wouldn't hear me anyway, and if Salina went at him head-on like I thought she would, then Cooper needed to focus on her—not me screaming at him. Besides, I didn't want her to realize I'd doubled back until she felt my knife slicing into her heart.

I made it up to the house and raced around the side, heading to the forge. Over the *thump-thump-thump* of my roaring heart, I strained to listen, but I didn't hear Cooper's hammer striking anything. That meant something had interrupted him—and I was willing to bet I knew exactly what that something was.

I sprinted into the backyard, looking right and left and doing a quick, visual sweep of the grounds, but no one was there, and I didn't see Cooper or anyone else lurking in the forge. I stopped on the stone patio, my head snapping back toward the house, wondering if they were inside. I'd just taken a step in that direction when I felt another cool gust of magic coming from the woods.

The sculpture garden.

Even though I wanted to get to Cooper as fast as possible, I forced myself to slow my steps and calm my racing heart. I'd need the element of surprise and every bit of magic I could muster up to take out Salina, so I palmed a knife and headed for the sculpture garden.

I'd only gone about fifty feet into the woods when I saw the first giant.

He stood with his back to me, facing the statues, his arms crossed over his chest. He didn't even have his gun out.

I slid behind a tree, hunkered down in the bushes, and scanned the rest of the landscape. The giant in front of me was the only one I could see, but there had been another one down at the moving trucks, and Salina would have been sure to bring at least a couple more, if only to move the last fountain more easily. That was what I would have done if our situations had been reversed. Besides, there was always a chance she couldn't finish Cooper off with her water magic and that she'd need the help of one of her bodyguards.

The faint murmurs of voices drifted out of the trees

in front of where the giant was standing. Good. Voices were good. They meant Salina was probably still talking to Cooper and hadn't gotten down to the business of actually killing him yet. Not that the dwarf would go easily. I imagined he would put up a good fight, but I'd felt how strong Salina was on the riverboat. The water elemental was in her prime and only growing stronger—just the way Jo-Jo always described me and my magic.

I wondered if Cooper had put it together, if he'd connected the stolen fountains to Salina as soon as Kincaid had mentioned her name. I wondered if that was why he'd been so insistent about not coming back to Ashland with us, if he'd wanted to catch Salina in the act, face her down and try to kill her himself. Didn't much matter now.

My fingers clenched around my knife, the small spider rune stamped into the hilt pressing into the larger, matching scar on my palm. Owen had made this and my other knives, crafting them with as much care and detail as Cooper did his sculptures, and I planned to put them to use—right now.

The giant never even saw me coming. With the voices still murmuring, I snuck out from behind the tree and headed toward him. At the last moment, I quickened my pace, launched myself upward, and leaped onto his back. As my knife punched into his spine at the base of his skull, he grunted like it was of no more consequence than a bee sting, rather than the lethal blow it was. He went down on one knee. I didn't give him the chance to scream as I yanked out my knife, reached around, pulled his head back, and slit his throat with the blade. The giant was dead before he thumped to the forest floor. One down, who knew how many more to go.

I crept through the underbrush, taking out another giant who'd been stationed at the perimeter the same way, before I was able to ease up to the edge of the sculpture garden itself.

Cooper and Salina stood in the middle of the clearing, their eyes glowing with magic, his a bright copper, hers shimmering from blue to green and back again. They were facing each other with about twenty feet of space separating them, hands down by their sides, intently studying each other. I'd expected nothing less, since they were getting ready to duel.

Elementals often fought by dueling, by flinging their raw magic, their raw strength, at each other over and over again until one person ran out of juice and succumbed to the other's power. Suffocated by Air, burned alive by Fire, frozen solid by Ice, encased in Stone, or some variation or offshoot thereof. None of them painless ways to die. Then again, elemental duels were only about one thing— destroying your enemy as quickly and brutally as you could.

"I was wondering when you would show up," Cooper said. "Seems like you've been busy since you've been back."

Salina smiled—that same cold, calm, serene smile she'd given me at the Pork Pit. "You might say that. You should have known better than to force me to leave Ashland in the first place. I always told you that I'd come back and kill you for it."

"And I always told you that I'd be right here to stop you. I only wish you'd come here first so I could have put you in your rightful place to start with. But instead, you decided on sneak attacks, just like always. Just like your father always did when he was alive. That's why he couldn't kill Mab, you know. Because his sneak attack to stab her in the back failed, and he just didn't have the raw magic to defeat her."

"Don't you dare talk about my father, you miserable little toad!" Salina screamed. "His plan would have worked! He would have killed Mab, if one of his giant guards hadn't gotten greedy and sold him out and told her what he was planning."

I winced at her screeching. Looked like daddy's death was indeed a sore spot, just like I'd thought. I wondered if that was another old score she planned to settle while she was in town, although I had no idea who she'd target, since Mab was already dead.

Salina made a visible effort to unclench her jaw and fists. A moment later, her stiff posture relaxed, and her features were smooth and serene once more. "But enough talk," she purred. "I've waited a long time for this moment, and I plan to savor every second of it."

She brought her hand up, curling her fingers into a loose fist. Then her fist seemed to almost . . . *liquefy*. Her skin became pale and glassy like, well, water. It almost seemed like I could hear her skin sloshing as she fully embraced her water magic. I could feel the cool, soothing wetness of her power all the way across the clearing.

But Cooper wasn't to be outdone, and the dwarf reached for his own Air magic. The wind seemed to gather around him, like he was standing in the center of a miniature tornado. Around and around the wind whirled, stirring up leaves, twigs, and rocks underfoot and making the trees creak and groan and the metal sculptures sway back and forth, despite their sturdy bases and heavy frames.

While the two elementals gathered their power for that initial strike, I turned my attention to the others, the five additional giants Salina had brought along. Three were about twenty feet behind Salina. They'd already grabbed the last fountain from its perch in the woods and were carrying it through the trees as fast as they could. I'd deal with them later. The other two stood behind Cooper, probably in case he tried to retreat from Salina and her magic. The dwarf didn't seem like the kind to turn and run, even when he knew he was on the losing side—like he was right now.

Oh, the dwarf was strong in his magic, but Salina was stronger. She was fully embracing her power now, and I could tell that she was almost as strong as Mab had been. That made her dangerous enough, but the wild card here was the type of magic she had. Like Cooper had said, Salina's water power was a tricky thing, hard to get a fix on, hard to defend against. It wasn't like any magic I'd ever felt—or fought—before.

But what most people forgot, even elementals, was that all the water magic in the world couldn't save someone from a knife in the heart—and I planned on driving mine into Salina's black one the second I got the chance. But first, I had to deal with the giants. Together, I knew that Cooper and I could beat Salina at her own game, but I wanted to level the playing field as much as possible. Besides, if I went after Salina first, there was too much risk of one of the giants pulling out a gun and trying to end things that way, with Cooper getting caught in the crossfire. No, I'd take out Salina's backup first, then go in for the kill on her.

I slithered through the underbrush, heading toward the first giant. He was focused on Salina and Cooper, instead of watching his own back, like he should have been. I reached the tree closest to him, then drew in a breath and rocked back on my heels, ready to surge forward at just the right moment.

"And now, Cooper, it's time for you to die," Salina said. "I'm going to enjoy marking you off my to-do list. Don't worry. You're not the only one I came back to Ashland to teach a lesson to. In fact, many people are finally going to get what they deserve. Very, very soon."

I frowned, wondering what she was talking about. With Cooper dead, the only people she would have left to go after would be Phillip again and perhaps Eva—and me, of course. So who else could Salina possibly be targeting? I didn't have time to puzzle it out, as a translucent, watery ball of magic appeared in her right hand.

"Good-bye, Cooper," Salina hissed, rearing her hand back to throw her magic at the dwarf.

Cooper didn't bother responding. Instead, he reached for even more of his Air power, ready to block her attack for as long as he could.

And that's when I pounced on my prey.

Just before Salina let loose with her magic, I erupted out of the underbrush and plowed into the giant closest to me. One, two, three quick cuts across his chest and stomach, and he was down for the count, without even really realizing what had happened in the first place.

But the giant's brain took over, causing him to scream and scream as he fell and bled out. I let him yell, because it had the desired effect of ruining Salina's concentration. The ball of magic she'd been about to toss at Cooper slipped through her hands and hit the ground, exploding like a water balloon someone had dropped from a high window. She cursed and reached for her power again, but Cooper was quicker. He snapped his hands up and in front of him. The wind that had been whistling around him coalesced into a shimmering blast of magic that zoomed through the air—hitting Salina in the stomach and throwing her back into a tree. If I was lucky, she would have a broken neck and be dead by the time I got around to dealing with her, but I wasn't holding my breath. My luck was never that good.

That left one giant standing in the clearing. I tightened my grip on my bloody knife and headed in his direction. But the giant was faster than I was, and he managed to get his gun out from underneath his suit jacket before I reached him. I grabbed hold of my Stone magic and used it to harden my skin the second before he pulled the trigger.

Crack! Crack! Crack!

The giant's bullets pinged off my body and rattled away into the woods, burying themselves in the leafy foliage. He frowned, wondering why I hadn't gone down when he'd just put three bullets in my chest, but I didn't give him a chance to get off more shots.

Slice-slice-slice.

Three quick passes of my knife, and the giant was down on the ground—never to get up again. Still, I cut his throat, just to be sure.

Then I hurried over to Cooper. "Are you okay?"

Instead of answering me, the dwarf lurched forward and shoved me out of the way. A second later, a ball of water magic slammed into the spot where I'd been standing—and hit him square in the chest. Cooper flew back through the air just like Salina had a moment before. My head snapped around. I'd foolishly assumed it would take her some time to recover from being tossed across the clearing, but the water elemental had already gotten back up on her feet and was forming another ball of magic in her hands.

"Cooper!" Kincaid shouted.

I turned and spotted him and Owen at the edge of the sculpture garden. Kincaid broke free of Owen's grip on his arm and raced over to the dwarf. I reached Cooper the same time Kincaid did, being sure to put my body in front of theirs to protect them from Salina.

I shouldn't have worried. Salina was too busy staring across the clearing at Owen—and he right back at her. Shock filled Owen's face—absolute shock that Salina had just tried to kill Cooper. Despite everything he'd learned about her, he'd finally seen her in action, finally seen Salina for her true self. I just hoped it was enough to break whatever hold she still had on his heart.

I knelt beside the dwarf. Salina had thrown her magic at him in such a way that it sucked the moisture out of his body, and Cooper's skin looked as wet and saggy as Antonio's had on the *Delta Queen* last night.

"It's . . . how she . . . fights," the dwarf wheezed, trying to breathe. "She pulls the water out of you and into her. It makes her . . . stronger."

I reached into my jeans pocket, yanked out a small tin I'd grabbed earlier at the Pork Pit, and thrust it into Kincaid's hands. "Here's some salve infused with Air elemental magic. I brought it along just in case. Rip open his shirt and put that on his skin, especially over his heart and lungs where Salina hit him the worst with her magic. It'll have to hold him until we can get him to the healer I know."

"Forget about me. Go!" Cooper rasped. "Go! I'll be all right!"

I could see the pleading in his eyes. No matter what happened, whether he lived or died, he wanted this thing with Salina finished—now.

And so did I.

"You stay here with him," I told Kincaid. "I'm going after Salina."

I scrambled to my feet. Salina saw me. She looked at Owen once more, then turned and ran into the trees. Owen just stood there, watching her go, and then me racing into the woods after her.

Salina darted through the trees like she was a deer—nimble, light, and quick. Too quick. I was losing ground on her, so I sucked in a breath and forced myself to move faster, to run harder. But I just couldn't seem to catch her, and I desperately wanted to. I wanted to end the threat Salina was to Owen and all the people he cared about—and the threat she was to us.

I caught a glimpse of Salina's long hair before she vanished around a large tree. If I'd had the breath for it, I would have cursed at how fast she was. Instead, I forced myself to pick up the pace that much more, despite the fact my heart felt like it was going to pound right out of my chest and my lungs burned in the warm, humid, spring air.

I rounded the tree, stepping into another clearing in the middle of the woods. About fifty feet ahead, I caught another flash of Salina's blond hair streaming out behind her, shimmering like melted gold in a patch of sunlight. I leaped over a fallen log, determined to catch her, but to my surprise, she did the most curious thing of all—she stopped.

She turned around and faced me, standing on a small rise at the top of the clearing, and I wondered if she was out of gas already. A satisfied smile curved my lips. If so, too bad for her. I put on a final burst of speed and surged up an incline to the edge of the clearing—and then I stopped too.

Because a creek lay between us.

The water had worn its way through the hill we were standing on, creating a slight dip in the landscape. About fifteen feet of water separated us, churning and frothing its way down the ridge to parts unknown.

Salina had already crossed the clear water, probably walking on top of it as she had the Aneirin River out by the *Delta Queen*. For a moment, I thought about saying the hell with it and plunging into the creek to continue my hot pursuit, but I knew better. Besides, I could easily blast her with my elemental magic from this side of the creek.

"You know, I'm getting rather tired of you interfering with my plans," Salina said in a mild, slightly amused voice. "And look at you—you're covered with blood, sweat, dirt, and who knows what else. Disgusting. What did Owen ever see in you?"

"Oh, I don't know," I said, my voice as cold and calm as hers was. "Maybe the fact that I'm not a psychotic bitch who tortures people for kicks. I'm also not the one going around Ashland killing his friends and family because I'm secretly jealous of them. Tell me, how many folks are you going to bump off before you're satisfied that you have him all to yourself? Call me crazy, but I don't think murder is the way to Owen's heart."

Her eyes narrowed in her beautiful face. "I think I know a lot more about Owen's heart than you ever will, Gin. I saw how he looked at me that night at Underwood's and just a minute ago in the clearing. He still loves me, and he'll always love me—no matter what."

I shook my head. "That's where you're wrong. Sure, he might have some feelings left for you, but believe me when I tell you they won't be enough to overcome you trying to murder Cooper—or what you did to Eva when she was a kid."

Salina gasped, surprised by the fact that her dirty little secret had finally come to light after all these years.

"Oh yeah," I said. "Cooper and Kincaid told him all about what you did to his baby sister. Owen's not the kind of man who forgets things like that. He protects the people he loves."

Salina stared at me, the rush of water the only sound between us. I kept my gaze on the other elemental, waiting—just waiting—for her to reach for her magic and try to blast me with it the way she had Cooper. I was ready for her, ready to reach for my own Stone magic and use it to harden my skin to protect the water in my body. Then I'd strike back at her with all the Ice magic I could summon and freeze her where she stood. I discreetly tucked my knife back up my sleeve and got ready to raise my hands up and throw my power at her.

Instead of being scared by me and the magic shimmering in my gray eyes, Salina still seemed amused. I was getting real tired of her laughing at me.

"You should have driven back to Ashland while you had the chance," she said. "I was going to be considerate and let you live a few more days. At least until after I finished my other business in town and could devote my full attention to Owen."

Once again, I wondered what she was plotting, but I pushed my questions aside. All that mattered was killing her before she could hurt anyone else.

"And you should have known better than to come up here," I snarled. "I warned you to leave Ashland. You really should have taken my advice. What did you think would happen? That you could just kill Cooper and go on your merry way? Fat chance of that now."

"Who said Cooper was the only one I wanted to kill?"

Then she smiled at me—smiled and smiled like she'd just won the lottery. My eyes narrowed. What was she grinning at? Salina wasn't in the clear—far from it. I wasn't going to be stupid enough to step into the water, and all I had to do was blast her with my Ice magic from this side of the creek—

My eyes dropped to the water that rushed in between us. Too late, I realized what Salina's plan really was. I tried to back away from the edge of the water, but I was too slow—too damn slow.

With a twisting motion of Salina's hand, water exploded out of the creek like a geyser. Even as I tried to lunge back out of its range, I could see the water arcing through the air, writhing and twisting into long, slender tentacles.

That happened in the first second. In the next one, the liquid tentacles wrapped around my legs. And by the third, they'd pulled me down into middle of the creek.

❖ 23 ❖

So this is what it's like to drown.

That was the thought that filled my mind as the cool creek water closed over my head. Oh, I struggled, of course, struggled with all my strength against the tentacles wrapped around my body. But it was like a hundred, cold, wet hands were twisting me around and around underwater, and I just couldn't get a sense of what direction was up.

Finally, I managed to break the surface of the water long enough to suck down a breath. Then the tentacles were around me again, dragging me under once more.

Over and over, the tentacles let me rise up just long enough to draw in precious oxygen. I knew what Salina was doing—the bitch was playing with me. She'd thought she'd already won, that she'd already killed me, and she was savoring the moment, savoring her victory over the Spider.

And I couldn't figure out a way to stop her. Cooper had warned me that her magic was wet, wild, and slippery. Every time I tried to pry off one of the tentacles wrapped around me, my fingers harmlessly slid through it like the water it was. Plus, she was strong in her magic, maybe even as strong as I was in mine, and now she had a whole creek full of water to use against me. I was in her element now—and it was going to be the death of me.

At some point, Salina must have gotten bored with making me bob up and down like a Halloween apple, because the tentacles wrapped me around a final time—and then dragged me down to the bottom of the creek. The water wasn't that deep, maybe eight feet, but there was more than enough for Salina to kill me with.

Mud and rocks ground into my back as I blinked, staring up through the creek. The water was pure, sweet, and clear this high up in the mountains, and I could make out Salina's wavy figure standing above me on the bank. I couldn't tell for sure, but I thought she was smiling.

But the worst part was that I could—I could see her through the water. Standing beside the tub watching me drown—smiling while I was drowning.

Eva's words whispered in my mind. I remembered what she had said about how Salina had watched her drown—and the pleasure the elemental had taken in it. Now, all these years later, Salina was doing the same thing to me.

Not if I could help it.

There was no use struggling against the tentacles, not now, when Salina had moved in for the kill, so I let my body go loose and slack against the water that surrounded me like a wet tomb, like I was already halfway to drowned.

Not much of a stretch. I had maybe two minutes' worth of oxygen left before I blacked out. After that, the end would be quick.

My Stone magic was useless in this situation, so I focused on my Ice power, gathering and gathering it around me. It was the only chance I had left—and I didn't even know if it would work. If I had enough power to do what needed to be done in order to survive.

Ten seconds passed . . . twenty . . . thirty . . . My lungs burned a little more with every passing second, the need for air so great I wanted to scream from it, but I forced myself to be calm, to wait to bring all of the Ice magic I had to bear, along with what I had stored in my spider rune ring. I thought about reaching for the Ice power that was in my knives as well, but my concentration was a little shaky, and I didn't know if I could tap into the magic of all six items at once. So I decided to focus on combining my magic with the ring's and releasing all of that power outward at once. I'd only get one shot at this, and I had to make it count—or I was dead.

So I gathered up the final scraps of my Ice magic . . . and let loose with it.

I sent out a blast of Ice, forcing the cold power out of my hands and into the water around me. I didn't know if I had enough strength, enough magic for what I needed to do; hell, I didn't even know if it would work at all.

The creek water that had been rushing by immediately froze. One second, I could feel the water flowing around me. The next, it had stopped cold—literally. The entire creek had frozen around me, including the tentacles of Salina's magic. They wrapped around my body like crystallized tendrils of ivy gnarled and knotted every which way. The whole scene, all the glittering, elemental Ice around me, was strangely beautiful—and still deadly.

I might have stopped Salina from drowning me by freezing the creek, but I still wasn't getting any air. I might have been an Ice elemental, but that didn't mean I could *breathe* through it. So I sent out another desperate burst of magic, hoping to crack the Ice that encased me like a crystal coffin.

But I'd already used up so much of my power, and the Ice was frozen solid. Again and again, I sent out burst after burst of magic.

And at last, slowly, much too slowly, the Ice around me began to chip and crack and fall away from my body.

But it still wasn't enough.

Running after Salina, fighting against her water tentacles, using my own Ice magic until there was none left—all of that had taken everything out of me, and I simply wasn't strong enough to claw my way out of the weight of Ice pressing down on me and get to the air I so desperately needed.

I thought I punched one hand free of the Ice, but I wasn't sure, and it wasn't enough to matter anyway. Bit by bit, the blackness crept over me before it rose up in a wave in my mind and blotted out everything else.

The last thought I had was of Owen, and what he would think when he realized that Salina had killed me.

❋24❋

Someone was pounding on my chest. Over and over again, a tight fist smacked into my ribs right over my heart. An uncomfortable sensation, especially when I'd been so peaceful just a moment before, drifting along in that calm, soothing, unending blackness . . .

"Come on, breathe, dammit, breathe!" a harsh voice barked at me.

Something hot and wet pressed against my mouth, forcing air down my throat and into my lungs. Again and again, that hot rush of air invaded my mouth, and there was nothing I could do to stop it. A few seconds later, my chest began heaving and convulsing, and I started coughing, spewing up all the water in my lungs and trying to choke down all the air I could at the same time.

Hands rolled me onto my side to make it easier for me to breathe. I just lay there, cold and half-frozen by my own Ice magic, my fingers curled into the dirt, my face resting on a bed of dried, cracked leaves, sucking down breath after breath. After a few moments, I managed to open my eyes and found a face right there on the dirt next to mine—but it wasn't the one that I expected. His eyes were blue, not violet, and his hair was as light as the sunshine kissing the forest.

Kincaid gave me a crooked smile. "Don't think you're going to weasel out of our deal just by dying, Gin."

Deal? We didn't have any deal. I'd never agreed to kill Salina for him. I opened my mouth to tell him that, but the words just wouldn't come. The blackness rose up in my mind again, and I was helpless to resist it once more.

The girl had finally quit screaming—if not crying.

Even though her father was dead and had been for a while now, the girl was still slumped over his body—or what was left of it—and sobbing like she would never, ever stop. Each one of her loud, wild, soul-wrenching cries was like a knife piercing my own heart. I knew that pain, I knew those screams all too well—they were the same ones that had torn my heart to pieces and spewed out of my mouth after the murder of my family.

I was still a little shocked by what had happened. Mab Monroe had spent the better part of an hour torturing Benedict Dubois, burning him with her elemental Fire, delighting in his tearful pleas and whimpers as he begged her to stop. And she'd made everyone watch—all the dinner guests, all the chefs, all the waiters, even Dubois's own daughter.

It had been like a nightmare come to life.

At first, Mab had toyed with Dubois, jabbing her red-hot fingers into his arms like they were slender cigarettes she was stubbing out. Then, she'd used her elemental Fire to burn the rest of him—his chest, his legs; she'd even used her power to singe all the hair off his head like she was scalping him.

Still, no matter what Mab did, I made myself watch the whole thing just like Fletcher did beside me. These were the realities of life in Ashland, especially for an assassin-in-training like me. Because if I was ever captured, especially by someone like Mab, I would face the same sort of torture. Fletcher didn't say the words. He didn't have to. Not tonight. Not when I was faced with something like this.

Once Dubois was dead, I'd thought the Fire elemental would turn her wrath on the girl to quiet her down, but Mab just let her scream and scream, as though the sound amused her. It probably did, given all the cruel things I'd seen the Fire elemental do tonight. Finally, the girl broke free of the boy holding her, threw herself on top of her father's body, and started crying, her sobs just as loud as her screams had been.

When it was finally over, Mab dusted the pieces of ash and burned flesh off her hands and turned to face the horrified crowd.

"Am I going to have any more problems from the rest of you?" she asked. "Or has this been an adequate enough display of my position in Ashland? I'm happy to demonstrate further, if you like."

No one said a word.

Mab let out a pleased, pealing laugh. "I thought not."

She turned and snapped her finger at one of her giants. "Bring the car around. I'm finished here."

And then she walked away—just picked up the skirt of her long, forest-green evening gown and calmly walked away *like she hadn't just burned a man to bits and enjoyed every second of it.*

Less than a minute later, the Fire elemental slid into the back of a black limo. One of her men shut the door behind her, then scurried around and got in the front. The driver put the vehicle in gear, and the limo coasted down the long driveway. Even when the car had disappeared from sight, everyone stood where they were, afraid to move, afraid that Mab might come back and do the same thing to them that she'd done to Dubois.

All the while, the girl kept crying. The boy who'd been holding her back went over, crouched down beside her, and put his hand on her shoulder. He didn't know what to do or say anymore than anyone else did. After a few seconds, the girl turned and threw herself into his arms, almost knocking him over onto the grass. He stroked her long blond hair and whispered words to her that I couldn't hear, although I imagined they were your usual sort of comforting lies about how everything was going to be okay.

I eyed Dubois's still smoldering body. No, everything was a long, long way from okay.

Eventually, the guests roused themselves out of their stunned state and began murmuring to each other.

"Can't believe Benedict thought he could really kill Mab . . ."

"He should have known better. . . ."

"If you ask me, he got what he deserved for being so foolish. . . ."

The last voice was a little louder and snider than the others had been—loud enough for the girl to hear. Her sobs stopped, and her head snapped around. She shoved the boy away and got to her feet, her hands curling into fists by her sides.

"Why didn't you help him?" she yelled at the crowd. "Why did you all just stand there? You were supposed to be his friends! Cowards! You're nothing but dirty rotten cowards! The whole lot of you!"

No one answered, but the guests edged away from her and dropped their eyes in shame.

Finally, a giant stepped forward, holding his hands out in a placating gesture. I recognized him as one of Dubois's bodyguards.

"Calm down, Salina," he said. "You know we couldn't save your father. Not from Mab. Not without dying ourselves. There was nothing we could do."

The girl stared up at the giant a moment, then smiled— a bright, sunny smile that was at odds with her red, tear-streaked face. Something about her expression made me uneasy. I started to move forward, but Fletcher grabbed my arm and held me still. The old man shook his head at me.

"You're right, Carl," the girl said in a sweet voice. "You couldn't do anything—but I can."

She reached into the giant's jacket, plucked his gun from the holster on his belt, and shot him in the chest with it.

Carl screamed with pain and surprise. He staggered back, but the girl went after him.

Crack! Crack! Crack!

She kept right on shooting him. Giants could take a lot of damage, but getting pumped full of lead at point-blank range will take a toll on anyone. Carl staggered back, his feet slid out from under him, and he landed on his back on the grass. But still, the girl wasn't done.

She walked over and stood by the giant's side.

"Salina . . . please . . . stop . . ." he said through a

*mouthful of blood. "It wasn't . . . my fault. . . . You have
to . . . know that. . . ."*

*That sunny, eerie smile curved the girl's lips again, and
her hand tightened on the gun.*

Crack! Crack! Crack!

She emptied the rest of the magazine into his head.

*Blood arced up through the air and spattered onto her,
but the girl didn't care. She kept pulling the trigger until the
gun was empty.*

Click.

*She let out a disgusted snort and threw the weapon down on
the giant's bloody chest. After a moment, she realized that everyone was watching her in horrified silence, just the way they had
Mab. Rage flashed in the girl's eyes, and she started forward to
do—something, I didn't know what exactly. The crowd backed
away from her, giving her the same wide berth they would a
wild, rabid animal that was about to charge at them.*

"Salina! Salina!" *the boy said, grabbing her from behind
and pinning her arms by her sides.* "That's enough!"

"No, it's not!" *she screamed, struggling to break free of
him, struggling to throw herself into the group of people in
front of her and claw at them with her bare hands.* "He
needed to pay! They should all pay for just standing there! For
just letting it happen! For letting my father die!"

*The girl struggled with the boy a few more seconds before
her screams dissolved into sobs once more. The boy put his
arms around her and held her again while she cried.*

*For a minute, everyone just stood there and watched.
Then, one by one, the guests began walking across the lawn,
careful to skirt around Dubois's and the giant's bodies as they
headed to their cars.*

Fletcher and I were among the last to leave. The old man looked at the still-sobbing girl with a grim expression on his face. "She's going to be trouble later on," he said in a dark voice. "For anyone who crosses her in any way."

"What do you mean?" I asked.

To me, she was just a girl—a girl who'd watched her father be horribly tortured and murdered, just like I'd seen happen to my mother and Annabella. My heart ached for her, and I wanted to go over to the girl and put my arms around her, just like the boy was doing. At least she had him to comfort her, to help her. That was something. I hadn't had anyone.

Instead of answering me, the old man shook his head. "Come on. Let's get out of here."

Fletcher put his arm around me, and we hurried across the lawn, going back to the kitchen with the rest of the staff under the pretense of getting our things and getting out of there. Before we went into the mansion, I looked over my shoulder a final time.

The boy had moved over to talk to another one of Dubois's bodyguards. He had his arm around the girl's shoulders, but he didn't seem to realize that she wasn't listening to what he was saying to the giant. Instead, the girl was staring down at Carl's body. But the weird thing was that she almost looked . . . happy. Satisfaction filled her face, and she was smiling again, although it seemed like there was something wrong with her expression, that it was somehow twisted into something far more sinister—

"Are you out of your fucking mind?" yelled an angry voice, startling me awake.

✻ 25 ✻

"Seriously, are you out of your mind?" that same voice asked again.

My eyes snapped open, and I realized I was staring at a ceiling that featured a soft, pretty, cloud-covered fresco. Jo-Jo's. I was in the dwarf's house. Somehow, I'd gotten all the way from Cooper's forge, down the mountain, and over to Jo-Jo's salon in a ritzy Northtown suburb. Since I was lying in one of her upstairs bedrooms, that meant she had already healed me, had already fixed all the damage Salina had inflicted when she'd tried to drown me with her water magic. Good. That was good.

What weren't good were the bangs, shouts, and general commotion I heard coming from downstairs.

"Just let me talk to Salina," another voice said.

Owen. That was Owen's voice.

"And do what?" demanded the first voice, which I now recognized as Finn's. "Ask her to apologize to Gin for almost drowning her? Or maybe you're going to get her to do a double apology, for almost blasting Cooper to death with her water magic?"

Silence. Then—

"I can't believe you're still defending her," a third, softer, feminine voice jumped into the mix. Eva, this time.

"I'm not defending her," Owen replied. "But Salina obviously needs help."

"Oh yeah," Finn sniped. "She needs help in the form of a bullet to the head—nothing else."

All the voices started talking at once, arguing with each other. I sighed, wondering how long my friends, family, and lover had been fighting. Probably since they'd brought me here. I glanced over at the window. Morning sunlight was creeping through the curtains, warming the entire room, and the clock by the bed read eight thirteen. We'd gone up to Cooper's about four o'clock yesterday afternoon, which meant I'd been in bed for more than twelve hours. Not surprising. Air magic always took a toll on you mentally as your brain tried to catch up to the fact that your body was well once more. Plus, I'd gotten my ass kicked. I still needed a few more hours' sleep to really be myself again.

The voices continued arguing, telling me it was time to rise and shine, whether I felt like it or not. I sighed again, threw back the covers, sat up, and realized I wasn't alone.

Kincaid was there with me.

The casino boss sat in a chair in the corner, reading one of Jo-Jo's beauty magazines. He looked up at the sound of me stirring in the bed.

"Getting some tips on how to keep your ponytail looking all nice and shiny?" I quipped.

He put the magazine on the table by his elbow. "Well, I always like to look my best. Apparently, it's all about which conditioner you use."

We fell silent. Kincaid sat there studying me, and I did the same to him. Instead of his usual suit, he'd dressed down today in a pair of black jeans, boots, and an expensive gray polo shirt that stretched across his shoulders.

"Welcome back," he said, for once without a trace of sarcasm in his voice.

"I suppose I have you to thank for that."

He nodded. "I saw you take off into the woods after Salina so I chased after you while Owen stayed with Cooper. I had an idea of where she would go."

"The creek."

He nodded again. "The creek. Salina used to spend hours there sitting by the water when we were younger and Owen was busy working with Cooper. She saw me coming and took off through the trees, and I realized you were in the bottom of the creek. I'd just started to wade in to try and get you out when this silver light erupted out of the water, and the whole creek froze over, like it was the dead of winter instead of early May."

Kincaid gave me a calculating look, and I knew he was thinking about my magic and what he'd seen me do with it. But I didn't volunteer any more information about my power. That was my business, not his. Especially when I still wasn't sure whether or not I could trust him. Kincaid might have saved my life, but he had his own reasons for doing so—like me killing Salina for him.

"Then what?"

He shrugged. "I saw you there under all that elemental Ice,

and I saw you blasting it again and again with your magic, trying to break free. I thought you were going to make it on your own. You got one hand loose and up into the air, but then it just sort of flopped there on top of the Ice. So I fished you out, dragged you up the bank, and did CPR."

I looked at his shoulders and at the muscles in his arms. "Guess that extra strength you have came in handy."

He shrugged. "You were right before. I don't know who or what my parents were. Maybe dwarves, maybe giants, maybe one of each. But I'm strong, and I use it to my advantage."

"Thank you," I said. "You saved my life."

He shifted in his chair, seeming uncomfortable with my thanks. "Just returning the favor you did me a few nights ago."

"I guess that makes us even then."

He didn't say anything, but for the first time, a hint of a real smile softened his face.

Below us, the voices kept arguing.

I jerked my head at the bedroom door. "What's all that about?"

Kincaid sighed. "Just Owen being Owen."

"Is he still defending Salina?"

"No. He's finally seen her for what she really is. But he doesn't want to cut off her head, mount it on a pike, and dance around with it like your pal Finn does."

I grinned. "Well, Finn can be just as violent as me. Sometimes even more so."

As if to prove my point, downstairs, Finn let loose with a very long, very imaginative string of words describing exactly what he thought should be done to Salina.

"You know, I'm actually starting to like him," Kincaid said. "He certainly has the right idea as far as Salina's concerned."

"Well, that will certainly warm the cold cockles of Finn's heart," I said, swinging my feet over the side of the bed. "Now, come on. Let's go before it escalates into fisticuffs."

I got up, and immediately had to lean against the nightstand for support. Despite the fact that Jo-Jo had healed me, I still felt weak and light-headed. I knew it was because I'd been so close to dying. Hell, maybe I'd even been dead for a minute or two there before Kincaid had revived me. Either way, it would take some time for my mind to figure out that I was still in one piece and not drowning one slow, agonizing breath at a time in that creek.

I managed to walk down the stairs without Kincaid's help. He seemed amused by my attempts to keep my legs under me, but he didn't make any move to help me either. I didn't want him to. The time for being weak was past.

I reached the salon that took up the back of Jo-Jo's house, and my eyes swept over the familiar furnishings. Cherry-red salon chairs. Stacks of magazines everywhere. Combs, scissors, curlers, and dozens of other beauty tools on the counters. Bottles of pink nail polish and matching lipsticks cluttered together. It was all as familiar to me as my own face, and I drank in the scene, grateful I'd survived another battle I shouldn't have.

Then I focused on the two men in the middle of the room. Finn and Owen stood toe-to-toe, their eyes bright, their bodies tense, and their faces flushed with anger, while Eva, Cooper, and Bria sat in the chairs behind them. The men's shouts had woken Rosco, Jo-Jo's tubby basset hound, who eyed them with lazy disinterest from his wicker basket in the corner.

Footsteps padded in the hallway behind me, and Jo-Jo came to stand beside me in the doorway, her perfume filling my nose with its soft scent.

Salina might pretend to be a genteel Southern lady, but Jolene "Jo-Jo" Deveraux was the real deal. She wore one of her many pink flowered dresses topped off by her usual string of pearls. Everything about her whispered of feminine poise, from the white-blond hair that was artfully curled over her forehead to the perfect makeup that softened the lines of her face to the effortless way she seemed to glide as she walked. Jo-Jo might have recently turned two hundred fifty-seven, but she was aging gracefully.

"How long have they been like this?" I asked her.

Jo-Jo glanced at a clock that was shaped like her puffy cloud rune, mounted on the back wall. "Ten minutes now. Apparently, Finn wants to kill Salina as soon as he can find her, while Owen at least wants to see if she'll surrender peaceably."

I was of the same mind Finn was, but I could understand where Owen was coming from. He'd once loved Salina, had wanted to marry her. It was hard to let go of those feelings, even now, when he knew exactly what she'd become—or maybe what she'd always been.

I might understand, yes, but that didn't mean that I wasn't seriously pissed about it. The bitch had tried to kill me—Cooper too—and yet here Owen was, still trying to protect her. What was wrong with him? Anger surged through me, along with doubt, worry, and fear. Not so much that Salina might kill me, but that she was going to be the death of me and Owen—of *us*. Try as I might, I just couldn't shake the feeling that Owen and I were headed for disaster, courtesy of Salina—and what I was planning to do to her.

At the sound of Jo-Jo's footsteps, Rosco peered in our direction, hoping she had a treat for him. The basset hound gave a happy woof at the sight of me, and his tail thumped against the side of his basket. Then he turned in Finn and Owen's direction and let out a low whine. Their argument had interrupted Rosco's nap, and it was obvious he wanted them to shut up so he could get back to it, pronto. Couldn't blame him for that. I'd only been in the room a minute, and their sharp voices had already given me a headache.

"Enough," I said.

Finn and Owen kept arguing, with Eva occasionally putting in her two cents for good measure. Cooper sat silent. I looked at him, and he shrugged his shoulders.

"Enough!" I repeated, raising my voice.

Finn and Owen were too intent on yelling at each other to hear me, so I did something Sophia had taught me—I put my fingers between my lips and let out a loud, earsplitting whistle. That got them to shut up and look at me in surprise.

"Morning, boys," I drawled.

For a moment, the two of them just stared at me. Finn recovered first. He usually did.

"I'm not sure how much of that you heard, but *he*"—Finn stabbed his finger at Owen—"actually wants to give that water elemental bitch a chance to explain herself. Apparently, he wants to know exactly *why* she tried to kill you, other than the fact that she's just mean as a snake and bat-shit crazy to boot."

Owen bristled. "That wasn't my point at all, and you know it."

Finn glared at my lover, but Owen ignored him and looked at me.

"My point was that Salina needs help," he said in a quiet voice. "She wasn't always the way . . . she is now. I want to at least give her a chance to do the right thing."

I thought the right thing for Salina involved stabbing her repeatedly with one of my knives and then slitting her throat for good measure, but I wasn't going to tell Owen that.

"Why don't you all leave us alone for a few minutes?" I said. "Owen and I have some things we need to discuss."

Finn shot Owen another hot glare, but he stormed out of the salon. Eva got to her feet and followed him, with Kincaid trailing along behind her. Cooper stood as well, walked across the room, and held his arm out to Jo-Jo, who blushed a little.

"My, what a gentleman you are," Jo-Jo said in a soft voice.

"I do try," Cooper said. "Especially with a pretty lady who saved my life."

Jo-Jo blushed a little more at that. So she had healed

Cooper with her Air magic too. Good. I was glad that Owen's mentor was okay, although I didn't know quite what to make of his shameless flirting with her.

Jo-Jo saw me looking at them and grinned. She let out a low whistle, and Rosco lurched up out of his basket and trotted after her, in hopes of getting a treat after all. Cooper leaned down to pet the dog, then the three of them set off down the hallway.

Bria stood up and came over to me. My sister gave me a critical once-over, then leaned forward and hugged me.

"I'm glad you're okay," she whispered.

I tightened my arms and returned her hug. "Me too."

She drew back. "What do you want to do about Salina? Cooper said he'd press charges against her, so I can arrest her for what she did to him."

I didn't want Bria anywhere near Salina and her magic, but I knew my sister was just trying to do her job. "I appreciate that, and I'm sure Cooper does too, but let me talk to Owen first, okay?"

She nodded, hugged me again, and left the salon.

Once she was gone, I shut the door for privacy. Then I turned to face my lover.

"So," I said. "Salina."

"Yeah, Salina."

Owen ran a hand through his hair and started pacing back and forth. I walked over, sat down in one of the padded chairs, and watched him. Waiting, just waiting, for him to let me in, to tell me exactly what was going on inside his head and his heart too—and wondering whether or not I'd like what he had to say.

I wondered if this was how Owen had felt when I'd

seen Donovan again. If he'd felt the same ugly pressure in his chest, the same paralyzing fear, the same sharp, niggling worry that the harder I tried to hold on to him, the faster I was losing him to Salina.

Not only was she stunningly beautiful and strong in her magic, but she was sly. To Owen, Salina had always presented a sweet, innocent, beguiling face, at least until today, but to everyone else, she had eventually showed her true, deadly nature. It was a sticky web she'd caught Owen in, pitting his feelings for her against how she'd hurt the people he cared about most. I wasn't sure if my lover could ever fully untangle himself from her and what she'd once meant to him—or if he even really wanted to deep down inside.

The idea of losing Owen scared the hell out of me, but I forced myself to stay calm and listen to what he had to say.

He finally stopped pacing and looked at me. "What Salina did to you and Cooper was terrible. And what she did to Eva and Phillip all those years ago is simply inexcusable. I know how you want to handle it now, and I can't say I blame you. If Donovan had done to me what Salina did to you, I'd take my blacksmith's hammer to the bastard's knees before I used it to cave in his skull."

I didn't respond.

"But she needs help, Gin. I wish you could have known her before Mab murdered her father. She was different then."

I wanted to point out that Mab had murdered my family too and that I hadn't let it turn me into a monster—at least not as much of one as Salina. I might have been an assassin, but I could keep my rage in check, whereas the water elemental couldn't, and I didn't blame people for things that weren't their fault. Most importantly, I didn't go around hurting innocent people.

But I kept those thoughts to myself. Instead, I just looked at my lover, that calm expression still fixed on my face. "What exactly are you proposing?"

"I want to go talk to Salina and get her to check herself into a facility."

As the Spider I'd once done a hit inside the confines of Ashland Asylum, and I'd have been quite happy knowing Salina was locked up there. In fact, there was no place I'd rather have seen Salina—except in the ground. But Owen was asking me for a chance. I owed him that.

"And if she doesn't agree?" I asked. "What happens if Salina doesn't want to get help?"

Owen's body swelled with tension, and a bit of fire flashed in his violet eyes. "Then I'll kill her myself for what she's done to you, Eva, Cooper, and Phillip. She either gets help, or she gets dead. Is that something you can live with?"

I would have skipped the getting help part and gone straight to getting dead, but I couldn't deny Owen what he was asking. I didn't want him anywhere near Salina, but I couldn't stop him from going, not without being a total hypocrite. Not after everything he'd seen and watched me do these past few months. Owen hadn't batted an eye at my killings. The least I could do was give him one more chance to get Salina under control before I plunged my knife into her heart.

I sighed. "I don't like it, but I understand why you

have to do it. But I have one condition—we go talk to her together."

Owen opened his mouth to protest, but I cut him off.

"No, I don't trust her, especially not with you. You saw her when she was attacking Cooper. How happy it made her to hurt him. You don't know that Salina won't turn on you too, especially given what you're asking her to do."

He shook his head. "She won't hurt me. Trust me. I know Salina better than anyone."

I wanted to point out how wrong he was. How he hadn't known what Salina was capable of when they were younger and that she'd likely only gotten crueler and more vicious over the years. But once again I held my tongue. Owen had stood by me plenty of times when I'd gone into dangerous situations, and he'd always let me do what I thought needed to be done. I had to do the same for him now. Besides, this way, I'd be there to protect him—and stop her for good.

"Okay," he finally said. "We'll go see her together."

Owen got down on his knees in front of my chair. He reached over and grabbed my hands, his fingers warm and rough against my own. Then he turned my palms up and slowly, gently, traced over my spider rune scars with his thumbs. He kissed first one palm and then the other, and I shivered at the feel of his lips on my skin.

"Thank you for understanding," he said. "For giving me this chance. It means more to me than you know."

Emotion clogged my throat, and I leaned forward and wrapped my arms around Owen, burying my face in his neck and breathing in his rich scent. I knew I had to let my lover speak his piece to Salina, but I also knew how things would play out—with me and Salina fighting to the death.

I only hoped I'd be the one standing in the end, and that Owen could forgive me for killing his first love.

❖ 26 ❖

Eventually, Owen and I broke apart. I opened the door, and we went out into the kitchen.

A butcher-block table with several stools stood in the middle of the room, while appliances done in soft pastel shades ringed the walls. Fat, puffy clouds—Jo-Jo's rune and the symbol for her Air magic—covered almost everything in the kitchen, from the oven mitts piled next to the stove to a set of plates stacked in the sink to the fresco that stretched across the ceiling. Jo-Jo and Eva sat at the table drinking pineapple juice, while Finn was over at the counter, brewing himself a fresh pot of chicory coffee.

"Where are the others?" I asked.

"Bria had to get to the police station," Jo-Jo replied. "She said she'd call and check in with you later. Phillip left too. Said he had some things to do on that riverboat of his. Cooper went with him to keep him company—although he's going to call me later on today."

I arched an eyebrow. "Do I sense a little romance in the air?"

"I just want to make sure that he's all healed up properly," Jo-Jo said, blushing again. "Besides, he's a true Southern gentleman. It's hard to find one of those these days."

I knew that Jo-Jo wouldn't have let Cooper leave if she hadn't completely healed him already, but I didn't tease her anymore. Instead, I nodded and headed over to the cabinets. My fight with Salina and worry over Owen had taken a lot out of me, and I was in the mood for some comfort food. So I grabbed all the fixings for a classic Southern breakfast—biscuits and gravy.

Flour, fresh buttermilk, and just a pinch of sugar and salt went into my biscuit dough, while I put a cast-iron pan into the oven to heat the shortening I'd coated it with. Once the shortening was melted, I cut the biscuit dough into rounds, coated both sides with the liquefied shortening, arranged them in the pan, and then slid the whole thing into the oven to bake. I also fried up some salty country ham, using the grease and drippings that were left in the pan, along with some evaporated milk and a generous dash of black pepper, to make my gravy.

Thirty minutes later, I slid the hot biscuits onto a plate and ladled the gravy into one of Jo-Jo's cloud-shaped serving bowls. We all gathered around the table and dug into my greasy feast. Yeah, it wasn't exactly health food, but the biscuits were light and fluffy and made a perfect base for the flavorful gravy.

"So," Finn drawled when everyone had finished eating, "what did the two of you decide to do about sweet, sweet Salina?"

Owen looked at me, then at everyone else in turn. "Gin and I are going to talk to her and try to convince her to get some help."

Eva's fork slipped from her fingers and clattered onto her plate. Her eyes snapped up to mine, and she gave me a sharp, angry look. I could see the accusation in her pretty face. She thought I'd betrayed her, that I was going back on my promise to kill Salina. She just didn't realize that I was only delaying the water elemental's death, nothing more.

My promise to Eva. Trying to understand Owen's feelings. Salina and her deadly magic. In a way, I had just as much of a noose around my neck as Kincaid had that night on the *Delta Queen*. A noose that was slowly tightening as a final battle with Salina became more and more inevitable—and there wasn't a damn thing I could do about it. If I didn't kill Salina, it was only a matter of time before she hurt someone else. And if I did take her out, it would impact my relationship with Owen—maybe even end it.

Eva, Owen, and Salina had all given me enough rope. All that remained to be seen now was when I was going to hang myself with it.

"I've got to get to class," Eva muttered, pushing her plate away. "Thanks for the juice, Jo-Jo."

"Anytime, darling."

Eva got to her feet and stomped out of the kitchen. A few seconds later, I heard the front door slam shut.

Owen sighed. "Sorry about that. I'll go talk to her."

My lover hurried out of the kitchen, leaving me, Finn, and Jo-Jo sitting at the table. My foster brother glared at me with the same fierce expression Eva had.

"You can't be serious, Gin. Salina tried to kill you, and you're going to go *talk* to her? In case you've forgotten, you're the Spider. You don't talk to people—you kill them. I'll ask you the same thing I did Owen. Are you out of your mind?"

"No, I'm not out of my mind. Owen asked me for this," I said. "He wants to give Salina one more chance, and I'm going to respect his wishes. He would do the same for me. Hell, he *did* do the same for me with Donovan."

Finn shook his head. "No, it's not the same thing. Not at all. Donovan just had a stick up his ass about you being an assassin. Salina likes to use her water magic to torture people. They are two very, very different things."

I could argue with him until I was blue in the face, and Finnegan Lane would still out-talk me, especially in this case, when we both knew he was right. So I decided to switch tactics.

"Forget about killing Salina for a second. I need you to look into something else for me," I said. "Cooper said that someone had stolen several fountains off his property. Fountains that had been commissioned a few months ago by a guy named Henley."

Finn's eyes narrowed. "One of Salina's husbands was named Henley. Her last husband, as a matter of fact. The one she killed a few months ago."

I nodded. "So I'm guessing she got him to order the fountains so Cooper wouldn't realize they were really for her. He wouldn't have made them otherwise. Then, instead of paying for them, she got her giant bodyguards to steal them, possibly out of spite and so she could thumb her nose at Cooper. But that's still a lot of trouble to go to. I think there's something else going on. I want to know what's so important about those fountains."

"I'm on it," Finn said, pulling his cell phone out of the pocket of his suit jacket and hitting some numbers.

While he reached out to his contacts, I gathered up the remains of our breakfast. I scraped a few leftovers into Rosco's bowl, then put the dirty dishes into the sink. Jo-Jo brought her plate over to the counter, and she got out some towels to dry the dishes as I washed them.

"I know you're worried about Salina," Jo-Jo said. "And Owen too."

I shrugged. "I only see this ending one way—with me killing Salina, or Salina killing me. She's not going to get treatment, or whatever Owen thinks. Roslyn told me that Salina was cruel even before her father died, and I think she full-on snapped the night Mab murdered him."

I told Jo-Jo about Fletcher's files and how they had triggered my dreams, my memories, of that night.

When I finished, she nodded and stared at me with her clear, almost colorless eyes. "That would be more than enough to scar anyone for life. Deep down, I think Owen realizes that Salina, or at least the girl he remembers her being, is gone. But he cared for her once, and he doesn't want to see her dead, even if he knows she's brought it on herself."

"I know, and it's one of the things I love about him . . . even though I have a feeling it's going to tear us apart in the end. Kincaid asked me to kill Salina, and Eva begged me to. I promised her, so that she wouldn't go after Salina herself. Now I don't know what to do."

"It'll be all right, darling," Jo-Jo murmured, reaching over to pat my hand. "You'll see. Everything will work out the way it's supposed to."

Faint, milky white clouds wisped through the dwarf's eyes, and I got the sense that she wasn't seeing me anymore. Jo-Jo had a bit of precognition. Most Air elementals did, since the wind whispered to them of all the things that might be, all the actions people might take, those events that might come to pass whether folks wanted them to or not. I wondered what Jo-Jo saw when she looked into Owen's future, but I didn't dare ask. I didn't want her to tell me I wasn't a part of it.

We split up. Eva left to go to her classes, Finn went out and about to see what his contacts had to say, and Jo-Jo geared up for a busy day at the salon.

Owen drove me over to his house. He insisted on tucking me into his bed, despite the fact it was after eleven and the day was already turning warm. He sat down next to me.

"I would offer to fix you breakfast in bed, but you took care of that already this morning," he joked.

I laughed. "It's okay. You know how much I enjoy cooking. It's therapy for me, as much as anything else."

"I know." Owen's face turned serious. "I'm sorry for what Salina did to you, Gin. Sorrier than you will ever know. But I'm glad you're going to let me talk to her, to give her one more chance."

I didn't say anything. I didn't trust myself to speak where Salina was concerned. Not right now, not to Owen. The last thing I wanted to do was push him away, but I knew that was what would happen if I told him Salina had run out of chances.

"Thank you for that, Gin."

Owen leaned forward and pressed his lips to mine. He started to pull back, but I deepened the kiss, drawing him closer to me. He hesitated, but his hands began to slide over my body in that strong, confident, familiar way that always made me shiver with anticipation.

"You should rest," he said.

"I feel fine now," I whispered against his mouth. "In fact, I want to show you exactly how fine."

I wrapped my arms around Owen and pulled him down on top of me. We took things slow and easy. We lay there on the bed for a long time, just kissing, our mouths pressed together, our tongues flicking back and forth, our hands gliding, gliding everywhere, just letting the need, the desire, build one soft kiss, one gentle caress, at a time.

But what started as a slow, simmering burn of want quickly escalated into hot, liquid, aching need. We undressed each other, and Owen grabbed a condom out of the nightstand drawer. I took my little white pills, but we always used extra protection.

We lay back down on the bed together and continued with our explorations. No matter how much I touched him, I always wanted more. I marveled at the feel of Owen's firm body under my hands, at the strength in his muscles, and the ever-quickening *thump-thump-thump* of his heart as he responded to my caresses. Owen lay back and let me take the lead. I pressed my fingers into his skin, kneading his warm muscles and trying to ease the tension in him—the tension we both felt.

When he was relaxed, I made my touch softer and lighter, more playful and teasing. A kiss here, a lick of my tongue there, a gentle nip or two with my teeth as I worked my way down his body.

I took him in my mouth, making my caresses hard, then soft, then harder still, until his eyes burned violet, and he trembled beneath me. But every time Owen was ready to let go, I brought him back down, just a little bit, before amping up his need once more.

Again and again, I did this. Hard, then soft. Quick, then slow. Playful, then seductive. I used every trick I knew to bring my lover as much pleasure as possible. Maybe it was selfish, but I wanted him to remember this. I wanted him to remember the way I made him feel and how good we were together. I wanted to do everything in my power to erase the memory of Salina from his body, his mind, and most especially his heart.

I *needed* to do it in a way I never had before.

"Gin," Owen rasped, the raw, aching desire apparent in his voice. "Gin."

I grabbed the condom from where he'd placed it on the nightstand and unrolled it over him, still teasing, still caressing, still sliding my fingers over him.

But Owen had other ideas. He reached up and drew me down on top of him. He crushed his mouth to mine and plunged a finger deep inside me. I gasped as he stroked me, hard then soft, fast then slow, over and over again until I was shuddering with the same pleasure he was.

"Two can play this game," Owen murmured in a sly, satisfied voice. "I don't know about you, but it's one of my very favorite games. I love the way you respond to me. I love the way you feel against me."

All I could do was clutch his shoulders and ride the wave of desire pulsing through me.

But it wasn't enough, and I rose up above him, then sank down, taking him deep inside me. Owen's hands wrapped around my hips, and he urged me on, urged me to give us both the pleasure we wanted, the pleasure we needed.

I took him deeper and rode him harder until we were locked together as tightly, as closely, as two people could be. The whole bed shook with our frenzied movements, and, still, it wasn't enough.

And when we finally reached that sweet, sweet pinnacle of pleasure, we exploded over the edge together—our desire finally satisfied and perhaps our hearts a little lighter too.

At least for this moment.

I must have been more worn out than I'd thought, because sometime after Owen and I finished making love, I fell asleep, nestled in his strong arms. My eyes still closed, I stretched, feeling completely, happily sated, and reached over for him. I didn't know about Owen, but I was ready for round two, maybe three—

Instead of the warm body I'd expected to find, my hands only met empty air and cold sheets.

My eyes snapped open. "Owen?"

No response.

I sat up, but my lover wasn't in the bedroom or the adjoining bathroom. He was probably just somewhere else in the mansion, snacking in the kitchen maybe. Still, something about the silence seemed ominous.

I picked up my clothes from where they had fallen onto the floor and quickly dressed. I left the bedroom and went to Owen's office, with its wall of weapons, but he wasn't there. The foreboding feeling welled up inside me like a storm cloud gathering strength. I searched the rest of the first floor of the mansion, but he was nowhere to be seen.

Finally, I came across Eva sitting at the kitchen table, a piece of paper in her hand and a stricken look on her face.

"Eva? What's wrong?"

She looked at me, and somehow I knew what she was going to say even before the words left her mouth.

"It's Owen. He's gone."

* 27 *

I frowned. "Gone? What do you mean Owen's gone?"

She waved the paper at me. "I mean I came home from class, and I found this on the kitchen table. Here. Read it for yourself."

I took it from her and realized that it was actually expensive stationery. The cream-colored paper smelled faintly of a sweet, cloying, floral scent—and it had Salina's mermaid rune embossed in blue-green ink across the top. But it was the handwritten message below that chilled me to the bone.

Darling Owen,
We need to talk about us. Come to my dinner party tonight, and I'll show you the marvelous plans I've made for us, for all of Ashland. Black tie dress only. And come alone— or your whore of an assassin dies.
XOXO
Salina

I didn't know what was more disturbing—the fact that Salina had threatened to kill me or that she'd signed the letter like a love-struck teenage girl. Then again, that was what she was when it came to Owen—obsessed and determined to get him back no matter what. I couldn't help but think that if Salina couldn't have Owen, then she would be more than happy to make sure that no one had him, especially me.

And Owen had walked right into her sticky web once more. I knew he'd gone to the water elemental to protect me from her threat, even if it meant putting himself in harm's way, but anger spiked through me just the same, that he'd left without telling me what was going on. Owen thought he could get through to Salina, that he could convince her get help, but he was wrong. I just hoped I could get to him in time—and bury the bitch once and for all.

"Damn and double damn," I cursed. "When did you find this?"

"About five minutes ago. His car was pulling out when I was coming in."

I looked at the clock on the wall. I'd fallen asleep in Owen's arms around one, and it was after seven. No doubt Owen was on his way to Salina's estate right now. I cursed again.

"I told you," Eva said in a cold, accusing voice. "I warned you about Salina—and Owen too."

I sighed. "Yes, you did. Don't worry, Eva. I'm going after Owen. I'll get him back—"

The front door of the mansion banged open.

"Are you expecting Violet or one of your other friends?" I asked in a low voice, already moving toward the butcher block on the counter and grabbing two of the knives there. I'd left my weapons in the bedroom when I'd come searching for Owen.

Eva shook her head, her eyes wide. I gestured for her to get down on the far side of the kitchen table, where she'd be out of sight, while I crept up to the doorway, ready to deal with whomever had decided to barge in unannounced. No matter what her note said, no matter what she promised him, I wouldn't put it past Salina to lure Owen away from the mansion and send some of her giant bodyguards to try to take me—or even Eva—out.

Loud, quick footsteps sounded in the hall, heading in our direction. My hands tightened around the knives, ready to cut down whomever was coming my way—

Finn hurried into the kitchen, walking right by my hiding spot, a thick manila folder in his hand. "Gin! Gin, are you here?"

"Right behind you," I said.

Finn shrieked and whirled around. I winced at the high-pitched sound.

"Dammit, woman." He clutched the folder to his chest. "Are you trying to give me a heart attack?"

"No, but it serves you right for walking in here unannounced. Come on out, Eva. It's just Finn."

Eva got to her feet and gave my foster brother an amused look. Finn winced, realizing she'd heard him shriek, but he still gave her a saucy wink anyway. He was rather incorrigible that way.

I stepped around him and slid the knives back into their slots in the butcher block. "Next time, I'd knock, if I were you. You almost got stabbed."

He shook his head. "That's the least of my problems right now. And yours too."

"What do you mean?"

Finn turned his green eyes to mine, concern and worry etching lines into his handsome face. "I finally figured out what was so important about those fountains. Salina stole them, all right, and I know exactly what she's going to do with them."

I frowned. "What? And why do you look so grim about it?"

"Because it's a trap," he said. "Salina's dinner party for the underworld muckety-mucks? It's nothing but a giant death trap."

"What do you mean?" I asked.

"I mean, Salina's gunning for everyone who shows up to her dinner tonight," Finn said.

I shook my head. "But how could she do that? From what you said earlier, Salina invited everyone who's anyone to the dinner. At a big to-do like that, all the crime bosses will have their bodyguards with them, and everyone will be on their best behavior. They'll all be sizing up Salina and each other, trying to figure out how she fits into things, but they won't make a move against each other. There's too much danger of it turning into a bloodbath otherwise."

Finn nodded. "And that's exactly why it's a trap. I was reviewing the information you had me dig up on Salina, comparing it with that old file of Dad's that you found, and I noticed something strange about the guest list for the dinner tonight."

"What?"

He pulled two pieces of paper out of his folder and spread them on the table in front of Eva. "Look at these, and see for yourself."

I stepped over and scanned the names on the lists. It only took me a few seconds to see what Finn was getting at. "Almost all the names are the same. They're even arranged in the same order. The only reason I can tell the one on the right is the new list for tonight is because I see Kincaid's name there on the bottom, along with those of some of the newer bosses in town. But still, it's just a list."

Finn tapped his finger on the paper on the right. "It may be just a list to you and me, but I'm thinking it's a little something more than that to Salina. This is the list of all the guests who were at the estate the night Mab killed Benedict Dubois."

"So what?" Eva asked, jumping into the conversation. "If Salina's trying to establish herself as the new Mab, these are the people she'd invite to her dinner, right? They're the ones with all the money, magic, and power, the people she wants to impress and get in good with."

"You're right, and she would have to do that," Finn said. "But this is where the fountains come in, all those fountains Salina had her giants steal from Cooper. The ones she got her dead husband to commission for her. Turns out Salina has been doing quite a bit of work out at the old Dubois estate, sprucing it up, updating, modernizing, and renovating everything."

"So what?" Eva asked again.

"Well, it just so happens that one of the new features she's had installed is a series of fountains. . . ." He pulled a map of the Dubois estate out of his folder and spread it out on the table so Eva and I could get a better look at it. "Right here, on the north lawn."

"So?" Eva asked for the third time. "What's so unusual about that?"

"For starters," Finn said, "there's already a series of fountains on the north lawn. It's costing Salina a small fortune to get even more installed just where she wants them. *And* she specified that the job had to be done by yesterday. But most telling? The north lawn happens to be the very place where dear old dad was murdered all those years ago—and where she's set up the dinner for tonight."

I thought about all the things Salina had said to me over the past few days. All the sly hints she'd dropped that she was in Ashland to pay back her old friends and any-one else who'd ever supposedly wronged her. All the com-ments about taking her father's place in the underworld. Even the mention of the future in her note to Owen. I thought that Salina had just been talking out of her ass with her delusions of grandeur, but I was beginning to get an idea of what the water elemental had in mind—and of just how devious she really was.

"She's going to kill them all," I said.

Finn gave me a grim look. "That's what I think too."

"What do you mean?" Eva asked. "How is she going to kill them all? Salina might be strong in her magic, but there's no way she can take on every single person on this list. Not if they're all bringing their bodyguards with them. And some of them are elementals too, or vampires or giants or dwarves."

"She's going to use the fountains to supplement her own magic," I said. "She'll use the water in them to put down anyone who challenges her. Salina's going to take her revenge on all the folks who stood by and watched Mab murder her father all those years ago. That's why she really invited them to her estate tonight—to finally get her revenge."

That also explained why she'd invited Kincaid and even me—so she could kill us along with everyone else.

"And while she's at it, she'll take out everybody who's anybody in the underworld," Finn added, "clearing the way for her to take control of all the crime in the city. Two birds, one stone. You gotta admit that it's brilliant, in a completely sociopathic sort of way."

Brilliant? No, it was ingenious. Whatever else she was, Salina was exceptionally clever. She was going to lure all the crime bosses onto her turf, ply them with food and booze, then turn on the waterworks when they were too drunk and full to defend themselves. The folks at the party wouldn't even know what hit them. With all those fountains, Salina could saturate the whole area with water. Then it would just be a matter of using her elemental magic to either suck the moisture out of people or drown them with all the water that would be available.

And Owen was on his way to her estate right now.

I had no doubt my lover would try to stop Salina, once he realized what she was doing. But by then, it would be too late for everyone—including Owen. He might not think Salina would turn on him, but I knew she would if he got in her way.

I immediately pulled my cell phone out of my jeans pocket and dialed Owen's number, but for once he didn't answer. Probably because he knew I'd be upset with him for leaving me to go see her.

"Dammit, Owen!" I snarled.

"What's going on?" Finn asked. "Where is he?"

Eva passed Finn the invitation Salina had sent Owen. Finn let out a loud curse.

I dialed Owen's number again. Once again, he didn't pick up. I knew that he wouldn't until he'd confronted Salina.

"There's no use trying that," Finn said. "If he's already at the estate, he won't get your call anyway. Among the many things that Salina has had delivered to her mansion in recent days is a series of cell phone jammers. No calls in, none get out. There's no way to warn anyone who's there."

I threw my phone across the kitchen. It hit the refrigerator and clattered to the floor. Emotion surged through me, and I wanted to go over and stomp on it until there was nothing left but tiny plastic pieces. I drew in a breath and forced myself to calm down, to go to that cold, calm, dark place where the Spider dwelt, as I had so many times before. Slowly, my emotions receded, leaving nothing behind but the black determination that beat in my heart to end Salina—once and for all.

I looked at Finn. "What kind of gear do you have in your car?"

"Enough. When I realized what Salina was planning, I grabbed everything I could get my hands on. I stopped by Dad's and got a few things for you, too. I'm loaded for bear."

"Good. Let me get my knives."

I started to head back to the bedroom, but Eva planted herself in front of me, her blue eyes flashing.

"I'm coming with you."

I sighed. "Eva—"

"No," she said, her hands clenching into fists. "Don't you dare tell me that I don't know what I'm doing or that it's too dangerous. Owen is my brother, and I can't just sit here and do nothing while he's in danger. Besides, this is my fight too. It was my fight before it was ever yours, Gin. I want to help you finish it for Owen's sake—for all our sakes."

I stared at her. Eva might only have been nineteen, but she'd been through a lot in her life. The death of her parents, living on the streets, being tortured by Salina, and now this. She was right. This was her fight too, even more than it was mine, and I'd be damned if I'd keep her from it.

"All right," I said, drawing in a breath. "Here's what we're going to do."

❖ 28 ❖

An hour later, just after eight o'clock, I slipped onto the Dubois estate.

The mansion was situated on a high bluff, and a set of stone steps led from it down to a large boathouse along the Aneirin River. I'd had Finn drop me off at a nearby bridge, then I'd hiked along the riverbank until I came to the steps. After that, it was just a matter of climbing up them, keeping an eye out for any wandering guards, and slipping into the woods at the top of the bluff. There weren't even any security cameras for me to avoid. No motion sensors. No explosive runes hidden in the steps. No magical trip-wires strung in between the trees in the woods. Lax security all the way around. Then again, Salina *wanted* people to come to her estate—she just didn't plan on them ever leaving again.

Now I was hidden in the trees, dressed in my usual

black clothes, and looking at the landscape through a pair of high-powered binoculars.

The woods bordered the north lawn, and I scanned the spectacle before me. I had to hand it to Salina—she'd gone all out. Tables covered with blue-green linens had been set up on the lawn, and I could see the glitter of crystal and silver on them, along with the faint flickers of lit candles. She'd even sprung for a couple of bars made of elemental Ice. Sharp peaks had been carved into the surface of the Ice, representing water, waves, and the ocean, along with Salina's mermaid rune. I eyed one of the grinning mermaids through my binoculars. Deadly beauty, indeed.

According to the information Finn had gathered, the dinner wasn't supposed to officially start until eight thirty, but a crowd had already gathered on the smooth grass. The men wore tuxes, while the women were dressed in evening gowns. Even from here, I could hear whispers from the gemstones the partygoers wore, as the jewels vainly murmured of their own faceted beauty.

I'd been right when I'd told Finn that all the power players would bring their bodyguards. Men and women wearing suits that obviously concealed guns could be seen among the glitterati. Most of them were giants, but there were a few dwarves, vamps, elementals, and humans in the mix too. All of them stayed close to their bosses and eyed the other guards with cold, hostile intent. Everyone was on their best behavior, and it was obvious they didn't like it one bit.

Waiters moved through the crowd, bearing trays of bite-size food, while several men and women worked the bars, pouring drinks as fast as they could. A couple of them were Ice elementals whose job was to keep the curved monstrosities from melting in the May heat. Their eyes flashed blue and white in the twilight as they held on to their magic.

But the fountains were what caught and held my attention.

There were seven of them, all featuring different shapes, all with a water theme. One fountain was relatively flat, with metal water lilies spiraling out from the edge, as if the flowers were really floating on the surface instead of being anchored in place. Another fountain featured metal koi half in and half out of the water, spewing steady streams of it up into the air. The other sculptures featured more fish and flowers, along with a few abstract designs. They were all beautiful, and I could tell that Cooper had crafted them with the same care he did everything else he made.

I focused on the largest fountain, the centerpiece of the lawn. It was another fucking mermaid sitting on a pile of rocks and grinning. Only her long, flowing, metal hair covered the mermaid's lush body, and she had her finger crooked out, inviting folks to come and take a closer look at her, not realizing that she was really luring them to their deaths with her shy, sweet, beguiling smile. Just like Salina had duped her guests into coming here tonight.

Finn had been right about what Salina wanted the fountains for. They were arranged in a wide circle, with all the tables and people situated in between them and the Ice bars filling in some of the wider gaps between the fountains. A kill zone if I ever saw one. Given Salina's magic, she could easily flood the whole area with water from the fountains, then let loose with her elemental power. No one would get out unless she wanted them to—and I doubted she'd offer anyone that mercy.

Eyeing the fountains, I wondered how long Salina would let the water just bubble, foam, and froth away before reaching for it and transforming the rippling surfaces into something deadly. Before finally taking the revenge she'd waited so long for.

On the ground beside me, my walkie-talkie crackled, and I heard a loud sigh.

"Do we have to do it this way?" Finn asked through the walkie-talkie for the fifth time since I'd gotten into position.

I didn't know how he'd done it on such short notice, but my foster brother had scrounged up a set that would work despite Salina's cell phone jammers. He'd even brought along a few tiny spy cams, which I'd hidden in the trees and pointed at the lawn so Finn could see what was happening there through a feed to his laptop.

"Yes," I replied. "We have to do it this way. Unless you have another idea for getting past that gate on such short notice?"

I looked off to my left. A ten-foot-high stone wall ringed the Dubois estate, typical for this part of Northtown. Several limos and town cars sat on the street outside the gate, the drivers waiting to take their bosses home later that night. It seemed like all of Salina's guests had already arrived, and the wide iron gate in the middle of the wall had been shut to keep any party crashers out—and everyone else in, even if they didn't realize it yet.

The plan was simple. I'd sneak into the mansion, find Owen and get him out of here, grab Kincaid on my way out, then go back and deal with Salina. If she made a move before then, Finn was going to crank the engine on his Escalade, zoom toward the gate from his position across the street, crash through the iron bars, and drive across the lawn to where the dinner was being held. Hopefully, the crowd would scatter in confusion and give my foster brother a clean shot at the water elemental with one of his omnipresent guns. If not, I'd take her down with my knives. Win-win, either way.

"But my car," Finn muttered. "Why do we always have to wreck *my* car?"

"It's not like you don't have another Escalade in your fleet. You'll barely notice the scratches on this one," I said, attempting to soothe his ruffled feathers.

"Hmph," he harrumphed in my ear. "Believe me, I'll notice. I just think you like destroying my cars on purpose. First, you get my new Aston Martin all scratched up and beat to hell, and now you want me to ram my Escalade through an iron gate. It's unseemly, I tell you. *Unseemly.*"

I rolled my eyes. "Oh yes. You've caught me. I confess. My sole purpose in life is to gleefully, willfully, maniacally destroy all of your precious chrome babies."

"I knew it!"

"What about Bria?" I asked, distracting him.

"She's on her way, along with Xavier and some other members of the po-po. Are you sure you don't want to wait for her?"

"Yes, I'm sure. If Salina sees the cops, she might decide

to start the show early. I doubt she'd have any qualms about killing the fine boys in blue along with everyone else. I at least need to get Owen and Kincaid away from her first before anyone goes in guns blazing. Just keep watch, and be ready if it looks like I'm in trouble."

"Roger that."

"Eva? How are you holding up?" I asked.

I heard Finn pass the walkie-talkie over Eva, who was in the car with him. I hadn't been able to stop her from coming, but I'd made sure she was on the outside looking in and well away from Salina and the danger the water elemental posed.

"I'm fine, but I'll be better when that bitch is dead. You promised me, Gin. You *promised*."

"I know," I said in a soft voice. "But I promised Owen too."

Eva sighed. "But he has such a blind spot when it comes to Salina. He always has."

I didn't tell Eva that I was planning to end that blind spot tonight—permanently. She knew as well as I did that Salina had to be put down. All that remained to be seen now was what Owen would think of me after the fact.

I looked through the binoculars a final time, then put them into the sack of supplies I'd grabbed from Finn's car. I pulled a few things out of the bag, including some extra knives, and slid them into the pockets on my vest, before hiding the bag in a pile of leaves. As a final touch, I picked up a long staff that Finn had gotten when he'd swung by Fletcher's house earlier—a staff that hummed with my Ice magic.

A few weeks ago, I'd used the staff to defeat Randall

Dekes, a nasty vampire who'd wanted to keep me as his pet. Dekes had stolen my magic by forcibly drinking my blood, but I'd tricked him into using my own power against me, and I'd had the staff ready when he did. Since the staff was made of silverstone, it had absorbed all the magic Dekes had thrown at me. Even now, all these weeks later, the metal felt cold to the touch.

My silverstone knives also contained my Ice magic, from my fights with both Dekes and Mab before him, and they were my backup plan, just in case I couldn't overcome Salina with the power within the staff. But if that was the case, I'd probably already be dead. Salina wouldn't be giving me second chances to kill her.

"All right," I said. "Stand by. I'm going in."

"Good luck," Eva whispered back.

I tucked the walkie-talkie into another pocket on my vest. I didn't tell her that I was wishing for every scrap of luck I could get tonight—and then some. We all knew what was at stake.

Fortunately, the area between the woods and the lawn was still a bit overgrown from all the years of neglect during Salina's absence, and several large holly and rhododendron bushes had sprang up, providing plenty of cover. I crept from the shadow of one bush to another, easing closer and closer to the mansion. I hadn't spotted Owen in the crowd with my binoculars, so I had to assume he was already inside—and that Salina was with him, since she hadn't put in an appearance yet.

The staff made it difficult to be as invisible as I wanted to be, since it was such a large weapon and the silverstone

that it was made of gleamed in the sunset. But the movers
and shakers were busy bullshitting and sizing each other
up, while their guards all eyed each other. The waiters
were just trying to keep everyone happy and their heads
attached to their shoulders. So no one noticed the dark
figure slinking through the shadows.

Finally, I came to the most dangerous part of my jour-
ney—a bush that was right by one of the Ice bars. It was
far too close to the crowd for my liking, but it was the
only way I could get to one of the mansion's side doors. I
waited until everyone was looking in the other direction,
then left my hiding spot and sprinted the few feet over to
the bush, crouching down behind it and making myself
as small as possible.

I counted off the seconds in my head. *Ten . . . twenty . . .
thirty . . . forty-five . . .* As the minute mark passed and
no one came to investigate, I figured I was safe enough
to make the final sprint from the bush over to the door.

I'd just started to move toward the house when someone planted himself on the other side of the rhododendron I was crouched behind, so close that I could see his
legs through the green, glossy leaves.

"Girl," a cold, familiar voice said.

I stiffened. I knew that voice, knew exactly who it be-
longed to—Jonah McAllister. Had he somehow spotted
me?

"Girl," McAllister repeated. "Come here."

I frowned. Those weren't the words of the man who'd
just spied his mortal enemy somewhere she shouldn't be. I
peered up through the branches at him and realized that he
was addressing someone else. He hadn't seen me after all.

The smarmy lawyer wore an impeccable tux like everyone else, and his wing tips had a higher shine than some of the necklaces the women wore. McAllister's silver coif of hair glittered with a hard, brittle light in the setting sun, and his face had an unnaturally smooth, almost waxy look to it. Jonah really needed to cut back on the Air elemental facials or soon he wouldn't have any skin left to exfoliate.

For a moment, I considered killing him where he stood. After all the trouble he'd caused me, I would have loved nothing more than to rise up and stab McAllister to death with my knives. But I couldn't do that without drawing attention to myself. With all the guards in attendance, I wouldn't get three steps before one of them realized what happened, pulled out a gun, and started shooting. Besides, I wasn't here for McAllister. No, tonight was about saving Owen and killing Salina—nothing else. So I swallowed my hatred of McAllister and kept quiet as a waitress shuffled over to him.

"Yes, sir. Champagne, sir?" she asked.

McAllister sniffed. "It's about time. I was wondering if Salina was going to make us all thirst to death."

I listened to the faint bubble of the fountains in the distance. I didn't think there was any danger of that tonight.

His champagne fix satisfied, McAllister dismissed the waitress with a wave of his hand and moved toward the center of the crowd. I waited until the woman had turned back toward the bar before racing over to the side door.

The door was standing open, and I slid behind it, using it to shield me from anyone looking in my direction. I paused and peered around the edge, making sure no one had noticed me and was coming my way, but I'd made it undetected. My eyes scanned over the crowd, taking in all the underworld sharks like Ron Donaldson, Beauregard Benson, and Lorelei Parker and the bodyguards they'd brought along with them.

I also spotted Kincaid, standing by himself next to an Ice bar. His blond ponytail glimmered in the sunset. Looked like he'd used the right conditioner after all. I wasn't surprised he'd shown up, even though Salina had tried to murder him. If everyone cut themselves off from all the folks who'd tried to kill them over the years, no one in the entire underworld would be able to do business.

The food, the guests, the lawn—the scene was disturbingly similar to the one I remembered from all those years ago when Mab had murdered Benedict Dubois, right down to the blue-green tablecloths gently flapping in the breeze. Everyone was a little older and grayer, but they still could have stepped out of one of the snapshots in Fletcher's file. Back then, everyone had laughed and talked and drunk themselves stupid right up until Mab had started barbecuing Dubois on the very spot they were standing on once again. I wondered if any of the guests were thinking back to that night. I wondered if any of them would appreciate the cruel irony of what Salina wanted to do to them.

As I looked at the crowd, I thought about walking away from the original plan—about finding Owen, grabbing Kincaid, getting them away from the mansion and lawn, and then just going on our way and leaving the sharks to

Salina to feast on. Her killing them all would make my life so much easier. More than a few of the people here had sent their goons after me these past few months, and they'd keep right on doing it as long as they thought they had a ghost of chance of taking me out. But if all the power players were dead, there would be a lot fewer folks interested in coming after me, at least in the near future, and my family and friends would be safer too. Yes, letting Salina have her revenge on them was a very, very tempting idea.

But in the end, I couldn't do it. Sure, I was an assassin. I'd killed people for money, but I couldn't condone mass murder, and that was what Salina had planned. She wouldn't limit herself to just the folks who'd stood by and done nothing while Mab had tortured and killed her father. Salina would eliminate everyone there, from the gangsters to their husbands and wives to the waiters serving them all. As the Spider, I'd always tried to avoid collateral damage, but it seemed like Salina delighted in causing as much of it as possible, given what she'd done to Katarina and Antonio.

Assassins chose to kill specific people for specific reasons. I didn't know if that made me better than her, but it at least made me different—at least I had a smidge of soul and a scrap of conscience left.

But first, I had to find Owen. I turned away from the crowd and slipped into the mansion. Lights blazed inside, banishing the shadows I would have hidden in, so I tightened my grip on the staff and hurried forward, determined to find Owen and get him out of here.

I eased down first one hallway, then another. I'd expected to see empty rooms or dusty, sheet-draped furniture, but everything from the end tables to the light fixtures gleamed, as though they had all just been polished. According to Finn, the Dubois estate had fallen into severe disrepair after Benedict's death and Salina's forced defection, but the place before me was immaculate, as if it had just been cleaned from top to bottom.

This wasn't the work of someone who'd come back to town a few days ago. Salina must have been planning her return for months, to get her massive house in such pristine shape. I wondered if she'd decided to come back to Ashland before or after I'd killed Mab. Didn't much matter. All that did was making sure I put a stop to her.

Every once in a while, footsteps would sound, signaling that a waiter or guard was coming my way, and I'd have to duck into one of the rooms, slide behind the curtains, or crouch behind a piece of furniture. But everyone was preoccupied with making sure the dinner went smoothly, so no one noticed me. No one realized the Spider was in their midst.

I moved deeper and deeper into the mansion, checking every room and every hallway I came to. Finally, I reached the center of the structure, which featured an open-air courtyard surrounded by balconies on all four sides. Another fountain, this one also shaped like a mermaid, gurgled in the middle of the area, and a variety of pink, blue, and green roses clustered together in urn-shaped, white stone planters that had been arranged around the fountain.

I'd just started forward to check the rooms that were attached to the courtyard, when I heard voices murmuring, one soft and sweet, one deep and masculine. It took me a moment to realize the sounds were coming from above my head. I craned my neck up and spotted Salina and Owen standing on a balcony on the second floor.

Kissing.

❋ 29 ❋

For a moment, everything stopped, and my heart clenched.

Salina looked as beautiful as ever, in a long, slinky dress made of aquamarine crystals sewn together in a scalloped, scale-like pattern. Her mermaid cuff bracelet flashed on her right wrist, and large diamond studs twinkled in her ears. She had her arms wrapped around Owen's neck, and her lips and body plastered to his. She let out a soft little moan in the back of her throat and pressed herself that much closer to him. Owen didn't seem to be returning her kiss, and his arms weren't even touching her, but still, it hurt all the same. I pushed the feeling aside and made myself stay cold, hard, and calm. That was what I needed to be right then to save Owen and everyone else there— whether they actually deserved to be rescued or not.

I'd just started forward to find a way up to the balcony when Owen pulled Salina's arms from around his neck and stepped away from her.

"Stop, Salina," he said. "Stop."

She sidled right back up to him, a pleased smile on her face. "I knew you'd come. I knew you couldn't stay away from me, any more than I could stay away from you."

Owen sighed, grabbed her hands from where they had crept back up to his shoulders, and stepped away from her. "That's not why I'm here tonight, and you know it. I came because you threatened to kill Gin. You need help, Salina. You're not well, and I think even you know it."

The smile never left the water elemental's beautiful face, but her eyes narrowed a little at his blunt tone. "I need help? Why? Because I want revenge for what everyone did to my father? For the horrible way I was treated? For the horrible way you let your so-called friends treat me? I don't see anything wrong with that. Besides, your friends are all still alive."

She didn't add *for now*. She didn't have to.

Owen shook his head. "And what about Antonio? Or Katarina? They had nothing to do with your father's murder or anything else, other than that they were Phillip's friends—but you still used your water magic to kill them. That was a horrible thing to do. It seems like I'm always talking about the horrible things you do, instead of the good ones."

Salina twined her arms around Owen's neck and raised her mouth to his, kissing him for all she was worth. He froze, apparently surprised by the fact that she just kept coming at him no matter what he said. I bit back a curse and scanned the courtyard, looking for the stairs that led up to where they were standing. Every few seconds, though, my eyes flicked up to Owen. I hated being indecisive, but I just couldn't stop myself from eavesdropping.

"Come on," Salina murmured against his mouth. "You remember how good it was between us? How alive we always made each other feel? I certainly do. No man I've been with has ever held a candle to you. I've spent too many nights to count dreaming about you, Owen. Dreaming about coming back to Ashland and being with you again. Can you tell me you haven't thought the same thing? Haven't dreamed the same thing? Haven't wanted the same thing?"

Once again, Owen pried off Salina's hands and mouth. This time, he pushed her away. "I'll admit I've thought about you over the years. Even dreamed about you and how things might have been."

Every word he said was like a dagger in my heart. This—*this* was how he really felt about Salina. This was how much he loved her, how much he'd always loved her.

"But that was before I knew why you really left Ashland all those years ago," he continued. "That was before I knew you tortured Eva with your water magic. That was before you tried to kill Phillip and then Cooper and Gin. I can't forget that, any of that—ever. Not even for you."

Owen took another step away from her.

Anger flashed in Salina's eyes, and her face tightened. "It's because of that assassin bitch, isn't it? That's why you're pulling away from me. Because of *her*."

"Yes, I met her, and I finally decided to quit thinking about the past, about you, and get on with my life." He stiffened. "Her name is Gin, and I love her, Salina."

"Love her? You couldn't possibly love *her*," she snarled.

"Not like you loved me. Not like you still love me. I know you still love me. Just give me a chance to remind you what it was like, what we were like—together."

She reached for Owen again, but he shook his head and stepped even farther away from her.

"No, Salina," he said. "Whatever we had was over the second you hurt Eva. I'm just sorry I didn't know what you were really like back then so I could have protected my sister from you and tried to get you the help you need. But know this: our history together is the only reason I'm not killing you myself for what you did back then and everything you've done since you came back to town. You can either get yourself some help, or you can leave Ashland and never return. There is no other option."

Let Salina leave Ashland? That wasn't what we'd talked about—not at all. Looked like I wasn't the only one who hadn't been completely honest about my intentions toward the water elemental.

If it comes down to Owen and Salina in the end, he won't be able to kill her—and then she'll murder him.

Eva's voice whispered in my mind. She'd said those words to me the night she'd told me what Salina had done to me. I hadn't wanted to believe they were true, but it looked like Eva had been right all along.

I stood there in the courtyard, torn between stepping back out into the hallway to find the stairs that led up to the second floor and staying put. Part of me wanted to continue eavesdropping on their conversation, but I also didn't want to leave Owen alone with the water elemental. Not now, when he'd just rejected her. If worse came to worst, and she made a move against him, I could blast her with my Ice magic from down here. It wouldn't be as good as ramming one of my knives into her heart, but it would probably buy me enough time to find the stairs, sprint up them, and get Owen to safety.

Salina looked stunned that Owen was rejecting her, that he didn't want anything to do with her anymore. The anger that had been simmering in her eyes boiled up into full-on fury, until her gaze was burning as bright as the bulbs in the crystal chandelier over her head.

"I can't believe you're taking her side over mine!" she hissed. "Do you know what a hypocrite that makes you? Your whore of an assassin's hands aren't any cleaner than mine. In fact, I'd be doing the world a favor by taking her out of it. How many people do you think she's killed over the years, Owen? And for what—money? How *cheap*."

Owen squared his shoulders. "Maybe that's true, but Gin has a good heart, something you lost a long time ago, Salina. She might have killed people, yes, but she would never hurt a child, and she would never hurt anyone I cared about. I'm sorry, but it's over. I love Gin, and she's who I plan on building my future with. Not you."

My heart lifted at his words, even as Salina's crashed and burned. She stared at him in shock, still not quite believing that things hadn't gone exactly how she'd wanted them to, how she'd imagined they would in her head. Then, all of the prettiness suddenly drained out of her face, replaced by something cold, ugly, and slightly unhinged.

"Very well," she said in a stiff voice. "You've made your choice."

Owen nodded his head, and some of the tension eased

out of his shoulders. He didn't notice the devious smile that curved Salina's lips—but I did.

"Guards!" she called out.

Heavy footsteps sounded, and a few seconds later, two giants stepped out onto the balcony. They must have been stationed right outside the door, waiting for Salina to summon them. Even though she'd expected the best, expected that Owen would come back to her, she'd still planned for the worst too. There was definitely a method to her madness.

"Salina, what are you doing?" Owen asked in a warning voice.

"Are the others in position?" she asked the giants.

"Yes, ma'am," one answered.

"Good. Make sure my darling Owen stays here until after I've seen to my other guests. Do whatever you have to in order to keep him under control—short of killing him."

Owen fought back when the two giants surged toward him, his fist connecting with the taller one's jaw, knocking him back. Owen growled and drew back his fist for another punch, but the other giant threw himself on top of him. All three men went down to the floor in a heap of arms and legs. I couldn't see exactly what was happening, not from this angle, but I heard Owen's grunts of pain.

"Don't struggle so hard, darling. You're only hurting yourself. It's most unbecoming," Salina murmured.

Then the water elemental turned and left the balcony.

"Salina!" Owen yelled. "Salina!"

But she didn't order the giants to stand down, and she

didn't come back. He kept fighting to get free, even as the other men kept hitting him. They were all tangled together, which meant that I couldn't risk using my Ice magic. I also abandoned my plan of searching for the stairs. That would take too much time now. Instead, I laid my staff down on the floor, grabbed a chair from against the wall, carried it across the courtyard, and put it right below the balcony where Owen was still struggling. I backed up to the opposite side of the courtyard, calculating the height and angles. Then, I ran forward, jumped up into the seat, leaped onto the very top of the chair, and launched myself into the air.

I managed to get high enough to grab hold of the bottom edge of the stone balcony. I hung there for a moment, like a spider dangling in the breeze, and then pulled myself up and over the side. The giants were too busy trying to pin Owen to the floor to notice me come up behind them, knives ready.

I fell on top of one, my blades punching into his back. He screamed with pain and clawed at me with his right hand. I pulled my knives out and plunged them into his body again, sawing through his thick muscles.

The other giant's head snapped around at his buddy's screams, and he lashed out at me with his fist. I managed to dodge his blow, yank my knives out of the first guy, and get back up on my feet. The giant I'd wounded tried to stand, so I kicked him in the head as hard as I could. He groaned and slumped back down on the floor.

The second giant scrambled to his feet and held up his hands in a classic boxer's stance.

"If I were you, I'd be running at this point," I hissed.

He came at me anyway. He swung his fist at my face in a quick jab, but I dodged the blow and stepped in closer to his body, ramming my knife into his chest. The giant screamed as I pulled the blade out and stabbed it into his chest a second time. He put his hands on my shoulders, trying to throw me off him, so I drew my blades across one of his arms, then the other. The giant fell to his knees, blood pouring out of his wounds. I kicked him in the head as well, and he flopped on top of his friend. Neither man was dead, but they'd bleed out soon enough. All I cared about right now was making sure Owen was all right—and stopping Salina.

I slid my bloody knives back up my sleeves and dropped to my knees beside Owen, who was on his back on the floor. "Owen! Are you okay?"

I helped him sit up. His face had already started to swell from where he'd been hit, and blood trickled out of his now-broken nose.

"Gin?" he said, struggling to focus on me. "What are you doing here?"

"Saving you. And everyone else here, despite my own best interests."

"What?" he asked, his eyes clearing and his voice sharpening. "What do you mean? What's going on?"

"Salina has a little more planned than just a simple dinner party and business powwow. I'll tell you about it on our way out of here. Let's move."

I managed to get Owen up onto his feet. My lover swayed back and forth, still dazed by the giants' blows. He shook his head, trying to get rid of the cobwebs.

"I'm sorry," he said. "I had no choice. Salina said—"

"That she'd kill me," I finished. "I know. Eva found the note."

I put my arm under his shoulder, and we left the balcony and stepped out into a hallway. I finally spotted a set of stairs, and I helped Owen walk in that direction and then down to the ground floor, filling him in on what Salina was planning and why she'd really asked all the Ashland crime bosses here tonight.

"Are you sure?" he asked. "Killing all those people is extreme, even for Salina."

"The fountains, the location, the guest list, it all fits. You told me yourself that Salina changed after her father's murder. I think this is the real reason she came back to Ashland—to get her revenge. I think this is all that she really cares about, except for you."

Owen stopped walking and looked down at me. "How much of that did you see on the balcony?"

"Enough." I couldn't keep the hurt out of my voice.

He sighed. "I'm sorry, Gin. Let me explain—"

I held up my hand, cutting him off. "We can talk later. Right now, I have to go after Salina. I have to stop her—"

A scream shattered the night air.

✸30✸

Owen and I stared at each other.

"Salina," I said, moving over to grab my staff from where I'd left it on the floor by the fountain. "She's started it already. Get out of here! Go!"

Owen shook his head. "No, I'm coming with you. Maybe there's still a chance I can talk her out of this."

I wanted to yell at him that it was too late for that, that Salina wouldn't stop until everyone was dead, but it was something he had to realize for himself. "Come on, then."

We hurried through the mansion and made it back to the side door that led out to the north lawn. The screams had quieted down by this point, and I forced myself to creep up, open the door a bit more, and peer around it.

Several giants stood on the lawn, positioned in the gaps between the bubbling fountains. Each had guns pointed in at the crowd they'd shepherded into a tight knot in the middle of the ring of fountains. Given the incredulous looks most of the folks were giving the giants, I was willing to bet these were the men Salina had stolen from the other underworld players the past few days. The water elemental had hired the giants to murder their own bosses, promising them who knew what to get their cooperation.

Whatever else she was, Salina was exceptionally clever. She played for keeps, and she never did anything halfway. I had to admire that about her. In her own way, Salina was as ruthless as Mab had been. No surprise, since she'd been twisted by the Fire elemental's cruelty, just as I had been.

A few of the folks crept toward the giants, as if they couldn't believe their own guards would turn on them, but the glares and guns pointed in their direction sent them scurrying back. Salina stood next to the mermaid fountain, beaming at everyone, as if she wasn't planning on murdering them in another minute, two tops.

I pulled my walkie-talkie out of one of the pockets on my vest. "Finn? Finn? Are you seeing this on your laptop?"

He got back to me a second later. "You mean the giants with the guns making sure everyone stays in Salina's little water trap? Yeah, I see it."

"Then get ready to move," I whispered back. "I'm going to take out some of the giants and create a way for folks to get away from the fountains and the water."

"I'll do my part," Finn said. "Bria and Xavier just pulled onto the street, along with another cop car. I'll tell them what's going on, and we'll be ready to go when it's time."

"Good," I said. "And tell them to be careful. Salina's too far gone now. She's not going to stop for anyone."

Owen stiffened beside me, but he didn't say anything. I put the walkie-talkie back in a pocket on my vest and looked at him.

"Do you think you can distract her long enough for me to deal with one of the giants?" I asked in a soft voice. "You're the only person she might listen to, even if it's only for a few seconds. But once she realizes what you've done, how we've tricked her, she won't be happy, especially not with you. She could attack you again."

He nodded. "I know. I can handle Salina."

"Okay. Then follow my lead."

I slipped out of the mansion and crept over to one of the Ice bars that had been planted on the lawn. The bartenders who'd been stationed there had been pushed inside the ring of fountains along with the others, giving me plenty of room to maneuver. Owen slid in beside me underneath the bar, his breath tickling the back of my neck.

"I'm going for the giant right there," I said, indicating the man closest to me. "You distract Salina. Wait for my signal, then move."

I crept over to the edge of the bar and peered around it, scanning the crowd for Kincaid. The casino boss stood on the far side of the giant I was targeting. Like everyone else, he was focused on Salina, but maybe I could change that. I palmed one of my knives and angled it into a patch of fading sunlight. Tilting the blade back and forth, I created a small sunspot flashing in Kincaid's eyes.

He grimaced, blinked, and turned in my direction, just as I'd hoped he would. Kincaid's eyes widened when he spotted me. I slid my knife back up my sleeve and held my finger up to my lips. Then I pointed at the giant and made a slashing motion across my throat with my finger, trying to let him know what my plan was. My crude signals must have worked because Kincaid nodded back and started sidling in the giant's direction, careful not to draw attention to himself. Kincaid wasn't my friend—not exactly—but I wasn't leaving him to Salina's wrath. If nothing else, I could at least get him away from the fountains as quickly as possible.

"I'm sure you're all wondering why I've asked you here tonight," Salina's voice floated over to me. "You've probably guessed by now that dinner will not be served."

She laughed at her bad joke, but no one else joined in. I peered around the side of the ice bar. Salina still stood by the mermaid fountain, addressing the crowd of angry, frightened people in front of her.

"Many of you here tonight may remember my father, Benedict. Many of you probably remember the last dinner party he gave."

Salina's eyes went from face to face, daring people to meet her cold gaze. Most of the guests stared back at her with blank expressions, not understanding what she was getting at, but a few shifted on their feet and dropped their eyes from hers.

"Of course, the real reason you probably remember that dinner is because that's the night my father died—the night he was murdered by Mab Monroe right on the very ground you stand on now. Many of you were here then. You saw exactly what Mab did to my father—and not one of you lifted a finger to help him or to try and stop her. Not a single one of you."

Murmurs of unease rippled through the crowd. I wasn't the only one who could hear the crazy loud and clear in Salina's voice now.

"Of course, Mab is dead," she continued. "But the rest of you *aren't.*"

More than a few folks sucked in breaths at the threat in her words.

Jonah McAllister pushed through the crowd until he was standing in front of Salina. The lawyer gave her an icy glare. "This is madness. Let us go, Salina. You can't possibly hope to get away with whatever it is you have planned. You don't know who you are dealing with."

"No, Jonah," she said. "*You* don't know who *you* are dealing with. But believe me when I tell you that you are about to find out."

She stared at the lawyer. McAllister opened his mouth to argue with her but then thought better of it and clamped his lips shut. Whatever he saw in Salina's face made him he realize that she was too committed to her plan to abandon it now—just like her father had been all those years ago.

"My father was known for his Ice magic," Salina said. "But I have a slightly different power—water."

Hoarse gasps of unease rippled through the crowd. People stared at the pretty fountains they'd been admiring earlier, awareness, horror, and fear filling their faces. They'd walked right into Salina's trap without even realizing it, and now there was no way out.

Again I hesitated. It would be easy—so damn *easy*—to let Salina kill the lot of them. It would solve so many of my problems, not to mention make Ashland a little safer for everyone. But, once again, I couldn't condone mass murder, especially when some of the people here tonight were innocents, just regular men and women waiting and bartending and trying to make a few bucks to support their families. I couldn't leave them to Salina's mercy—or lack of it. It would go against everything Fletcher had ever taught me about being an assassin—and a halfway decent person too.

"The reason I invited you here tonight was to remember my father." Salina's voice was as calm as ever, which made her words that much more chilling. "To honor him—and to watch you all die screaming, just like he did."

That was my cue if ever there was one. Still holding my silverstone staff, I surged to my feet and sprinted to the giant closest to me. He saw me out of the corner of his eye and frowned, as if he couldn't believe I would actually run toward him while he was holding a gun on the crowd. He swung his weapon around to me, and I reached for my Stone magic, using it to harden my skin.

Crack! Crack!

The crowd screamed at the gunshots, and many folks ducked down and started shoving each other, scrambling to put their neighbors between themselves and this new danger.

The giant got off two shots at me. One was off the mark and plowed into the bar, shattering part of the elemental Ice, while the other hit my shoulder and bounced off my hardened skin. Cursing, the giant started to pull the trigger a third time, but Kincaid snuck up behind him and chopped the gun out of his hand.

My turn. I brought the staff up and around, slamming it into the side of the giant's head. He staggered back. I palmed a knife, followed him, and shoved the blade deep into his chest, sliding it in between his ribs and slicing it into his heart. The giant screamed, but I was already pushing him out of the way and stepping over to Kincaid.

"Fancy meeting you here," Kincaid said, grinning.

"Uh-huh. Now shut your mouth and start running."

I tucked the bloody knife back up my sleeve, grabbed the woman closest to me, and shoved her toward Kincaid and the opening I'd just created in Salina's trap.

"Move! Move! Move!" I screamed at the people in front of me. "Run! Now, while you still can!"

For a moment, there was shocked silence; then folks began to stampede in my direction. I leapt up onto the rim of the closest fountain so I wouldn't get dragged down to the ground and trampled. Looking over the crowd to where Salina was standing in front of the mermaid fountain, I could only hope I'd bought everyone enough time to get out of her watery web of death.

But it was already too late—Salina's eyes began to glow, and I knew she was reaching for her magic.

Normally, I would have enjoyed being so close to such beautiful fountains. I would have been happy to relax, sit on one of the rims, and listen to the water merrily gurgle away while a bit of cool, refreshing spray wafted over me.

Not tonight.

The water that had been bubbling so peacefully in the fountains took on a harsher, more ominous sound. It surged out of the metal sculptures with all the force of a fire hose pointed at the crowd—seven of them, one from each fountain.

People screamed as the water slammed into them, and the jets of it were so powerful they knocked over tables, chairs, and everything else in their paths. In a second, everyone was soaked to the skin, which was just what Salina wanted. People fell to the ground, which had already turned to mud, and they wrestled with each other, trying to get on their feet or crawl over the tops of their enemies to safety. Others weren't so lucky. They were picked up by waves of water, dumped into the bottoms of the fountains, and held there, only to surface when they were good and dead. Salina wasn't using her magic to dehydrate anyone. No, tonight, she was intent on drowning everyone she saw.

"Salina! No! Stop!" I heard Owen yell. "Don't do this!"

Owen pushed his way through the crowd until he was standing before the elemental. He held out a hand, pleading with her. She looked at him. Her face softened, and I could see all the love she had for him, all the love she'd always had for him, crazy and twisted as it was. For a moment, I thought she might actually reconsider, that she might actually stand down and give up her deadly plan. But then her eyes found mine, and her face hardened once more.

"You made your choice, Owen," Salina snarled. "And *this* is mine!"

She waved her hand and a jet of water roared out of the fountain behind her, slamming into Owen, knocking him back thirty feet into the Ice bar we'd been hiding behind.

"Owen!" I screamed.

But my lover didn't respond, and his body slumped to the ground at an awkward angle. At the very least, he was unconscious. I didn't want to think about the very worst.

"Owen!" Kincaid yelled the same thing I had and started shoving his way over to the bar. I leaped off the fountain rim and took a step toward Owen, too—

And that was when Finn finally crashed the party.

His Escalade rammed through the front gate, followed by Bria's sedan and another cop car with flashing blue and white lights. Finn forgot about following the driveway. Instead, he turned the wheel hard, accelerated onto the lawn, and slammed the vehicle into the koi fountain. He knocked the metal off its foundation, busting the pipes hidden beneath it and causing even more water to shoot up into the air. Finn had also clipped the giant who'd been guarding that spot, creating another opening in the ring of death, which was quickly filled with more fleeing people. They stumbled away from the pulsing jets of water, out onto the lawn, and then picked up their sodden dresses and pant legs and ran for all they were worth.

I noticed Jonah McAllister was leading the pack of escapees. A pity the lawyer had gotten away, but my eyes snapped back to Salina. Even though I desperately wanted to check on Owen, first I needed to make sure she didn't hurt anyone else.

I pushed my way through the screaming crowd, heading toward her and avoiding as many of the sprays of water as I could. They blasted out of the fountains like geysers, and Salina laughed with delight as she used the water to push one man over the rim and into the bottom of the mermaid fountain. He didn't surface after that.

Salina was having so much fun murdering that poor soul that she didn't notice me sprinting at her. I managed to get within arm's reach of her. I raised my staff, intent on bashing her head in and putting her down before she could kill anyone else—

My foot slipped in the mud.

Instead of killing Salina, I merely slammed into her, and we both went down in a heap in the mud. The staff fell from my fingers and flew out of reach, so I palmed one of my knives, got up, and turned to face her. She was already back up on her feet.

"You bitch!" she screamed. "You've ruined everything!"

I didn't respond—I was too busy throwing myself forward and trying to end her existence.

Salina might have presented herself as a sweet Southern belle, but she clearly knew how to fight. She punched me in the face, knocking me back, then lashed out with her hand and slapped my knife out of my fingers. I palmed another blade and threw myself at her again, but once again she was ready for the move and landed another punch, this time to my stomach, knocking my second knife away as well. But still I managed to latch onto her, and we fell to the ground. We rolled around and around in the mud for several seconds before getting up on our feet and turning toward each other again.

All around us, water continued to spray, but the panicked screams had faded as most of the guests had managed to get away from the fountains and onto the relative safety of the lawn. Even the giants who'd been standing guard had turned tail and run.

Crack! Crack! Crack!

Gunshots sounded behind me, probably Finn, Bria, and Xavier dealing with the rest of Salina's men, but I didn't dare turn around to look. No, this moment was about me and her—nothing else.

We circled each other, going around and around in a silent dance, our feet sending up sprays of mud. The water continued to rain down around us. Salina's aquamarine dress was plastered to her skin, the crystals tinkling together like wind chimes, and even more water dripped out of the ends of her blond hair, making her look like an evil twin to the crazy grinning mermaid of the fountain beside us.

Her eyes narrowed as she glared at me, the color shifting from blue to green and back again, the orbs glowing with her water magic—along with more than a touch of madness. For the first time, I saw what Owen did when he looked at her—someone who needed help.

Salina might need help, but she wasn't going to get it from me.

❈ 31 ❈

The water continued to rain down all around Salina and me, like the two of us were standing in the middle of a thunderstorm. We faced each other in the midst of the downpour. Her eyes flicked around, scanning the overturned tables, the broken dishes, the crushed chairs, the shattered Ice bars. Then, her gaze swung back to me, hurt and accusing.

"This is your fault," she muttered. "All your fault. You've ruined everything! Owen! My revenge! Everything!"

I grinned. "I have a way of doing that."

Salina smiled, baring her teeth at me. "Well, this is going to be the last thing you ever ruin, you assassin whore. And once you're gone, Owen will come back to me. I know he will."

I looked at her, wondering if she really believed that, if she really believed Owen would come back to her after everything that had happened, after everything that she'd done to the people he cared about. But her conviction filled her face, making her eyes burn that much brighter. For a moment, I almost felt sorry for her.

Then the bitch blasted me with her water magic, and I got over it.

Salina raised up her hands, and the water droplets that had been clinging to her skin began to move and writhe like kudzu vines sprouting and growing all around her. I realized we were in a different kind of garden now—a water garden in which Salina was the queen and I was just her unfortunate victim.

"You really should have drowned in the creek while you had the chance," she hissed. "Because now, I'm going to tear you limb from limb."

She waved her hands again, and the water vines shot out from her skin and slammed into mine. It was the same sensation I'd had when she'd tried to drown me in the creek—all of these tight, tiny vines wrapping around my whole body.

Only this time, instead of pulling me under the water, they were ripping me apart.

I watched in horror as the water vines began to sprout long, sharp, curved thorns. For a moment, the vines arced out away from my body before shooting forward, the thorns ripping into my skin. I screamed, but the thorns continued to burrow deeper and deeper into my body with every breath I took. It felt like my skin, my muscles, even my bones were on fire, and I could feel the blood gushing out of the hundreds of tiny pricks the thorns had made in me. I had no doubt Salina could do exactly what she claimed—she would tear my arms, legs, hell, even my head from my body. I wondered if she'd go that extra step and pop my eyes out of my skull like she'd done to Antonio. Either way, it would be a horrible, painful way to die.

I reached for my Stone magic, hardening my skin against the thorns' intrusion. But that only slowed the onslaught—it didn't stop it.

I stood there, pushing back against Salina's water magic with my Stone power. She let out a frustrated scream that I'd stalled her initial attack and she wasn't going to immediately kill me the way she wanted to.

"Fine," she snarled. "If I can't rip you to pieces, I'll just drown you like the rat you are."

Using her left hand, Salina grabbed the silverstone cuff bracelet on her right wrist and made a twisting motion, tapping into the power stored there. The water vines wrapped around me started pulling me over to the closest fountain, the one shaped like a mermaid. I dug my boot heels into the ground, but since it had turned to mud, it didn't slow down the vines—not even for a second.

I couldn't let go of my Stone magic or Salina would rip me apart with her water thorns, and I couldn't fight back against the vines that held me tight. The vines had trapped my arms by my sides, making it impossible for me to reach for one of the knives still left on me. So I skidded along in the mud, the mermaid fountain getting closer and closer with every second. I knew that if she got me in there I was dead. Salina would just keep pouring more and more water on top of me until I either drowned or was crushed, or she broke through my Stone magic and could tear me to pieces like she'd promised.

I only had one chance left—the staff.

My eyes landed on the weapon, which had slid over to the base of the mermaid fountain. It was covered with mud, like everything else was, but I could still see the long, distinctive shape of it. The staff was the only shot I had left to get out of this alive and turn the tables on Salina. It wasn't the weapon itself so much that mattered—it was the Ice magic it contained.

My Ice magic.

I didn't have enough Ice magic on my own to stop Salina. There was just too much water puddled on the ground and spewing up in the air for me to do that. Besides, she was using the extra power stored in her cuff bracelet to augment her already strong magic. But the staff had soaked up a fair amount of my power when I'd been battling Dekes, power that I'd added to over the past few weeks, just in case I ever needed it—which I desperately did tonight.

Now all I had to do was be very, very good—and very, very lucky.

I quit struggling against the water as it dragged me closer to my death. Instead, I started calculating distances and angles. I also reached for my Ice magic, bringing it to bear, right along with my Stone power. I'd only get one shot at this, and I had to make it count.

"I can't believe you're the one who killed Mab," Salina said, walking through the mud right beside me as if we were out for an evening stroll instead of marching toward my waterlogged demise. "She was so strong. But you? You're not strong at all, are you, Gin? Or at least not strong enough. Not to keep Owen, and not to keep me from killing you."

I didn't bother answering her. There was no point in it. I doubted she'd hear me through her own ego anyway. Instead, my eyes locked on the staff lying in the mud. I was only ten feet away from it now.

Nine . . . seven . . . five . . . three . . . one . . . go!

The vines dragged me right by the staff. I let go of my Stone magic for one precious second, letting the water thorns rip into my skin again, and reached for my Ice power instead, using it to freeze the vines that trapped my right hand down by my side. The water froze, and I sent out another blast, shattering some of the vines—just enough of them.

Beside me, Salina stopped. "What do you think you're doing? That won't save you—"

Once my arm was free, I used it to push her as hard as I could. She stumbled back against the fountain. She didn't hit it very hard, since my blow was so weak and awkward, but it was enough to break her concentration on her water magic, just for a second.

That was all I needed.

The remaining vines loosened around my body, and I threw myself forward and down into the mud, reaching, reaching, reaching for the staff with all the precious Ice magic it contained.

My fingers closed around it just as her magic tightened around me once more.

"Die, bitch!" Salina hissed.

"You first!" I snarled back.

Struggling against the vines, I managed to get to my feet, bring the staff up over my head, and slam it down into the mud—releasing every last bit of the Ice magic stored inside.

For a moment, nothing happened.

Then, in the space between breaths, everything around me just—*crystallized*.

The second before the staff plunged into the ground, I reached for all the Ice magic—my magic—stored in the silverstone. I combined that power with what was flowing through my veins, pouring it all into the staff and using the weapon to focus my energy, my will. And when the metal tip of the staff buried itself in the mud, I forced all of the power out of the weapon, lashing out with it as hard, fast, and brutally as I could. The silvery color of my magic filled my vision, blotting out everything else, as though I was standing in the middle of a cold, burning star.

I wasn't sure if it would be enough to overcome all the water on the ground and still arcing up through the air. I wasn't sure if I had more magic stored in the staff than Salina did in her bracelet. I wasn't sure if my magic would be enough to cut off her power source.

But I tried it.

And it *worked*.

For a few seconds, there was just—cold. This blast of cold that overcame everything else, like a nuclear winter. Ice zipped along the ground, the jets of water froze in midair and glittered like giant ocean waves, and everything became cold, hard, and slick. And the elemental

Ice didn't stop at the edge of the fountains—it kept right on going, spreading out across the lush spring grass like a sheet unrolling, killing the blades instantly, and causing the people still running from the scene to slip and fall as the Ice crystals caught up with and then spread past them.

When it was over, when the silvery light of my magic finally faded away, I slowly stood up, the staff still in my hands. Empty now of all its power, just like me. I'd put every last bit of my elemental magic—Ice and Stone—into that blast. Now, I had nothing left. A wave of exhaustion washed over me, and the staff slipped through my fingers and clattered to the ground.

Behind me, someone let out a low whistle. I whirled around to find Finn casually gliding on his wing tips across the sheet of Ice with all the easy grace of an Olympic figure skater.

"Damn," he drawled, sliding to a stop beside me. "I knew that staff had some of your Ice magic in it, but not *that* much. It looks like the middle of January instead of May."

That was something of an understatement. Ice stretched out as far as the eye could see, glittering like a field of frosty diamonds in the growing darkness. Two inches of Ice encased all of the fountains, and not so much as a single drop of water flowed out of the busted pipes. The ground had also frozen solid and was as slick and glossy as an ice-skating rink.

I'd been the closest to the mermaid fountain, and it had taken the brunt of my attack. The Ice had blasted it into pieces. The mermaid was missing her tail, while her head and long, wavy hair were now just barely clinging to the rest of her body, although she still had that crazy, crazy grin on her face—one that still made me shiver, even now, when it seemed like I'd survived after all.

✳ 32 ✳

I let out a shaky breath and ran my trembling hand through my hair. At least, I tried to, but my ponytail had frozen just like everything else had, including my clothes. Jo-Jo had always told me my magic would just keep growing and growing, but sometimes it still amazed me to realize the dwarf was right. Sure, there had been a lot of power stored in the staff, but most of this—most of this had been *me*.

"No!" a voice screamed. "No, no, no!"

Salina stood in the middle of the garden of elemental Ice, her gaze frantically searching the ground for any sign of free-flowing water that she could use against me. But there wasn't any. I'd frozen it all with my Ice magic—every last fucking drop.

Salina saw me staring at her, and rage filled her features once more. I thought she might reach for her magic to try to pull the water out of my body, but her eyes caught on something black that was half-buried in the Ice, and she bent down and yanked it free. Too late I realized it was a gun, one that the giants or her guests must have dropped in their rush to escape.

I put myself in front of Finn and instinctively reached for my Stone magic to harden my skin—only this time, I was all out of juice. I'd used up all my magic, and there just wasn't time to try grab one of my knives and use the Ice magic stored there to form some sort of shield. My spider rune ring was empty too, gone since the battle at the creek yesterday.

I still had on my silverstone vest, but Salina was aiming the gun at my head.

I'd finally beaten Salina, finally used my elemental magic to overpower hers, and now she was going to kill me with a simple gun. Ah, the irony. Going to be the death of me—right now.

Behind me, Finn noticed what was happening. "Gin!" He yelled. "Get out of the way!"

He tried to shove me to one side, but Salina was quicker. She must have realized I was out of magic because she smiled—a smile that was just as crazy as the mermaid's was.

Crack! Crack!

Gunshots reverberated through the air. I stiffened, waiting for the bullets to slam into my skull and put my lights out for good—but two red splotches blossomed on Salina's chest instead of mine. My head snapped to the left, and I realized why.

Eva.

She ran around Finn's car, a gun clutched in her hands.

Salina crumpled to the ground, and Eva rushed over and kicked the water elemental's gun from her hand, almost falling on the Ice as she did so. Then, Eva stood over Salina, a grim, tortured expression on her face. Finn started forward, but I put my arm out.

"No," I said. "Let me handle it. You go check on Owen. Salina used her magic to knock him around before I could stop her."

He nodded and hurried across the Ice as fast as he could to where Owen lay. Kincaid was there too, tending to my lover, but I pushed my worry for Owen out of my mind.

"Eva," I said in a soft voice, walking toward her, "it's over now. You can put the gun down."

A dazed look filled her blue eyes, and it took a few seconds before she actually seemed to hear my words. Eva shook her head, and her hand tightened around the gun. "No, it's not over yet. I haven't killed her yet."

I glanced down. I'd thought Eva had hit Salina square in the chest, but she'd only winged her in the shoulder and arm instead. One wound looked like a through-and-through in her upper left bicep, while the other had punched into her skin just below her collarbone. Painful wounds—but not fatal ones.

I looked at Salina a second longer, making sure the water elemental wasn't going to get up, but she only moaned, clutched her shoulder, and rocked back and forth on the ground. So I reached over and put my frozen fingers on top of Eva's hand, the one that was still holding the gun.

"It's okay, Eva," I said in that soft, soothing voice

again. "You did it. You got her. You saved me and Finn. It's over now."

Eva shook her head, mutely telling me that it wasn't over, but this time she let me lower the gun, slip it out of her hand, and tuck it against the small of my back right next to my knife. I put my arm around Eva, carefully hugging her to my chest, despite the fact my clothes were as cold, stiff, and frozen as everything else was.

A sob escaped her throat, then another one, then another one. Her whole body trembled with emotion—so much emotion—as wave after wave of it lashed through her. All the terror, all the helplessness, all the rage she'd felt because of what Salina had done to her and how she'd threatened to hurt Owen and Kincaid.

I held her and let her cry, let her scream, let her beat her fists against my back, even as I stroked her hair and murmured nonsense words to her, telling her it was okay. Sometimes there was more comfort in lies than the truth.

Finally, Eva's sobs died down, and she drew back and looked at me. Tears kept streaming down her face.

"Please, Gin," she whispered. "*Please.*"

I nodded and stepped away from her. By this point, Bria and Xavier had worked their way over to us. Xavier grabbed Eva's shoulders and pulled her away from me and Salina. Bria helped him. Looking at me as she passed, my sister tilted her head the tiniest bit. I nodded back and grabbed the silverstone knife from against the small of my back, ready to end this once and for all.

Footsteps shuffled behind me. I turned to see Finn and

Kincaid helping Owen walk toward me. Owen held a hand to his side, as though he had some broken ribs. A bloody gash marred his forehead and his face was swollen from the giants' blows, but other than that, he looked okay. Some of the tightness in my chest eased. He was okay.

Salina caught sight of him too, and she stretched out her bloody hand toward him.

"Owen," she rasped. "Help me. Please. You were right, and I was wrong. I'm sorry. So sorry. I'll do whatever you want me to. I promise I will."

I bit back a bitter laugh. She wasn't sorry—she wasn't sorry for one damn bit of it, except that I'd stopped her and she hadn't gotten the revenge she wanted.

But Salina's plea had the desired effect on Owen. My lover turned to me, aching pain, regret, and sadness in his eyes.

"Gin . . ." he said. "Don't. Let Bria take her away. She's sick. You know she's sick."

I did know that Salina was sick and that it could have just as easily been me lying there on top of the Ice instead of her. The irony of the situation wasn't lost on me—not at all. Mab had murdered my family; I'd felt the same pain, loss, and rage that Salina had. Maybe it would have consumed me the way it had her if Fletcher hadn't helped me channel my anger, if he hadn't taught me his code, if he hadn't trained me how to control my emotions and do what was necessary no matter what.

For a moment, I considered walking away. Just turning, walking away across the Ice, and letting Bria, Xavier, and the other cops haul Salina off to Ashland Asylum. But that wouldn't end things. It would just postpone them—and someone else would get hurt when Salina escaped or was finally cut loose.

I looked at Owen and then my gaze went over to the cops and Eva, who was still crying. Across the field of Ice, her eyes met mine, blue on gray, and I saw all the innocence she'd lost tonight—all the innocence she'd lost all those years ago to Salina. I saw the worry and the fear and the waking nightmare that just wouldn't end as long as Salina was alive.

And I made my choice.

Maybe I'd made it the night Eva had first told me about Salina, the night she'd compared her to Mab. Maybe I'd known what I would do even back then— and what it would cost me. I didn't know if it was right or if it was wrong, but it was my choice, and I made it, the way I had so many other hard, ugly ones over the years.

"Gin," Owen said again, an edge in his voice now. "Don't."

I drew in a breath, knowing there was no going back. This time, I looked at Finn instead of my lover.

"Keep him back however you have to," I said, not quite echoing the orders Salina had issued to her guards earlier tonight.

Owen let out a curse and started forward, but Kincaid held on to his arm. A second later, a distinctive *click* cut through the night air. Owen looked down in disbelief at the gun Finn had pressed to his side.

"I don't want to hurt you, Owen," Finn said in a regretful tone. "But we both know I will. So why don't you just stand still while Gin does her thing."

"Gin," Owen said a final time, that same plea in his voice.

I stared at my lover a moment, looking into his beautiful violet eyes. Then I turned away.

Behind me, I heard Owen let out another curse and start struggling with Finn and Kincaid, but I shut the sounds out of my mind.

I dropped to a knee beside Salina. The water elemental drew in short, ragged breaths, her exhalations turning to frost given how cold the air was from my blast of magic. Blood had already frozen on the Ice beneath her body, and her blond hair fanned out around her in lovely waves, as though she were underwater.

Salina looked at me, then turned her head to stare at Owen. She smiled at him, that crazy, crazy love still shining in her eyes, before she looked at me once more.

"I won't stop," Salina rasped in a low voice only I could hear, as the blood continued to pump out of her gunshot wounds. "I can't stop—ever."

"I know, sweetheart," I said softly. "I know."

And then I leaned over and cut her throat.

"No!" Owen shouted. "No! No! No!"

But it was too late, and the cut I'd made in Salina's neck was too deep. She gasped, arched her back, and clawed at the wound, but she knew it was over, just like I did. Salina looked at me, something almost like relief flashing in her blue-green eyes, then lolled her head to the side to stare at Owen. She smiled at him a final time and held out a bloody hand, reaching for him—still reaching for him, despite everything that had happened, everything she'd done, everything that had passed between them.

Then the light went out of her eyes, her hand fluttered to the Ice, and she was still, as cold and dead and still as the shattered, frozen mermaid that loomed over us.

* 33 *

I crouched there and watched Salina bleed out. Finn and Kincaid let go of Owen, who rushed over to the dying elemental. He hunkered down on the other side of her, staring at her open, sightless eyes and the deep, ugly gash I'd sliced in her slender throat.

"I'm sorry," I said. "But it had to be done. I think you know that, deep down inside."

Owen looked at me, old memories and grief and pain swirling in his eyes—so much pain. Over Salina, over what she'd done to the people he'd cared about—and what I'd just done to her, the woman he'd once loved.

Owen didn't say a word as he watched Salina die. But when her blood slowed and finally stopped, he got to his feet, turned, and walked away from me—and he didn't look back.

All I could do was just watch him go, my heart shattering into smaller and smaller pieces with every step he took.

I stayed in that one spot, feeling as cold inside as the landscape was around me. A minute passed, maybe two, and the world kept on turning just like it always did.

I sighed, and got to my feet. Then I fished my knives from where they had been buried in the Ice, grabbed the staff as well, and sat down on the edge of the fountain, right next to the almost decapitated mermaid with her missing tail. The figure seemed to fix her eyes on me, accusing me of murdering the woman whose rune she'd represented.

"What are you staring at?" I muttered.

The mermaid kept grinning at me with her crazy smile. There was nothing else she could do. Just like Salina. Just like me too. I grimaced and turned away.

Bria and Xavier must have called for reinforcements, because more and more cops started showing up on the scene. Portable lights were rigged up so the po-po could see what they were doing. Crime scene tape was strung up here and there. Evidence was gathered. At least, what could be pried out of the elemental Ice that still covered most of the lawn.

I sat there on the rim of the fountain in the middle of it all. A few of the cops gave me sideways glances, but no one dared approach me—except Finn, who once again skated over to me.

"I'm sure you've realized by now that it won't be too much longer before the media arrive," he said. "So I suggest we make our exit now—unless you want your face all over the morning news."

I nodded.

"Good," he said. "I made the same suggestion to Owen and Eva. They're already waiting for us in the Escalade. Kincaid is taking his own wheels home."

I blinked. "How the hell did you manage that? Seeing as how you were holding a gun on Owen not twenty minutes ago?"

Finn flashed me a grin. "I pointed out that Owen needs to get Jo-Jo to look at those bumps on his head and his cracked ribs. I also suggested that, unless he wanted Eva to be on camera, we should skedaddle as quickly as possible. For once, he was sensible about things."

I shook my head. "You mean you wheedled and probably browbeat him into it until he gave in."

"Would I do something like that?"

"Absolutely."

Finn grinned a little wider.

I followed him over to the Escalade, which was a mess. The front had been smushed in like a tin can where he'd rammed the car through the gate and then into the koi fountain, and the windshield had splintered as a result. More scratches and scrapes could be seen on the passenger's side where the vehicle had slammed up against the side of the fountain. It was like a group of giants had pounded on the car with their fists. Just about everything on it was either smashed, cracked, or broken.

"By the way," he said, opening the driver's side door. "You *will* be paying for every bit of the damage."

Despite the situation, his words brought a ghost of a smile to my face. It was somehow comforting to know that Finnegan Lane was still looking out for number one—himself.

I slid into the front passenger's seat, Owen and Eva already in the back. Eva nodded, but Owen just stared at me, a blank look on his face. As though we were strangers.

Nobody spoke on the ride over to Jo-Jo's. Finn parked in the driveway, and we all got out of the car. Owen headed toward the house without a word, without even looking at me or giving me a hint of a smile, letting me know that everything between us was going to be okay.

"Just give him some time," Eva whispered. "He'll come around eventually, Gin. I know he will."

I nodded, not trusting myself to speak, not trusting myself to give voice to all my fears that by killing Salina, I'd also killed the love between me and Owen.

She squeezed my hand, hurried after him, and slipped inside the house. Finn stepped up on the porch. He started to go inside when he realized that I hadn't moved.

"Gin?" he asked. "Are you coming?"

I shook my head. "Not right now. Let Jo-Jo see to Owen first. He got the worst of it tonight. Tell her that I'll be along later."

Finn nodded and stepped inside, letting the screen door bang shut behind him.

When I was sure that he wasn't going to double back and check on me, I walked around to the other side of the SUV, putting the vehicle in between me and the house. I kept going until I was at the edge of the yard just before it started sloping down to the street. It was full dark now, and only the fireflies glimmered in the quiet night, weaving in and out through the trees where the crickets and cicadas sang their midnight song, punctuated here and there by the bellow of a bullfrog and the low hoot of an owl.

But I didn't really hear the noises of the night. Only one thing echoed in my head again and again.

Daddy! No! Daddy! Daddy—

I breathed in, letting the soft, humid scent of the night air roll across my tongue. I scrubbed my hands over my face, as if I could wash away the memories of tonight, especially the image of Owen turning his back on me.

But I couldn't—and I didn't know if I ever would.

❋34❋

I stayed outside for a long time—long enough for Jo-Jo to heal Owen and for him and Eva to go on their way.

The porch light snapped on, and my lover stepped outside, followed by Eva and Sophia. The Goth dwarf rounded the house, and I heard her convertible start up a minute later. She must have been taking them home.

Sure enough, Sophia drove her convertible around to the front of the house. Eva opened one of the passenger doors and slid into the backseat. Owen grabbed hold of the front passenger door. He started to open it and get inside but paused, his eyes scanning the yard. He couldn't see me in the shadows, and my heart rose in hopes that he might come looking for me.

But he didn't.

Instead, he got into the car and shut the door. Sophia steered the vehicle down the driveway, and her red taillights—shaped like little skulls—disappeared into the darkness.

When I was sure they were gone, I walked over, trudged up the porch steps, and shuffled inside. I plodded back to the salon, where Jo-Jo and Finn were talking in low voices. The two of them looked at me. I knew they could see the raw emotion in my face, but for once I was too tired to hide my feelings.

Everything about tonight had simply hurt.

I settled myself in one of the cherry red salon chairs. Finn gave me a sympathetic glance, murmured something about calling to check in with Bria, and left.

"Finn told me what happened," Jo-Jo said, reaching for her Air magic. "What you did to Salina."

"I killed her, Jo-Jo. She was down for the count, but I went ahead and killed her anyway—even though Owen asked me not to."

In a flat, dull voice, I told the dwarf everything, starting with Owen leaving me to go confront Salina to Finn figuring out her plan to my putting a stop to it and her—for good. All the while, the dwarf worked her magic on me. The feel of the tiny needles pricking at all my cuts, lumps, scratches, and bruises and making them whole again didn't bother me tonight.

It was nothing compared to the ache in my heart.

Finally, the dwarf finished healing me and dropped her hand. The magic faded from her eyes, and she looked at me once more.

"It was an awful choice you had to make, darling. But Owen wouldn't have wanted Eva to be a killer. Not like that."

"No, he wouldn't have, and I was trying to protect Eva from that." I let out a breath. "But part of me killed Salina because I wanted to, Jo-Jo. Because she was a threat to me and Owen, and not just physically. I didn't want to lose him to her, but it looks like that's what's happening anyway."

She nodded. "Maybe that's what it feels like now, but we both know Fletcher trained you better than that, Gin. He might have raised you to be an assassin, but he taught you to respect his code, your code. You don't kill for the pleasure of it—you do what you have to in order to survive. Nothing more, nothing less. Like it or not, sometimes people just get broken, and nothing and nobody will make them whole again. Some of them even enjoy what they become. If you hadn't killed Salina tonight, how long do you think it would have been before she made another run at you? Or Eva? Or even Owen?"

Jo-Jo was right, but that didn't make me feel any better. It didn't heal this rift between me and Owen.

"She would have killed one of you sooner or later," Jo-Jo continued. "And then how would Owen feel? He's already full of guilt that he didn't realize what she was doing to Eva and that he believed her lies about Phillip. If you'd let Salina live, and she'd hurt any one of you, Owen would have felt even guiltier that he didn't kill her when he had the chance. It would have eaten him up inside until there was nothing left."

I didn't say anything. I didn't know there was anything left of me and Owen.

Jo-Jo's eyes clouded over, as though she was peering into the future. "Don't worry, darling. It may take some time, but it everything will work out all right in the end. You'll see."

She patted my hand and started moving around the salon, straightening up. I sat in the chair and thought about her words.

But try as I might, I couldn't convince myself that things would ever be the same again.

I spent the night at Jo-Jo's. The next morning, I was sitting in one of the rocking chairs on the front porch, brooding into the sunlight, when Bria's car pulled into the driveway. Xavier was with her, and he waved at me from the passenger's seat. I waved back.

Bria got out of the car, walked to the porch, and sat down in the rocking chair next to me. For a long time, the only sound was the faint *creak-creak-creaks* of the wood. Finally, my sister spoke.

"I thought you'd want to know that there are fifteen folks dead, including Salina and the giants you killed, and almost two dozen with injuries," she said.

I nodded. I'd expected the damage to be something like that, given how much water had soaked the area and how much glee Salina had taken in using her magic.

"Still, it could have been worse, a whole lot worse, all things considered," Bria said. "She would have killed everyone with her magic if you hadn't stepped in. The folks who survived owe you their lives, Gin."

I tried to smile at her, but it didn't come off very well. "Yeah, well, maybe the mayor will finally break down and give me that medal I've always wanted."

My sister reached over and squeezed my hand, which

was cold despite the growing warmth of the day. "Maybe. But I want you to know that I'm proud of you. I know it would have been better for you if Salina had killed everyone, especially Jonah McAllister. I know it wasn't easy for you to save all the people who've been trying to murder you these past few months."

I shrugged. "Maybe I'm getting soft in my old age, wanting to protect my enemies instead of executing them like I should have. Like they would have done to me."

Bria's eyes met mine. "Not too soft. You killed Salina in the end."

I let out a breath. "No, not too soft."

"What does Owen think about that?"

"Nothing good."

"I saw what happened, what you did for Eva. You killed Salina so she wouldn't have to, so Owen wouldn't have to. He'll come to see that in time." She echoed what Jo-Jo had said to me last night.

I shrugged. I wished I shared her confidence, but I didn't—I just didn't. I'd seen the way Owen had looked at me after I'd slit Salina's throat. How angry and hurt he'd been by my actions. I didn't know if he could recover from that. I didn't know if I could either.

"Bria!" Xavier called out, waving his hand at my sister through his open car window. "We have to go!"

Bria waved back, telling him that she'd be there in a minute. "Duty calls," she said, and got to her feet.

"I made quite the mess for you to clean up, didn't I? You'll be dealing with the aftermath of this for weeks."

She shrugged. "What are sisters for? Besides, you just helped me close two other homicides—Katarina and

Antonio. Plus, the families of the men Salina married and murdered can finally get some closure, too. All in all, not a bad night's work for the Spider."

"You know, I think that's the first time you've ever said my assassin name in a happy tone," I said.

Bria looked at me, her face somber. "Do you remember what you said to me the night you saved Elliot Slater from beating me to death in my own house?"

"Something like there were worse things in the world than me."

She nodded. "I think we saw one of those things last night. There are worse things than assassins in the world, Gin. A hell of a lot worse things. Some of them are even disguised as love."

She leaned down and hugged me, then headed back over to her car, where Xavier was waiting. A minute later, they were gone, off to deal with the rest of the fallout.

The attempted massacre of Ashland's underworld leaders dominated the news for the next few days. Story after story filled the newspapers and airwaves about Salina Dubois and her twisted plan to get revenge for her father's murder.

When those stories became old news, the survivors told their harrowing tales for the local media, Jonah McAllister chief among them. Even though he'd been working with Salina, had helped her arrange her deadly dinner, he still painted himself as just another victim. The smarmy lawyer gave an interview to anyone who came calling until you couldn't turn on the TV or open the newspaper without seeing his smooth face. Smug bastard. He was worse than a cockroach, always finding a way to survive no matter whose boot heel he was being crushed under.

But slowly, life got back to normal—except for the fact that I didn't hear a word from Owen.

He didn't call or come by to see me, and I didn't try to contact him. I knew he needed some time, some space, and I was determined to give it to him, no matter how much I just wanted to hold him in my arms and pretend like the last few days had never happened. Like I'd never heard of Salina Dubois or discovered just how much she'd meant to my lover.

Eva called me every day, but she didn't have much to say either. She was trying to deal with Salina's death and her part in it just like I was.

Finally, a week after I killed Salina, Owen dropped by the Pork Pit. My lover stepped into the restaurant, making the bell over the front door chime. It was five minutes before closing time, and the restaurant was deserted except for me and Sophia. The dwarf jerked her thumb over her shoulder at him.

"Privacy," she rasped.

"Thanks, Sophia," I murmured. "I'll finish locking up. See you tomorrow."

The dwarf gave me a hopeful smile, then pushed through the double doors and went into the back of the restaurant.

Owen waited until she left before squaring his shoulders and walking over to the counter. "Hi."

"Hi, yourself."

I smiled at him, trying to tell him that I understood, trying to tell him that I wanted to move forward. But he didn't return my smile, and his eyes were dark and troubled in his rugged face. Not a trace remained of the giants' attacks on him or the injuries he'd gotten when Salina had used her magic to throw him against the Ice bar. No, Owen looked just fine on the outside. Inside, though, I knew it was a different story—for both of us.

"I'd like to talk, if that's okay with you," he said.

I nodded. I locked the door and turned the sign there over to *Closed*. We moved to a booth out of sight of the storefront windows. The honk and hum of the cars sounded on the street outside, but we sat in silence.

Finally, Owen drew in a breath. "I'm sorry about how I acted the other night. When you . . . killed Salina . . . it affected me more than I thought it would."

"I know, Owen. And I'm sorry about that. Sorrier than you will ever know."

I didn't apologize for killing her. I didn't say that it simply had to be done, that Salina wouldn't have ever stopped, that I'd probably saved Owen's life—all our lives—by cutting the water elemental's throat. He knew all that as well as I did. And if he didn't, well, then we had an even bigger problem than I'd imagined.

"One of the things that bothers me the most is that you had Finn pull a gun on me," Owen said, his violet eyes harsh and accusing. "You let him hold me at gunpoint while you killed Salina."

I wasn't surprised he was upset by that, by how I'd had Finn keep him out of the fight. Not only had I killed Salina, but I'd also taken away Owen's choice in how things would go down. I would have been just as angry if our positions had been reversed.

"And what would you have done if I hadn't? You would have tried to stop me, Owen. Hell, you told me to stop—more than once. I was trying to protect you, trying to keep you safe."

Trying to spare you from having to kill someone you once loved.

I didn't say the words, but they hung in the air between us, weighing everything down, weighing us down, with their many ugly implications.

Owen shook his head. "No, you just didn't trust me enough to do what needed to be done where Salina was concerned. You didn't trust me at all, Gin. Not with her. When we went to Blue Marsh, and you ran into Donovan again, I trusted you to make the right choice. I trusted in your love for me. I trusted you not to hurt me. I expected the same courtesies in return, but you didn't give them to me with Salina."

I didn't say anything at first. I couldn't, because his words were too true. I hadn't trusted him with Salina because I hadn't wanted to get my heart broken when he chose her over me. When you cared about someone, you gave them the power to hurt you, and I'd feared that Owen would throw away my concern just like Donovan had once done. Deep down, I knew it was irrational, that Owen was nothing like Donovan, but I'd still felt that paralyzing fear all the same.

"But I did trust you," I replied. "Did I have doubts? Sure. Was I worried that Salina was coming between us? Absolutely. But I handled all that as best I could. Even when you went to see her alone, I came after you—and that's when I heard you tell Salina that she could *leave*

Ashland. That wasn't what we agreed on. Not at all. You didn't tell me what you were really going to say to her, so I'd say that you didn't trust me either."

To that, he didn't say anything. He couldn't, because my words were as true as his had been a moment ago. For once, I let my emotions show. Let him see my clenched jaw, the tightness in my face, the cold, harsh accusations in my eyes. I let him see my anger and my hurt and my disappointment—in him.

"I'll admit that I was jealous of her," I finally said in a soft voice. "She was everything that I'm not, and she was a part of your past that you couldn't seem to let go of. That maybe you didn't want to let go of."

Owen sighed. "Salina and I were finished the moment she first hurt Eva, even if I didn't realize it back then. But as soon as she came back to Ashland, I should have made it crystal clear to her that we were long over—and to you too. I thought I did that day at the Pork Pit. But that doesn't change the fact that you killed her, Gin. Right in front of me. I asked you not to, and you killed her anyway."

"I didn't kill her for you. So I could have you or keep you."

No, I killed Salina for Eva, for Kincaid, for Cooper—and for myself too and everything she represented to me. What I could have become if not for Fletcher. Maybe what I was anyway.

Owen's face tightened. "I know that. Over these past few months, I've watched you do what you thought needed to be done, no matter how dangerous it was. Even when other people told you not to do something or tried to get you to stop, you went ahead and did what you thought was right anyway."

"Is there something wrong with that?"

He shook his head. "I can't say that there is. Not after I've seen how you've helped people. But I never thought you would tune me out the way you sometimes do Bria, Jo-Jo, and even Finn. I never thought I would ask you for something—something important—and you would just ignore me."

I could have protested. I could have told him that he was wrong. That I listened to my family and friends, that I didn't just tune them out, but he was partially right. Because in the end, someone had to make the hard decisions, had to do the dirty work, had to be the bad guy, and, like it or not, it seemed that quite often that someone was me.

I thought about telling him what I'd promised Eva, about how I'd promised his baby sister that I would protect Owen no matter what—even from himself, if it came down to that. But I kept my mouth shut. Owen had to accept what I'd done on his own and not just because I wanted him to. He had to forgive me on his own terms, in his own way, and not because I gave him an excuse to.

We didn't speak for several minutes. Outside, folks went about their day, talking on their phones, getting into their cars, driving home, but inside the restaurant, it was like Owen and I were frozen in place, stuck in this one awful moment, and not sure where we went from here. I could almost see our future swinging back and forth like a clock pendulum.

Tick-tock, tick-tock. Together, apart. Together, apart.

"So where does all of this leave us?" I finally asked.

Silence. Then—

"I need . . . I need some time, Gin. To think about things. You. Me. Us."

Those were the words I'd been dreading hearing, and they caused my heart to crack, splinter, and disintegrate into black dust, leaving a hollow, cavernous space in my chest, an ache that just pulsed and pulsed and pulsed with pain.

Owen hesitated. "And it's not just about Salina. It's about me too. All these years, I believed her lies, and I hurt Eva, Phillip, and Cooper because of it—and you too. Because I believed in Salina when I shouldn't have. I feel like such a fucking fool. I said before that you didn't trust me. Maybe you were right not to, because I've clearly been wrong about this most basic thing. I just—I just don't know anymore. What to do, what to say, what to feel about any of this."

Bitterness colored his voice, and the guilt he was feeling made him grind his teeth together. His mouth twisted with disgust—at himself.

I wanted to reach out to him, wanted to put my hand on top of his and tell him that it wasn't his fault. That Salina had fooled a lot of people.

But I didn't.

I knew that I had to give Owen some space. I had to give him some time to come to terms with what had happened, work through everything, and settle it for himself. He had to come back to me on his own, he had to find his way back to me on his own. Otherwise, we'd never truly recover, and we'd only be going through the motions, pretending to love each other, and it would eventually eat away at and undermine everything we had together. I'd rather have lost Owen completely than have had him by my side when I knew he didn't really want to be there.

And the truth was that I needed some time too—time to think about Salina, what she'd meant to Owen, and how I felt about all that. I needed some time to convince myself that I wasn't like Salina, that Mab hadn't ruined me the way she had the water elemental, that she hadn't twisted me into something sad, dangerous, and grotesque.

That I wasn't a threat to the people I loved.

Owen slid out of the booth and got to his feet. I did the same. He started to go, but I caught his hand in mine. He turned to meet my gaze.

"I understand," I said, "and you take as much time as you need. But know this, Owen. I love you. Now, today, tomorrow. That won't ever change, no matter what happens between us."

I moved closer, cupped his face in my hands, and kissed him.

For a moment, he gathered me up in his arms and kissed me back—kissed me back with all the passion, all the concern, all the love I felt for him.

Then he broke off the kiss and stepped away. I curled my hands into fists so I wouldn't be tempted to reach for him. He'd asked for space, and I was going to give it to him.

No matter how much it fucking *hurt*.

"Take care of yourself, Gin." Owen hesitated. "I'll be seeing you."

I forced myself to smile. "Yeah. We'll see each other again real soon."

Owen nodded, then turned and walked out of the restaurant. The bell over the door chimed as he stepped outside, ringing like a dirge for the dead, and the end of our relationship.

Or was it? Was this the end? Could we get past this? I didn't know. I hoped so. Oh, how I hoped so. But my hope was as useless as tears would have been. So I stood there in the shadows staring out the storefront windows for a long time, the dust of my heart quivering with sadness and a chill creeping into my bones, despite the warm spring sunshine outside.

❊ 35 ❊

The next day was business as usual at the Pork Pit. I still had a barbecue restaurant to run.

I cooked food, waited on tables, and cleaned up after my customers. But for once, my mind wasn't really focused on the tasks at hand and I was just going through the motions. My misery must have shown, because Sophia stopped chopping onions long enough to give me a tight hug. I thanked the dwarf and got back to the macaroni salad I was making.

About three o'clock that afternoon, someone not entirely unexpected walked through the front door—Phillip Kincaid.

The casino boss was once again in a suit and tie, and he had his blond hair slicked back into his usual ponytail. Kincaid surveyed the other customers in the storefront, then walked over and took a seat on a stool right next to the cash register.

"Gin."

"Phillip."

I didn't ask why he was here. I was still too preoccupied with Owen. Besides, I figured Kincaid would get to it sooner or later.

Kincaid ordered a couple of hot dogs, coleslaw, fries, and three of the chocolate cupcakes that I'd baked fresh that morning. I fixed his food, set it in front of him, and picked up my copy of *Little Women*. Normally, I would have breezed through the rest of the book hours ago, but I was having a tough time concentrating. Still, I gave it a shot, even though I had to go back and skim the paragraphs so I could recall the words I'd just read moments before.

Kincaid ate his meal in silence. He didn't bother me, and I didn't speak to him, but the quiet between us wasn't hostile. If anything, it was almost . . . friendly.

He finally let out a satisfied sigh, pushed his empty plates away, and untucked the napkin in his collar. "Another fine meal."

"That's what I do here."

I thought he might pay up and leave, but instead Kincaid threaded his fingers together on top of the counter and looked at me.

"I went to see Owen last night," he said. "He invited me out to his place for a drink. Cooper too. The three of us spent most of the night talking. It was . . . nice. Like the old days."

It didn't surprise me. Now that the truth was out and Salina was dead, there was nothing standing in the way of Owen and Kincaid resuming their friendship. I was happy for them. They'd been family once upon a time, along with Cooper and Eva, and I thought they could be that again.

"I know the two of you are having trouble right now," Kincaid said. "I'm sorry for that. Really, I am. It was never my intention to cause those sorts of problems for the two of you. I just . . . I just wanted Owen to know the truth. Finally."

I shrugged. Kincaid being sorry didn't change things between me and Owen, but it made me feel a little better.

"You know, I'd enjoy getting to know Owen again while you can," I said in an easy voice. "Because once he realizes that you're in love with Eva, he's going to morph right back into that overprotective, big brother, bear mode."

Kincaid froze, his glass of iced tea halfway between the counter and his lips. "What? What are you talking about?"

I laughed, a genuine, bona fide, amused laugh. "Oh, come on. It's so obvious. The way you were looking at Eva on the riverboat, you hiring me to be there to protect her in case Salina showed up, the fact that you still let Eva get away with calling you by that ridiculous childhood nickname. If that's not love, I don't know what is." I gave him a hard stare. "But you need to keep in mind that she's only nineteen. And you're not exactly the safest guy to be around in Ashland."

Kincaid shrugged, but he didn't deny any of it. If anything, his eyes brightened at the thought of her. "Eva Grayson was the first person who ever gave a damn about me. That's not the sort of thing you forget."

"No," I agreed. "It's not."

"And that's why I'm going to give Eva some time to grow up—a lot of time, actually. Like you said, she's still young. She hasn't figured out what she wants out of life yet. I'm going to give her that chance. And in the meantime, I plan to have plenty of fun."

I arched an eyebrow. "And if it comes to pass that she doesn't want you?"

He grinned. "Oh, she'll want me. I'm even more irresistible to women than your friend Finn is."

I had to laugh at his confidence, if nothing else. My chuckles were just fading away when the bell over the front door chimed and a guy stepped inside the restaurant. He was a dwarf wearing a plaid shirt that was too tight for his muscled upper body, jeans, and a pair of dusty cowboy boots. He started flexing his hands as soon as he stepped inside, and his gaze cut right, then left, like he was looking for someone specific to give a beat-down to.

I sighed. I knew the type—some low-level hood who wanted to move way, way up in the underworld food chain by taking out the Spider.

The dwarf looked in my direction, and his eyes narrowed, indicating that he'd found his target—me. I put down my book, straightened up, and gave him a cold smile. Kincaid noticed my evil grin, and he swiveled around to see who I was glaring at with murder in my eyes.

The dwarf took a step forward, like he was going to charge me right here in the storefront, but he froze when he saw Kincaid. The dwarf's eyes widened, and he started chewing on his lip—thinking hard. Kincaid arched his eyebrows in a silent command, then made a shooing motion with his hand.

The dwarf didn't have to be told twice. He turned around and practically ran out of the Pork Pit as fast as his cowboy boots would carry him. Kincaid turned back around to me.

"Funny thing," I said. "Since that night at Salina's, no one has come into the restaurant and tried to kill me. Until right now."

"That *is* funny . . . since we both know how infinitely lovable you are."

"Why, Philly," I drawled. "If I didn't know better, I'd almost say that was a joke."

Kincaid grinned at me. "What can I say, Gin? You bring out the worst in me."

I thought of Owen, and my chest tightened. "Yeah, I tend to do that to people."

He looked at me, but he didn't get up to leave. Instead, he stared at me, an amused smile on his face. "Don't tell me you've forgotten already."

"Forgotten what?" I asked, having no idea what he was talking about.

"We had a deal, remember? You kill Salina, and I get the folks gunning for you to back off. As many as I can, anyway. You held up your end, and I intend to do the same with mine."

I frowned. "That dwarf? He was one of yours?"

"Of course not. I would never be so crass as to send a hit man after you. Let's just say I've let it be known that I've developed something of a grudging fondness for you. He saw me, and he thought better of things. That's all."

I might have mocked him about it on the riverboat, but Kincaid was one of the few people in Ashland who actually had that kind of clout. If he wanted to throw a little goodwill my way, fine by me. Still, I couldn't help but point out the obvious.

"Technically, we never had a deal because I never agreed to kill Salina for you."

He grinned. "I know, but she's dead all the same. And I couldn't be happier about that."

I snorted. "Despite how happy you are, it won't last, and you know it. I'm too tempting a target for folks to ignore me for very long."

"I know," he replied. "But I figured you could use a break, after everything that's happened the past few days."

I couldn't argue with that.

I worked at the restaurant the rest of the day, then went home. Normally, I didn't mind being alone, but tonight, Fletcher's house felt especially empty, despite all the odd knickknacks stuffed inside. Or maybe that was just because my heart felt like a hollow shell now that Owen and I were . . . well . . . I didn't know what we were right now, but we weren't together.

And it fucking hurt.

I didn't have an appetite, so I poured myself a glass of gin and took it and the rest of the bottle into the den in the back of the house. I downed the drink, relishing the sweet burn of the liquor as it slid down my throat. I reached for the bottle to pour myself another round, but I stopped. Getting stinking drunk wouldn't ease the ache in my heart, and it sure as hell wouldn't make me feel better in the morning. So I pushed it aside and leaned back against the couch.

My eyes lifted to the mantel and the four framed drawings there. My mother, Eira's, snowflake, representing icy calm. Annabella's ivy vine for elegance. Bria's beautiful primrose. The one of the neon sign outside the Pork Pit that was my homage to Fletcher. My gaze lingered on each one of the runes, and a strange mood seized me.

It had been a while since I'd taken any art classes at the community college, but I still had some supplies on hand. I rummaged through one of the drawers in a table in the den and found a sketchpad and some pencils I'd stuffed in there when I'd moved back into Fletcher's house last year.

I put the pad on my lap, grabbed a pencil, and started drawing. Thirty minutes later, I had a fifth rune—Owen's hammer. The symbol for strength, perseverance, and hard work. All things he had, all things he excelled at. My fingers traced over the symbol, and I wished that I could show it to Owen, wished he was here with me now.

But he wasn't—and I didn't know if he would ever be here again.

I was sitting there staring at the rune when a sharp knock sounded on the front door, followed by a key turning in the lock. Besides me, only a few people had a key to the house—and Owen was one of them.

Heart pounding, I put the drawing aside, got to my feet, and went out into the hallway, hurrying toward the front of the house. I skidded to a stop just inside the door, waiting for whoever was outside to come on in and show himself. The lock clicked open, and the door swung forward.

But it wasn't Owen standing on the other side—it was Bria.

My baby sister stepped inside the house and held the door open for someone coming in behind her—Roslyn. Both women were carrying canvas bags full of . . . something. I couldn't quite tell what.

"Hi, Gin!" Roslyn called out, putting both of her bags into one hand so she could pull the door shut behind her.

"Roslyn. Bria. What are ya'll doing here?"

Bria raised an eyebrow. "You told me to come by anytime."

"Me too," Roslyn chimed in.

I shook off my confusion. "Of course, and you're always welcome. Both of you—you know that. I'm just . . . surprised, that's all."

Bria and Roslyn exchanged a look. Then they both came in farther, passing me in the hallway and heading toward the kitchen. They dumped their bags on the table and started unpacking the items inside, which included some cheeses, crackers, chocolates, fresh fruit, a bottle of wine, and a couple of books.

"What's all this?" I asked.

I picked up one of the books and turned it over so I could see the cover. The words *Little Women* glinted in silver foil.

"Book club," Roslyn said, opening the kitchen drawers in search of something.

"Book club?"

"Remember, you were joking the other day at the Pork Pit that we should start our own book club. Well, I talked to Bria, and we both thought it was a fine idea, especially now . . ." Roslyn winced, and her voice trailed off, but I knew what she'd been about to say.

Especially now that you and Owen are having problems.

My heart twinged with pain, but I was gracious enough not to call her on it.

"We thought it would be fun," Bria said in a quiet tone. "For all of us. Roslyn and I have spent the last few days reading *Little Women*."

The two of them looked at me, the question of whether they should go or stay clear in their eyes. They were obviously trying to cheer me up, and their gesture touched me. I knew they wouldn't have read the book if Roslyn hadn't seen me with it at the restaurant. I hadn't had many true friends in my life, and I was glad that I'd found them. So even though I didn't really want company, I plastered a smile on my face.

"I think book club sounds like a great idea. Thanks for thinking of it—and me."

"Excellent!" Roslyn said and turned her attention back to the drawer she was rifling through. "Although where's your corkscrew? I don't see one in here."

"I think Finn stuffed it in one of the drawers in the den the last time he was here. I'll get it."

Bria and Roslyn started chatting about how good the food looked and what sort of plates they should put everything on, while I went into the den. After a couple of minutes of searching, I found the corkscrew stuffed down behind one of the couch cushions.

"Finn," I said, laughing a little and shaking my head.

I'd just turned to go back to the kitchen when my eyes landed on the drawing I'd done of Owen's hammer rune.

I stopped and picked up the paper, my fingers tracing over the rune, a sharp, pulsing ache in my heart once more.

But like it or not, the pain and the uncertainty were things that I just had to live with, like I had so many other hard, painful things in my life. Owen and I had hit a rough patch, thanks to my actions, and his too. Now we had to deal with the consequences and fallout as best we could. Owen had asked for some time, and I needed the space and separation too. Maybe more than he did. Time to realize that Owen had loved someone before me. Time to realize that part of him would probably always love Salina. Time to realize that her death had hit him harder than I'd thought it would—harder than I thought it should. But who was I to judge? I wasn't exactly the poster child for emotional health. Quite the opposite.

Besides, Jo-Jo had said that everything would work out the way it was supposed to. I'd taken her words to mean that Owen and I weren't done, that she saw a future for us. It might take a while, and there might be a lot of heartache along the way, but we'd get there. I knew we would. I had to believe we would.

I just had to.

I carefully tore the sheet with Owen's rune out of my sketchpad and propped it up alongside the others on the mantel. Maybe it was time for a change regarding the drawings. I'd always thought of them as the runes of my dead family, but maybe, maybe I could start thinking of them as tributes instead. A way to celebrate the people I loved.

Or maybe the love Owen and I had shared was just as dead as my mother, sister, and Fletcher.

No, I thought. Our love wasn't dead. It was just a little battered and bruised. It would eventually heal, and I was determined to do everything I could to help it along. If that meant giving Owen time and space to himself, then that was what I was going to do—no matter how much I just wanted to be in his arms right now.

"Come on, Gin," Bria said in a loud voice. "The wine isn't going to open itself!"

"Be right there!" I called back.

My friends had come to cheer me up, and I was going to let them. So I had a broken heart—so what? I'd gotten through worse, and I'd get through this too. This time, I was just grateful that there were people here for me, people who cared about me.

I looked at Owen's rune a final time, then fixed a smile on my face and headed into the kitchen to eat, drink, talk, and laugh the night away with my friends, my family.

Turn the page for a sneak peek at the
next book in the Elemental Assassin series

DEADLY STING

by Jennifer Estep

Coming soon from Pocket Books

❊ 1 ❊

"That would look *fabulous* on you."

Finnegan Lane, my foster brother, pointed to a tennis bracelet in the middle of a glass case full of jewelry. The shimmer of the gemstones matched the sparkle of greed in his eyes.

I looked at the price tag beside the diamond-crusted monstrosity. "You do realize that the cost of that bracelet is within spitting distance of my going rate as an assassin, right?"

"You mean your going rate back when you were actually killing people for money," Finn said. "Or as I like to call them—the good ole days."

Finn gave the diamond bracelet one more greedy glance before moving over to a display of shoes. He grabbed a purple pump off a shelf and waggled the shoe at me before holding it up and inspecting it himself. He gazed at the shoe with a rapt expression, as though it were a work of art instead of merely overpriced pieces of leather sewn together.

"It's the latest style," he said in a dreamy voice. "Hand-stitched lavender suede with custom-made, four-inch heels. Isn't it marvelous?"

I arched an eyebrow. "Have I ever told you how scary it is that you know more about shoes than I do?"

Finn grinned, his green eyes lighting up with amusement. "Frequently. But my impeccable fashion sense is one of the many things you love about me."

He straightened his gray silk tie and winked at me. I snorted and moved over to look at some dresses hanging on a rack near the wall.

The two of us were out shopping, which was one of Finn's favorite things to do. Not mine, though. I never paid too much attention to what I was wearing, beyond making sure that my jeans and boots were comfortable enough to fight in and that my T-shirt sleeves were long enough to hide the knives I had tucked up each one. As the assassin the Spider, I'd learned a long time ago not to invest too much money in clothes that were only going to end up with bloodstains on them.

But here I was, along for the consumer ride. Finn had shown up at the Pork Pit, my barbecue joint, just after the lunch rush ended and had dragged me all the way up to Northtown, the part of Ashland that housed and catered to the wealthy, social, and magical elite. We'd spent the last hour traipsing from store to store in an upscale shopping development that had just opened up.

Now we were browsing through Posh, the biggest, fanciest, and most expensive boutique on this particular block. Racks of ball gowns and evening dresses filled the store, starting with all-white frocks on the left and darkening to midnight black ones on the right, like a rainbow of color arcing from one side of the store to the other. There wasn't a dress in here that was less than five grand, and the shoes arranged along the back wall went for just as much. Not to mention the minuscule handbags that cost ten times as much as a good steak dinner.

"Come on, Gin," Finn wheedled, holding the pump out to me. "At least try it on."

I rolled my eyes, took the shoe from him, and hefted it in my hand. "Lightweight, nice enough color. Not the worst thing you've shown me today. And that skinny stiletto would make a decent weapon, if you took the time to snap it off the rest of the shoe and sharpen the end of it."

Finn sighed and took the pump away from me. "Have I ever told you how scary it is that you think of heels in terms of their possible shiv potential?"

I grinned at him. "Frequently. But my impeccable sense of improvised weaponry is one of the many things you love about me."

This time, Finn rolled his eyes, and then started muttering under his breath about how he couldn't take me anywhere. My grin widened. I loved needling Finn as much as he enjoyed teasing me.

"Tell me again why I have to go to this shindig with you?" I asked when he finally wound down.

"It's not a mere *shindig*," he huffed. "It's the opening gala for an exhibit of art, jewelry, and other valuable objects from the estate of the late, not-so-great, and certainly unlamented Mab Monroe. Everyone who's anyone will be there, underworld and otherwise, and it's going to be *the* social event of the summer. Besides, aren't you the least bit curious to see what the old girl stashed away over the years? The things she collected? What she thought was beautiful or valuable or at least worth hoarding? She *was* your nemesis, after all."

Mab Monroe had been a little more than my nemesis—the Fire elemental had murdered my mother and older sister when I was thirteen. She'd also tortured me. But I'd finally gotten my revenge when I shoved my silverstone knife through the bitch's black heart back in the winter. Killing Mab had been one of the most satisfying moments of my life. The fact that she was dead and I wasn't was the only thing that really mattered to me.

"Sorry," I said. "I have no desire to go gawk at all of Mab's shinies. They're not doing her any good now, are they? I'm quite happy simply knowing that she's rotting in her grave. And I still don't understand why you insisted on dragging me out to buy a dress. I have plenty of little black numbers in my closet at home, any one of which would be perfect for this event."

Finn snorted. "Sure, if you don't mind wearing something that's ripped, torn, and caked with dried blood."

I couldn't argue with that. Funny how killing people inevitably led to ruined clothes.

Finn sighed and shook his head at my lack of interest in Mab's many treasures. "I can't believe you won't go out of simple curiosity and unabashed greed. Those are certainly the reasons *I'm* going. And probably half the folks on the guest list. We've just covered why you need a new dress. As to why you have to go with me, well, naturally, I asked Bria first, but she has to work. I need *someone* to drink champagne with and make snide comments to about everyone else in attendance. You wouldn't deny me that pleasure, would you?"

"Perish the thought," I murmured. "But what about Roslyn? Or Jo-Jo? Why don't you take one of them instead?"

"Roslyn is already going with someone else, and Jo-Jo has a date with Cooper." Finn used his fingers to tick off our friends and family. "I even asked Sophia, but there's some classic Western film festival that she's planning to catch that night. Besides, she'd probably insist on wearing black lipstick, a silverstone collar, and the rest of her usual Goth clothes instead of an evening dress. Since I don't want to be responsible for any of the old guard having conniptions or coronary episodes, you're it."

"Lucky me."

"Besides, it's not like you have plans," he continued as though I hadn't said a word. "Other than sitting at home and brooding over lost love."

My eyes narrowed, and I gave Finn a look that would have made most men tremble in their wing tips. He just picked up a strappy, canary-yellow sandal and admired it a moment before showing it to me.

"What do you think? Is yellow your color? Yeah, you're right. Not with your skin tone." He put the shoe back on the shelf and turned to face me.

"Look," Finn said, his expression serious. "I just thought it would be good for you to get out of the house for a night. You know, dress up, go out on the town, have a little fun. I know how hard this last month has been, with you and Owen on the outs."

On the outs was putting it mildly. I hadn't spoken to Owen Grayson, my lover, since the night he'd come to the Pork Pit a few weeks ago to tell me he needed some time to himself, some time away from me, from us.

But that's what happens when you kill your lover's ex-fiancée right in front of him. That sort of thing tended to make a person reassess their relationships—especially with the one who'd done the killing.

No matter how much I missed him, I couldn't blame Owen for wanting to take a break. A lot of bad stuff had gone down in the days leading up to me battling Salina Dubois, a lot of terrible secrets had been revealed, and he wasn't the only one who'd needed time to process and come to terms with everything. I might understand, but that didn't make it hurt any less.

Even assassins could have their hearts broken.

"Gin?" Finn asked in a soft voice, cutting into my thoughts.

I sighed. "I know you're just trying to help, but I'm fine, Finn. Really, I am. The important thing is that Salina is dead, and she can't hurt anyone else ever again. Owen and I . . . we'll eventually work things out."

"And if you don't?"

I sighed again. "Then, we'll both move on with our lives."

I kept my face calm and smooth, although my heart squeezed at the thought. Finn started to say something else when one of the saleswomen sidled up to him.

"Good afternoon, sir," the woman, a gorgeous red-head, practically purred. "What can I do for you today?"

We'd already been in the store for five minutes, and I was mildly surprised that it had taken someone this long to come over to us. In my boots, worn jeans, and grease-spattered black T-shirt, I didn't look like I had two nickels to rub together, but Finn was as impeccably dressed as ever in one of his Fiona Fine designer suits. The perfect fit showed off his strong, muscled body, while his walnut-colored hair was artfully styled. Add all that to his hand-some features, and Finn looked just as polished as the jewelry he'd been admiring earlier.

The saleswoman's eyes trailed down his body and back up. After a moment, she smiled at him, and then subconsciously licked her lips as though Finn were a hot fudge sundae that she wanted to gobble up. In the back of the store, a second saleswoman eyed her associate with anger. While Finn had been waxing poetic about bracelets and shoes, the two of them had been having a whispered ar-gument about who got the privilege of waiting on him. Looked like Red here had won.

Finn, being Finn, noticed the woman's obvious interest and immediately turned up the wattage on his dazzling, slightly devious smile. "Why, hello, there," he drawled. "Don't you look lovely today? That sky-blue color is *amazing* with your hair."

Red blushed and smoothed down her short skirt. Her gaze flicked to me for half a second before she focused on Finn again. "Do you and your . . . wife need some help?"

"Oh," he said. "She's not my wife. She's my sister."

The woman's dark eyes lit up at that bit of information,

and Finn's smile widened that much more. Despite the fact that he was involved with Detective Bria Coolidge, my baby sister, Finn still flirted with every woman who crossed his path, no matter how old or young or hot or not she was. Dwarf, vampire, giant, elemental, human. As long as you were breathing and female, you could count on being the recipient of all the considerable charm that Finnegan Lane had to offer.

"But my sister could definitely use your help, and so could I. What do you think about this color?" he asked, picking up the purple pump once again. "Don't you think it would look fabulous on her?"

"Fabulous," Red agreed, her eyes wide and dreamy.

I might be standing right next to Finn, but I was as invisible as the moon on a sunny day. I sighed again. It was going to be a long afternoon.

Twenty minutes later, after being dragged from one side of the store to the other, Red showed me to a fitting room in the back. Rightfully insisting that he knew more about fashion than I did, Finn had picked out several dresses for me to try on. Red placed the gowns on a hanger on the wall before brushing past me.

"I'm going to check on Mr. Lane and see if he needs anything," she said.

"Of course you are."

Red hightailed it over to the jewelry case where the other saleswoman, a well-endowed blonde, was leaning over and showing Finn the diamond bracelet he'd been admiring earlier—along with all of her ample assets. Red stepped up next to Blonde and not so subtly elbowed her out of the way. Blonde retaliated by shoving her breasts forward that much more. The two of them might as well have filled up a pit with mud and settled their differences that way. That would have been far more entertaining than the petty one-upmanship they were currently engaged in.

I rolled my eyes. Finn was the only man I knew who could inspire a catfight just by grinning. But it was a show that I'd seen many times before, so I stepped into the fitting room, closed the door behind me, and started trying on the dresses. The sooner I picked something, the sooner I could get back to the Pork Pit.

Too tight, too short, too slutty. None of the garments was quite right, not to mention the fact that Finn had chosen more than one strapless evening gown. My cleavage had never been all that impressive—certainly not on par with Blonde's—but of more importance was the fact that strapless gowns were not good for knife concealment. Then again, Finn didn't care about such things. He didn't have to. He could always tuck a gun or two inside or under his jacket, which suited him just fine, as long as the weapons didn't mess up the smooth lines of the fabric.

I was just about to take off the latest fashion disaster—this one in that awful canary yellow that definitely wasn't my color—when I heard a soft electronic chime, signaling that someone else had come into the store. I wondered how long it would take Red and Blonde to tear themselves away from Finn to see to the new customer—

A surprised scream ripped through the air, along with a sharp, smacking sound. The pain-filled moan that followed told me that someone had just gotten hit.

"Don't move, and don't even think of going for any of the alarm buttons," a low voice growled. "Or I'll put a couple of holes in you—all of you. Maybe I'll do that anyway, just for fun."

Well, now, that sort of threat implied that the person making it had a gun—maybe even more than one. I perked up at the thought, and a genuine smile creased my face for the first time today. For the first time in several days, actually.

I cracked open the fitting room door so I could see what was going on. Sure enough, a man stood in the storefront, right in front of the jewelry case. He was a dwarf, a couple inches shy of five feet tall, with a body that was thick with muscle. He wore jeans with holes at the knees and a faded blue T-shirt. A barbwire tattoo curled around his left bicep, which looked like it was made of concrete rather than of flesh and bone. He held a revolver in his right hand, the kind of gun that could definitely put a large hole in someone, especially if you used it at close range.

Since it didn't look like the dwarf was immediately going to pull the trigger, my gaze went to the other people in the boutique. Blonde was the closest to the gunman. She had her one hand pressed to her cheek, probably from where the dwarf had reached across the counter and slapped her, and her other hand was clamped over her mouth to hold back her screams. She wasn't entirely successful at that, though, and a series of high-pitched squeaks filled the air, almost like a dog whimpering.

Finn stood about ten feet away from the dwarf. He must have been talking to Red when the gunman entered the store, because he'd put himself in between her and the dwarf. Red had the same stunned, horrified expression on her face that Blonde had.

Finn had his hands up, although his eyes were narrowed, assessing the dwarf and the danger he presented, just like I was.

The first thing I did was look past the gunman and through the boutique windows, just in case he had a partner waiting outside, but I didn't see anyone loitering on the sidewalk or sitting in a getaway car by the curb. A solo job, then.

The second thing I did was study the dwarf to see if it looked like he was searching the store for someone else—me, Gin Blanco, aka the assassin known as the Spider.

By killing Mab, I'd inadvertently made myself a popular target in the underworld, and more than one of the crime bosses had put a bounty on my head, hoping to establish themselves as Ashland's new head honcho by taking me out. It wasn't out of the realm of possibility to think that the dwarf had followed Finn and me to the boutique on someone's orders.

But the only thing the dwarf was interested in was the jewelry. His eyes glinted and his mouth curved up into a satisfied smile as he glanced down at all the expensive baubles. So this was nothing more than a simple robbery, then. Plenty of those in Ashland, even up here in the rarefied air of Northtown. Really, if the Posh owners were going to keep all those diamonds around, then they should have at least hired a giant or two to guard them.

"Move!" the dwarf barked, pointing his gun at Blonde. "Over there with the others. Now!"

Blonde, who'd been behind the counter, hurried around it and stopped next to Red, putting the other woman and Finn between her and the robber. Well, at least she had a good sense of self-preservation. Red knew it too; she gave her coworker a hostile glance over her shoulder.

I turned my attention back to the robber, wondering if he might have any magic to go along with his inherent dwarven strength and the hand cannon he was sporting. But the dwarf's eyes didn't glow, and I didn't sense anything emanating from him. No hot, invisible waves of Fire power, no cold, frosty blasts of Ice magic, and nothing else to indicate that he was an elemental. Good. That would make this easier.

"Give me the key!" the dwarf snapped at Blonde as he moved behind the counter. "Now!"

With a shaking hand, Blonde pulled a set of keys out of her pants pocket, stepped around the others and over to the robber, holding them out to him at arm's length. The dwarf grabbed the keys and used one of them to open the lock on the jewelry case, instead of just smashing the glass and setting off the alarms. He threw the keys down on the floor and started shoving bracelets, rings, and necklaces into his jeans pockets.

I looked at the knives I'd piled on the bench inside the fitting room alongside my clothes. Normally I carried five silverstone knives on me—one up either sleeve, one against the small of my back, and two in the sides of my boots—but I'd removed them when I'd started trying on the dresses. I couldn't exactly go outside with a knife in my hand, since that would ruin whatever element of surprise I had, and there was no time to change back into my regular clothes. Cursing Finn under my breath, I hiked up the long skirt of the dress I was wearing and opened the fitting room door.

"Darling!" I squealed, rushing into the storefront. "Isn't this dress just the most divine thing you've ever seen!"

I twirled around and managed to put myself in between Finn and the robber. With the yellow dress, I might as well have been a mother duck, watching over her little ones.

"Darling? I thought you said she was your sister!" Red hissed.

A dwarf had threatened to shoot her and was now robbing the store, and Red was still more worried about Finn's marital status than all that. Someone's priorities were a little skewed.

Finn winced and gave her an apologetic shrug, but he never took his eyes off the dwarf.

The dwarf's head snapped up at the sound of my voice, and the gun followed a second later. He stepped to the end of the counter and grabbed hold of my bare arm, his fingers digging into my skin as he pulled me next to him. His hot breath wafted up my nose, reeking of onions and garlic. I hoped he'd enjoyed whatever he'd had for lunch today because he was going to be eating through a straw soon enough.

"Who the hell are you?" he growled, shoving the gun in my face. "Where did you come from?"

"I was . . . I was . . . I was in the back, trying on some evening gowns," I said in the breathiest, most terrified and helpless voice I could muster. "I don't want any trouble. Please, please, please don't shoot me!"

The dwarf stared at me for several seconds before he lowered his gun and let go of my arm.

"Just so you know, that's the ugliest damn dress I've ever seen," he said. "You look like a fucking daffodil."

He shook his head and reached inside the case to grab another handful of jewelry. The second his eyes dropped to the diamonds, I stepped forward, yanked the gun out of his hand, and drove my fist into the side of his face.

With his dense, dwarven musculature, it was like smashing my knuckles into a cement block. My punch didn't have much effect, except to make him stop looting the jewelry case and focus all his attention on me, but that was exactly what I wanted.

"Stupid bitch!" he growled, stretching his hands out to grab me. "I'll kill you for that—"

I pistol-whipped him across the face with the gun. My fist might not have had much of an impact, but the sharp edges and heavy, solid weight of the weapon did. His nose cracked from the force, and blood arced through the air, the warm, sticky drops spattering onto my skin.

The dwarf howled with pain, but he reached for me again. I tightened my grip on the gun and slammed it into his face once more. And I didn't stop there. Again and again I hit him, smashing the weapon into his features as hard as I could. The dwarf fought back, wildly swinging his fists at me over and over again. Despite the blood running in his eyes, he was a decent fighter, and so I grabbed hold of my Stone magic and pushed the cool power outward, hardening my skin into an impenetrable shell.

Good thing, since the dwarf's fist finally connected with my face.

Given his strength, the blow rocked me back, and I felt the force of it reverberate through my entire body, but it didn't shatter my jaw like it would have if I hadn't been using my magic to protect myself. Still, the dwarf took it as a sign of encouragement that he'd finally been able to hit me.

"Not so tough, now, are you?" he snarled, advancing on me again.

"Tough enough to do this," I said.

I waited until he was back in range, blocked his next blow, and then used the gun to coldcock him in the temple. His eyes widened, taking on a glassy sheen, and then rolled up in the back of his head as he slumped to the floor.

"You know, Gin, you really should warm up before you tee off on somebody like that," Finn murmured, leaning across the counter and staring down at the dwarf. "Wouldn't want you to pull a muscle or anything."

"Oh, no," I sniped, letting go of my Stone magic so that my skin would revert back to its normal texture. "We wouldn't want that. Have I told you how much I hate shopping?"

Finn just grinned, and pulled out his cell phone from his pocket to call Bria and report the attempted robbery. I used the long skirt of the dress to wipe my prints off the gun, and then put the weapon down on top of the jewelry case.

I'd just started to head to the fitting room to change back into my own clothes, when the two saleswomen blocked my path. They both looked at me with serious expressions. They were probably going to thank me for saving them—

"You know you have to pay for that," Red said.

"Oh, yeah," Blonde chimed in. "That's a ten-thousand-dollar dress you just got blood all over."

Blood? There hadn't been that much blood. It wasn't like I'd sliced the dwarf's throat open with one of my knives, which is what I usually did when bad folks crossed my path.

I opened my mouth to respond, when I caught sight of my reflection in one of the mirrors on the wall. Dark brown hair, gray eyes, pale skin. I looked the same as always, except for the flowing yellow dress—and the blood that covered my hands, arms, and chest. Actually, being covered in blood pretty much *was* the same as always for me. But the dwarf had bled more than I'd thought, and the fancy gown now looked like it had come straight out of a horror movie where everyone dies at the big dance.

I started to push past the two women, but they crossed their arms over their chests and held their ground. Apparently, the sight of a ruined dress was more offensive than the fact that I'd just bludgeoned someone unconscious right in front of them.

"I just saved your snotty little store from getting robbed, not to mention kept that dwarf from probably killing you both, and you actually think you're going to charge me for it?" I stepped forward. "Keep talking, and this dress won't be the only thing in here with blood on it, sugar."

Red paled. After a moment, she stepped aside. I turned my cold gaze to Blonde, who sucked in a breath and stepped aside too.

I stomped past them, went into the fitting room, closed the door behind me, and peeled off the gown. I put it on its hanger and placed it on the back of the door. Now instead of being canary yellow, the top of the dress had taken on a bright crimson color, and blood had even oozed down the full skirt, giving the whole garment a garish, tie-dye effect.

Still, as I stared at the disastrous dress, I couldn't help but smile.

Finn was right.

Yellow really wasn't my color—red was.

More bestselling
URBAN FANTASY
from Pocket Books!

More Bestselling Urban Fantasy
from Pocket Books!